HEADHUNTER

The totem pole – a Dogfish Burial Pole – was fifteen feet high. The crosspiece was carved with a figurehead from an Indian myth. Hanging between the struts was the body of a woman. Her hands had been nailed to the crosspiece and her head had been cut off. The carved face of the Dogpole appeared to take its place.

D1639169

HEADHUNTER
MICHAEL SLADE

A STAR BOOK
Published by
the Paperback Division of
W.H. ALLEN & Co. PLC.

A Star Book
Published in 1985
by the Paperback Division of
W. H. Allen & Co. PLC
44 Hill Street, London W1X 8LB

First published in Great Britain by
W. H. Allen & Co. PLC, 1984

Printed and bound in Great Britain by
Anchor Brendon Ltd, Tiptree, Essex

ISBN 0 352 31518 0

for all the
Fathers/Mothers

PROCLAMATION.

ABERDEEN.

(L.S.)

CANADA.

VICTORIA, by the Grace of God, of the United Kingdom of Great Britain and Ireland, *Queen,* Defender of the Faith, &c., &c.

To all to whom these presents shall come, or whom the same may in anywise concern,— GREETING :

A PROCLAMATION.

E. L. NEWCOMBE,
Deputy of the Minister of Justice, Canada.

WHEREAS, on the twenty-ninth day of October, one thousand eight hundred and ninety-five, **COLIN CAMPBELL COLEBROOK**, a Sergeant of the North-West Mounted Police, was murdered about eight miles east of Kinistino, or about forty miles south-east of Prince Albert, in the North-West Territories, by an Indian known as "Jean-Baptiste," or "Almighty Voice," who escaped from the police guard-room at Duck Lake;

And Whereas, it is highly important for the peace and safety of Our subjects that such a crime should not remain unpunished, but that the offenders should be apprehended and brought to justice;

Now Know Ye that a reward of **FIVE HUNDRED DOLLARS** will be paid to any person or persons who will give such information as will lead to the apprehension and conviction of the said party.

In Testimony Whereof, We have caused these Our Letters to be made Patent and the Great Seal of Canada to be hereunto affixed.

Witness, Our Right Trusty and Right Well-beloved Cousin and Councillor the Right Honourable Sir JOHN CAMPBELL HAMILTON-GORDON, Earl of Aberdeen; Viscount Formartine, Baron Haddo, Methlic, Tarves and Kellie, in the Peerage of Scotland; Viscount Gordon of Aberdeen, County of Aberdeen, in the Peerage of the United Kingdom; Baronet of Nova Scotia, Knight Grand Cross of Our Most Distinguished Order of Saint Michael and Saint George, &c., Governor General of Canada.

At Our Government House, in Our City of Ottawa, this Twentieth day of April, in the year of Our Lord one thousand eight hundred and ninety-six, and in the Fifty-ninth year of Our Reign.

By command,

CHARLES TUPPER,
Secretary of State.

DESCRIPTION OF THE AFORESAID INDIAN "JEAN-BAPTISTE" OR "ALMIGHTY VOICE":

About twenty-two years old, five feet ten inches in height, weight eleven stone, slightly built and erect, neat small feet and hands; complexion inclined to be fair, wavey dark hair to shoulders, large dark eyes, broad forehead, sharp features and parrot nose with flat tip, scar on left cheek running from mouth towards ear, feminine appearance.

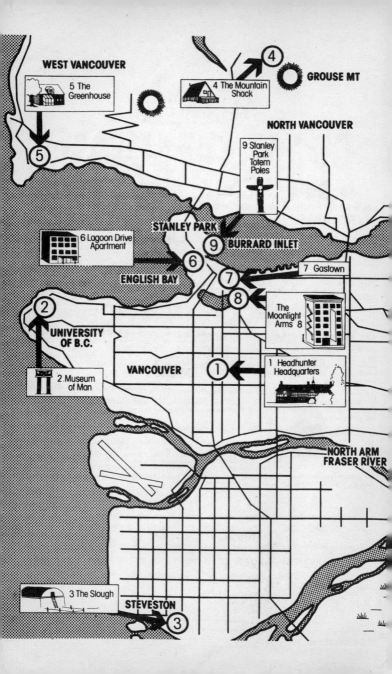

PART ONE

The Seed

The mind of man is capable of anything –
because everything is in it, all the past
as well as all the future.

Joseph Conrad

The Nightmare

Medicine Lake, Alberta, 1897

The body hung upside down from the ceiling by nails driven through both feet. The head was missing, the neck severed to expose vein and muscle, artery and bone in a circle of raw flesh. What was left of the man was still dressed in the bright scarlet tunic of the North-West Mounted Police, the arms, with their sleeves decorated with gold braid now dangling down toward the plank and sawdust floor. A pool of blood as red as the tunic spread out beneath the corpse. There was blood dripping from the tips of the dead man's fingers but the splash of each drop as it hit the pool was drowned out by the slow, incessant, monotonous thud of a drum beating overhead. The drumbeat came from up on the roof beyond the trap door in the ceiling.

Thump . . . thump . . . thump . . . thump . . .

He awoke with a start.

His muscles tense.

His mind alert.

His nervous system taut like a bowstring at full draw.

Under the blanket Blake used as a pillow, his right hand closed on the Enfield's grip and his thumb eased back on the hammer. There was a click as the hammer cocked but its sound was smothered and lost among the coarse cloth folds of the blanket. Slowly, Blake eased the revolver out from under his head and into the bitter cold. Then he lay shock-still in his buffalo robe. Silent. Listening. Waiting.

Thump . . . thump . . . thump . . .

The night was cold and moonless. To the North the

aurora borealis flashed and trembled across the frozen landscape, the sheeted light fading in and out with that weird flicker the Indians say is 'the Dance of the Dead Spirits'. Above Blake's head countless stars pierced the inked-out sky; while off to the East, in the vault of space, rose-coloured streaks from a meteor shower stabbed the first faint smudge of dawn. The time was 6 a.m.

During the hours that Blake had slept a storm had burst in from the Arctic, and once more reburied this valley beneath a weight of thick-fallen snow. By 3 a.m. the blizzard had passed. Now frost came down from the cold, dark sky to shroud his camp with ice – and all the world seemed to sleep in savage desolation.

Thump . . . thump . . . thum-thump . . . thump . . .

Blake was camped four hundred and fifty feet west of Medicine Lake. It was here in the lee of a clump of pine that he strained his ears to the silence. There was not a sound in the air nor from the frozen earth, yet in his gut, his primal core, Blake – *knew* something was out there.

Enfield in hand, breath held, slowly he rose from the ground.

Wilfred Blake was a tall man with a firm, unflinching eye. He was dressed by regulation in a thick black buffalo coat. Though he was almost sixty years of age, the decades of fighting and exposure had failed to sap his strength. This strength was moulded in his shoulders and chest, in his neck, in his backbone as straight as a ramrod down a rifle barrel.

Wilfred Blake was not a reckless man. He had not survived for nineteen years in the British Imperial Army by disregarding his instinct, for instinct had saved him more than once in those many Colonial Wars.

In 1857 Blake had been with the Highlanders stationed on the Ganges, and during the Sepoy Mutiny he had been garrisoned at Cawnpore. It was there that he had slept through the screams of soldiers skinned alive and nailed to makeshift crosses, had seen that well near the Bibighar filled with the heads and limbs and trunks of

12

dismembered British women and children. It had been instinct that had guided his arm for the revenge that was wreaked at Lucknow, where kilted and bloodstained and shrieking 'Cawnpore!' again and again and again, Blake had spiked and had slashed with his bayonet, taking no prisoners and feeling the Glory as the bagpipes had driven him on.

Fifteen years later Blake had been with the Black Watch in Africa: in fact Viscount Garnet Wolseley himself had chosen Blake for the Ashanti Campaign. In 1825 Sir Charles Macarthy had foolishly crossed into Ashanti-foo where the Africans had killed him and cut off his head, parading the skull once a year through the streets of Comassie. In 1872 London had ordered Wolseley to even the score. It had been strictly on instinct that Blake had survived the Battle of Armoafo, for in wave upon wave the Ashanti had hurled a force five times as large upon the British Colonial Army. Through ambuscade after ambuscade in ever increasing numbers, Blake had ordered the Square to 'fire low, fire slow' as a mountain of African corpses had piled up in front of the Black Watch rifles. Later, Blake had found Macarthy's skull and had been awarded the Victoria Cross.

Thus over the years this man had been taught the soldier's ultimate lesson: that intelligence tempered by instinct was the only key to survival.

Instinct had ruled him then, for sure. And instinct ruled him now.

Blake listened. As dawn began to stain the jagged ice-capped peaks to the East, he crouched on his heels and shivered in the keen hoarfrost. The hand which held the Enfield was beginning to go numb.

Thum-thump . . .

Lake water was lapping against the ice ring that crept in from the shore.

Thum-thump . . .

From far away, at intervals, came the lonely hoot of an owl.

13

Thum-thump . . .

Every now and then a passing breeze would bend the fir trees until their branches whispered like conspirators.

And then there was silence.

Thum-thump . . .

Almost total silence.

The only sound that Blake could hear was the blood-pump in his ears.

When Wilfred Blake had awoken he had been in the grip and torment of an unrelenting nightmare. This black dream had come to him with the hour preceding dawn, and as with the tension that ran through him now, it too had commenced with a pounding in his ears. He began to wonder, as he crouched listening to the beat of his own heart, if perhaps it was only this nightmare that had wrenched him wide-awake. Eventually this line of thought brought the nightmare creeping back.

Thump . . . *thump* . . . *thump* . . . *drip* . . .

It is not the throbbing that bothers him. Nor is it the dark. It is the bullet marks and knife hacks that slash and scar the walls. For this is a room that has lurked in his mind for almost thirty years. The walls without windows – the plank door studded with nails and now firmly bolted shut – the hand-hewn logs stacked one upon the other, some with shavings of bark like skin still clinging to the fibre – the mud packed between the trunks to fill the gaping spaces: every detail of this room is just as it was back then.

He knows it is a winter month in 1870.

He knows this is the room in the fort where they conduct the Indian Trade.

For close to him are sacks of feed and crates of ammunition. Off to his left against the wall, there leans an open box. The lid of this box, prised off, is lying on the floor. Inside a ruddy smear of candlelight shimmers on a barrel, while next to it are seven crates, one just like another. At twenty carbines to the case, there are one hundred and –

The attack came without warning.

As happens in the mountains, the wind had changed

direction. A light breeze barely strong enough to turn smoke or twist a feather had sprung up from the West. Instantly two dogs awoke and turned in that direction. The dogs had been sleeping near the sled fifteen feet north of Blake.

For a split second Blake thought, *why the dogs? They're nae in this dream.* Then he realized this was not the dream and that his hunt was over.

Blake turned.

Fast. Fast enough to meet the attack now coming through the snow.

The Cree was no more than eighteen years of age. He wore the usual winter dress of his tribe and it offered little protection against the elements. A breechclout of leather hung down over a narrow belt tied around his waist. His leggings reached from ankle to groin. On his head, he Cree wore a buffalo horn cap adorned with feathers and weasel skins. There was no covering for the upper part of his body save a buffalo robe. In his right hand, he clutched the barrel of an old Winchester that he now held above his head like a club.

Iron-child, Blake thought. *At last the search is over.*

A sudden jolt of adrenalin hit the white man's blood, for this was when he was most alive and knew it most completely.

Raising his gun, he sighted the Indian down its barrel. Then he pulled the trigger.

The Enfield, however, refused to fire. For either his finger was frozen or the mechanism was jammed.

The sudden shrill pitch of a war whoop shattered the brittle air. Iron-child had come out of a thicket forty feet to the west, and now he was churning and floundering and clawing his way through the stretch of snow between them. He was out of shells, that was obvious.

Blake jammed his left mitt into his mouth, bit down hard, and wrenched the glove from his hand. Then he gripped the revolver with both hands and once more tried to fire. The wood of the handle was smooth to his touch, the trigger a curl of ice.

Iron-child had discarded his robe and was now naked above the waist. Stumbling and faltering, his breath billowing out before him in great white clouds, he staggered through the snow drifts ten feet from Blake. The rifle was grasped in both hands high above his head. When he saw Blake about to fire, he ducked and dropped to his knees.

There was a flash of yellow from the muzzle, and then a shocking explosion. With a lurch of the pistol, the blast roared out at the solitude, only to be repulsed and echo back again and again.

But the bullet missed.

It passed two feet over Iron-child's head and hit the breech of the Winchester. There it splintered and ricocheted off the metal. One careening fragment hit the Indian just above the temple. It slashed his cheek in a downward course before it lodged in his shoulder. The velocity stunned him. His right arm went numb. And the force of the shot hitting the rifle threw his body backward into a drift of snow.

Iron-child's right leg snapped at the ankle.

Then he passed out.

Thump . . . thump . . . thump . . . drip . . .

When Iron-child emerged from the shock of his wounds he found himself staring down the barrel of a gun.

'Aye, lad,' Blake said softly in English, 'I can see that you're alive. Are you in pain now . . . lad?'

Blake was standing between the Cree and the blazing ball of the sun. Around his neck he wore a high black scarf. With his left hand he was rubbing his temple as if it caused him agony. Yet strangely he was smiling. His head was large and his forehead, square-cut and massive, was almost hidden by bushy white eyebrows. His skin was ruddy and weathered from years of exposure to the elements, but his eyes were pale and grey and steady above a snow-white moustache. From a

16

thong around his neck his gloves hung at his sides, while numb and naked in the cold his right hand held the pistol.

'One dinnae fight because there is hope of winning. It is much finer to fight when it is nae use. That's Cyrano d'Bergerac, lad. Would thet be your philosophy?'

Iron-child did not understand a word that the white man was saying, but he sensed that it would not be safe for him to make a sound. So the Cree said nothing. Blake pulled the black scarf down from his chin, then he squatted on his heels. The muzzle of the Enfield was four feet from Iron-child's head.

'Aye, you dinnae understand English? Or is it the clout to your head that the bullet gave you? It dinnae matter to me, laddie, for we're going to have a wee talk anyway while we got the time.'

Just then one of the Eskimo sled-dogs came trotting over to sniff at the blood that had spread over Iron-child's face. The Cree did not move, for numbness was seeping through his body. The mountain air was beginning to warm as the sun reflected off the dazzling snow. Blake shook his head and once more rubbed his temple. Then he removed the scarf and loosened the throat of his buffalo coat. In the V at Blake's neck Iron-child could now see the scarlet uniform and one shiny button.

'Ye see, lad, I've been trackin' you for a long time now, and I want you to know the trouble that you and your red brother Almighty Voice have caused. And it's a wee bit of trouble indeed.

'Now I can see how the Crees on Chief One Arrow's Reserve dinnae like being boxed into sixteen square miles when they once had a thousand miles of prairie to roam. And I can see how they dinnae like starving because there are nae buffalo. But laddie, that's part of the price you Crees must pay for backing Riel in his Rebellion against the Government. You cannae stop th' settlers from coming.

'This Almighty Voice, he was a piss poor leader for you

17

to follow in your recent escapade. What did you three young Cree think, that he'd bring back the old days and drive the white man from your land? Well, lad, it's our land now: that's a lesson for your learning.'

Iron-child's body was now racked by shivering and his broken leg-bones had begun to rattle one against the other. He hoped that shock would take him soon and set his spirit free, that he could die with dignity and cross the Bridge of the World. For the pain and the cold and the loss of blood were beginning to make him weak. As he listened to the words that meant nothing as they rolled off the white man's tongue, he found himself being mesmerized by the sound of the Scotsman's rumbling *r*.

'Now laddie, I'm nae saying that Sergeant Colebrook was the best of officers. True, he had a chequered record and had been up for breaches o' discipline. But when he caught up with Almighty Voice that morning just as he was breakin' camp, he dinnae draw his pistol. This is nae Tombstone nor Dodge City, lad, and the Mounted Police are nae Yankee barbarians. So you tell me, why did Almighty Voice have to shoot Sergeant Colebrook through the neck with a double barrelled shotgun?'

Blake let the question hang in the air for a moment.

'That put pressure on us, aye. But the real pressure, Cree, that came from within. It came from the Force itself. Cause, laddie, no one – Indian or white – gets away with the murder of one of our own.'

Suddenly Blake stopped talking and his eyes lost their focus. Almost hypnotically he was staring at a scatter of blood drops spattered across the snow. *Drip . . . drip . . . drip.* He began to hear sounds in his head. His left hand went to his temple. Then when he resumed talking his voice seemed far away.

'Do ye think I'm ramblin', lad? Well I'll tell ye something. I once picked up a spot of malaria in the tropics, the Ashanti War it was. And it still bothers me every now and then, though it's been twenty-five years.'

Without warning, Blake lashed out with his left hand

and yanked the buffalo horn cap from Iron-child's head. In doing so he smeared blood across the heel of his palm. As he brought his arm slowly back he stared at the liquid red. Then with his tongue he began to lick the blood from his hand.

Blake held up the cap.

'Nae much of a trophy, is it Cree? Nae like my scalp would have bin. Aye, that brings you pride among your people, taking a grey-haired scalp.'

Then once again he stopped talking. Blake shook his head. He rubbed his temple. He licked a final drop of blood from the bristles of his moustache.

'Well, boy, you renegades made a mistake. You made a very bad one. It was nae killing Colebrook. And it was nae killing the others. Your mistake was in prodding Herchmer to put me on your tail.'

Suddenly Blake lashed out with the Enfield, striking the Cree in the mouth. With a sickening crack Iron-child's front teeth exploded in a spray of shattered enamel. His screams of shock and pain ran up and down the Rocky Mountains. Then Blake grabbed him by his braided hair and yanked his head up off the ground.

Iron-child choked on the fragments of teeth as the Mountie spat out his words.

'Herchmer says I'm excessive, lad, but you'll nae find a bad mark on my record. Cause, Cree, the Mounted Police need me much more than I need them. When there's a job of tracking, you know who they call on? And if they hadnae sent me away last year after that mess in Manitoba, they'd have had Almighty Voice just like they'll have you.

'A legend is born, lad, when a man beats the probabilities of life. And I'm the one that gets the ones that ought to get away. Believe me, Cree. The legacy of this Force will be the legacy of me!'

Blake let go of the Indian's hair and threw him back on the ground. Then Iron-child heard the hammer snap as the policeman cocked the Enfield. He watched as Blake once more stood up and began to rub his temple. He saw the pistol rise. He saw the bore of the muzzle. He saw the sunlight glint off the metal of the barrel.

'Dead or alive,' Blake said, 'it's all the same to them. But believe me laddie, it's nae the same to me.'

Then Wilfred Blake pulled the trigger and shot Iron-child between the eyes.

The blast from the shot rang up one side of the valley and down the other.

Blake listened. Then he drew the Enfield muzzle close and sniffed gunsmoke into his lungs.

Thump . . . thump . . . thump . . . drip: sounds ran through his head.

After several minutes, Blake turned from the body of Iron-child and trudged through the snow across to the un-hitched dogsled. He unpacked its contents, rearranged what he did not need, then he built a fire, filled the kettle with snow and put it on to boil.

While the sled-dogs fed on dry moose meat, Blake ate biscuits and pemmican. Eventually he brewed some tea, hot and strong, and filled his pipe with tobacco. He sat in the snow drawing deep puffs of smoke into his lungs while he waited for the throbbing to cease.

Thump . . . thump . . . thump . . . thump . . .

It wouldn't go away.

What bothered him most of all was that each time the nightmare came, its aftermath took longer. And the dream was occurring more often. Always when he was alone. And always on the hunt.

That worried him.

This time it might have cost him his life, for the night-mare's echo had distracted him right when he required his wits. For almost a quarter century, Blake had lived with the occasional bout of malaria – but this was different. This was far more severe. First the nightmare, always the same. Then on and on, the throbbing. Then the echo daydream.

If only that damn echo would come, then the throbbing would cease.

Thump . . . thump . . . thump . . . thump . . .

He'd have to wait it out.

But the pressure in his head was worse, and getting worse each minute. A crushing weight was sending streaks of red pain whirling around his skull. With every beat of his heart, darts of agony like nails were rammed into his temples. *Please*, he thought, suffering, *please let the echo come!*

Drip . . . drip . . . thump . . . drip . . .

Blake buried his face in his hands . . . *thump* . . . He slammed the heel of his palm against one of his temples . . . *drip* . . . Then he bunched his fists, threw back his head, and let out a gut-tearing scream.

Thump . . . thump . . . thump . . . drip . . .

Suddenly Blake leapt to his feet. He had an uncontrollable urge to move. He kicked the fire savagely, sending sparks and flaming brush exploding across the snow. He trod to the unhitched sled and whistled for the dogs. Running from all directions, they came bounding through the drifts. As he attached the train to the sled, the huskies jumped on one another in play, tangling the traces and back-bands and collar-straps into knots and interlacings. Spanker and Cerf-vola began fighting over the lead.

Blake left them to their frolic, once the train was secure. He busied himself with breaking camp and packing up the sled. Finally, he trudged over to where Iron-child lay sprawled in the snow.

The Enfield had blown out an exit wound the size of a navel orange. Blood spread out like a halo from behind the Cree's head.

Blake grabbed hold of the two hair braids and dragged the corpse to the sled. He tied it securely diagonally with a crosshatch of leather lashings. Then climbing onto the rear runner skates he flicked a whip at the dogs.

With his head bent low, Cerf-vola tugged at the load.

The other dogs followed and the sled began to move.

For hours the huskies panted as they hauled the heavy load, biting frequent mouthfuls of the soft snow through which they toiled. At noon, clouds settled over the mountains; then the upper layer broke to reveal the outer spurs of the Rockies that now flanked Blake on both sides. Blake pulled in on the dog-train and brought the sled to a halt.

This was it. They'd reached it, the Indian's 'Bridge of the World'. That hinge where the Rocky Mountains front on a thousand miles of plain.

Blake climbed off the sled.

Then while moving forward to take the lead for the stretch where a false step could mean a fall to the gorge beneath, the Inspector glanced at Iron-child. He saw the open skull, the shattered brain, the tissue hanging in bloody strands out of the cranium. Blood was dripping into the snow. A trail of crimson drops marked the route that the sled had taken. Drops dripping, dripping, dripping drips, *drip . . . drip . . . drip . . .*

Blake slammed his fists into his eyes as the nightmare came flooding back.

Drip . . . thump . . . thump . . . thump . . . thump . . .

It is not the throbbing that bothers him. Nor is it the dark. It is the bullet marks and knife hacks that slash and scar the walls.

For he knows this is a Hudson's Bay Company fort along the Saskatchewan River.

He knows it is a winter month in 1870.

And he knows this is the room in the fort where they conduct the Indian Trade.

For close to him are sacks of feed and crates of ammunition. All around the log walls — at least in that half of the room lit by the light of a single candle — are piles of fur stacked up to the ceiling. Buffalo and mink. Bear and otter. Beaver, black fox, and marten. Off to one side, to trade for these pelts, are blankets, beads and coloured cloths, handkerchiefs and ribbons. From the

22

ceiling hangs the carcass of a deer, strung up to age, its head thrown back and its antlers pointing like fingers of crooked bone.

Wilfred Blake is sitting at a table near the door, his elbows on the tabletop, his chin cupped in his hands. He is watching the wick of the candle drown in a pool of its own melted wax. This candle casts the only light within the Indian Room.

Wilfred Blake is afraid of the part of the room he cannot see.

Outside, the pounding is closer now, as it begins to mix with another sound within this room.

Thump . . . drip . . . thump . . . drip . . . thump . . .

Suddenly there is a shriek of pain from just beyond the door.

Blake springs to his feet. He draws the bolt. He throws the barrier open.

Then he gasps and turns away – for what he has seen is far worse than he has imagined.

The fort is a five-sided structure with flanking bastions and a stockade twenty feet high. It stands high on a level bank one hundred feet above the Saskatchewan River. The gate is open. Through the gate, Blake can see the wigwam poles outside, can see a solitary horse far down in the river meadow. On both sides of the water, discoloured by smoke and mud, stand rude and white crosses to mark the place of the dead.

It is snowing.

Large wet flakes tumble out of the sky and land on the windows of several buildings huddled within the stockade. Blake can see the frightened faces masked by these window panes.

Blake can see the Indians swarming into the fort.

The Indians are everywhere.

Now a Medicine Man materializes from out of the driving snow. He walks to the centre of the yard and holds his hands up to the sky. This man is dressed in a deerskin shirt embroidered with porcupine quills and ornamented with hair locks from his enemies. His headdress is of ermine skins; his face has clawed out eyes. Tears of blood are trickling down his wrinkled cheeks.

Thump . . . thump . . . thump . . .

The drumming is getting louder, filling the air with sound.

Thump . . . thump . . . thump . . .

Now all the whites are on the ground, crying, moaning, wail-

ing, bleeding, all without a scalp. Then the Indians all stand up at once, erect and motionless – and in that instant Blake knows what has brought them here.

The Indians have come to bring the smallpox back.

He sees each face distorting and shrivelling in decay, each one a leering travesty of the human form, each foetid apparition melting and flowing like tallow. What was once flesh is now putrid and dripping, now bone-revealing carrion slowly being eaten away. He sees the Indians, dying and disfigured, move to the doors of the houses. He watches as they spit on the handles and smear pus from their faces across the windows, each throat evoking a plaintive cry to take this demon back.

Then Wilfred Blake slams the door and rams the bolt into place.

Now the pounding has stopped. Blake sighs. Then the candle sputters and dies. Darkness, blackness. Drip . . . drip . . . *The sound is across the room.*

The first smash of a tomahawk cracks through the wood of the door.

Groping in his pocket, he finds a match and strikes it. Sulphur flashes yellow against the tinderbox. Then with the match before him, he starts across the room – into that part he could not see by the candlelight.

Here the floor is strewn with broken bottles, and kegs, and overturned medicine chests. Glass is smashed; powders have spilled; tinctures seep from lead containers to stain everything in reach. Blisters, pills and fluids mix with whisky, high wine and rum.

Crack! Crack! Crack! *Tomahawks splinter the door.*

The match dies. Find another! *Again the yellow light. And this time he sees the bones and skulls upon the floor.*

Now Blake has a sudden frantic wish to exclude this scene from his mind. He claws his eyes and begins to turn around and around and around. For he has seen the fang marks scratched upon each bone, has seen the skulls sawed open and picked clean of their contents, has seen how those skeletons still collocated show postures of frenzy and panic. The bone tangle stretches for yards in every direction.

Drip . . .

The second match frizzles and dies.

He strikes his last match. He crouches. His fingers examine the floor. Blood, a pool of sticky blood, soaks into the sawdust and planks.

Drip . . . drip . . . *A drip from above lands on the back of his hand. For blood is raining in slow drips from the ceiling of the room. Blake wrenches his head up and shivers at what he sees.*

Then the drumming starts up again.

The drumbeat comes now from up on the roof beyond a trap-door in the ceiling, a relentless thumping echoes around in his head.

The body hangs upside down from the ceiling by nails driven through both feet. The head is missing, the neck severed to expose vein and muscle, artery and bone in a circle of raw flesh. What is left of the man is still dressed in the bright scarlet tunic of the Northwest Mounted Police. And Blake knows somehow that the tunic is his own. Good Lord, *he thinks,* why must I be so –

Clink

What was that?

Clink

There it is again!

The skeletons are all beginning to move. Each bone joins to another. Then another. Then another. Then each skull looks at Blake.

The Inspector rips open his holster and grasps at empty air: his Enfield is gone.

With a crash the door breaks open and the drunken Indians enter the room.

'We've got him now, brothers,' *one skull shrieks in glee, its skeleton slowly creeping across the floor, its ivory cranium straining forward to reveal razor-sharp teeth.*

A hand of bones grips Blake's leg as the final match goes out. Fangs sink into his thigh. Kicking, fighting, Blake lashes out, stumbling in the dark. His hand brushes against a ladder.

With a snarl he breaks free, and suddenly he's climbing.

A skeleton starts after him.

25

Reaching up with both hands, Blake pushes against the barrier. It begins to yield, squeaking up on rusted hinges. He swings it open. He gets his head and shoulders through – and then the pounding encircles him.

Thump . . . thump . . . thump . . . thump . . .

'Nae!' Blake screams aloud.

For sitting cross-legged in front of him is a naked Ashanti warrior. All he wears are bells and shells and a leopard tail tied round his waist. The black man is grinning through sharp, pointed teeth at the drum that sits before him, for on this drum is a severed head wearing a white pith helmet.

Blake gasps.

For the black man beats upon Blake's head with a massive buffalo bone.

Thump . . . thump . . . thump . . . *A relentless, monotonous pounding.*

Though a scream starts deep in the white man's throat, it never reaches his mouth. A hand now grabs the Inspector's hair and yanks his head around. Blake feels his chin caught in the crook of someone's naked arm, feels his head being jerked back and his jaw being raised. A sudden searing line of fire cuts across his throat, then with a gush a waterfall cascades down the front of his chest. Coughing and choking and gasping for air, Blake shrieks out inside his head, but the sound just echoes round and round unable to escape. His last view is a bloody knife in Almighty Voice's hand.

Thump . . . thump . . . thump . . . th-

The pounding came to a halt.

The echo finished; the nightmare gone.

And once more it was over.

The spell broken, Blake turned his eyes away from the sight of Iron-child's head. He began to take deep breaths counting up to fifty. When that was finished he felt better, and he looked out through the gap.

The Rocky Mountains stand sentinel over the plains of North America. The mist had now burned away, and

26

stretched before him lay an expanse so vast that every hill and lake and wood seemed dwarfed into one continuous level. Alberta, Saskatchewan, Assiniboia had all ceased to exist. What remained was one surface of lakelets glittering in the bright sunshine and spread out in sheets of dazzling white and blue.

Suddenly Blake thought of Jenny, her blue eyes laughing underneath that large, lace-bordered cap.

Aye, he thought to himself, *she's a bonnie lass. Admit it, man, the prettiest in all of the North-West.*

Her image made him smile.

And as for him, Blake thought, *a child is a serious matter at any point in a man's life.*

Then he walked back to the sled and climbed onto the runners. A moment later, with a flick of the whip, Cerf-vola began to lead the slow and long descent down the mountain side.

God willing, Blake thought, *I might be home for Christmas.*

EYES

New Orleans, Louisiana, 1957

Jazz was in the streets, and it wafted up on the warm night air, a musical mix of ragtime and bop and boogie-woogie and swing, drifting up over the heads of the Mardi Gras revellers snaking through the French Quarter, up over the mingle and jumble of rich and poor, of black and white, of priest and libertine, up, still up over the surging crowd of people lined eight deep, some on scaffolds, some on stepladders, some on the tips of their toes. The music rose over the parents who sipped pink liquid from hurricane glasses as they pushed and shoved their children to the front of the line, children munching on peanuts and popcorn and hot dogs and apples-on-a-stick, everyone shuffling through a carpet of confetti and broken bottles. The jazz rose up over the sea of costumed masked revellers infiltrating the crowd, the 'He-Shebas' dressed in drag as butterflies and snails, a King Kong here, a Zigaboo there, the Queen of Hearts and a big-leafed Adam and Eve. Away from 'the Big Shot of Africa' and the Zulu King's retinue, away from a one-eyed cyclops, away from the white leather cowboy garbed in front and bare-ass naked behind, up and away from Royal Street with its banners and its streamers, up until the jazz slid softly through the wrought-iron balcony where the black girl stood at the window.

The black girl was naked.

Crystal stood with her back to the room, swaying, her breath quietly hissing through white, even teeth. A trickle of sweat ran down between her shoulder blades toward the small of her back. As her body was still tingling with the aftershock of orgasm, the fireworks that exploded over the city seemed to explode in her head. She felt good. Secure. For just a moment she wondered if her father would turn his sexual advances on her younger sister now that she was gone, then she managed to push the thought aside since it spoiled her mood. From fifteen feet away, Elvis begged her, *Don't be cruel.*' Crystal smiled and slowly rocking, began to sing along.

'You want some of this?' a voice asked, louder than the radio. 'It'll ice the top of your head.'

Crystal turned from the window and walked over to where Suzannah sat at a glass table chopping up cocaine. The razor blade cut through the powder and tapped on the glass to the music. Finished, the white woman put the blade down and picked up a crisp $100 bill, rolling it into a tube and handing it to the girl.

Crystal plugged one nostril and put the tube to the other. Leaning over the table, she inhaled the drug. Then she switched hands and sniffed cocaine into her other nostril. During the process, she felt a hand cup one of her breasts. The nipple puckered.

'That ought to cool you, honey,' Suzannah huskily whispered into her ear. The woman's other hand slipped up between the girl's thighs.

Crystal shuddered, uncertain whether it was Suzannah's touch or the spreading effect of the snow. But she didn't care, for all that mattered was the warm shiver tingling through her body. After a while she closed her eyes and abandoned herself to the woman.

Suzannah laughed and said, 'Better watch that, Crystal dear. Pussy is addicting.'

Then the woman turned her back on the girl and herself bent over the table. She ran the bill around the glass and sucked up most of the powder. Finished, she wet her index finger and washed it across the surface, completing the ritual by rubbing its tip around her gums.

Suzannah was a woman who dripped sexuality. Twenty-eight years old, she stood five-foot-ten in her bare feet and had a luscious figure. Her head was shaved bald, and she too was naked. As Suzannah bent over the table, from behind her Crystal could see six small gold rings piercing the labia and glittering among the hairs of the woman's crotch.

Suzannah straightened up. Pinching her nostrils several times as she sniffed in deep breaths of air, she glanced up at the Gustav Becker clock ticking on the wall. The time was 11.33. She turned to Crystal and said: 'We haven't much time, dear, until our guest arrives. He'll be here in an hour.'

Frowning, Crystal walked over to the window. At the end of the side street, where it intersected with Royal, she could see the parade of floats and, for a moment, even the figure of Comus holding his goblet high. The crowd cheered as he went by, swept away as if caught up in a surging tide. Crystal sighed.

'Must we miss the party?' she asked.

'Sweetheart,' the woman said softly, her eyes now glazed and her face flushed by the cocaine's effect, 'you must realize that some things are more important than others. Like this man tonight. He is *very* important *for us*.'

Crystal nodded absently, suddenly feeling the jittery intoxication of the drug. Her face felt frozen and there was no sensation in her teeth. When she looked down at her chest it seemed as though her heart was beating wildly in an effort to break free, each tick of the clock vibrating this room into sharper focus.

The room would have been similar to any other rich, elegant parlour in New Orleans were it not for the walls. To Crystal, it was eerie to have so many empty eyes watch her every move. Suzannah had decorated this half of the upper floor of the ancient Lafon house entirely in antiques. Most of the furniture was by the cabinetmaker Prudent Mallard, immense, ornate, and Victorian. Though Mallard had used carved rosewood, Suzannah had used the masks.

There were more than a hundred different masks covering the walls.

On the wall opposite the window were the masks of Africa: an Oulé Mask from Bobo and a Senufo Fire-spitter; a Nalindele Mask and an Ashanti Fertility Head.

On the wall to the right of the window were hung the masks of the Near and Far East: a Mummy Mask from Egypt and a Roman Mask of Pan; a Japanese Gigaku and a Chinese T'ao t'ieh Face.

In the wall to the left of the window there were three closed doors, and around the jambs, framing them, were the masks of America: a Death Mask from the Inca and a Salish Spirit Mask; a Six Nations Iroquois False Face and a Hopi Katchina Doll.

And on the window wall were the modern masks. To the left of the pane was a Beelzebub by Theodore Benda and a German Executioner's Mask. From above it leered a Corbel from England, a Creon Mask from Stratford, a Death's Head Hussars Busby. While to the right hung a New York Yankee's catcher's guard, a World War I gas mask and a shroud from the Ku Klux Klan.

30

Out beyond the window were the masks of Mardi Gras.

Catlike, Suzannah padded across the floor and began to stroke Crystal's hair. Together they watched the parade.

'What does all this *mean?*' Crystal asked. 'That's what I'd like to know.'

'Mean? It doesn't *mean* anything. It's just something you feel. You let yourself go.'

Crystal closed her eyes, moving her head in time to the stroking of her hair. It felt so good.

'You see,' Suzannah added, 'Carnival appeals to a basic human urge. Almost everyone has the desire hidden within them to occasionally don a mask. There is *no* culture in history in which masks have not played a part.' Suzannah whispered, 'Come with me.'

Together they walked to one of the doors set into the wall to the left. The woman swung it open and they entered the bedroom beyond.

This was a room in conflict, a riot of red and black. The walls were of red satin, the curtains of red velvet, the spread draped across the bed a red patchwork quilt. The carpet, however, was black. The furniture – a dresser, a wardrobe, and a mirrored washstand – was of black ebony and onyx. And attached to each of the four posts supporting the canopy bed were chains and handcuffs of forge-blackened steel.

Suzannah crossed to the washstand and sat down on its chair. As she picked up a jar of makeup, she was staring at her own face in the mirror, thinking the reflection was showing signs of age. The small creases at the corners of her full mouth and green feline eyes had been there last week. The lines on her forehead had not. Concerned, she rubbed one hand across her shaved head, noting the blue veins that spread like fingers reaching up from her temples, counting the pulse-rate at which her heart pumped blood.

Suzannah opened the jar of stage makeup and began

31

to blacken her eyelids. Spreading the grease with her index fingers, she worked the shadow in a narrowing slit around the sides of her head. Then she cleaned her hands with cream and began chalking her entire face white. As she did this, her eyes seemed to sink further and further back in her head. Fascinated, Crystal sat down at the foot of the bed and watched.

When she had finished, Suzannah painted her finger-nails a bright scarlet red – the same colour as the satin walls of the bedroom. Then fanning her hands to dry the lacquer, she turned to the girl and said: 'You and I, Crystal, we have a lot in common.'

'We do?' the girl said, surprised.

'Well, of course. That's why I asked you here. A few years ago, after I got rid of my husband, I did just what you've done. I too escaped down the Mississippi River. Only I made a mistake. Whereas you were smart enough to get a job in a laundry, I spent half a year removing my clothes in a sleazy Bourbon Street strip joint. It was awful!'

'You were married?' Crystal said, surprised again.

'Yes, dear. We lived at the top of the world. But let's not talk about that. The man turned out a bum. Oh he was tough on the outside, shiny buttons and all, but inside where it counts he was a snivelling little boy – lost and living in the shadow of his father. In fact, love, he was the *last* man to lay a hand on me. But I took care of him. He doesn't matter now.'

'When were you divorced?' Crystal asked with interest.

'Divorced? We were never divorced. The man just died. That was Christmas Eve, 1955.'

Suzannah stood up and crossed to the dresser and pulled open one of the drawers. From it she removed a pair of sheer stockings, then carried them back to the washstand. As she walked her breasts swayed, her shoulders softly rolling to keep them moving. Crystal stared transfixed.

'Good coke, eh?' the older woman said.

'Can I have some more?'

'Later, dear. This stuff is stronger than you think. Believe me.'

Suzannah sat down on the chair and raised one of her legs to pull a stocking on.

'Do me a favour, love. You see that drawer second down? Open it and bring me one of the scarlet ones.'

Crystal moved to the dresser drawer and pulled it open. Inside, it was filled with wisps of lace and nylon, all of them black or red. The girl removed the tiniest of garter belts and brought it to the woman. Suzannah fastened it around her waist, tethering the stocking tops with two snaps at each thigh. Then she looked up.

'How do I look, sweetheart?'

'Stunning!' Crystal said. She was beginning to shiver, her throat suddenly dry. She tried to wet it by swallowing, but all she got was a taste of bitterness running down her throat from her nose.

Suzannah stood directly in front of the girl. Her suspenders ran like blood-red transversal lines down to the white of her thighs. Crystal could hear the material rasp ever so softly.

'Do you understand, love, how men make women whores? You can see them in every city, every house, every office building. Well, it makes me sick. Women like I was, stripping in clubs and letting men ogle their tits and ass. Millions of women sitting on their bums adding up figures or typing words. Women working in laundries and washing dishes. You want to know a secret, love? Just between you and me? Each day those women peddle their ass for peanuts – never once realizing that there is a market just waiting to be tapped. A market where women can get back their own.'

Suzannah flicked her eyes at the clock. The time was 12.09.

Turning from the girl, she walked over to rummage in the wardrobe and remove a set of clothes. She carried the

33

outfit over to the bed and set part of it down on the quilt. Then as Crystal watched, Suzannah wiggled her body into a black leather corset.

This corset was cut low in the front to accentuate her cleavage. It ended just above her groin. Two leather straps ran from the armpits up to her neck where they fastened to a black studded collar. The sides of the garment were stitched with red laces, the bodice cut in circles to reveal her nipples. To complement the corset, Suzannah pulled on two shoulder-length black gloves also stitched in red, and snapped them to the collar. The fingers of the gloves had been sliced off, and revealed her scarlet nails. Then she pulled on a pair of spike-heeled, red-laced, knee-high boots and picked up a thin-lashed leather cutting whip. The handle of the whip was decorated with a pretty blood-red ribbon tied in a large bow.

Returning to the washstand, Suzannah removed a flat bottle of rouge from its onyx surface. She held the container out to Crystal and said: 'Would you colour my nipples while I paint my mouth?' Shivering, the girl nodded.

When they had finished, Suzannah bent over and sucked on Crystal's breasts until both tips were hard buds. Dipping a finger into the makeup, she slowly rouged each nipple until it was a brilliant red. Then with one hand she took the girl's face in her fingers and looked deeply into her eyes. The bow on the end of the whip brushed Crystal's cheek.

'Men are swine, lover, *please* remember that. You and I are linked by what we have in common. I was also raped by my father.'

Crystal blinked, her eyes locked with the woman's, unable to break away.

'Yes, dear. You are not alone. And believe me, – *no* man will ever hurt you in *my* house. You're safe here.'

'How did it happen to you. Please tell me. I want to know.'

34

Suzannah sighed. 'All right,' she said. 'I was born on a vineyard in the south of France. In 1934 – when I was five – I was sent to school in Paris. During the War my father collaborated with the Vichy Government. He was a traitor. Anyway, in 1941 my parents called me home. By then the Germans were in Paris and they thought me safer on the family estate.'

'You lived under the Nazis!' Crystal exclaimed, wide-eyed.

'Yes, dear. But they weren't my problem. Near the end of the War my father started drinking heavily. And he beat my mother up. By then the Allies had landed and the Germans were retreating. My father was living in fear of reprisals for his collaboration.

'Anyway, this one day I was home alone. My mother was in the hospital, he had beaten her that bad. She lied about the reason.

'In the early afternoon, my father began drinking. By suppertime, he was drunk. He started punching me, calling me by my mother's name, swearing and screaming at me. Then he raped me. I was then fifteen years old – a year younger than you – and I was a virgin.

'I remember lying there, feeling torn and battered, empty, mostly empty as if I were not in touch with myself. And I remember his breath foul with garlic.

'After a while he began to sober up and realize what he had done. He begged me for forgiveness, but I just lay there. Eventually he fell forward with his head on my breasts, sobbing like a baby. I was filled with revulsion.'

'Did you tell anyone?' Crystal asked softly.

'No, but my mother suspected. Shortly after that I was sent to Montreal to continue my education. That's where I met my husband. That's where I got married. And that's the end of the story.'

'I hate men!' Crystal said. 'Especially *my* father.'

'Well that's good, sweetheart. That's the way to be. Besides, I can satisfy you like no man *ever* can.'

'Then why did you get married if you feel the way I do?'

'That's a long story,' Suzannah said, glancing at the clock. 'I don't have time to tell you, though I wish I did. I don't want you *ever* making the same mistake. Let's just say that I was blinded by the colour red. The man was old enough to be my father and maybe that's what I wanted – a replacement. I was young and stupid. What more can be said?'

Suzannah let go of the girl and retreated several paces. She stood with her legs apart, her head held high, her backbone erect. She looked the girl up and down, smiling, and thought: *I can't wait any longer. It's time to reel her in.*

According to the clock on the wall, it was 12.28 a.m.

'Crystal,' Suzannah said slowly. 'I must ask you a question. Listen before you answer. Okay?'

The girl nodded.

'The moment I saw you this afternoon, I knew we were the same. That's why I followed you from the laundry after work and sat beside you in that greasy little restaurant. You looked so alone. Have you enjoyed what we've done this evening?'

The girl nodded again.

'Well, there's no reason in the world that this must ever end. No one knows that you're here. No one knows that you're with me. And no one needs to know. Would you like that?'

Once more the nod.

'Good. Cause tomorrow night I'd like to take you to Europe. To London, Paris, Rome. I'd like to buy you fine clothes. I'd like to give you all the cocaine you want. I'd like to spend just hours and hours playing with your pussy, getting you so hot you think you're going to melt. Sound like fun?'

The girl swallowed.

'Here,' Suzannah said. 'Let's run away for good.' She pulled open a flat drawer in the washstand and removed a stack of $100 bills which she tossed to the girl. Crystal's mouth dropped. The bills slipped through her fingers and tumbled to the floor.

'Go on. Pick them up. They're yours,' the woman said. 'That's $10,000 lying at your feet. And that's just spending money.'

'Where did you get that?' the girl exclaimed, her voice breaking in a croak.

'Why, from the man *before* the guest who comes tonight. The one this evening will bring another twenty grand with him. And once he's finished, well then we're off and free. I'll have made $100,000 off Mardi Gras this year. Not bad for two weeks' work, eh?'

The girl said nothing. She stared at the stack of money with a dumbfounded look on her face.

'Crystal,' Suzannah said softly, 'it's time to answer that question. Do you want to stay with me – or shall we call it a night and you can return to your job at the laundry? The decision is yours.'

In a flash, the girl was across the space between them and cradled in the woman's arms. Warm tears touched Suzannah's shoulder where the glove joined her corset. As the woman whispered, 'That's my girl,' over and over again, she caught a glimpse of the two of them in the washstand mirror. *This one was easy*, she thought with a smile. *Once you know the market of life – and what people need to buy*.

For a moment longer she held the girl, then gently pulled away. 'No turning back, dear, is that agreed?'

'Yes,' Crystal said.

'Good. Let's have some more cocaine.'

Back in the room with the masks, Suzannah drifted over to the middle door in the wall on the left and pulled it open. Beyond the jamb a spiral staircase disappeared below. 'Come on,' Suzannah said, 'there's something weird to see.' Her words held out adventure like honey to a cub.

Together they descended, twisting round and round on the iron steps, past the main floor and on down to the basement. Suzannah opened a hidden trap door and a gust of stale damp air swept up and out of the black pit that yawned beneath it.

Ever so faintly from below came the murmur of running water. Then as Crystal's heart pounded against her rib cage, Suzannah picked up a torch, climbed into the hole and disappeared down a rusted iron ladder.

Crystal followed.

As she descended the girl could feel the walls sweating and dripping with the ooze of centuries. When the ladder ended the two of them continued on down a narrow flight of stone steps. Crystal had counted twenty-six before a wail of anguish from off to the right brought her to a halt. Her muscles locked tight and for a second she froze.

The noise was a low-keyed godless gibber that seemed to burst forth from no discernible point. It appeared to issue from several sources off to the right side.

Crystal turned to run – when Suzannah grabbed her by the arm. 'Look,' the woman said.

Continuing her grip on the girl, Suzannah swept the torch in an arc that sliced through the darkness around them. Crystal could see that they had reached a vaulted corridor. The floor was of chipped flagstone, the arched walls and roof of dressed masonry. The corridor stretched away before them into indefinite blackness. To the left there was a closed wooden door. To the right were five black open archways through which came the wail.

'What you hear,' Suzannah said, her words sucked away almost the second they were uttered, 'is wind off the Mississippi River. What you see is an old smuggler's vault dating from the seventeen hundreds.'

As she spoke the woman stabbed the flashlight toward one of the open archways on the right. At the outer-reaches of its beam Crystal could just make out the stone-banked channel of a stream.

'You see that underground river? It connects with the Mississippi. It was once used by French pirates, back in the early days. Now its mouth on the river is sealed by a mesh of iron bars.'

'Is this what you wanted to show me?' Crystal asked, now embarrassed by her attempt at flight.

'No,' Suzannah said, 'I want you to see this.' She walked over to the wooden door and ushered Crystal in.

'What's in here?' the girl asked, standing in the pitch dark as the woman reached up to light a torch set into the wall beyond the doorway and off to their left.

Crystal choked in fright. Her neck hairs stood on end. Never before had her eyes seen – or even imagined – the instruments that cluttered this hellish room.

'This is a *torture chamber!*' Crystal shrieked with a spine-jarring shiver.

'Correct,' Suzannah said. Then she laughed out loud, her voice hard and brittle.

This vault was a stone crypt, twenty feet by thirty. The chimney of a fireplace ran up one wall like a great grey sucking vein, cobwebs hanging like veils from several of its bricks. Beside this hearth stood a brazier with seven branding irons dangling from its rim. Along the opposite wall there was a Medieval rack, its wheels and clamps cast in mimicked shadow by the torch, dark stains discolouring the upper surface and spreading down the sides in thin drip-lines. An Iron Maiden crouched waiting in the far corner with its door gaping open on several hundred spiked teeth. Turning in panic, Crystal saw a gibbet iron hanging from the ceiling – that one wall was covered with whips and manacles and cat o' nine tails – that a skull rack containing seven leering ivory grins hung on the stone surface behind the door – that knives and needles and surgical instruments were laid out in tidy precision on a flat surface to her left – and, worst of all, that Suzannah stood guarding the doorway with her arms folded across her breasts. Reflected torch-light glinted off the metal rings in her crotch.

As the vault began to echo with the dull hideous whine that Suzannah had said came from the wind off the river, Crystal's mind screamed at her *A knife! Grab a knife!*

The girl ran to the dusty surface spread with polished,

gleaming blades. Then with a butcher knife in one hand and a skinning knife in the other, she turned to face the door.

Suzannah grinned. 'Crystal, you are *precious!* What a scene,' she said.

'I want out of here,' the girl hissed through tightly clenched teeth.

'Good. Then it works,' the woman replied, never moving an inch. 'For that is precisely the thought, my dear, that this theatre is designed to induce.'

'Yeah! What's this place for? You just tell me that!'

'Crystal, Crystal, Crystal,' Suzannah said, shaking her head. 'This is where I work.'

'Work!'

'Yes, *work*, silly. What do you think it's for?'

'What sort of work would ever need a place like this?'

'The sort of work, sweetheart, that pays a hundred grand in two weeks. The work of relieving guilt.'

'Go to *hell!*' Crystal screamed. 'Let me outa here!'

'So what's stopping you? You're the one with the knives.'

The girl blinked. For a split second she glanced down at her own hands and the two razor sharp instruments that they held. Then, fearing a trick, she flicked her eyes back to the door. Suzannah had not moved.

'What you see around you, dear – what you seem to be so afraid of – is really nothing more than a million-dollar fantasy – the essence of masochism. These are just a few of the props.'

Crystal shook her drugged head. 'But why would anyone *want* this?' She gestured at the walls.

'Ah, now that's the question . . . and it shows you don't know men.'

'Tell me,' Crystal said. And she put down the knives.

The man with the briefcase chained to his wrist was thinking about his rabbit.

40

He sat on a chair to one side of the dance floor, watching all the pompous people in their ties and evening gowns oozing etiquette and snobbery, only half aware of the pageantry of the 'Rex Ball' that was now in full swing around him.

At 12.41 he glanced at his watch and felt a chill of excitement. Then the thrill made him remember.

He recalled how as a young boy he so loved to climb into his mother's lap and nuzzle his face between her soft warm breasts. How she would lock him tenderly in her arms, at the same time kissing him, then press him against her so tightly that it almost hurt. Sometimes his mother would take a nap on a very hot afternoon, sitting him on the bed as she removed her clothes, letting him lie beside her with his body nestled to hers. On those days she would dab the perfume that he liked so much on the secret parts of her body and he would lie in that hot room almost drunk on the fragrance of her skin.

That, of course, was only if his father wasn't home.

For his father abhorred coddling. 'I'll raise no Mama's boy!' he'd shout every time he caught them. And that happened often.

On those occasions when his father surprised them, his mother would act as if she were suddenly angry with him and push him violently away. Grabbing her hairbrush from the dresser, she would lock his head firmly between her legs and bend over his back to smack his buttocks till he screamed. Crying he would desperately try to straighten up, but he never could. For his neck would merely slip up her thighs and hit her body above. And strangely at that moment her perfume was twice as strong.

'Give him a tanning,' his father would shout, grinning at the performance. 'Show me I'm wrong in thinking that you spoil him too much.'

Then – except for one occasion – it would always end the same. He'd be sent to his room to 'smarten up', and as the hours ticked away, utterly confused by the chaos

41

of his feelings, he'd sit on the floor and have a talk with Freddie.

Freddie was his rabbit.

The one occasion that was different was what he remembered now. Again his father had come home, and again he'd had the spanking. Once more he was in his room talking softly to Freddie. Then the rabbit's ears jerked up at the sound of his mother's scream.

On that day he had run to the door, his heart in his throat, flagrantly transgressing his parent's sternest warning. 'And don't you dare leave your room until you get permission.' The warning didn't matter. His mother was being hurt.

He was five years old.

Even now the man could vividly recall what the boy saw in that room. For his mother's hands were tied to the headboard of the bed. She was dressed in underwear, her body shining with sweat. Her pants were torn and she was moaning as his father moved up and down between her thrashing legs. Then his mother screamed again – and the boy rushed in to save her.

He began to hit his father who wrenched around in surprise. 'What are you doing here?' the man shouted, his face livid with rage.

'Get out!' his mother cried, her reaction shocking him.

Then his father leaped off the bed and grabbed him by the arm. His 'thing' was pointing at the boy as he shoved him out the door.

'I hate you, Daddy,' the boy said, surprising himself when he heard the words come out of his mouth. And that was his mistake.

For a moment his father said nothing as his eyes narrowed to slits. Then he dragged his son to the kitchen where he removed a butcher knife from the drawer. Together, the boy struggling, they both approached his room.

Poor Freddie, the man thought, recalling that look in his rabbit's eyes. *He knew before it happened*.

That night the boy spent locked up in his room. For hours he cried, shaking and sobbing as he desperately tried to put the animal back together. For his father had cut off Freddie's head, forcing the boy to watch. Then after a while he gave up. He spent the remaining dark hours gently stroking both of the pieces on the floor. In the morning his mother came once more to take him in her arms. 'I'll replace him,' she said.

The man looked at his watch. It was now 12.49. Time to go. He found the Men's Room where he waited till he was alone. Then he removed the mask from his jacket and adjusted it over his face.

Two minutes later, he opened the exit door.

For an entire year this man had waited for the excitement of tonight. Now his anticipation was almost at an end.

Tonight – at least for a while – he knew he would forget.

Suzannah walked over to a cabinet near the rack. She opened two leaded glass panels and removed a tray from inside. The tray contained ten 8" needles, each one shining silver-gold in the firelight. Then she placed the needles in a medical sterilizer that was housed in the lower cupboard. Her words, silken, vicious, washed through Crystal's drugged mind. The girl didn't know what they meant, but she knew they sprang from a hatred deeper than any she could imagine.

Suzannah walked over to the wall of whips and took two of them down. She carried them back to the girl.

'This, sweetheart, is a Scottish tawse, about seventy years old. You'll note that it is a tailed strap with a fire-hardened tip. The tip bites like an adder at the end of a cut.

'This other one is an English birch – the closest you'll find to poetry in all these flogging instruments.'

Suzannah handed the tawse to Crystal and stepped back several paces.

43

'Have you ever been to the circus,' she slyly asked the girl.

'Yes.'

'Well then you know how they train lions?'

'Uh. Huh.'

'Well, love, you can train a man the same way.'

With a pirouette, the woman spun around in a circle and lashed out with the birch. She hit the tawse in Crystal's hand and sent it spinning like a pinwheel to clatter on the floor. Then in one fluid motion Suzannah danced before the rack, slowly, methodically, rhythmically beating the wood with the whip. Crystal stared aghast, for with each relentless stroke the woman's lips grew thinner and drew back from her teeth. Her nostrils flared. Her breath came in gasps. And dust exploded in the anxious air.

Then suddenly in midstroke, Suzannah stopped.

'Men are such donkeys,' she said with a hiss. 'They think themselves superior to their own psychology.'

Crystal backed away.

'They are no more than animals, just programmed machines – and sex is the clockwork which winds up the engine.'

Suzannah hung the whips back on the wall. Slyly she smiled. 'In my house, Crystal, in this room – and as long as he's got the money – give me a naughty little boy and *tailored* punishment is what he gets. Behind the mask of Mardi Gras Jekyll really can turn Hyde loose.'

'And just where do I fit in?' Crystal asked dryly.

'You're my assistant.'

'Assistant! What do you need me for?'

'To answer that, sweetheart, I must tell you about our guest.'

It was his mother who had first told him about the Axe-Man of New Orleans. That was shortly before she died.

44

He had later found out that the Axe-Man had killed six people and injured several others during a brief reign of terror at the end of the First World War. Each victim was selected at random, access gained to each dwelling house by chiselling through the back door. Once inside, the killer had chopped his victims up with a long-handled axe. The axe, as a calling-card, was invariably left at the scene.

The Axe-Man was never caught.

His mother had told him none of this. The job of the Axe-Man, she had said, was to hunt for those young boys who did not love their mother. He would hack them up and then devour the pieces. His mother had told him this when they were both in bed.

The man now came out through the main door of the Municipal Auditorium, away from the Mardi Gras Ball. For a minute he stood in St Peter Street, scowling at all the drunken fools staggering all around. Then a black girl dressed in sequins stumbled and bumped against him. She smiled and mumbled ''scuze me' and quickly passed on.

'Slut!' the man spat after her.

He watched the woman walk away in the direction of St Louis Cemetery, his mind recalling painfully the black girl who had been in the street the night his mother died. That girl was not from the neighbourhood; he had never seen her before. Just a passerby. Hurrying down the sidewalk. With tears in his eyes and a choked voice he had begged her to run for the doctor. He had pointed up the street toward the doctor's office. Then taking the steps three at a time, he had scrambled back upstairs.

His mother was bleeding profusely. Her skin was as pale as tissue paper and her tongue was flicking wildly between her pearl-white teeth. Oh God, what teeth she had – the straightest he'd ever seen. And now he remembered those happy days, sitting in his mother's lap, listening to the words of love humming from her mouth.

The man turned left on Bourbon Street, glancing at his watch.

Why does it still bother me when I did nothing wrong? Why? the man thought.

For if only that girl had done as he'd asked, his mother would still be alive. And then he'd still have her love. Eight years old was far too young for a boy to lose his mother.

Perhaps I blame myself, he thought, *for hating the child inside her. But I never, never, never meant for her to die.*

No, the blame falls on the nigger. And now she has to die. For if she had only fetched the doctor, the death of the unborn child would not have taken my mother.

The man stopped walking abruptly, for he'd reached the mouth of the alley.

Nonchalantly he paused and lit a cigarette. The smoke felt good as the nicotine played with his nerves. He waited for a break in the crowd, then he darted down the passage.

Crouching down, he reached out and groped behind a trashcan. It was still there, exactly where he'd left it before attending the ball. Removing it, hefting it, he placed it under the jacket of his formal evening clothes. Then he stood up swiftly and returned to Bourbon Street. At the next corner he turned right and made for the French Quarter.

As he walked it felt good, the object hanging in the sling beneath his left armpit. For even through his ruffled shirt, the metal of the axe-head was cool against his heart.

With her arm around Crystal's shoulders, Suzannah walked the girl out through the door of the vault and into the corridor beyond. The whine from off the river had started up again.

'Love, we're running short of time, so I must ask a favour. Take the flashlight with you and go back upstairs. Turn on the outside lights. The switch is near the door. There's something down here I must do in order to get ready. I'll join you in a minute for another snort of coke.'

The thought of wandering through the cavern by herself was not an enticing one. The girl hesitated.

'Well go on. Be a sport. Only one more night's work – and then the thrills of Europe!'

Crystal took the electric torch and began to walk away.

Suzannah waited until the footsteps had died away. She was definitely worried about the girl's commitment to tonight. And for this sort of money, she couldn't take a chance. But all the doors were locked; Crystal had no way out.

The way Suzannah figured it, if she kept going two more years she'd have a million dollars. Just three more sessions in London, three in Bonn, and two more sessions here. Plus tonight, of course.

Now if only Crystal held together and played her part to the hilt.

The man who would arrive tonight was her favourite john of all. Filthy rich from some business that had to do with nuclear arms (she suspected a past involvement with the Manhattan Project) he had already paid her twenty grand just to set it up. The twenty thousand coming tonight merely reserved him a place next year. *What would you say, Crystal, if you knew what you were worth?*

Suzannah returned to the torture chamber and took the torch from the wall. Shining it up to the ceiling she located the meat hook in its vault. Next she removed the drip-tray from under the rack and centred it in the floor. She wanted the john to see it the second he entered the room.

Good! she thought, smiling. *Now the place is ready.*

Leading with the flambeau, Suzannah left the chamber, crossed the hall, and made for the underground river. Finding a bucket, she dipped the container into the stream and carried the water over to a large stone trough. When the trough was a third full, she added the plaster of Paris. A plastic bag around the sack had protected it from the dampness.

She was stirring the powder and water together when once more from far away came the whine of a howling. In this part of the cavern, it sounded nothing like the wind.

She stood up listening, then began to walk the bank that led to the mouth of the river. The wailing grew louder, now a dismal moan.

Half way toward the mouth that joined the Mississippi, the torchlight from the flambeau glinted off some metal. Here a rusting iron ladder climbed the side of a cylindrical stone bin. The howling – more insistent now – was coming from inside.

'Easy boy,' Suzannah said. 'Just wait a little longer. You will get what remains when our friend is finished.'

Howling mad with frenzy, the Dobermann pinscher gnashed its teeth.

'Put these on!' Suzannah snapped as she threw the lingerie at Crystal. They were back in the bedroom on the second floor. Crystal looked at the white cotton bra and pair of white panties and then began to cry.

'I said put them ON!' The woman almost screamed.

Shaking, Crystal did as she was told. The white garments stood out against her rich, dark skin.

Suzannah crossed to the wardrobe and swung the right door open wide. Inside it was covered with numerous clumps of different coloured hair hanging on metal hooks. The woman selected one of the wigs and sat down at the washstand. She pulled on the hair piece and adjusted it just right. When she stood up once again, long black snake-like strands writhed about her shoulders.

She grabbed the girl by the arm and dragged her out of the bedroom. Suzannah then went to one of the walls and took down a half-face mask. It was white with vision slits shaped like cat's eyes and two horned ears. 'Put this on,' she ordered, handing it to the girl.

Again Crystal did as she was told.

'Now, I don't care *what* happens, that mask does not come off. Understand? Neither does his. You deride him, shame him, spit on him – and most of all laugh at him while I work. Do you comprehend? All right. Now let's have that cocaine.'

Once more Suzannah sat down at the glass table and delicately opened up a bindle. She selected a large rock from the powder and placed it on the surface. When it was chopped and lined she turned to the girl and said: 'You snort first.' Crystal did.

It was as Suzannah was leaning over to inhale her second line that the girl found the courage to whisper again: 'I won't do it!' She was staring at the empty eyes all around the room.

The blow hit her square on the cheek as the cocaine powder went flying. The tremendous force in the slap sent Crystal sprawling across the floor. The drug settled like snowflakes on the surface of the table.

Seeing this, Suzannah's mind flashed with a vivid thought. For there he was once again dying in a wasteland of snow. She could see his face contorted as the poison took effect, the yellow spittle caking his moustache and freezing to ice as it dribbled from his lips. Outright terror was registered in his eyes.

Suzannah pulled her gaze away from the cocaine on the table. She jerked a leather thong from off a hook in the wall. Then she pounced over to stand straddled above the girl.

'Eat me, sugar!' she ordered. 'Then lace my cunt up good!'

Crystal shook her head.

She refused to look at the rings glinting in the hair.

The second blow was harder, almost lifting her off the floor. It sent the girl crashing against one of the wooden doors. This door was the third one in the wall on the left.

Suddenly Crystal yanked her hand away as if the partition had burned her. Suzannah laughed, then smiled.

'When you don't have the one you hate, you work on what you've got. What you're hearing, Crystal, is my very *special* project.'

Low and muted behind the door, a child's voice was sobbing. 'Mommy! Mommy, I'm sorry! Forgive me, Mommy! Please!'

At 1.13 that morning, the doorbell rang.

THE HIPPIE

On the Santiago River, Ecuador, 1969

'Wanta do some acid?'

'Huh?'

'LSD. Wanta do some?'

'Oh . . . uh, . . . no . . . no, I don't think so.'

Selena cocked her head to one side, arching her right eyebrow. 'What's the matter, Sparky? Why the hesitation? You have done dope before, haven't you? I mean you can't be *that* straight.'

'Yeah, I've done drugs.'

'Well then . . .' Selena said, shrugging her shoulders. 'I mean acid ain't a turn-down, now is it? It's not like I'm offering you grass or coke or bombers or speed or something else like that. This is acid, babe. The ultimate. Straight from God to Owsley to me to you . . . I mean you have done acid before, haven't you?'

There was a pause of silence, then Sparky replied quietly, 'No. No, I haven't done that.'

'Well then, look at the living you're missin', the fun you've never had.' Selena chuckled. 'Try *everything* once I say. Don't you agree?'

There was a second pause of silence. Then with hesitation Sparky said: 'Yeah . . . yeah, I guess so.'

'Good! Then it's settled.' And with that Selena held out her hand. In her palm two small tablets of White Lightning were washed by the tropical sun. The woman wet the index finger of her other hand and touched it to one of the hits, then she transferred the drug on her fingertip to the end of her protruding tongue. Closing her mouth, she swallowed.

'Okay, now it's your turn. Go on, Sparky, take one.'

Taking the tab, Sparky examined it, swallowed it, and waited for something to happen.

Nothing did.

It was strictly by chance that they had met in the jungles of Ecuador. Though this meeting was set on collision course through a faulty aircraft engine, to be precise, the die had been cast four months earlier. On that particular day – one fine California Saturday morning – Selena awoke to find that she had passed out the night before on the floor of a dirty artist's loft in Haight Ashbury. This floor was carpeted with soiled mattresses which were littered with approximately twenty sprawling, intertwined human bodies. Most of the bodies were naked, some of them coated from head to toe with sweat, red wine, Acapulco Gold ash, and a body massage oil that came in a bottle labelled with a picture of a Hindu Goddess waving her eight arms. That morning, to Selena's eyes, most of the people in the loft had just as many limbs.

It had taken her several minutes to figure out just where she was, an arduous process in which fragments of the Filmore West and the Grateful Dead were jumbled together with a raucous car ride up one San Francisco hill and down another.

Yes, Selena decided, it had been quite a party. In fact it had probably been as wild a gathering as any of the other hundred or so happenings that had gone down this year. *Jesus, how fuckin boring*, she thought: Selena wanted out.

And in less than a week she had done just that.

First the young woman had hit her father up for several thousand dollars, the money supposedly destined for tuition and room and board at Berkeley University. Next she had put the money into American Express Travellers cheques. After that she had found a muscular ex-guitarist from Sweet Stuff who was disillusioned with America and who had a big cock. Then finally, once they had secured the necessary passports and visas, the two of them had set off South in an old jalopy in search of adventure and sun.

The trip was great while it lasted – and that was just over three months. Then, within the last week, the whole thing had fallen apart.

On Monday they had been driving past the Plaza Independencia in the heart of Quito, the square dominated on one side by a grim cathedral, when the jalopy broke down for good. Thus gone was their transportation.

On Wednesday they had reassessed their finances to discover that all that remained of Selena's bankroll was ninety dollars in travellers' cheques. So almost gone was their means of subsistence.

And then on Thursday they had been walking through the steep, winding, cobbled streets of the old south-western section of Quito when the Sweet Stuff guitarist had been side-tracked by a rich middle-aged Argentinian woman. Selena never saw him again.

Bright and early the following morning, Friday, the young woman went to the local American Express Office and telephoned her father collect to ask for the money to fly home. He agreed to wire it to her. Then she hung up and caught a bus to Mariscal Sucre Airport to embark on one last adventure. For fifty of her ninety dollars it would be a good one.

The aircraft was a single engine affair that should have

had Band-aids on its wings. It was an old Piper that had seen service in Alabama, in Barbados, in Costa Rica, and now in Ecuador. The sides of its nose cone bore the scars of grease and oil and scorch marks. The pilot, Juan Garcia, was in the same shape as his plane. He was a short greasy man in a baggy blue suit with a taco-stain on his shirt. When he smiled – which he did every time he glanced at Selena's breasts and whispered '¡Que bonitos pechos!' – a gold tooth gleamed in his mouth.

The flight took almost an hour. Mount Sangay was still about forty miles away when Selena first glimpsed the rather symmetrical cone that rose well above the intervening ranges. As they drew closer, she could make out the large snow-beds near its summit, the apex of the peak now black and covered with a fine volcanic ash. Selena had never seen an active volcano before.

As the aircraft closed on Mount Sangay from fifteen miles away, a sudden outrush of steam rapidly shot up to five or six thousand feet above the cone. It spread out in a mushroom cloud as a wind-shock buffeted the plane, then it began to dissipate southward as a fresh explosion occurred. This time there was lava.

'Far out!' Selena cried, excitement filling her voice.

And it was then that without warning, the Piper engine gave a spluttering cough and died.

Selena nearly shit herself.

In panic she looked at Garcia, and that made matters worse. Frantically the pilot was flipping switches and turning dials and pumping at the throttle. A bead of sweat had formed on his forehead. When Selena looked out the window, her hands gripping the arms of the co-pilot's seat in a vice-lock, it seemed to her that the jungle was rushing up to meet them. She swallowed dryly and closed her eyes. *We're gonna hit!* she thought – and was very surprised when they didn't.

Instead, the Piper continued flying as a glider. First Mount Sangay slipped by on the right as fiery fingers of lava poured down its snow-capped slopes; then the rain forest of the Oriente spread out to the southeast like a rich green carpet. Opening her eyes and taking this in, Selena had all but resigned herself to a crash in the trees of the jungle, when straight as a sword-slash a broad band of water opened up in the forest beneath them. This break was none too soon – for the wheels of the airplane missed the treetops by inches as they came in over the river. Then, miraculously, Garcia made a perfect two-point landing, surprising Selena who was unaware of the pontoons above the wheels.

The Piper waterskied to a halt.

'Well, fuck me,' Selena sighed, letting out her breath. 'I didn't think we'd make it.'

Garcia, very pleased with himself, flashed his gold tooth at the woman. 'Don' worry,' the pilot said, patting the instrument panel. 'She good plane, lady. Very good plane.'

'Yeah, right,' Selena said. 'She good plane. Now where in hell are we? And how do we get outa here?'

'This is Rio Santiago,' Garcia replied, with an expansive sweep of his arm. 'Very big river. You look an' I fix plane.'

With that the pilot swung open his door and climbed out onto the left pontoon.

For the next forty-five minutes, Juan Garcia busied himself working with a large wrench under the engine cowling.

Selena looked out through the window of the cockpit. She estimated the Santiago, at this point, to be approximately a third of a mile wide. Its swift, deep, slightly turbulent waters were carrying the plane downstream. There wasn't a human in sight. *Just great!* she thought.

When Juan Garcia finally climbed back into the Piper his hands and the sleeves of his uniform were coated with grease and oil. Reaching out to twizzle a radio knob, the man proudly looked at her and said: 'Is fix, lady.'

Oh God, I hope so, Selena thought.

Though the radio had come to life, its sound was

nothing but static. Garcia tried for several minutes to pick up an active band, then finally he abandoned the task, shrugged, and said: 'Is volcano make radio no good.'

Turning around in her seat, Selena looked back at the fiery eruption of Mount Sangay off to the northwest – and that was when she noticed the dugout canoe. The canoe had emerged from a small stream to the rear and the right of the plane. The canoe carried a single occupant, sitting at the helm. The occupant was Sparky.

'Hey, look!' Selena said, tugging at Garcia's arm. 'There must be a town or a village or something very close to here.'

The pilot nodded. As he climbed back out on the left pontoon, the boat approached from the right. Garcia dipped under the belly of the Piper and waited for the dugout to come alongside, then he helped Sparky aboard. Together, they fastened the canoe to the right wheel strut.

'God!' Selena said, her head out the co-pilot's window. 'Am I ever glad to see you. Who the hell are you – a saviour sent from heaven?'

'My name's Sparky,' the stranger said, smiling.

'Yeah, well I'm Selena Benton and this is Juan Garcia. What brings you out here?'

'Right now I'm working with the US Peace Corps.'

'Doin what?'

'Today I'm taking water samples. Typhus. Malaria checks. That sort of thing. Where you from?'

'Up there,' Selena said, pointing to the sky. 'We got a fucked-up engine that almost got us killed.'

'Plane is fix,' Garcia said sharply, defending his own Latin machismo and the reputation of his beloved Piper.

'Yeah, sure,' Selena said, 'I'll bet you fix plane good.' Then she turned back to Sparky and asked: 'Is there a land route outa here?'

'Sure. The way I got in. Down the river to Macas and out from there.'

'Can you get me outa here?' Selena asked Sparky.

'As long as you're willing to rough it, and you've got a little time.'

'Babe, I've got all the time in the world. I just missed losing my life.' She turned to the pilot. 'Well, Juan, thanks for the thrill, but I fear this is where I leave you. You can keep the return fare and have a drink on me in Quito. *Buenos dias, Señor.*'

Garcia did not look happy. He stood for a moment looking from Selena to Sparky and back to Selena again. He would never understand *gringos* as long as he lived: they just threw their money away. Finally he resigned himself to losing a passenger, and with a sigh caressed Selena's breasts one more time with his eyes before he climbed back into his plane. Five minutes later the boat pushed off, this time with two paddlers. When the dugout was clear by twenty feet Garcia kicked in the engine. There was a cough, a splutter, sparks and smoke – and then the Piper was moving. Gaining speed, gaining altitude, soon the airplane was gone.

'Well, saviour,' Selena said, shaking loose her hair. 'Take me away from here.'

'Aye, aye, captain,' Sparky said, pointing the boat downstream.

Ten minutes after take-off and twenty miles from the river, Garcia's engine failed once more. Only this time there was no liquid landing-strip and the plane hit a mountain side.

Garcia's end went unknown in Quito because the static had not cleared.

Selena and Sparky, floating south, never heard the crash.

They were too deep in the jungle.

And too far away.

Selena awoke on Saturday morning to dawn in the Ecuador jungle. She rolled over onto her back and looked up at the sky, awed by what she saw. Here the huge

56

equatorial forest was set in an eternity of sombre gloom – a gloom as silent as a cellar filled with clinging mist. Enormous trees with trunks almost forty feet in diameter stretched two hundred feet above her head, their lower branches rich with every shade of green, their dense leafy canopy almost white where the sun had bleached the life-blood from the leaves. Already it was stifling down here, yet it was only 6.00 a.m.

What struck Selena most of all was the network of parasitic growths that hung down in a tangle from the armpits of the trees – bright purple orchids adhering to gum-tree trunks, spiral creepers hundreds of feet in length that twisted like gigantic serpents slithering from branch to branch, poisonous fruits that fell down into the undergrowth emitting noisome odours. It was a world so strange, so alien, that down here among the ferns that held the low ground mist she felt as if she lay at the bottom of an ocean.

Selena looked around for Sparky but her companion had left the campsite. Climbing to her feet and rubbing the sleep from her eyes, she began to head for the river a hundred feet away.

The two of them had spent the previous day drifting lazily down the Santiago. As the afternoon wore on the sun leaned out of heaven to beat down harshly upon the surface of the water; a shimmering haze hung between the trees and a languorous smell of vegetation drugged Selena's senses. Occasionally Sparky would tap her arm and point to the riverbank.

On one occasion Selena heard a *woof* of displeasure and saw an evil eye go blank, a long snout and grey-green body sinking into the water. When she looked toward the brown mud-bank not twenty yards from the side of the boat she saw another knobbly reptile with a pale throat, its eyes glassy and half-closed, its jaws wrinkled and half-open, its expression as wicked as a Notre Dame gargoyle. 'They're called *jacare*,' Sparky said, 'or sometimes *cocodrilo*. They make nice handbags.'

Another time she saw a covey of vampire bats hanging upsidedown in a hollow tree, their bellies bloated with blood that their victims could ill afford.

Then yet another time she heard the crack of twigs and voices murmur with a low, guttural sound. Scanning the riverbank to the right and squinting her eyes, Selena could just make out the features of several dark faces peering from behind the trunks of trees. It shocked her to notice that some of their mouths were filled with sharpened teeth. Then they were gone, these furtive men, leaving only the rustle of disturbed leaves and the soft smack of released branches.

Abruptly a disagreeable stench, a foetid musky odour came off the riverbank. Wrinkling her nose, Selena turned in that direction just in time to see something detach itself from the ground and flap up into a tree. As she watched, another followed. Then another. And another. And another, until the foul air resounded with the flap of wings and the branches of the vegetation lining the river were covered with black and white *urubu*.

'Vultures,' Sparky said, as the boat nosed toward the shore. 'They're Nature's grave-diggers. They bury the jungle dead in the warmth of their gizzards.'

As the dugout neared the bank, the birds sat in glum silence along the limbs of the trees. The meal of which they had been deprived still lay on the sundrenched mud. The back of the animal was now a sea of blood, clotted and sticky where the hide had been wrenched from the muscles of the flesh. Great strips of skin dangled downward from these wounds, and the horns of the bullock had been smashed and splintered by savage blows from wooden clubs. The intestines lay looped about the hooves and a number of broken spears stuck out from the haunches of the beast. Most unsettling for Selena, however, was the fact that no sooner had the *urubu* abandoned the corpse than it was covered with a blue and white and yellow flock of butterflies. She could plainly see brilliant wings fluttering in ecstasy as their slim legs pressed into the flesh and their faces sank into the prey.

With eyes wide Selena said: 'I thought butterflies lived on flower dew.'

'Even the world's most beautiful hunger with hidden desires,' Sparky replied.

'Yeah, but who butchered that animal and smashed it up like that?'

'Probably Jivaro. In a violent mood.'

'You mean those Indians I saw back there? The ones along the river.'

'The same ones,' Sparky said, guiding the boat back out into the stream. 'They used to be headhunters not so long ago.'

'Fuck me! I hope they're civilized now.'

'They are,' Sparky said. 'Or at least that's what I'm told.'

As the boat passed on, Selena saw the vultures dropping one by one back down to their interrupted meal.

But that was yesterday.

Now Selena reached the bank of the river. Sparky was in the dugout thirty feet from shore.

'Hey good mornin, saviour. What the hell ya doin?'

Sparky turned to look at her while screwing the lid on a jar. 'Just taking the last of the water samples. I'll only be a minute.'

'Take your time,' Selena said. 'I ain't going nowhere.'

As she sat down on the riverbank, the young woman took a long, slow look around her. Late yesterday afternoon, they had abandoned the main channel of the Santiago River for a small sidestream. Two miles up, this tributary had opened into a lagoon, and they had pitched their camp for the night by its shore. Sitting now at the water's edge, Selena let herself relax and revel in the morning – for gone here was the oppression of the forest with its constriction and decay. Gone too was the dirty flow of the Santiago, its current opaque with loam scraped from its banks in the scurry to connect with the

Amazon. Here instead was stillness, peaceful and serene. The mud-flats, barren and free from life, were shadowed purple by massive overhanging trees that paddled their roots in the water. The fireflies were not awake. No fish mottled the surface of the river. The bull-frogs were asleep, preparing for their nightly choir practice.

Low in the sky to the east, the sun and the moon had paired off to spend the day blazing at each other, while down on Earth their light shone on the clear lagoon, forging it into metal. The eastern side was silver, tinged here and there with mauve; the western part was glaring like a sheet of hammered bronze.

As Selena watched, through the water, slightly raised by the weight at the helm, foam creaming around its prow, the blunt nose of the dugout came in toward the shore.

'Jesus!' she said, standing up. 'This place is a blow-away.'

'Like it, eh?' Sparky said, as the canoe bumped against the bank.

'And how! What a day! Here, you want some help?'

'Sure. Take these jars up the bank while I moor this thing.' Sparky passed the water samples to Selena, then stepped out of the boat.

'How long ya been with the Peace Corps, out in this wilderness?'

'About six months,' Sparky said. 'I'm not a member though. I just work with them.'

'Yeah? Why's that?'

'I'm not a US citizen. That's a bar to volunteering.'

'Well then how the fuck did you ever end up in this lost neck of the woods?'

'It's a long story,' Sparky said, trudging up the bank. 'When my mother died some years ago, my maternal grandmother took me in. She liked the sun, so we lived for awhile in Tahiti. Then Martinique. Then finally French Guiana. Eight months ago my grandmother passed away and I started kicking around the north coast, trying to decide where to go from there. One day I met these two guys in Venezuela, down on the beach. They were with the Peace Corps and had just been reposted to Ecuador. Anyway, one thing led to another. I had some money from my grandmother's estate, so I asked if I could tag along and pay my own way. They said yeah.

'When we got to Quito, where I was to leave them, one guy came down sick. Dysentery or something. The other guy didn't want to go into the jungle alone, and I was looking for adventure. Anyway, he arranged with the Corps to take me on as local labour, or some such lie. They don't pay much, but that doesn't matter. I like it here. I can do what I want. Mostly I take river excursions by myself. I like my own company.'

'Yeah?' Selena said. 'Well I like your company too.'

Sparky smiled. 'Here. You hold the jars while I tape them and mark the sample location.'

As Selena held the first container Sparky removed a knife from its belt-sheath and cut a piece of adhesive tape from a larger roll. Together they labelled the jars.

It was as Sparky was resheathing the knife that a yellow and blue macaw, four feet from beak to tail, shrieked in the branches above them. Selena glanced up just in time to see a flight of green parrots rise from the tops of the trees. Then there was silence. Again nothing stirred in the brazen sunlight. Not a cloud flecked the hard blue of the sky. And with the silence came a thought. Selena looked at Sparky.

'Are you finished your work?' she asked, digging into the breast pocket of her shirt and removing a small glass vial.

'Uh huh,' Sparky said.

'Then we got some time to relax?'

'Sure. I don't see any hurry.'

'Good,' Selena said grinning, and removing the lid from the vial.

'Why?' Sparky asked. 'What have you got in mind?'

'This,' Selena said, and she tapped the contents of the container into the palm of her hand.

'What's that?'

'Just *heaven*, babe, that's all. Wanta do some acid?'

'I don't feel so good.'

'It'll p a s s.'

No, really. I don't feel well a t a l l.'

'Hey don't freak-out on me, Babe. Acid a l w a y s starts in the gut.'

'It's not my gut I'm talking about. It's my *h e a d!*'

'Shush. Just listen to the sounds.'

It was forty minutes since they had dropped the acid, and now it seemed to Sparky as though the slow moving river had become a great sound conductor, an evil whispering gallery that gathered the noise of an entire continent and delivered it in distorted form to this very spot. It was as if the world had gone electric, each tiny movement adding to an increasingly tinny hum that rose eventually into a nerve-shredding, brain-vibrating crescendo of metallic abuse. This jungle was altering in its very form, transmogrifying into something evil, miasmic, swampy – like a warm festering wound. Sparky was afraid.

Soon loosely associated thoughts were slipping through Sparky's mind . . . *nothing to fear but fear itself . . . fear itself afraid of fear . . . nothing but fear . . . fear . . . fear . . . help! I've got to get out of here. . . .*

Abruptly Sparky stood up, almost stumbling in the effort.

Before the rush hit, they had broken camp and moved their supplies down to the bank of the river; they had then sat down by the water and waited for the effect of the drug. But whatever Sparky had expected, it certainly wasn't this.

Oh God! What's happening to me?

Unchecked and coming in sporadic flashes, refusing to fall into any scheme of order, sharp barbs of unwanted thought now pierced the flesh and hooked themselves inside Sparky's brain. With each tug on a fishing line, fear moved up a notch.

Nausea! Weakness! Tremors! Distortion! *My body is out of control!*

Sparky's heart had lost its rhythm and began a crooked beat. Lungs now choking, unable to squeeze oxygen out of this atmosphere of decay. Throat dry, very dry, tasting the colour grey. Each sound, each slight insignificant noise, had now begun to form its own geometric pattern before Sparky's eyes – weird objects in a phantasmagoria of kaleidoscopic colours seemed to change in size and shape, to fuse with the background until the very boundaries of life, the body, the self were fluid and disintegrating. Sparky had become a part of this vast, foul-smelling, oozy stretch of bog that undulated with the motion of an unsqueezed sponge. *Oh God! Now my brain is out of c o n t r o l!*

Then Selena started to go.

At first it was gradual, like the rot that comes with death. Her skin began to fluctuate between pallor and flush. Her pupils dilated, her eyes beginning to bulge like a fish. And then rapidly her body took on a terrifying pulse, each throbbing vein and artery visible just beneath the surface of her skin. The skin itself was changing, half flesh, half metallic blue and the muscles below the outside shell seemed to give off a succession of silent cues. Her face distorted into a frightening caricature, a perversion of woman incarnate, lips, eyes, nostrils flaring and dripping with sex . . . *sex . . . sex! Oh no! Let me out of here!*

Then something broke inside Sparky's head. It was like a total letting go, an overload, a chemical psychosis that fractured Sparky's id.

Reality broke away.

The real world had become as elusive as the fragments

of a dream. Vision after vision began to waver in the flicker of after-image. Details – unnoticed before – now seized and demanded attention.

All that was left of Sparky's life was creeping paranoia. Danger was *everywhere*. Inside and out.

Then Selena stood up and took off her shirt.

It was not a fluid motion, for the young woman seemed to disintegrate as she moved, recovering her image just in time to disintegrate again. Transfixed, frozen, mesmerized, Sparky watched this slow strip that seemed as if it had been planned a century in advance. For Selena uncoiled from the ground like a waking cat, standing, stretching her arms skyward as though in worship of the sun. Then with button after button, she released the flaps of her blouse.

Sparky could see the deep valley that ran between her breasts.

A tiny white tick called a *garapate du chão* had adhered itself to one milky mound and now grew pink as the woman's blood filled its transparent body.

Then the cloth fell away and Sparky shivered as Selena's breasts burst forth in nakedness, exposing every little pocket of fat, every vein, every highlighted blemish. One breast now grew larger than the other, then smaller, then bloated larger again. The nipples were dry and cracked like a sun-baked riverbed.

'God!' Selena shouted, shaking loose her wild mane of black hair. 'It's positively primal. This place is f u c k i n alive!'

Rocking her body and rolling her shoulders and moving to some hidden rhythm, she stepped toward the lagoon.

Don't, Sparky's mind screamed. *Watch out for the leeches!* But the thought never found words; it just fell unspoken like a bird shot bleeding from the sky.

Selena had reached the mudbank and was now buried knee-deep in ooze. The mud seemed to suck at each sinking foot as the woman threw back her head and laughed wickedly out loud: 'Eat me, Mother Nature! S u c k your daughter dry!'

To Sparky, the voice seemed detached, unnatural, little more than a growl that scraped from Selena's throat. Yet two of the words, echoing, hooked into Sparky's mind: – *Eat me . . . Eat me . . . Eat me, Sparky! Yes, child, I've come back!*

Sparky stopped dead.

Now only Selena was moving, turning, holding out her arms. And her face was ageing fast.

I said 'Eat me, Sparky!' Take your Mama away.

'But . . . but you're not alive! You're buried in the ground!'

Selena frowned and mouthed the words, 'Who are you talking to?' Then abruptly she laughed, reaching for the waist button to her shorts, fumbling, getting it loose, pausing for effect before she pushed them down.

Heat flamed up from the sun-drenched bank.

Small deep pools now studded the surface of the mud, each one gleaming like a crystal against the background of lacquer green.

Then the mud seemed to climb Selena's legs, reaching out for the shorts that were coming down, coming off, first one leg sucking out of the goo, then the other, then the woman standing spread-eagled and naked before Sparky's terrified eyes.

And that was when the thought unwanted ripped through Sparky's mind: *tzantza!* Again: *tzantza!* Again: *tzantza!* It would not go away.

Suddenly the strain of gazing at the brilliant sheet of mud became too much; Sparky's eyes sought relief in other details of the scene. Like the purple wasp with dull orange wings that slipped by to the right. Like the were-wolf wail of the howler monkey lost somewhere in the canopy of gloom above and behind. Like Selena's tumbling black hair with one long loose strand that –

No! Not a strand of hair – but rather a slow, regular, unhurried movement – a slithering, sliding, swaying

65

black, heading toward Sparky. Now Selena was approaching Sparky, her feet sucking through the mud as she reached for her shoulder bag lying on the bank. Selena now dripping sex from her Medusa smile as the anaconda wrapped its coils round and round her head, the jaws of the snake snapping open for a quick glimpse of small white teeth, its dark eyes black with fury and hate as it lashed like a whip with its tail.

A series of hot shivers passed through Sparky's gut.

Time had become a drone; Pandora's Box opened.

Now there was fear in the hair-snake, all slimy with muscles that appeared from nowhere to play beneath its skin, rising up in knots or dissolving into jelly at the command of the small brain within the spade-shaped head.

There was fear in what Selena now held in her hand, the object emerging from the shoulder bag like some two-faced Janus-head, like tongues of the Devil curving up to lick the jungle air.

And there was fear in Selena's voice, her words steamy and sultry in Sparky's tortured ears: 'Don't you look away, Babe. I got the hots for you. Just walk right i n t o me and let that a n i m a l loose. Come on – '

and eat me, child. Take your Mama away!

Selena reached out and with a growl grabbed Sparky by the arm as her other Devil's hand went for the shorts. In panic Sparky pulled away sharply, and slipped and fell in the mud. Selena laughed as the shorts ripped, baring Sparky's groin. Then she tossed the garment up on the bank and stood with her legs spread, towering above the figure sprawled on the ground at her feet. On hands and knees, through tear-filled eyes, ripped and stoned by the acid, Sparky looked up.

It was at that moment that Sparky's hand touched the handle of the knife still in its belt sheath.

Then Selena was squatting slowly, her groin now coming to life.

Tzantza? No, not tzantza but . . . but –

A black mass of hair rose up on its haunches from the

woman's crotch to wave several strands of pubic wisp hypnotically in front of Sparky's face. Within moments the patch of black had eight legs of various lengths covered with long coarse hair. Then it had become an obscene fat sack, round and bulging with a pair of unpleasant eyes that glared forth from a kind of watch tower above the body. Next the spider sat back on four of its legs, the other four raised in the air – then it dropped and moved with a furtive, sinister motion back into the swamp of Selena's crotch.

A second later, Selena sat down on Sparky and her Devil's hand issued forth.

'F e e l   t h a t, babe, just feel that. Have I got a t r e a t for you.'

'No!'

Sparky!

'GO AWAY!'

'Ah ya, slip it deep inside. Now fuck me, babe.'

I hate you, Mother! Daddy, help me please!

Selena bucked with a sudden jerk, the forceful thrust of her body slamming Sparky against the ground. Then she began to thrash convulsively, her limbs now twitching and her eyes bulging wide. At first there was just an unearthly sound from where the knife had pierced her windpipe, a noise half-way between a bubble and a hiss as if someone were sucking at a clogged tube. Then Sparky yanked the blade savagely to the right, tugging it when it caught. And with a gargle, Selena's throat slit open and a fountain of blood in pulsing spurts sprayed the air with a crimson fog.

Sparky started to scream.

Silence.

A vast silence that was no silence at all – but more a holding of breath. For though all sound had ceased and a hush had come over the forest, this was *jungle* silence, watchful and alert. This was the silence of the snake, the tiger, and the bat. This was a silence to call forth the self-protective in man. This was the sort of silence that said: 'Seize the nearest weapon – for that which comes, will come too quick for thought.'

The woman knew this jungle, so she put down her bowl of *chicha* and cocked her head to one side.

She was an ugly Jivaro woman, clothed as was the custom with the left shoulder bare. Her hair was filthy with dirt and infested by lice, her face painted in wild designs. Listening, she sat in front of a poorly-constructed, thatch-roofed hut the bamboo walls of which seeped quantities of smoke. A *tzantza* hung above the narrow door.

In front of this woman, a fire was burning under a clay pot filled with a muddy stew. Beyond the pot, a young child with spindly legs and a swollen stomach was pulling the tail of a mangy, flea-bitten dog. The dog had ceased to play and now listened like the woman.

The first sign of anything unusual was a dull, high-pitched screaming that came from the trees above. First a colony of monkeys worked themselves up to a feverish excitement, then all the other creatures of the jungle seemed to join in – only to stop abruptly. This left an eerie path of silence down which came a shriek of such terror and ecstasy, each emotion bouncing wildly off the other, that the woman jumped up sharply and ran to retrieve her child. In fear she clutched the infant to her breast, her eyes darting about in the forlorn hope that her mate might suddenly return to their home.

Then she shuddered violently, for it froze her to the bone.

This wrench of primal passion.

Sparky's first orgasm.

PART TWO

Horseman

Old is the tree, and the fruit good
Very old and thick the wood.
Woodsman, is your courage stout?
Beware! The root is wrapped about
Your mother's heart, your father's bones,
And like the mandrake comes with groans.

Robert Louis Stevenson.

Is Someone Hunting Heads?

Vancouver, British Columbia, 1982

Monday, October 18th, 5.00 a.m.

In this city, it often rains. Geography demands it. For beyond the islands scattered west roll endless miles of ocean, while northeast at the city's back jut jagged mountain peaks. With the slate-grey skies of autumn come the cyclone westerlies, raging winds and boiling clouds that sweep in from the sea. In waves these bloated clouds tear open on the peaks, and the rain which fills each gut spills and rattles down.

To live in this city, you learn to like rain.

The woman stumbling through the early morning storm was soaked right to her skin. She staggered up Pender Street in Chinatown with one arm clutched to her abdomen, the other thrown wide to grasp support from the buildings that lined the road. Her feet splashed through the puddles stained with neon tint. She was tall and slender, this woman – a long-legged, black-haired Caucasian in her early twenties. Though the chill of October hung in the air her coat flapped open to expose a scooped-necked blouse that bared her upper chest and a pair of tight blue jeans. The wet fabric of the blouse clung to her puckered nipples. She was cold. She was tired. She was hungry and wet. And she was badly in need of a fix.

The woman was heading for the Moonrise Hotel and 'The Wall' where, by tradition, hookers write their messages to each other. The neon sign which sputtered a block ahead was her destination. There was mist inbetween.

At the corner of Pender and Main the woman slipped and her feet skidded out from beneath her. There was a bone-jarring wrench as her hip collided with the pavement. She gasped in pain as severe withdrawal cramps seized her. A cold burn spread over the entire surface of her body. Ants seemed to crawl through her muscles. And now as she sat quite still on the pavement, her head bent, the rain plastered her black hair against her pale white forehead. She began to cry.

Johnnie, you rotten bastard! Won't somebody help me, please!

It had now been twenty minutes since the police had let her go.

The bulls had stopped her on the street at nine the night before. 'Routine check,' the bulls said. 'We roust all the working girls.' At first she had thought they were vice bulls working the pussy patrol. But of course they were narcs.

'Lemme alone,' the woman said. 'I know my legal rights.'

One cop riffled her wallet, then gave her a wan smile. 'You don't *have* rights,' he said. 'This ain't the USA.'

Then they had found the junk hidden in her shoe. Ordinarily she would have carried her stash in a plastic balloon in her mouth, hoping to get it swallowed before they clamped on a choke hold. Work, however, made that very difficult. How do you chat a john up when your mouth is stuffed with balloon?

The worst part of all was that the cap was for her fix. Just five more minutes, count 'em, and she'd have cooked it up in a spoon.

The bulls had dragged her down to the cop shop at 312 Main. She was already sweating by the time they booked her in, took her prints and snapped a mug-shot full of anguish. They had caged her on the fourth floor, then left her alone to stew. Lack of junk had done the rest.

It was only a short time before her nose and eyes began to run and sweat soaked out through the pores of her skin to drench her already rain-damp clothes. Hot and cold flashes hit her as if a furnace door were swinging open and shut. After awhile she lay down on the springs of the bunk – for there was no mattress – and curled up into a ball. She felt too weak to move and her legs twitched and ached. A soft blow hit her heart. The cell went black around the edges.

The woman wanted to die.

It seemed like months before the narcs removed her from the women's jail upstairs and put her in the interview room. By then she was clutching her guts with both arms just to keep them inside. The room was ten feet square with a table and two chairs. One cop, young and muscular, remained standing by the door. The other narc sat down. He was much older, a man with a waxy embalmed complexion and a silky black moustache. He looked like a Mississippi gambler from the 1880s. He was the one who grabbed her arm and slapped it down on the table.

'You been hookin' that spot so much it's about to get infected.' He pointed to the needle welt in the crook of her elbow where the vein had almost disappeared, retreating back toward the bone to escape the probing needle.

Black Moustache then dumped her purse onto the table between them. Combs, cosmetics, condoms and tissues scattered across the surface. He placed the cap of junk seized from her shoe in the centre of the contents. Then he began the spiel.

'The law allows, lady, up to seven years for possession. With the sort of shape you're in even minutes will seem like years. You make the decision.'

'Back to your cell,' Muscles said, 'or walk right outa here.'

'Pick up the contents of your purse and sashay out the door.'

'*All* the contents of your purse. *Everything* on the table.'

Black Moustache tapped the cap and rolled it an inch toward her. 'Name your pusher.'

73

'Name your pimp.'

'Give us something better.'

'We're reasonable men.'

'Poor sick girl like you.'

'Don't tell us,' Moustache said, 'and what else can we do?' He shrugged his shoulders, palms up, like the Frenchmen do.

But she did nothing. Said nothing. And the narcs made good their threat. It wasn't until 4.30 a.m. that they issued her an Appearance Notice and let her out of the can.

Johnnie! I gotta find Johnnie! she thought. *Please Johnnie, get me a fix!*

She had gone first to the room they shared in a rat-infested hotel. A sign outside advertised: *Hot and Cold Water in Every Room. Reasonable Rates.* But Johnnie wasn't there. And all their stuff was gone.

When she reached the exit onto the street a drunk was sprawled in the doorway. The wino had a pale thin face and long yellow teeth. He looked like a rodent. Flicking her a blank, cold smile, the man took a deep slug from a bottle of Aqua Velva shaving lotion. On the ground beneath him was a puddle of piss and rain.

Disgusted, the woman squeezed herself flat against the brick wall near his feet. 'Gimme a kiss,' the drunk slurred as she stumbled out onto the pavement. Then the woman turned down Carrall Street and made for China-town. The feel of the bricks on the skin of her palm had reminded her of The Wall.

Now the traffic light at the empty intersection of Pender and Main turned red, suffusing the mist with a colour so intense that it seemed as if a rain of blood dripped down on the city. The woman glanced down Pender Street, back the way she had come.

Chinatown at five a.m. could be in another century. For at this hour the mystery and inscrutability that the West sees in the East is almost tangible. The woman could see a line of buildings stretching out in the rain,

74

their façades as ornate as Chinese theatre masks. Windows looked out on the road like dead man's eyes. In one of these buildings Sun Yat-sen had lived out part of his exile. In others Secret Societies had met in an atmosphere as thick with mystery as the smoke which fumed from their opium factories. While under the street – where she sat now – fabled tunnels had snaked from somewhere to somewhere else for some forgotten reason.

This woman, of course, knew none of this – for she was new to this city. She had lived within it for a total of four days.

Slowly struggling to her feet, she lurched toward the hotel.

The Wall was right next door to the Moonlight Arms, the pub of the Moonrise Hotel, and it was built of old brick painted with the red and white stripes of a skid row barber shop. The white stripes had become a hookers' message board. For it was here that the prostitutes who worked the Downtown Eastside warned their sisters of the night about certain kinky johns. Messages like: *Light blue Pontiac: This one's a cutter* or *Look out (shank!)* and then a BC licence number. Occasionally pimps used The Wall to contact their stables. Pimps like Johnnie.

With a rising panic, the woman frantically searched for Johnnie's characteristic scrawl.

Oh, God, no! He hasn't left a message!

She didn't notice the vehicle that came around the corner.

The car crept down the block from Main Street, its tyres hissing over the rain-soaked tarmac, its licence plate covered by mud. Ten feet from the woman, it headed for the curb. The passenger's window was open. The engine idled.

The woman heard the motor purr and she slowly turned around. Then she stumbled to the window.

'Want a date?' she croaked.

On instinct she bent down to get a look at the driver,

75

for hers was a dangerous business. Only yesterday afternoon she had heard that a working girl had been snuffed by a john. The guy had used a nylon to strangle her to death.

Though the driver's face was shadowed, she could just make out the eyes.

'Forget it,' the woman said sharply, and she went to turn away.

'Hey, wait a minute, lady. You don't look so well.'

'Fuck off,' the woman said, glancing back over her shoulder.

'You strung out, lady? I can fix that up. I want you for a friend of mine. He'll throw in some junk.'

'No!' the woman said – and then the cramps hit her again, worse this time.

Ten seconds later, she climbed into the car. The driver eased the vehicle away from the curb and they drove off into the night.

11.45 a.m.

The maple trees were turning. Earlier that morning the rain clouds had blown inland and now, out beyond the panes of the greenhouse, the leaves were a riot of colour. Hues of red and yellow and orange stood out sharply against the backdrop of English Bay with its blue-green waters whipped into foaming whitecaps. Bright October sunshine slanted in through the glass, hitting a row of prisms that threw rainbows across the floor. Inside there were also other colours in profusion, for they liked it here, the roses.

The plants were growing in tropical wells and artificial gardens, row upon row of them, spread out around the greenhouse.

Over near a door which led to the house was a section for 'hybridizing'. In this section stood a single plant that flowered deep maroon.

The man was sitting in one corner in a large white

wicker chair. He was a tall, slender individual with piano-player hands. His hair was dark and wavy with a trace of grey at the temples, his eyes dark and brooding. There was a slight shadow of beard showing through the skin of his finely-chiselled jaw, and his aquiline nose, on first impression, hinted at arrogance. It was only if you heard him speak that his humility came through.

The man was sitting cross-legged with a pad and clipboard on his knee. Scattered about him, covering the surface of a library table, hiding the tiles on the floor, were several dozen volumes of history on the First World War. The floor space left between the books was littered with crumpled paper.

Engrossed in what he was writing, the man failed to notice that a woman had entered the room. She stood for a moment just inside the door to the house, contemplating him. Her eyes were large and green and sparkling with life. They were set in a flawless face. Her cheekbones were slanted high and her lips were full. Her hair was auburn. She was twenty years younger than the man, in her early thirties. She wore a maroon silk blouse and a tailored suit over her full figure. The suit was grey.

'Eh bien, Robert,' she said in French, *'Est-ce qu'on prendra un* lunch *aujourd'hui?'*

The man looked up from his work and smiled. He put the clipboard down. *'Oui,'* he said. *'J'aimerais bien. Combien de temps as-tu?'*

'Juste une heure,' the woman replied. *'J'ai une classe de seminaire en fin de la journée.'*

The man stood up and crossed over to where she waited at the door. She touched his arm as they turned to leave but the man paused for a moment. He looked at the single plant in the hybridizing area, picked up a pair of shears and snipped off one of the buds. The rose was from a strain that he had bred himself. Up until now it had remained unnamed.

'As-tu pensé au nom que tu lui donnerais?' the woman asked him.

He held out the rosebud just in front of her heart, maroon on maroon for a perfect match.

'*Genevieve*,' he answered, now giving it a title.

With a light laugh, Genevieve DeClercq broke into a smile.

And in that moment, it seemed to him even brighter in the room.

Monday, October 25th, 6.30 p.m.

It is common knowledge that for physical setting there are only six great cities in the world. Rio de Janeiro, Sydney, Cape Town, Hong Kong and San Francisco: these are five of them. Vancouver is the sixth one.

The young man who leaned on the port rail of the BC Government boat was watching the city pass by on the left. He was six feet tall and lanky, with a long face, good teeth, and blond hair that blew in the wind.

The boat was returning from a salvage check up the bite of Howe Sound. The Sound lay just north of the city harbour, one of the million indentations that make up the ten thousand rugged linear miles of the British Columbia coastline. The boat had just reached the mouth of English Bay, the gate to Vancouver Harbour. Point Grey lay ahead, Vancouver to the left.

It was the shank of the day; the sunset, the time Heller enjoyed the most. His work completed, he could now relax with nothing more important to do than breathe in slow, deep lungfuls of the salt-sea air. To the north and left the backdrop peaks of Hollyburn and Grouse and Seymour Mountains were burnished copper by the sun. In the foreground where slope met sea the Point Atkinson Lighthouse was winking. Far away in the distance which comprised the State of Washington, the volcanic cone of Mount Baker stood guard above the scene.

Heller loved the sea because the sea knew no control. Here English Bay one moment was a sheet of calm green glass, its freighters and tugs and sailboats slipping among the tide lines like small fish through a net. Then the sky would change suddenly as a storm came crashing in, the boats then tossing in the wild waves like corks in boiling water. From all around would come the shouts of men in rubber raingear, and the clouds would open up to pelt the angry waters.

It had been like that this morning, but now the sea was calm.

Dan Heller turned around and waved to the man in the wheelhouse. Glen Simpson gave him a thumbs up back.

Now the boat had crossed the harbour mouth and the city lights slipped away. Looming up before him were the sandstone cliffs of Point Grey. Down near the water Heller could see the tower gun emplacements which had waited for the Japanese during the Second World War. High on the cliff were the buildings of the University of British Columbia, the glass walls of the Museum of Anthropology ablaze with the setting sun. Behind Point Grey lay the Fraser River.

Ten minutes later, as the boat turned into the North Arm of the Fraser, Heller saw a heron lift off from Wreck Beach. A log in the water thumped along the hull. Then they were home and the boat bumped the dock.

Glen cut the engines and left the wheelhouse once Heller had secured the lines. They were moored to the Government Wharf of the Provincial Ministry of Lands and Forests. A helicopter was landing on the helipad, its rotors flashing and throwing off rays of blood-red sunlight. Glen joined Heller at the rail.

'Like a cup of coffee?' the wheelman asked.

'Thanks,' Heller said, taking the mug. The brandy warmed his stomach.

The two men were silent for several minutes as they watched the hustle and bustle in the estuary. Log booms lined the river and boats were everywhere. Jets came and went from the International Airport on Sea Island, across the water.

'How many boats you think'll be gone by this time next year?'

'Who knows?' Heller replied. 'Maybe twenty per cent.'

'That high? Man, oh man. What a change in the weather. Want another coffee? There's some left in the pot.'

'Why not?' Heller said. 'But you better hurry. Less than a minute till the sun sinks in the sea.'

'I'll make it,' Glen said, heading for the wheelhouse.

But he didn't make it – and both men missed the sunset. For as Glen Simpson grabbed the rail that ran up to the pilot's station, he happened to glance at the water and his eyes caught something floating.

'Hey, Dan! Come here! And bring that gaff behind you.'

'What's wrong?' Heller asked, joining him at the boat rail.

'You see what I see?' Glen pointed at the water.

And there, half submerged and bumping the hull, was the body of a woman. Naked. Bloated. Just a body ending at the neck. The corpse was missing a head.

11.31 p.m.

Commercial Crime Section (Special 'I')
Target: Steve Rackstraw (aka 'The Fox')
Tape installed: October 25th. 0900 hours. (Tipple)
Tape removed: October 25th. 1130 hours. (Tipple)
u/m only known as 'The Weasel'.
Outgoing local call.

Weasel: Hey.
Fox: Hey. Hey.
Weasel: Sorry I forgot to call ya . . . forgot all about it.
Fox: Ya did, huh?
Weasel: Sorry.
Fox: Well ya better grab your ride and get your black ass over here. Now.

Weasel: I can't, not now. Later maybe.

Fox: Is that our lady, Ms Billie Holiday, I hear behind you, man?

Weasel: Yeh, you know how pussy reacts to that. I need time man, time to get this horse in the stable.

Fox: Yeh?

Weasel: Time to get this here filly broken, ya know, broken, so I don't need no rope, ya know, to keep the bitch from leaving.

Fox: So? So what?

Weasel: Stay cool . . . Hey, just a moment (Shouting: Turn that music down. U/f: Come on, Baby. Make me fe-e-el good. Weasel: In a bit, just git your selfishness ready.) Ya still there, man?

Fox: Okay. Okay, a bit more time. But I'm warning you, cousin, get your priorities straight. Important things are beginning to break and you had better be ready.

Weasel: Yeh, yeh, I be ready.

Fox: When the Wolf calls, you had better have your shit together, man. Don't use your dick, use Sister M.

Weasel: What, what the . . . (inaudible) . . . zombi walks.

Fox: By the by, man, where is H.G.? She been missing for a week.

Weasel: Yeh, I know, like that's cold, real cold.

Fox: You better find her, man, before the Wolf finds out, or you'll be cold, stone dead cold if there's a leak.

Weasel: No, no worry. I can do . . .

Fox: We will be waitin' on you all.

Weasel: Bye.

Fox: Huh. Huh.

(end of call)

Tuesday, October 26th, 8.15 a.m.

Winter had arrived early within the four walls of the room. It was that cold. The air had a chill, brittle quality to it and there was a light condensation on the stainless steel surface. The pathologist wore gloves.

Doctor Kahil Singh was an elderly man with close-cropped silver hair. His face was long and angular and he wore rimless glasses. Dr Singh was one of three pathologists at the Richmond General Hospital. Today he had drawn duty in the hospital morgue.

He had arrived for work at 7.30 this morning to find three accident victims waiting for him in their drawers. Two of the bodies had come from a motor vehicle collision last night on Highway 99, the police report stating that a bottle of Cuervo Tequila was found smashed on the road. The third corpse was a floater fished out of the Fraser River.

Dr Singh did not like floaters. So he took that one first.

This had been Singh's practice ever since medical school, for as one of his professors way back then had so wisely put it: 'If you take the ugly ones first, the worst is over.' And this one was certainly ugly. Bloated and immense, the girl's body was partly decomposed and here and there fibrous strands of muscle clung to exposed bone.

Singh assumed at first that the skull had been sliced away when it met with a boat propeller. *A drowning suicide*, he thought, *with a subsequent clean cut*. So the doctor peeled back the waterlogged flesh that had closed around the neck, and using a strong magnifying glass examined the top vertebra.

Two minutes later, Singh called the RCMP.

Corporal James Rodale was not pleased with the telephone call. It was not that he was a lazy man neglectful of his duty, it was just that Rodale was one of those men with a weak breakfast stomach. He did not need the scales of nausea tipped by a morning autopsy. Luckily,

Singh was a perceptive man. When the doctor noticed the look on the Corporal's face as he entered the autopsy room, he suggested that Rodale wait for exhibits on the far side of the morgue. Rodale was grateful.

'There's a phone on the table,' the doctor said. 'Use it if you want.'

Corporal James Rodale was slim and his movements precise. He wore the brown serge working uniform of the RCMP. His hairline was receding so he always wore his hat, and the regimental badge sat square in the centre of his forehead. Rodale had since birth had different coloured irises: the left eye was reddish brown, the right one green. At school the other students nicknamed him 'Stoplight'.

As the autopsy was performed, Rodale sat at the table with his back to Dr Singh. Though he kept his eyes averted he knew what was going on. The pathologist was recording his findings by means of an overhead microphone. Between the calls that Rodale made on his other investigations, some of the comments got through.

'The body is that of a white female in her early twenties. Needle marks cover the interior aspect of both arms . . .'

'There is a 4.5 cm. incision on both the left and right sides of the neck close to vertical plane. There is a horizontal cut from the anterior to posterior aspect of the neck 6 cm. superior to the suprasternal notch . . .

'The heart weighs 280 grams. The coronary arteries show minimal atherosclerotic streaking and are widely patent. On sectioning, the myocardium is of a uniform tan brown colour. The aorta is intact . . .

'The labia are bruised. There are a few adhesions of the fallopian tubes . . .'

Almost an hour later, Dr Singh was finished. He wiped his gloves on a clean cloth and walked over to where Rodale waited. As yet the RCMP exhibit jars on the table were empty.

'May I have a print sheet?' the pathologist asked.

Rodale found the requested form and handed it to the doctor. Singh then crossed back to the stainless steel table that held the cut-up remains of the woman. He injected glycerine into all ten wrinkled fingertips and then one by one he rolled each fingertip across a pad of ink. He fingerprinted the form and returned it to Rodale. The officer put it on file.

'Well?' the Corporal asked finally, meeting the doctor's eyes.

'She didn't drown,' Singh said. 'The lungs are free of water. That means she was already dead before she entered the river. There's a perpendicular slit on both sides of the neck, consistent with a stab wound sideways through the throat. The weapon has a thick blade. A second horizontal cut removed the head from the body.'

'A sex attack?' Rodale asked, writing in his notebook.

'I can't tell from the genitals though there's bruising in the area. We'll do a smear for sperm, but she spent at least a week in the water. The only other injury is a slash across both breasts. It cuts right to the sternum that joins the ribs together. It bisects both nipples.'

Rodale nodded. 'Is the cut that took the head away from a motorboat propeller?'

'No,' Singh said, removing a jar from the table. He walked back to the body.

The Corporal averted his eyes as the pathologist picked up a scalpel from a tray of shiny instruments to his left. Rodale felt bile rise to his mouth as Singh returned to the table. Fighting it down, angry with himself, he forced his reluctant eyes to focus on what the doctor held in one blood-streaked hand. The glove contained a single human vertebra.

'See these marks?' Singh said, indicating the upper surface.

Rodale stared at several lines scraped into the bone.

'They move in a zigzag pattern like you get from a saw-ing cut. There are two of them, a quarter centimetre apart. Perhaps a nick in the blade. I don't know a propeller that moves with that sort of motion.'

The pathologist dropped the neck bone into the jar he held and passed it to the Corporal. Rodale sealed the bottle, labelled it, and marked the paper square with time, date, place, and his regimental number.

Singh said, 'You'll have the autopsy report before the day is over.'

'Thank you, Doctor,' Rodale said, picking up his brief-case and exhibit and turning to leave.

'One moment,' Singh said, peeling off his gloves. He scrubbed his hands in a nearby sink then pulled the table drawer open. 'Here,' he said, removing a packet of Alka-Seltzer and giving it to the Corporal. 'For the next time I call you.'

Rodale took the lift down one floor. He found a men's washroom and prised the package open. Popping a lozenge in his mouth, he glanced at the cop in the mirror. 'Forget next time,' he said to the reflected image. 'Worry about now.' Then he left the building.

12.15 p.m.

To: Richmond Detachment,
        RCM Police,
        6900 Minoru Blvd.,
        Richmond, BC.

                            Attn. Cpl. James G. Rodale.

From: Vancouver Police Dept.,
        312 Main Street,
        Vancouver, BC.

                            Repl. Det. Bernie Zebroff,
                            Drug Squad.

Re: Fingerprint Enquiry/Floater (Fraser River).
        ID confirmed.
        Helen Ann Grabowski aka Patricia Ann Palitti.
        Outstanding charges: NIP (heroin). Vancouver.

DOB June 12, 1961 Topeka, Kansas.
Check with FBI.
Picture to follow.
Description from booking sheet: white female, height (175 cm) weight (50 kg), slim build, large breasts unusually firm (believe me, that's what it says here), black hair to collar, brown eyes, needle tracks both arms, long scar down centre of spine (skin search by nurse).

B. Zebroff (Det.)

3.45 p.m.

'E' Division, RCM Police,
Richmond Detachment.

Attn.: J. G. Rodale (Cpl.)

From: 'N' Division, RCM Police,
        Ottawa, Ontario.

Re: 4722067.

FBI confirmation print record: Helen Ann Grabowski aka Patricia Ann Palitti.
New Orleans Police Department.
Fraud with Intent (April 12, 1980) Suspended Sentence.
Known prostitute. Pimp: John Lincoln Hardy aka 'The Weasel'.
No Record.
Pictures to follow.

5.30 p.m.

It hit you as soon as you came through the door. Nothing definite, nothing concrete, just a vague amorphous atmosphere that hung in the air like opium smoke. You knew at once without being told that this place was junk city. That junk time ruled here, with reality suspended.

There were fifty patrons in the Moonlight Arms making the noise of twenty. Most of them just sat around, nursing a beer, hanging out, watching each other furtively through tombstone eyes. The only animation in the pub came from a fat, slovenly woman who leaned on the jukebox and drunkenly pounded its top. Loverboy was playing. You knew also that likely as not, upstairs in the rooms, a dozen hypes were sprawled on beds, nodding in and out of life, outfits clinging to their arms like a dozen glassy leeches.

Then perhaps, having sensed this, you backed out through the door.

The woman slouched against the wall off to the left of the bar. In looks she would have been striking if she had taken care of herself. She was just short of six feet tall with a full and muscular figure. Her features hinted at Ursula Andress in the movie *Doctor No* – same high cheekbones, same honey-coloured hair, same almond eyes. But there the likeness ended. For this woman was dressed in a set of filthy clothes. Her fingernails were cheap and fake and painted with chipped red lacquer. It had been a full two weeks since her hair had felt a brush. Her make-up was sloppy. And there were circles under her eyes.

Today, this woman was nervous and jumpy.

Her blue-grey eyes were piercing as they jerked about the room, telling all and sundry what she was looking for. *I need junk*, they pleaded.

'Are you lookin', baby?' It was a whispered voice to her left.

'You got?' she asked, flicking a glance at the man.

The Indian rolled his own eyes toward the pub's back door. He was a short, stout man with thick biceps circled by copper armbands. His arms were naked from the shoulder to the fingertips. The frayed jean jacket was open at his chest exposing a leather thong with a whale's tooth at its end. His soiled jeans were suspended from a thick black belt with a Harley-Davidson buckle. His face was pockmarked and his eyes, which peered out from under the brim of a Stetson, were cold with the meanness of the streets. When he smiled, as he was doing now, his lips opened over stained and rotting teeth.

'What's it for?' the woman croaked, leaning toward his table.

'Sixty for one,' the Indian said. 'Meet me in five out back.'

Then the man stood up abruptly and quickly walked away.

5.45 p.m.

The little girl was laughing and no more than five years old. She was dressed in a waterproof snowsuit that covered her from head to toe. Her face was flushed and rosy-cheeked and here and there a red curl poked out from her hood. Squealing and chuckling with delight, she came tumbling down the wooded hillside, part running, part sliding, part rolling toward the harbour water. Every inch of her clothing was caked with thick, wet mud.

'Wait up, Cindy!' her sister yelled from behind. She was going on seven, so a little more reserved. Age does that to you.

They had seen the tent all ripped to tatters from the top of the hill. The hill was in North Vancouver, a quarter mile from their home. Already it was nearing dark and the fir trees cast deep shadows across the slope to the water. Dianne didn't like the shadows: to Cindy it didn't matter. She had plunged on ahead.

'Wait up, I said!' Dianne shouted, sliding down beside her sister. It took her a full five feet to stop. 'Who do you think lives here?' the older girl asked.

'Oscar the Grouch, you nose-honker,' Cindy replied.

As she approached the tent, crouching, Cindy whispered softly: 'Oscar. Hey, Oscar. You hiding from me in there?' Then suddenly her foot sank into the ground with mud up to the ankle.

'You're such a gumby, Cinders. That's where the creek runs down.'

The little girl ignored her and took another step. It didn't work. Her left foot came out of her rubber boot and for several seconds she stood waving her arms in the air like a trapeze artist losing balance. Then inevitably – and with a shriek – Cindy toppled over. Flat into the mud.

'Boy, are you gonna get it! Wait till Mom sees your clothes.'

Cindy struggled to her feet and finally stood up in the muck. Reaching down she grabbed hold of the top of her gumboot and gave it a hearty tug. With a sucking sound the boot came loose – but then the girl immediately fell over again. Only this time she didn't get up. Instead, with eyes as big as searchlights she stared at the ground, for there where her boot had disturbed the mud as she had yanked it out of the earth, a clutching hand of rib bones now reached out from a shallow grave.

8.05 p.m.

They had set out flares to mark the way down to the scene of the crime, but still it was dark within these woods and the underbrush was threatening. Tonight the sky above was clear, a million pin-prick stars visible in space, but the ground was partially hidden by creeping fingers of fog. Up ahead a knot of men stood washed by the glare of floodlights, all but one in uniform, and all with plastic cups. The steam from the coffee held in their hands mingled with the fog from the ground.

As Corporal Rodale moved toward this group, the man without the uniform turned in his direction. 'Is that you, Rodale?' a voice asked, with a stern edge of authority.

'Yes, sir,' the Corporal answered, emerging from the shadows.

'Good. I want you to look at this. I think we've got a problem.'

The man who spoke was now a black silhouette in

front of the portable arc light. He was somewhere in his early fifties, and barely reached the minimum height required by the RCMP. As Rodale moved up beside him, the light shifted to reveal a pair of intense blue eyes above a neat clipped military moustache. The man's mouth was stretched into a grave and determined line. He wore a blue blazer and grey flannel slacks. Sewn to the pocket of the blazer was the crest of the Mounted Police, a buffalo head beneath a crown and surrounded by maple leaves. The man's name was Jack MacDougall.

For a moment Corporal Rodale paused to take in the work in progress. An Ident. member from North Vancouver Detachment was already busy snapping photos of the scene. A constable beside him was making a sketch of the ground, while off to the right a dog master was reading his German shepherd. The animal moved back and forth as if along the lines of a grid, sniffing the leaves in front of him and advancing on the water. Down on the beach, just a black outline against the refinery flames of loco, a member with a metal detector was scanning and sweeping the sand.

'I had you called,' MacDougall said, 'just to be on the safe side. The site was already damaged before we got the call. The bones were discovered by two little girls who reported the find to their father. Instead of calling us right then, he came out here for a look. He's the one who cleared the leaves and mud and sticks from the grave. By the time we got here it was already dark.'

Sergeant MacDougall directed Rodale to an area marked with rope. A beam from one of the arc lights made the ground seem white. Within the square delineated, the Corporal saw what looked like a shallow creek bed beneath a mass of bones. Though the flesh had long since rotted away from the skeleton's upper torso, the trousers that clung around the lower legs had preserved some skin and muscle. Here the maggots were still at work.

'Come dawn I want you to work this scene independently as a backup. I want *everything* done twice. Including a sifting of the soil for two hundred yards around. If what I suspect actually happened here, we can't be overly careful. Do you see what I mean?'

'Yes,' Rodale said, nodding. 'The skull is missing.'

Wednesday, October 27th, 10.34 a.m.

They don't make newspapermen like 'Skip' O'Rourke anymore. Too bad.

The Skipper was a rotund man late of Her Majesty's Navy who sported a belly made of Guinness and a tattoo from Taiwan. The tattoo was a reminder of the perils of too much drink, for when O'Rourke sobered up from his final shore leave before obtaining his discharge, the needle portrait was waiting, engraved on his lower left arm. How he obtained it, where he obtained it, or why he obtained it, O'Rourke had no idea. What he did know, however, was he hated the thing from the moment his sober eyes saw it. The tattoo was one of Popeye, spinach can in hand.

Today, as always, O'Rourke was sporting one of his longsleeved shirts.

He sat at his City Editor's desk, butt in mouth, reviewing the four star page proofs when Edna approached him from the left. Edna was a skinny, flat-chested woman. To Skip O'Rourke she looked like a reincarnation of Olive Oyl.

'This just arrived,' Edna said in her squeaky voice. 'Someone's marked it *Personal: eyes of Editor Only*.' In her hand the woman held a brown manila envelope.

'Put it in the basket. Can't you see I'm busy?'

'Yes, *sir*,' Edna squeaked, then she huffed off back to the mailroom. The Skipper merely grunted, but he was smiling to himself. *The Headhunter*, O'Rourke thought, *I think that's what we'll call him. It's got a catchy ring*.

'Skip' O'Rourke was an editor straight from the dinosaur school. In these times of Visual Display Units

91

(VDUs to those in the know), cold process web-offset, and computer pasteups, O'Rourke still longed for the old days of yellow copy and hot metal type. To the Skipper the word 'scoop' meant more than an ice-cream cone. Thank God, at least the page proofs still came down like before.

Page proofs were the first take before a print was run – and each day O'Rourke read them almost religiously. You never knew what embarrassments a typographical error could throw up.

Completed, the Skipper sat back and put his Hush Puppies up on his desk. He lit a wooden match with his thumbnail and passed it back and forth across the end of the cigar. Then he thought about the bodies and how to handle the story. He was hoping for a connection.

In this city, both *The Vancouver Sun* and *The Province* were owned by Pacific Press. This was just a minor monopoly in a world of shrinking presses – and nothing to worry about. Besides, who cares if bad news comes from one or many sources? Bad news is bad news, right, no matter how you print it.

That morning both papers had used an identical headline. In 96-point type they had asked their readers: IS SOMEONE HUNTING HEADS? Skip O'Rourke had decided that the final edition of the *Sun* should be different. It would ask commuters: HEADHUNTER ON THE LOOSE?

Once you're dead you're dead, O'Rourke thought philosophically. *What's the difference to the victims, may they rest in peace? But a homicidal psychopath – ah, that would sell some papers*.

The Skipper was an editor, true, blue and – well, tattooed.

His job was selling newsprint. And that was what he'd do.

Satisfied, O'Rourke sat up and reached for the envelope that Edna had found in the mail. He ripped it open with a letter knife and dumped the contents onto his desk. All that fell out were two photographs and a magazine clipping. The pictures landed face down.

O'Rourke picked up the clipping and shook his head in wonder. It was a printed subscription form for a sophisticated men's publication called *Buns And Boobs Bonanza*. At the top of the form was depicted a woman naked to the waist. She had the biggest pair of breasts he had ever seen. The caption under the picture read simply: *Looking for These?*

O'Rourke shook his head once more and picked up the photographs. He turned them over. Then the cigar dropped abruptly from his lips and the Skipper yelled out those magic words at every editor's heart: 'Jesus Christ, somebody stop the bloody presses!'

For each picture was of a woman's head, severed at the neck and stuck on an upright wooden pole.

THE BURIAL POLE

10.45 a.m.

The first Headhunter Squad was not a squad at all – it was a co-ordinating centre. In fact were it not for Clifford Olson and his murder rampage in the summer of 1981 there would have been no squad at all. But the RCMP had learned a bitter lesson about lack of co-ordination in that previous case, and so the squad was formed. The first Headhunter Squad consisted of Sergeant Jack MacDougall and Corporal James Rodale. They met in the Headquarters building at 1200 West 73rd.

'That was Dr Kahil Singh,' MacDougall said as he replaced the phone. 'He's at Lion's Gate Hospital where we sent the bones. The marks on the skeleton's vertebra are a match with those on the floater. That means we've got a killer.'

Rodale nodded. 'Where to from here?'

'I think the concentration will have to be on Grabowski. So far our soil sift has turned up nothing. We can't expect very much if we don't know when she died. I'm having Vancouver Harbour Patrol check their back records to see if something was noticed from the water. And I've got a helicopter on order to infra-red the slope. So far the only bit we've got is the tent manufacture. It's Swiss, from Zurich – we're checking all the outlets. Also Interpol.'

'You think she's a foreign national, camping in those woods?'

'Perhaps,' MacDougall said. 'Now how about you?'

'As far as we can tell, this Grabowski woman was here only three or four days. New Orleans wired pictures and they're checking things that end. We don't know what she's doing here and neither do they. We're looking for her pimp. Our best guess at the moment is a john who likes to snuff. One like that knocked off a girl late last week. We're keeping an ear to the street.'

'That it?' MacDougall asked. It was hardly worth a note.

'I'm afraid so,' Rodale answered, shrugging his shoulders. 'A pile of unidentified bones and a transient American hooker – that's not very much to go on.'

MacDougall had to agree.

Thursday, October 28th, 5.15 a.m.

What a day! she thought. *Isn't it amazing that any of us survive?*

The man with the red hair and freckles had brought his wife into St Paul's Hospital at 7.05 that morning. The woman's water had broken forty minutes before, so the man was apprehensive, this being their first child. One of the nurses had taken him aside and had tried to calm him down.

'Now, I want this natural,' the man had said, reaching

for a Kool cigarette and fumbling in his pocket for matches. 'I don't want drugs. Or forceps. Or trauma. Do you understand? Who's your obstetrician and where was he trained?'

The nurse had asked him calmly not to smoke in the Admitting Hall.

Snapping the cigarette in two and tossing it into a trash can, the man had watched his waddling, bloated wife disappear into an elevator.

'I don't trust hospitals,' he said. 'I want that clear from the start. Isn't this the place where they left a sponge in some guy?' Again removing his pack of Kools he had shook a cigarette loose.

The nurse had asked him calmly not to smoke in the Admitting Hall.

The complications had started at 5.21 p.m., not long after Joanna Portman's shift began.

Joanna had found the next five hours draining. She enjoyed working as a nurse in the Maternity Ward, for although a hospital by definition was a place of sickness and death, here she was located at the wellspring of life. She thrived on the feeling of her own rebirth that each delivery gave her. And besides, she liked the mothers. She felt needed, the way they depended on her to see each one of them through.

Mrs Walker, however, had been a tough one.

For hours the poor woman had been tortured by labour pain, awaiting each coming contraction with terror in her eyes. Joanna had held her in her arms. She had soothed her and calmed her with quiet words of encouragement, and toward the end she had even quoted from the Bible. It had never ceased to surprise her how even with agnostics and atheists that seemed to do the trick.

That night Joanna's nursing shift had ended at midnight. The Walker baby, however, had waited till 4.19. So as usual Joanna had remained and seen the delivery through: when a mother had come to rely on her she just couldn't desert in the crunch.

95

Never bail out, she told herself, *until the bomb is dropped. What a day! Isn't it amazing that any of us survive?*

It was now 5.15 in the morning. Joanna was sitting on a bench waiting for the Macdonald bus. There was a smile on her face.

Joanna Portman was a petite woman, twenty-two years of age. On shift she wore her hair in a bun, but now she had released it and let it tumble free. A breeze down Burrard Street blew black strands across her face so she turned part way round on the bench back toward the hospital. Founded by the Sisters of Providence in 1894, St Paul's was a rambling red brick building right in the heart of town. Over the years as the city had grown, additions had been added. Now the plan was to tear it down and build another in its place. Joanna looked up at St Paul's statue in its alcove below the roof. *Will you still look down and protect me*, she thought, *once the new hospital's built?*

The Macdonald bus arrived and Joanna climbed on board.

Ten minutes later when she alighted at Macdonald and Point Grey Road, a cold wind from off the water slapped her across the face. She pulled her collar up and thought, *It almost feels like snow!* But that, of course, was ridiculous. After all, this was Vancouver. Lotusland. And it was only October. *Still, it feels mighty cold*. Joanna started walking.

The shortest route to her upstairs suite in a house three blocks away was through Tatlow Park. Normally, she would skirt the side of the tennis courts and cut across the grass until she reached Bayswater Street. From there it was but a quick walk up to the corner of Third.

This morning, however, that route was unthinkable.

For one thing, it was still pitch dark, and what with the newspapers screaming about this Headhunter being on the loose . . . well, she'd just have to resign herself to taking the long way round.

Joanna Portman was less than two blocks from her home when she heard the car, in low gear, coming up behind her.

With it came apprehension.

Easy girl, she told herself, *let's not get too jumpy. (Jumpy! That's a laugh. I'm scared shitless!)*

There was not a single light burning in any one of the old houses that lined the tree-shadowed street.

Well, go on and take a look. You can scream and run if you have to.

So she took a glance, a quick one, over her left shoulder. And then, relaxing, she sighed with relief as the car pulled up beside her.

Friday, October 29th, 2.03 a.m.

The sweet pungent smell of marijuana began to fill the car. The windows fogged. As the young man puffed on the joint, drawing rapidly in order to fill his lungs to capacity, the burning tip of the cigarette pulsed orange in the dark. Then he blew out a stream of grey smoke that swirled around Val's face.

'I think I'm off,' he said, his voice vague and far away.

'You know what's wrong with you, Chris? You're never serious.'

'About you, I'm serious,' he said, moving over on the seat and giving her breast a squeeze.

'Get serious,' Val muttered, then she closed her arms tightly across her ample chest.

The young man laughed and retreated. He took another long drag off the smouldering joint. 'This is good shit, Valerie. You don't know what you're missing.'

An hour ago they had parked the car at the Simon Fraser Lookout, a pulloff on the University cliff road that marked the spot where the explorer had first sighted the Pacific Ocean. A few minutes later the RCMP had checked them and shone a light into the Volkswagen, so Chris had moved on, muttering something about Trudeau having promised to keep the State out of the bedrooms of the Nation.

Now they were parked on an access road near the

Museum of Anthropology. Normally they would have been able to see the building in the distance with its great glass walls sixty feet high, a modern showcase for the totem art of the Pacific Coast Indian tribes. They would have looked out through the windshield on several carved poles that stood in front of the Museum. But tonight a fog rose from the ground and they could see nothing at all.

Chris reached for Val's breast again.

'Hey, listen, Chris. Really, we've got to talk. I do not want to fail.'

'Fail?' he said, laughing at her. 'You're not going to fail. This is only October. Exams aren't till December.'

Chris Seaton was a blond-haired youth, eighteen years old. Val Pritchard had met him at a freshman dance four weeks ago. She had liked his mirthful eyes, his strong, square chin, and the fact he was always laughing. Now she was beginning to realize that he laughed a little too much.

'You know your problem?' she said. 'You got laughter anxiety.'

'Great. The chick enrolls in first year psychology, attends four or five classes, and she's got me analyzed. Did it ever occur to you that maybe I'm just horny?'

'You're horny cause you're anxious. You got a buried neurosis.'

'And you? What's your cop-out for fucking like a mink?'

'You pig! I do not fuck like a mink.'

'Oh, yeah. You should hear my tapes. I keep a little recorder hidden in the back seat.'

'You don't!' Val said, though she wouldn't put it past him.

'How much money you got? Buy 'em back right now or I send them to your mother.'

'You asshole,' Val said, and both of them laughed.

It was beginning to get cold in the car so Chris cranked over the engine and kicked in the heater. The defrosters started blowing. The windshield began to clear. And that was how they noticed that it had begun to snow. Large but scattered fluffy flakes were landing on the glass, melting, and slowly slipping down to the hood of the Volkswagen.

'Will you look at that?' Chris said, and he blew out a low whistle.

'I thought it rarely snowed down here on the coast.'

'It doesn't. I've lived here all of my life and . . . I mean this is mid-October. It's not supposed to *snow*.'

'Well it is.'

'Yeah, I can see that, silly. Come on. Let's fuck.'

'Not tonight,' Val said. 'Let's go back to the dorms.'

'Jesus, Val. We always fuck when we park.'

'Not tonight, I said.'

'Why?' Chris asked.

'Why? Because I want to get some sleep and it's already 2.00 a.m., that's why. Because I want to pass my exams, that's why. Because my mother works her ass to the bone up in Quesnel cooking in a restaurant so I can go to university, that's why. I get a little freedom and what do I do? Smoke my bloody brains out and hump each night away. Well I'm not going to fail. Come on, let's go to the dorms.'

Chris slipped his hand up between Val Pritchard's thighs.

'JESUS!' the girl shouted, and she pushed him away. 'Don't I have any say around here?'

Before the youth could answer, she swung the car door open and jumped out into the night.

'Get your shit together, man. And get off my self-esteem!' Val slammed the door shut and stomped off through the curtain of snow.

'Women,' Chris muttered.

For several seconds he just sat in the driver's seat, rubbing mist from the inside of the windshield, trying to catch a glimpse of the girl through the tumbling snow. She was heading toward the totem poles, of that he was certain. From there Val would pick up one of the paths that led back to the campus. That is unless she lost her way, walked off the cliff, and fell over one hundred feet to Wreck Beach below. So he opened the door, climbed out, and started after her.

Now it was really coming down. He couldn't see her for the wall of flakes that pressed in around him. *Snow in October. Man, oh man. What a freak*, he thought.

He broke into a light jog so as to catch up to Val.

Cherchez la femme, Chris old boy. Cherchez la big-boobed fe-

He was twenty-five feet from the car when Val screamed. It was not the cry of a woman falling; it was a shriek of raw terror. The scream seemed almost to ricochet among the crystals of snow.

Chris decided to turn and run: Val could take care of herself.

But just then he slipped in the snow, skidded crashing into Val, and the force of the collision knocked both of them to the ground.

Now the girl threw back her head and let out a second scream. Chris almost pissed himself. He took one look at the lines of horror etched into her face and that was enough. The youth scrambled around, clawed the snow, tried to gain his feet. He looked up, himself terrified – and that was when he saw what was hanging in the air.

There was a light at the foot of the totem pole ten feet off to his left. This light shone up to illuminate two vertical support struts that held an ornate crosspiece suspended above the ground. The totem – a Dogfish Burial Pole – was fifteen feet high. The crosspiece was carved with a figurehead from an Indian myth. Hanging between the struts was the body of a woman. Her hands had been nailed to the crosspiece and her head had been cut off. The carved face of the Dogpole appeared to take its place.

Chris' mouth dropped open, but he managed to stifle a scream.

Then he noticed that the body was wearing a nurse's

whites. The garment had been torn down the front, revealing a strip of naked flesh from the neck to the hair of the crotch. Blood was trickling down this strip, down the legs, dripping off the feet dangling eight feet up from the ground. The pool of blood at the base of the totem measured four feet across.

'Oh my Jesus,' Chris said.

Then he turned away and threw up into his hand.

CALL TO DUTY

2.19 a.m.

The call clocked into the VPD at 2.19 that morning. The telephone call shouldn't have come through to the Vancouver Police at all, but the dispatcher didn't catch the error. He had spent the previous evening drinking at the Police Athletic Club and even now his head felt as though the iron ball of a wrecking crane was demolishing it piece by piece. At the mention of the words dead body, however, he sat up straight at the switchboard and pushed the headphones to his ears.

'Where's this body?' the dispatcher demanded, a whisky growl to his voice.

'Man, it's hangin' from a totem pole. And it doesn't have a head!'

'The totems in the Park?'

'I said a totem pole, didn't I?'

'Who's calling?' the dispatcher enquired of the nervous and jumpy voice at the end of the line.

'Chris. Chris Seaton.'

'Well, hang on, Chris, while I patch this through. I'll get back to you.' The dispatcher disconnected the line and then threw a toggle switch to feed into the street patrols. 'We've got a possible 212. Stanley Park. Brockton Point totem poles. Code 4 response.' Then he switched back to Chris.

'Okay, Mr Seaton. Full name and date of birth.' The dispatcher picked up his pen and quickly began to write.

2.20 a.m.

Within a minute of the emergency broadcast hitting the police airband the first blue and white car from the street patrol of the Vancouver Police Department tore into Stanley Park, its tyres squealing off the Causeway and then skidding in the snow. The moment the patrol car hit the park, the cop riding shotgun kicked-in the siren and started the wig-wag lights. Blue, then red, blue, then red, reflected off the snow. It took no more than three minutes for the car to reach Brockton Point, and its totem poles.

Even before the car had stopped moving the officer riding shotgun was out the door and running. The driver quickly followed twenty feet behind him. Fifteen seconds later they found the totem poles, each one of the mythical giants now shrouded by crystalline snow.

What they didn't find was a body.

2.22 a.m.

It was Detective Al Flood of the VPD who first caught the squeal. Because the call came into his building. Because it was a possible murder. And because he was catching up in Major Crimes.

Flood was thirty-eight and stood six feet tall exactly. He was large boned with broad muscular shoulders. His fair skin was a backdrop for freckles surrounding sharp blue-grey eyes. His hair was strawberry blond. Whenever he walked to the watercooler – as he was doing when the squad room phone rang – he moved like a natural athlete.

'Major Crimes,' Flood said, catching the phone call on the third ring.

'It's Jenkins in Dispatch, Detective. We got a possible 212. Caller says the totem poles in Stanley Park.'

Flood moved a pad into place. 'Where's the caller now?'

'At a phone booth.'

'Which phone booth?'

'Uh . . . I forgot to ask him.' The dispatcher's head was still pounding.

'Well, if he's still on the line, do it now. I'll wait.'

The phone went dead.

For about two minutes Flood remained standing where he was. It was now 2.25 a.m. on a snowy grave-yard shift and the squad room was practically empty. It felt like a deserted cavern of unmanned desks and stilled typewriters. One of the fluorescent lights was failing and it softly strobed the floor space about him. In some other part of the building a telephone was ringing. It wasn't answered. As he stood by the desk biding time until the dispatcher came back on, Flood picked up a circular put out by the RCMP. It was a Coordinated Law Enforcement Unit request for any information remotely connected to either of two deaths. Both bodies, CLEU said, had been found without a head. Flood was still reading when the line reactivated.

'Detective. It's Jenkins again. You still there?'

'Of course. Where is he?'

'Out at UBC. Guy says he's phoning from the Museum of Anthropology, a phone booth nearby.'

'That's at least five miles from Stanley Park. How does he know of the body?'

'Well, it seems it's not Stanley Park. It's the totems at UBC.'

'I thought you said that he said that it was Stanley Park.'

'I made a mistake.'

'Uh. Huh. Didn't I see you, Jenkins, yesterday, sur-rounded by empty bottles in the Athletic Club?'

'Uh . . . yeah, maybe.'

'Well get onto the Mounties. The stiff's in their jurisdiction.'

'Right. Thank God it's not in ours. The body's got no
head.'

Flood almost dropped the phone. As with most people in
this city who could read, he had consumed the front page
story on the headless bodies in one of the two major newspapers. And he had seen it on TV. He had just read the
RCMP flyer on the crimes sent out to the private municipal
police forces – and then to top off all this, here he had a
hungover police dispatcher telling him there was yet
another headless body around and that for those most
important moments in any police investigation – namely the
first few minutes when the force reacts to the squeal – they,
the VPD, had been fumbling the ball. Flood did not need to
remind himself of the police response equation: that for
every initial minute lost the chance of a case being ultimately
unsolved went up by mathematical proportions.

'Well, go on! Move it, man! Get the Mounties on the
line!' Flood almost shouted the words into the phone. It
was out of character, for usually he was an easy gentle-
mannered man.

'Right!' the dispatcher said, and the line went cold.

2.31 a.m.

Constable Ron Mitchell stood among the tumbling flakes
and stared up in disbelief. The scene was almost surreal:
it was that weird. The body nailed to the Dogfish Burial
Pole was now illuminated not only by the light at the base
of the totem but also by the headlamps of Mitchell's
patrol car. He had driven the vehicle down the access
road off Chancellor Boulevard and right out on to the
plaza in front of the Museum of Man. Then careful not to
get too close and do damage to the scene, he had climbed
up on to the hood of the car to get a better look. What he
saw was diabolical.

For whoever had carried the body out here and nailed it to the wood had also dumped a container of blood over what remained of the corpse. The plastic container, an Imperial gallon in size, was lying on the ground and Mitchell could make out streaks of dried blood on the body in amongst the wet ones.

2.36 a.m.

The phone beside the bed rang and wrenched him out of sleep. He reached for it quickly, fumbling in the dark, hoping that he would catch it before it woke his lover up. He yanked the receiver from its cradle before the second ring. There was a mumble from across the bed as he spoke in a whispered tone.

'Hello,' Jack MacDougall said, glancing at the clock.

'Sergeant, this is Constable Ron Mitchell. University Detachment. I don't think you know me.'

'I don't,' MacDougall said frowning. Then he waited.

'I'm sorry to bother you, sir. I hope it's the right decision.'

MacDougall felt like telling him that for his sake he hoped so too. 'Well,' he said.

'We've got another body. One without a head.'

The Sergeant threw back the covers and sat up on the bed. 'Where?' he demanded, abandoning the whisper.

'The Museum of Anthropology. Nailed to a totem pole.'

'Where are you, Mitchell?'

'I'm right at the scene.'

'Well you stay right where you are, I'm on the way. You guard that area with your bloody life. Nobody goes near it. Nobody, you hear. You report directly to me.'

'Yes, sir.' Then Jack MacDougall hung up.

The Sergeant was already off the bed and half way into his clothes – same blue blazer and crest, same grey slacks – when there was the squeak of bedsprings and a sleepy voice from the sheets. 'Is something the matter, Jack?'

'We've got another body. This one's worse.'

'Oh God no. Want some coffee?'

'I haven't got time, love. One quick phone call and then I'm out the door.'

'Will I see you later? Spend another night?'

'I hope so,' MacDougall said, glancing at the bed, taking in the gymnast's body outlined beneath the covers. Chances were good that body would perform in the next Olympics.

'I hope so, too,' Peter Brent said.

Ottawa, Ontario, 6.11 a.m.

When Commissioner François Chartrand put down the phone, he carried his cup of coffee through to his study overlooking the Ottawa River. There he lit a Gauloises and stood smoking in contemplation in front of the double-glazed window. Off to the east the first faint light of predawn was advancing slowly to engage in battle with the silver beams of the moon. A wind down from the Northern Tundra was whipping up the metallic waters that flowed before him, while waves of Canada geese flying in V formation slipped across the pale orange lunar surface above. Finished with the cigarette, Chartrand lit another.

The Commissioner was a stout man who had struggled for most of his adult life with a recurring weight problem. At one time he had also tried to control his habit of chain-smoking, but quickly found that fighting a double front was beyond all human effort. Besides, he enjoyed cigarettes.

Chartrand was the sort of man born to be Commissioner, for he was a natural leader. His face was nondescript – short hair cut high above the ears in military fashion and balding at the crown, sparse restrained eyebrows, an easy mouth, soft perceptive eyes – and not in the least threatening. Chartrand gave orders by advising you of his opinion and asking if you could help. He took

106

you into his confidence – or at least seemed to – from the very first moment you met him. No one likes to be told what to do and Chartrand would no more think of doing that than asking you to help where your help wasn't needed. And yet no matter what happened, if he was involved he always assumed complete responsibility for the outcome. No sloughing off of blame, no sacrificing of those who gave him aid. He was the sort of man who commanded voluntary respect.

As Chartrand stood now in front of the window contemplating the implications of what the Attorney General for British Columbia had told him, the telephone rang. He put down his coffee cup and caught it on the third ring.

'Chartrand,' he said quietly.

'François, this is Walt Jessup. I'm calling from the coast. We've got a serious problem.'

'I've already heard, Walt. By a different chain of command.'

The Deputy Commissioner of 'E' Division snorted. 'I'm going to need muscle and machines, François. This'll be worse than Olson. Even there we had vigilante squads and private police forces and phony ransom demands and God knows what else. I don't expect the feminists to be as restrained as parents.'

'You'll have them.'

'What else are we going to do? What shall I tell the press?

'Leave that with me, Walt. I'm thinking about it now. I'll call you back shortly once I've made a decision. I promise I'll give you something. You just give me time for a second cup of coffee.'

The Deputy Commissioner managed a shallow laugh. 'All right. But no longer,' he said. 'Or I'm going to sneak out of town.'

After replacing the receiver, Chartrand walked through to his kitchen and poured himself another cup. He lit a third cigarette and went back to his study. And it was then, with the advancing light of dawn, that the idea struck him.

He knew what had to be done.

For when you are the head of an organization with both a sacred duty and a mythical legend in trust.

You use the very best you've got.

Even if you no longer have him.

Vancouver, British Columbia, 8.15 a.m.

Genevieve was dying.

He held the rose bush gently in his left hand and carefully examined it for signs of blight or disease. But all he could find were two minuscule white dots where the flower joined the stalk. Whatever they were, he had never seen this symptom before. *That's the problem with exotic plants,* he thought. *They contract exotic diseases.*

Outside the greenhouse lay a world of dazzling snow. The maple trees, and the city far beyond were blanketed with white and the sun now blazed down, bouncing off the snow crystals and the prisms in the greenhouse's glass walls. Rainbows were everywhere.

Except for the weather, it was a bad day all the way round.

As usual, he had begun his work this morning at five-thirty. But the moment he sat down in the white wicker chair and placed the clip-board on his knee was the moment that he knew the block had settled in for good. He merely sighed with resignation. To be honest with himself, there had been a lethargy about the project from its very beginning. Did the world really need another history of the First World War? Hadn't Fay and Albertini, Tuchman and Falls and Liddel Hart said what had to be said?

He put the plant down gently and in the doing knew that the book had died.

Now *Genevieve* was dying too.

While lost in thought he had not heard his wife open

the door of the greenhouse that led to their home. She touched his arm as she always did and spoke to him in French.

'Robert, on tu demande au téléphone.'

He looked at her for a moment – the auburn hair now piled on top of her head, here and there a wayward strand tumbling down to her shoulders, then he nodded and went quietly out of the greenhouse and into the living room, across the pegged wood floor with its Persian carpet, and into the entrance hall where he picked up the telephone.

He felt a little depressed. The day was shot. What else could go wrong?

'Hello,' he said in English. 'This is Robert DeClercq.'

4.55 p.m.

He was smiling as he stopped just inside the door to the pub, his eyes skipping from table to table, checking to see who was strung out and twitching and looking for some smack. He knew that for a moment all eyes in the Moonlight Arms were furtively sizing him up to see if he was holding. Especially the blonde jerking and jumping in the corner. She was always here, waiting – but then she was a big girl and a fix wouldn't hold her long.

The Indian moved among the tables, closing in on her.

Not ten minutes ago he had been fronted two bundles of junk. The Man had said it was the best around since the last time the Horsemen had done a sweep of the street. 'But move it fast,' the Pusher said. 'Harness bulls get a wiff of this an' they'll kick in the door ablastin'.' 'Why the front?' the Indian asked. 'That's not usual practice?' 'I trust you, my man,' the Pusher said. 'Now where would a motherfucker like me be without a little trust? Just move it *fast* my man.'

The way the Indian figured it, he'd push forty-five caps and save five for the fix. Mixed with a little bouncing powder, the blast of a Belushi speedball would have him in space by eight. It had been at least a month since he had done a borderline fix and his heart was beating fast.

Tonight would be the night. As soon as he moved the bundles.

'My man,' the blonde whispered as soon as the Indian came within earshot. 'Am I glad to see you.'

Her face was twitching like dead matter coming alive.

'Sorry to disappoint you, blondie, but I couldn't score.'

But it was just the old pusher joke, getting off on the interplay of hope and anxiety on a junkie's face, tasting the feel of power, the power to give or withhold, then opening his mouth a little bit to reveal the balloon behind rotting teeth, revelling in her sigh of relief as he said 'Oops, my mistake. I had some all the time. You got a place?'

The blonde shook her head. 'Not near here. Fix me, my man, fix me. Then just let me split.'

'You want one or two, lady? It's seventy-five a hit. This is de-e-e-lux goods.'

There was a slight flicker in the blonde's eyes, but that didn't matter. She was in no position to balk.

The blonde nodded twice.

'Meet me out back in five,' he said. Then the Indian turned away.

It was at that moment that they both saw the black man who had just walked in through the door. His shoulders were thick, usurping the space where his neck should have been, and his chest strained the material of his blue denim shirt. He wore wide bell-bottom blue trousers without a belt which looked as though any second they'd be down around his ankles. Under the edge of his white toque peeked a receding hairline. His face was round and he sported a pencil-thin moustache on his upper lip. The man was weighed down with jewellery: several gold chains in the hair of his chest, eight small rings on his manicured hands, a single stud in his left ear. Judging from his look, however, there was little chance that even in this part of town anyone would try to take them off him.

110

The Indian blinked at the man who nodded toward the back door. Then the black turned on his heels and left by the front. The Indian slipped among the tables and went out through the rear.

When they were gone, the blonde stood up and quickly made her way to the back of the pub. As she entered the hall leading to the washrooms a man of about fifty with running pimples all over his face slipped a hand between her thighs. She pushed him away and entered the women's room.

The room stank.

There was the smell of urine everywhere and three separate puddles where people had puked on the floor. A soiled Kotex floated in one of the puddles. The only window was open to the alley as if the smell of garbage would somehow freshen the air.

The blonde entered the toilet cubicle that was directly beneath the window. The seat was missing from the toilet. She stood up on the edge of the porcelain bowl and peeked out through the window.

For less than a minute the woman watched the black man and the Indian talking. They exchanged something. Then they turned away from each other and walked in opposite directions.

Once they were gone from sight, the blonde climbed down, took out a pen and a matchbook, and began to make some notes.

5.40 p.m.

From somewhere out there came the squeal of wheels on rails and the smash of train cars being shunted. From somewhere else came the sound of a foghorn lost on the edge of the harbour. For now the fog had come rolling in from the sea, swallowing up the physical world and disembodying its sounds. For the month of October, the weather was back to normal.

The railroad hut sat on the edge of the National

Harbours' Board property, twenty feet from the Pacific Ocean and several thousand yards from the western terminal of the Canadian Pacific Railway. It was here in a synapse now shrouded with vapour that four thousand miles of rail linked up with the shipping routes of the Pacific Rim. Here was the reflex ganglia of the country's nervous system.

The man who sat at the single window of the railroad hut was smoking yet another cigarette. It was an Export A, no filter. He was one of those men who are politely described as being corpulent. His beer belly pushed out the front of his suit, permanently stretching the leather of his belt out of shape. The butt of a Smith and Wesson .38 stuck out from the top of his pants.

He turned at the sound of the door behind him being opened.

It was the blonde from the beer parlour.

'I think I'm onto something,' she said. There was excitement in her voice.

'Yeah?' the man replied with no emotion in his tone.

'Problem is I might just blow my cover getting to it.'

As she spoke, the woman removed two No. 5 gelatin capsules from the pocket of her jeans. She walked over to a shelf on one side of the hut and picked up an envelope, then she sealed the caps inside it and marked the exhibit with her name, her Regimental Number, the date and the designation 56 C. In an RCMP undercover drug operation each person the operative scores from is given a number. Their picture then comes down from the target board and goes up as a hit. The letter 'C' in this case indicated that this was the blonde's third buy off this particular hit.

'Outrageous price,' the woman said, handing the envelope over to her cover man. He put it in an 'E' exhibit pouch. Then the blonde sat down by the heater near the door and began making notes in a large black court book.

'You said you were onto something,' the man reminded her. Again without emotion.

She looked up. 'Before the buy, 56 made connection with this black dude in the alley. He had that swagger of the *nouveau riche*, you know what I mean? Flaunted jewellery. Arrogant air. That sort of shit. I think he's one step up and probably a link. I'd like to go after him and forget single cap sales.'

'Well you can't,' the man said, bitterly. 'Spann, you've been pulled.'

'What do you mean "pulled"?' the woman asked, frowning.

The man grunted and lit another cigarette. His fingers were dark orange from nicotine stains.

'What do you mean "pulled"?' the woman asked again.

'Clean up. Fuck off. Report to Heather Street. They just sent word down you made the Headhunter Squad.'

The woman tensed, involuntarily. Now her heart was pounding fast.

'It should have been me, lady. It should have been me.' Then he turned back to the window to stare out at the fog. 'Write out notes on this big connection before you go. Give me something to do.'

'Yeah, sure,' the woman said, almost in a daze. Then she added very quietly, 'Who do I report to?'

Snorting, the Corporal turned slowly from the window. On his face there was a faint sardonic smile.

'The news is big, Spann. About as big as it comes. Chartrand, our bloody Commissioner, is bringing back Robert DeClercq.'

THE GRAVEYARD

Sunday, October 31st, 5.30 a.m.

Twelve years, and he could still get into the uniform. The fact made him feel good.

It was usual for the Superintendent to be at work before dawn, and most mornings he would climb quietly out of bed so as not to disturb his wife, make his way into the kitchen to drip a pot of coffee, then carry a steaming cup of it, strong and black, out into the greenhouse where he would sit among his plants. For it was here at this early hour, alone with his thoughts and away from the sensory input that would come with the light of day, that Robert DeClercq would run the gauntlet which stretched back into his past. With each new day the same ghosts were lined up and waiting for him, all of them with knives. And each morning he would subdue them in that hour before dawn.

Most mornings DeClercq would then pour himself another coffee, dress for the weather and go out through the back door of the greenhouse and down to the edge of the sea. There he would sit very still in the old driftwood chair on a knoll above the ocean, the sundial at his left, and think about the day's work while he awaited dawn. Only when the eastern horizon was ablaze with shafts of glory would he return to the greenhouse, to the wicker chair, and place the clipboard on his knee.

That, of course, was most mornings. Today was different.

DeClercq put the kettle on and ground the coffee as usual, then he went to the closet in the spare bedroom and took his uniform down from the rack. For eleven years it had hung there, unused and untouched. Finding a soft-bristled brush, he sat down on the bed and with short brisk strokes removed the lint of a decade from the dark blue serge. He pressed his trousers and shined his shoes. Then sitting in the greenhouse with his first cup of coffee, Superintendent Robert DeClercq polished each brass uniform button until it gleamed in the light from the desk lamp. Only then did he return to the spare bedroom and put the blue serge on.

The man who stared back at him from the closet mirror was a man who had not been seen since the Quebec October Crisis of 1970.

Twenty minutes later when DeClercq closed the front door and stepped out into the dark, the chill of autumn was in the air and maple leaves scraped the ground. For a fleeting moment his mind was touched by a sense of *déjà vu*, a pale glimpse of that other autumn many years ago, of dead leaves in a moaning wind moving through the graveyard – but he shook it off sharply and began to climb the driveway. He had parked the cars up near the road after the freak snowstorm. He warmed up the engine of his Citroën, then drove off down Marine Drive and toward the centre of town.

Dawn was yet an hour and a half away.

6.35 a.m.

They had set up Headhunter Headquarters in the old Command Building of the Royal Canadian Mounted Police. Located at the corner of 33rd Avenue and Heather Street, this was a structure of massive stone blocks and acute-angled timbers that very much resembled an Elizabethan mansion. The Maple Leaf was flying on the flagpole outside. Once the Vancouver Headquarters of the Force, the building had more recently found use as an officers' mess and a police training academy.. Even more recently it had been gutted, and was now in the process of reconstruction. Gutted or not, however, it still looked from the outside like a Headquarters should. That's more than could be said for the *real* Headquarters building up on 73rd. It looked like a transistor.

It was now just after 6.30 a.m. and a light rain overnight

had washed the mist from the air and left the lights of the city sparkling like diamanté on black velvet.

As DeClercq walked toward the doorway at the front of the Headquarters building the air felt crisp and clean within his lungs and the freshness of the morning seemed to add a clearness to his sense of purpose. It had been a long time since he was last a cop. *It feels good to be back*, he thought.

The first day of his resurrection – October 29th, the morning of Chartrand's call – DeClercq had met Sergeant Jack MacDougall of North Vancouver Detachment and Corporal James Rodale of Richmond Detachment to form the second Headhunter Squad. Earlier that morning while the Sergeant was overseeing the investigation out at the totem poles in front of the Museum of Man, Rodale had done a computer projection of the manpower available to the Force. A printout on the background and service record of each member in 'E' Division was ready by noon that day.

That same afternoon, DeClercq, MacDougall and Rodale had put together the squad. Then the duty calls had gone out.

The second day of his comeback DeClercq had spent shut up in his new office working over the files. He had read, digested, culled, and reconstructed each report on each crime at least seven times. The room now showed his work.

The office was at the end of a corridor that met the top of the stairs. A spacious room, thirty feet square, with a bank of windows along one side that looked out at St Vincent's Hospital across 33rd, it had once been an officer's billiard room and an adjunct to the mess. But whatever purpose it had once served, it had now been modified to DeClercq's specific instructions. For on the first day of his resurrection – while he had been putting together his squad – a team of workmen had stripped the place and then reconstructed the three windowless walls with floor to ceiling corkboard. And it was the Headhunter's work that now adorned the corkboard walls.

116

For furniture the office contained three Victorian library tables arranged in a horseshoe surrounding a single chair. The chair – which had once been at the centre of the commanding officer's quarters generations ago and only just discovered in the basement – was highbacked with a barley-sugar frame and the crest of the RCMP carved in wood to crown its user's head. The chair faced six seats in front of the desk.

It was now 6.46 a.m. on the third day of the return of Robert DeClercq – and it was time to take off his jacket and sit in the chair and analyze yesterday's work. It was time to ride out on the hunt for the ghoul who was standing in the graveyard.

DeClercq sat down and rolled up his sleeves.

At the centre of the wall across from his chair a large map of the Lower Mainland of British Columbia was pinned to the corkboard.

Next to it was a section of wall visually depicting the North Vancouver murder. In the centre the Superintendent had pinned the unidentified Polaroid photograph sent to Skip O'Rourke at the *Vancouver Sun*. The Polaroid had itself been photographed and blown up, but though this enlargement was also on the wall it was too grainy in texture to add very much. The photo was of a young woman's head – she was probably in her teens. Her eyes were rolled back into her skull with just the barest trace of pupil moon peeking out beneath the eyelids. Her hair was black and tangled and matted with blood, her mouth open slackly as if stopped in a scream. Shreds of skin at the base of her neck dripped gore and curled toward the pole like several thin snakes.

What struck DeClercq was the fact that except for the head and the top of the pole on which it had been stuck, the photograph revealed nothing. No ground. No backdrop. Just a white surface as though the snap had been shot facing a linen sheet set up to highlight the head and the pole. *A specially constructed pose*, was the thought that entered his mind.

To the right of the Polaroid of the victim's head, DeClercq had attached two helicopter shots of the area around the bone site. They both revealed the North Shore hillside from about two hundred feet. With a sharp eye it was possible to make out the tattered tent half hidden by the bushes.

To the left of the Polaroid photograph, beside the police blow-up, DeClercq had yesterday tacked up four Ident. section pictures taken on MacDougall's orders. Two of the photos were shots of the shallow creekbed grave. Though the bones could clearly be seen, the amount of dirt dug away from them by the two girls' father – plus the statements later taken from the three of them – indicated that before the disturbance the remains had been hidden from sight. The creekbed was clogged with autumn leaves and broken branches, several of which appeared to have been cut and placed over the grave. One of the other two Ident. shots was of the cut ends of several of these branches. On later examination, the police lab had found striation marks identical to those discovered by Dr Singh on the neck bone of the river floater and of the skeleton in question. The fourth photograph was a blow-up of the marks on the upper neck of the unidentified corpse where the head had been cut from the body.

Put together, DeClercq thought, *these pictures raise a number of questions. They offer very few answers*.

He removed a sheet of paper from the drawer of the library table that formed the bottom of the horseshoe and began to write:

    1. Was the woman killed at the location of the tent? Or was she carried there after her death by the Headhunter? If the latter, then a strong person indeed! It's very rugged terrain.

    2. If deposited there after death, was the corpse carried down from the road up above? Or up from a boat on the sea? Or along the shore? It was probably done at dusk or in the early morning – dark enough for cover, but light enough to see.

3. Was the body meant to be found? Cut branches indicate that it was purposely hidden. Was the stream running at the time that it was left? Was it buried mainly by the act of nature?

Looking over the questions, DeClercq's gut reaction was that the woman was killed at the tent site, that she was probably camping there, and that the killer had then cut off her head and buried the body and in a frenzy ripped the tent to pieces. His reasoning was that up in the North Shore mountains there are a thousand sites more deserted than this one where a body would never be found. Here the risk of being seen was just too great. But the corpse *was* left at this location – so that indicated that either the Headhunter had stumbled upon her in the wood, or they had met at some other location and returned to the murder scene. If the Headhunter was camping here, one of the people in the houses nearby might have seen him coming and going. And that could lead to a description. No, the chances were the victim was the one who pitched the tent. But even that was conjecture. It might have been there before.

What concerned him most and tugged at his mind was not, however, the answer to these questions. It was the question that arose from these questions in the light of subsequent facts. *For if this corpse was meant to be hidden, why had the Headhunter changed his style?*

Look at the case of Joanna Portman.

Tacked to the corkboard wall in the section for the North Vancouver crime there were many other sheets of paper: lab and autopsy reports, police memos, witness statements, interforce enquiries – but these added little to his knowledge. From the angle of the cuts on the branch ends (plus the blade shape left in the flesh of Grabowski and Portman) the lab had determined that the weapon was probably a large Bowie knife. That was more an American instrument than one found in Canada. The autopsy report revealed that there were cuts on several of the rib bones indicating that the North Van corpse might also have suffered a slash through the breasts. The time of death was estimated at between three and five months ago, but probably closer to three since the last days of August had been very hot and decomposition would have advanced rapidly. A soil search of the entire gravesite was negative; a diver search of the shore waters by the RCMP frogman team had turned up nothing; an infrared helicopter scan of the area recorded no temperature differences that might indicate other rotting human remains. A check of the Harbour Patrol had proved fruitless and not one of the neighbours living on top of the hill had noticed anything suspicious. In fact only one had known that the tent was there.

The only positive fact in the investigation so far was that the tent had been traced to an outdoors shop in Luzern, Switzerland. It had been purchased eight months ago.

DeClercq rose from his chair and crossed over to the wall. For the next twenty minutes he again reviewed the entire North Vancouver case as reconstructed and focused on the corkboard. At the end of that period he had confirmed that on this part of the investigation there were only two constructive things to do: wait for the European Missing Persons reports requested through Interpol.

And have Joseph Avacomovitch go to work on the bones.

It was 7.23 a.m. when the Superintendent turned his attention to the Helen Grabowski case. Though technically the corpse had been found within the jurisdiction of University Detachment, because that outpost was so small the investigation had been usurped by Rodale out of Richmond. DeClercq was pleased to see that the Corporal had done a thorough job.

Again, however, there were questions – and not very many answers.

As with the case of the North Van bones, this display centred around the Polaroid print sent to Skip O'Rourke. Once more there had been a blow-up by the lab – same grainy quality – and this along with the subscription form from *Buns and Boobs Bonanza* was pinned up to the left. MacDougall had determined that the form came from the July 1982 issue of the publication which was available at any corner store. DeClercq's eyes moved back and forth from the clipping to the Polaroid.

The picture was of another head with the eyes rolled back in the skull. Helen Grabowski had black hair, a narrow face, and her mouth hung slackly open. Even in the photograph she looked like a junkie, the ravages of the drug having pinched and lined her skin. Blood ran from both corners of her lips. And again the picture was confined to the head and the top of a pole, no ground, no backdrop except for the same white surface.

Another pose, DeClercq thought.

It also occurred to him, judging from the lack of decomposition and freshness of the blood, that both photos had been taken immediately after the killings. The bodies had probably then been dumped very shortly after. Obviously the pictures were saved for the killer's titillation and his subsequent taunt. But what had then happened to the heads?

Immediately to the right of the Polaroid was tacked an aerial shot of the wharf where Heller and Simpson had found the floater, and next to that a close-up of the bloated nude remains stretched out on the dock. The slash through her chest had halved her breasts, each withered wrinkled quadrant pointing in a different compass direction. Bare ribs could be seen. Two other photographs were off to the right of these. One of them showed the striation marks on the vertebra that Dr Singh had removed. The other the woman's fingertips. DeClercq could see that Dr Singh had injected glycerin beneath the fingertip skin to smooth out the washerwoman's wrinkles before printing the remains. Singh was obviously a very cautious man. He knew that without the head a dental identification was gone forever. And that left just her prints. In the photo – which was a blow-up – the fingers of the corpse were positioned below the individual print of each one on a fingerprint sheet. Thus, though the flesh would have long since rotted before any case got to court, Singh's opinion on identification could withstand any cross-examination. Look for yourself, counsellor!

Beside that photograph was Rodale's earlier fingerprint sheet. And tacked next to that the reports from New Orleans.

The Superintendent picked up his pen and turned to his question sheet. He began to write:

1. Where was Grabowski killed? No water in the lungs so it wasn't in the river. Was it on a boat, the best of murder scenes? Is that a connection between the two remains? The North Van woman killed at sea and then taken ashore? If so why not just use a sea dump like Grabowski?

2. Does bruising to vagina mean sex attack? Is vertical stab to the throat made during intercourse? Sexual stimulation connected to female death throes? Slash to the breasts significant as mother mutilation?

3. Was Grabowski picked up hooking by a sadistic client? Perhaps the North Van girl too? Perhaps, but then Portman doesn't fit. Drugs?

4. What about John Lincoln Hardy aka 'The Weasel'?

5. Connection with New Orleans?

DeClercq once more got up from his chair, crossed over to the wall, and scanned the papers and reports pinned there.

Helen Grabowski, also known as Patricia Ann Palitti, was an American heroin-addicted prostitute from New Orleans. Dr Singh, in his report, estimated that her body had been in the Fraser River approximately a week. Just over a week before the body was found she had been arrested on a charge of junk possession while hooking near the Moonlight Arms. She had been released in the early morning and no one had seen her again. Rodale had done a blanket sweep through skid road questioning the street people and greasing the palms of the stoolies but all to no avail. As near as anyone could tell, Grabowski had been in Vancouver no more than three or four days. She had been identified from her mugshot by several working girls – and one or two had also tentatively fingered John Lincoln Hardy as being around from a rather poor stake-out photo wired up from New Orleans.

The follow-up from Louisiana did not advance things much further. Grabowski was a runaway from Topeka,

Kansas – then a fresh-faced country girl. Her family had not heard from her since January 1980. At the beginning of April that same year she had been arrested in the city of New Orleans defrauding a restaurant of food. She had pleaded guilty and been given a suspended sentence. Though she had run up no subsequent record or charges, she and one John Lincoln Hardy, also known as 'the Weasel', had been under suspicion of being involved in a prostitution ring. Four persons had been charged out of that investigation, but not Grabowski and Hardy. And that was it, the lot. New Orleans had sent up Grabowski's 1980 mugshot for fraud and a surreptitious undercover snapshot of Hardy taken from the back seat of a car.

So where did that leave the Headhunter Squad? DeClercq saw nothing but questions.

Unless these were random killings, what was the connection? Although it was not uncommon for the murderer of a *particular* person to attempt to mask his crime within the hysteria of a false psychopathic rampage, could that apply to Hardy given the short time he'd been in town? Not unless this was at least his second trip.

Was the most sound conclusion not the obvious one: Grabowski had been killed by a marauding john?

If so, DeClercq thought, *then why Joanna Portman?*

The Superintendent took one last look at the remaining photographs on this part of the wall. Above the Polaroid of Grabowski's head on a pole, he had yesterday pinned up both the Vancouver and New Orleans police mugshots of the woman. In both of them the fresh-faced innocence of a Kansas prairie girl was gone forever. Instead, all that remained was a wasted subservient woman. The final photograph was of her pimp – a black male with a receding hairline and a pencil-thin moustache whose massive shoulders were so thick that they totally usurped the space where his neck should have been.

It was now 7.55 a.m. and DeClercq was about to move on

to the Portman killing with its macabre implications.

The focus of this section of the corkboard was a Catholic nurse's graduation photograph, all black hair and happy mirthful eyes.

She reminded DeClercq of his first wife Kate, when she was young, and he turned his gaze away.

Outside dawn was just beginning to break in a wash of molten copper. Across 33rd Avenue the glass panes on the top two floors of St Vincent's Hospital were dazzling sun-smeared mirrors.

'You're looking for me?' a voice asked from the door behind DeClercq.

'Am I?' the Superintendent asked, starting around.

'Yes,' the man in the doorway said. 'Somebody moved my hat and I think it was you. It was put down exactly the way it was found, only reversed around. Shows a person of precision, distracted by other things.'

'Well, I declare. You must be the great Sherlock Avacomovitch,' DeClercq said with a smile. 'I've heard of you.'

'Hello, Robert,' the Russian said. 'Long time no see. How about some breakfast? My treat.'

'You're on,' the Superintendent said – and that was the moment he saw it. Strange that he had not noticed the fact before, it was a detail of importance. He had been looking at Joseph Avacomovitch, having just turned from the window, and in that turning his eyes had brushed over the wall with the photographs of the two heads on the two poles and had then touched on Portman's picture. The section of corkboard reserved for the last crime was just off to the right of the door. It took about a second for the connection among the three pictures to register on his mind. Then his thoughts turned inward.

Avacomovitch was too sharp a man not to notice the signs. 'What just struck you, Robert?' he asked of the Superintendent.

DeClercq was a moment coming around, then he pointed at the pictures of all three victims.

'Notice anything,' he asked the scientist.

For a moment the Russian thought, then he nodded his head. 'Yes. All three women have raven black hair.'

Joseph Avacomovitch's background was unique.

He had been born in the Russian Ukraine of parents who worked on a rural collective. Both were slaughtered during the Nazi advance on Stalingrad when the boy was fourteen. Avacomovitch had been brought up by the state and selected early because of his academic brilliance for a first class Soviet education. By the early 1960s when he was in his thirties he held four university degrees and was a leading forensic scientist in the Soviet Academy of Sciences. Even then, the techniques that he developed were being recognized and picked up for use in the West.

In 1963 Moscow had sent him to the city of East Berlin. Shortly after President John F. Kennedy had made his statement *'Ich bin ein Berliner!'* to the ecstatic response of West Germans, the East German police had been confronted by a baffling series of homosexual slayings. In each case a middle-aged German man had been found sodomized and strangled with both hands tied by rope to the sides of the neck. In the clutched hand of the fifth victim had been found a button from a Soviet soldier's uniform. The day that this news leaked out the East German Army had had to crush an anti-Russian riot. That night there had been a sixth victim, minutes before Avacomovitch had arrived.

It took the Russian scientist fourteen hours to break the case. He did it by examining a rope.

The first five murder victims had been found indoors. But the last one had been different. It had the same MO of sexual assault, trussing, and strangulation – but a second rope had been looped about the neck and the corpse tossed out through a fifth floor window above a darkened street.

Every rope has properties peculiar to its fibres. Avacomovitch found several points of fibre rotation twist. Then he discovered at the points of the twist flakes of either car paint or chrome plate. After two hours' work by chromatography he had isolated the vehicle year and make. It was a Nazi Volkswagen, vintage 1943.

Two hours after that East German Motor Vehicle Records had found the registration, for after the Soviet bombardment of East Berlin at the close of the Second World War there had not been that many intact Nazi vehicles left. Then an hour and a half later an East German was arrested. The KGB linked him to the American CIA. Avacomovitch linked him to the body hanging from the window. Then the case itself was closed – and passed on to Propaganda.

The points of stress and the location of the paint and chrome deposits on the rope used to hang the sixth victim indicated that the same rope had been tied around the vehicle's roof rack and then run down the back of the car and wound several times around one side of the bumper.

When the East German agent of the CIA had been arrested, an examination of his car revealed that one of two ropes used to support the right rear bumper had recently been removed and had gone missing. It was unfortunate, however, that the man never came to trial and that Joseph Avacomovitch was once more denied an opportunity to test his precision in a case. Inexplicably, the man had suffered a heart attack under KGB questioning – but not before he had blown a network of seventeen NATO spies.

The next day all seventeen were summarily shot and it was announced in Moscow that forensic scientist Joseph Avacomovitch had been awarded the Order of Lenin for his deductive achievement.

The day after that Avacomovitch defected to West Berlin.

After his defection to the West in 1963, Avacomovitch had been debriefed in London by both British and American Intelligence Units. After that he had been offered a sizeable 'resettlement' fee. He had chosen to move to the Canadian prairies and was reported to have given this as his reason: 'I long to return to the Ukraine in the years of my early childhood. That I cannot do, but this land serves my purpose. This land is like Russia – minus the Russians.'

Two days after Avacomovitch set foot on Canadian soil in the city of Calgary, Alberta, the RCMP – ever pragmatic when it came to top notch personnel and well aware of his forensic exploits – had offered the Russian emigré a non-security-access laboratory appointment. From then on Joseph Avacomovitch was employed on Her Majesty's Service – and five years later he was granted Security Clearance.

DeClercq and Avacomovitch had first worked together in Montreal in 1965. One night that November, with baby Jane sitting on his knee, Robert DeClercq had asked Joseph Avacomovitch the reason for his defection. 'That's if you don't mind telling,' he said.

It was after dinner and they were sitting, the four of them, Robert, Kate, Joseph and Jane, in front of a cracking fire while the snow once more tumbled down beyond the frosted windows. Old Man Winter already had one icy toe in the door.

'I don't mind,' the Russian said, 'it's all a matter of record. The reason's half political and half academic.'

Avacomovitch took a sip of cognac then rolled the glass in his very large hands.

'The political part is straightforward. I was never a member of the Communist Party at heart and I didn't believe in the system – although it was good to me. One look at East Germany and I knew I wanted to go. Besides, except for position I had nothing to leave behind.' He smiled down at Jane who was rapidly falling asleep.

'But it was really intellectual incentive which gave me the mental push.' Avacomovitch looked from the baby directly at Robert DeClercq. 'When I was involved in studies toward my final two degrees, we were encouraged to pore over all the classic works on famous Western murderers. The official line was that they revealed the sickness in bourgeois society. The ones who intrigued me most of all were the killers who slaughtered for no other reason than the fact they enjoyed it. The Germans have a word for this – they call such a motive *lustmord*.

'Now it just so happens that we don't have such murderers in the Soviet Union. At least not that I could hunt – and that's a realistic fact. Those with the *lustmord* instinct are recognized early in that country and channelled into the Secret Police. Their aggression is utilized, and as a group of natural killers they are jealously protected like an endangered species.'

Jane had fallen asleep, cradled in Robert DeClercq's lap. Raising his glass the Russian drained the last of his cognac.

'The reason I defected was to find an adversary. That's why I came to the West. There are so many of them here.'

8.25 a.m.

Joseph Avacomovitch was a giant of a man. He stood 6'4 in his stocking feet with shoulders and chest as massive as an old-fashioned, wood-staved beer barrel. Like most men his size the Russian had a slightly stooped posture, as if subconsciously attempting to shrink to the size of the majority of men around him. Although it had been twelve years since Robert DeClercq had last laid eyes on him, the Russian had changed little. His hair was still almost albino white and luxurious, combed back in a pompadour. His grey eyes still twinkled behind a pair of wire-rim glasses. He still wore no jewelry on his large hands, save a ring removed from his father's body when the Nazis left the old man sprawled in the blood-splashed Ukrainian snow. And he still wore the hat.

The hat was a prairie Stetson, worn and slightly off-colour, the sort of headgear that was common in Alberta and in Texas and in John Travolta's closet. At the base of the crown and above the rim was wound a thin Indian bead hatband and sticking out from this on the left side was a tiny flag pennant. Small words printed on the pennant read: DALLAS COWBOYS.

The two men were sitting in the White Spot coffee shop at Cambie and King Edward, several blocks north of Headhunter Headquarters. They had both ordered bacon and eggs poached, with brown toast on the side. They both drank their coffee black. The Stetson lay on the table between them and off to the right.

'Is that the *same* hat you were wearing in 1970?' the Superintendent asked.

'Yep. The same one.'

DeClercq shook his head. 'I don't understand,' he said.

'Don't understand what? The hat or the pennant?'

'Both,' the policeman said.

The Russian grinned. 'Have you ever been around immigrants, newly arrived? Well when you first set foot on foreign soil and know you're there to stay, that you can never go home, a kind of depressing alienation inevitably sets in. Clothes, food, language, manner, cut of hair, way of walking – everything around you is so vastly different. You know you don't belong. And you fear you never will.

'When I arrived in Calgary in 1964 the Stampede was in full swing. Indians dancing in the streets, chuck-wagon breakfasts, rodeo acts, everyone walking around in a ten-gallon hat.

'There I was walking the streets surrounded by pseudo-cowboys. I bought the Stetson and was immediately lost in the crowd.

'When the Stampede was over I kept the hat – it keeps my head warm.'

The waitress refilled their coffee cups and in doing so glanced at the hat. Arching one eyebrow slightly, she looked at DeClercq. 'Want some oats for your horse?' she asked with a smile. The Russian laughed.

'Okay,' DeClercq said. 'What about the pennant?'

'In Russia everybody plays chess. I've played since I was five. Here few play chess, but a lot follow football. In both games the win depends on psychology and strategy. And to really enjoy the football spirit you need a team. Mine's the Dallas Cowboys cause I like their style of play. People see the pennant and if they share my interest they start a conversation. It provides an opener – and like the hat itself, helps me find some friends.'

DeClercq had interrogated too many people in his time not to have learned that it mattered less what was said than how it was delivered. Too long an explanation meant lack of conviction.

I think you're very lonely, Joseph, the Superintendent thought. *Same hat. Same fear you don't fit in. Now I do understand.*

Robert DeClercq said: 'I don't think it's possible to leave your roots behind. That's what I tried to do by leaving Quebec. After what happened to Janie and Kate all I wanted to do was run and try to escape. I discovered you can't. It's been twelve years, Joseph, yet every day the memory still comes back to me. It'll haunt me till I die. Particularly my child. All I did was take my roots and transplant them out here. I suppose that's the real reason I came back to work. Time to stop running. Life's too short. Do you know what I mean?'

Avacomovitch nodded, but didn't meet his eyes. 'Some days I worry that I'm not even alive. That somehow I've turned life into an empty game of chess. That all I've got waiting is checkmate at the end.'

'Then welcome to the West Coast,' Robert DeClercq said. 'You don't escape from here. You either go back where you came or sink into the sea. And that's a narrow choice.'

For a moment they both were silent, as if each was using the other to assess where he had been, to put twelve intervening years into some rough perspective. Finally Joseph Avacomovitch shrugged and said: 'Chartrand told me you made a special request.'

'I told him I'd only take command if he put you on special assignment to the case. He agreed.'

'Just like the old days,' the scientist said.

'Just like the old days,' the policeman repeated.

'And we'll have a celebration if we nail this guy?'

'I'll have you out to my house, to meet Genevieve.'

'Then no more crying in the beer. Let's pick up the pieces. Robert, I really mean it. I'm damn glad you're back and it's good to see you again.'

'And I feel the same way. Let's get to work.'

They paid the cheque and walked out onto Cambie Street. All the way back to Headhunter Headquarters the pale October sunshine shone down on the park to their left, bringing the colour of the grass to a vibrant green, dazzling off the patches of snow which remained in the shadier parts protected from rain by the trees. Several small children were throwing slushy snowballs.

'Last night I took the red-eye special out from Ottawa,' Avacomovitch said. 'I got in at five and couldn't sleep so I went to the lab. I spent about an hour on the envelope sent to the *Sun*. This one's smart, Robert. There are no prints on either photo, on the subscription form, or the envelope – except for employees at the newspaper. I did a serology examination on the gum of the manila flap, hoping to show the saliva was from a particular blood-type secretor. I found nothing. I don't think the Headhunter even licked the envelope. I think water was used to wet the sealing gum. It's almost as if the killer *knew* that we'd do such a test. I did manage to isolate the type-face on the address. It's from a small portable Commodore, made in Toronto. If you find the typewriter, I'll be able to match it. The letter 'C' is off-mark and holds up the carriage.'

As they entered the Headquarters building the sun was still shining. Off to the west there were storm clouds on the horizon, boiling in from the sea.

8.55 a.m.

If DeClercq had found little to work with in the files on Helen Grabowski and the North Vancouver skeleton, the case of Joanna Portman presented other problems. Her file was over three inches thick already, and the body had only been discovered two days before. MacDougall and Rodale had obviously been working around the clock. Their squad had interviewed over a hundred people already: doctors and nurses and administrative personnel at St Paul's Hospital; the BC Hydro bus drivers on the Macdonald route; Portman's landlady in Kitsilano and every neighbour in every house between the bus-stop where she had alighted and the home she had never reached. Nothing had come up. Nothing had been seen.

A team of detectives had been dispatched to Regina, Saskatchewan where the nurse had grown up. They had interviewed her mother, her high school friends, the staff at Gray Nuns' Hospital where she had been trained. The victim profile that emerged was of a well-liked, kind-hearted young woman strong on religion and love of human beings. She didn't have a boy-friend. She had her work instead.

As DeClercq had read the Portman file again and again, he had been confronted with evidence that conclusively proved that Jack MacDougall was an officer of high calibre. All the reports as they came in had been digested, analyzed, indexed, and then cross-referenced into a cohesive whole. More than most, DeClercq knew the prominent role that morale had played in the history of the Force. Indeed it was that history which was their greatest strength, that sense of continuity that lies at the heart of the world's most elite fighting machines. Had the RCMP not evolved from the British Imperial Army? And who revered tradition more than the British did? Indeed that had been the thesis of DeClercq's first book: that the sheer weight of experience handed down from officer to officer over the years remained the Force's most powerful weapon, the feeling that they were a team. The Superintendent was well aware that he had stepped in to take command of MacDougall's squad and that it was only human nature to resent such a usurpation. For the sake of morale and that sense of team if for nothing else, DeClercq knew that no matter what the Sergeant's ability it would be necessary to find a place for him. It was a God-given bonus that MacDougall was this good.

On the wall of DeClercq's office the visual on the Portman case revolved around the nurse's graduation picture. To the left of that was a large Ident. blow-up of her body hanging between the struts of the Dogfish Burial Pole. Several aerial shots of the Museum of Anthropology high on the cliffs of

Point Grey overlooking the entrance to the Harbour were tacked up to the right. A photo of her vertebra revealed the same striation marks found on the other two victims. Police, autopsy, and serology reports completed the visual.

Sitting at his desk DeClercq reviewed the Portman case. To his mind certain points stood out and seized his attention.

In the first place, though MacDougall's squad had found no footprints in the snow nor in the earth beneath it – in fact the area around the totem poles was covered with loose gravel – it had discovered a line of deep indentations among the stones like those that might be left by a person over-weight – or someone carrying the load of a body. These indentations ended at a paved loading area beside the museum itself. No tyre tracks had been left on the tarmac.

In the second place, according to the autopsy performed on her remains, Joanna Portman had been dead for about eighteen hours before her corpse was found by Valerie Pritchard and Chris Seaton. Her head had been cut off just after she died. The killing had produced a lot of blood which had pumped out over her body, but this had dried and clotted within a matter of hours. What was strange was that the Headhunter had apparently collected most of the blood at the time of the murder and then poured it over the corpse after nailing it to the totem pole.

Put together, these facts worried DeClercq. For it appeared to him that the Headhunter had hoped that the North Vancouver body would not be found. It was buried in an isolated location and cut branches had been placed on top of the remains. Likewise, it was possible that the floater in the river might wash out to sea and never be discovered. So why, all of a sudden, had the murder pattern altered? For here in the Portman case the Headhunter had killed his victim, then at great risk of detection transported the body to the University, carried it down to the totem poles, climbed up on some sort of ladder and nailed the corpse through both palms to the crossbeam of the Dogfish Burial Pole. And then poured collected blood over his creation.

Was this bizarre scene meant as some sort of statement?

Had the finding of the first two victims and the subsequent publicity given the killer a thrilling taste of notoriety?

And if so then next time, next murder, would he try to outdo the last one? DeClercq believed he would.

Several other matters were also playing on his mind.

Grabowski's body had been found at the foot of the University cliffs. Portman's body had been found on the campus itself. Was the killer therefore connected to UBC? Was he perhaps a student or member of the staff?

The autopsy on Joanna Portman had revealed that as with the other two victims, there was a vertical wound to the throat. In addition the pathologist had been able to take swab smears from her vagina and anus for an indication of whether or not there had been a sex attack. The slide prepared from the vagina swab had shown sperm. The sperm were immotile and few in number. DeClercq knew from Portman's file that the investigation had not turned up a boyfriend. One unkind staff member had even termed her 'prissy'. From previous cases the Superintendent was well aware that the detection of sperm in the vagina and the determination of the length of time since intercourse depends on a number of inter-related factors: the amount of ejaculation and the depth at which it occurs; the condition of the vagina for acidic/alkaline balance, menstruation and infection; sterility of the male; whether the woman has rested prone or walked around in the interim. As a general rule sperm will not be found thirty-six hours after intercourse. By twenty-four hours the tails of the spermatozoa will have broken away. Mobility is lost at about the six-hour point. In the case of Joanna Portman, the sperm found in her body were immotile with the tails snapped off. That, plus quantity, would indicate intercourse had occurred during the time-span of twenty-four to thirty-six hours before the autopsy. Death and body cooling was a complicating factor. Though the presence of semen itself does not indicate rape, here the pathologist had also noted that both the vagina and external genitalia were bruised and traumatized. His conclusion, therefore, was one of a murder/sex attack. And with that DeClercq agreed.

He reached for his question pad. This is what he wrote:

1. Sexual psychotic or sexual psychopath?

2. Is each victim's gender their only connection?

3. Does the killer get sexual release from ending the lives of women?

4. Does immotile sperm = sterility?

5. Is it the memory of the crimes which enables the killer to maintain a normal relationship with his wife or girlfriend? Is his subsequent arousal secretly based on the thought of what he did before?

6. Does he pathologically hate all women?

7. Or is it all a smokescreen for some personal reason connected to one of his victims?

8. *Will we ever know?* he thought, but didn't write it down.

That left the totem pole.

During the winter of 1973 to 1974 the city of San Francisco was stunned by the so-called Zebra killings. Zebra was the investigative name for a cult of Black Muslims who systematically attacked twenty white victims, killing four of them. Several years earlier in Los Angeles, Charles Manson's Family cult of 'creepy crawlies' had butchered seven 'straights' in the hope of bringing down 'Helter Skelter'. Then there was the 'Reverend' Jim Jones. And of course there had always been the Ku Klux Klan.

These days there were cults everywhere, at least one for every motive.

The totem pole bothered DeClercq.

It bothered him partly because the Portman murder marked a change in the pattern. The killer had taken a great risk to make some form of statement. Perhaps that statement was nothing more than a sudden demand for attention, the totem being nothing more than a random method to get it. Or perhaps the totem pole was a part of the statement itself.

135

What bothered DeClercq even more, however, was the positioning of the body. Just nailing the woman to the totem pole was attention-getting enough. Yet in this case the Headhunter had hoisted her up almost fifteen feet and then hammered her hands to the cross piece so that the carving on it provided a substitute for her head. That was too much work and risk unless there was a reason.

And finally it bothered him because of the totem itself.

It is difficult to live in the Pacific Northwest without picking up at least a rudimentary knowledge about the myth of the Indian totem. In the case of the Superintendent, he knew more than most.

Joanna Portman had been nailed to a mortuary pole. The Dogfish carving on it was a form of Pacific shark.

DeClercq was too experienced a policeman to overlook any possible motive, no matter how remote. Over the years he had learned the hard way that often the most stunning insight in any investigation will come from some small, almost insignificant detail that rises from the subconscious like a piece of driftwood floating up from a sunken wreck on the ocean floor. Any cop will tell you that the psychology of murder is a bizarre wasteland indeed. Had David Berkowitz not been ordered to kill by his neighbour's talking dog?

There had never been to DeClercq's knowledge an Indian cult like Zebra. The basis, however, was there. Recently British Columbia had been the focus of an awakening Indian movement.

Was it not fact, DeClercq now thought, *that during the civil rights movement in the United States, most black leaders consciously sought out the roots of their people's past? Did some like the Black Panthers and Black Muslims not seek out the most violent traditions? And did the women's liberation movement not react the same? In this city, had the Wimmin's Fire Brigade not torched pornographic outlets? And what about the Indian? Did he not also look to the roots of his past? And would some not eventually seek the more violent traditions? Was that not the psychology of the frustrated everywhere?*

DeClercq looked back at the corkboard wall, at the photo of Joanna Portman nailed to the Burial Pole.

All right, he thought to himself. *Freefloat for a while.*

You've got a mortuary pole. Of what significance?

It was the practice of many Northwest tribes to erect a mortuary pole near the burial place of the dead.

Give me another tradition.

Among the Kwakiutl, it was the rule to have people unrelated to the dead cut the hair of the mourners.

Is that why the head is missing? A symbolic cut of the hair?

No, it doesn't fit the ritual. She's dead, not a mourner.

Then give me a ritual which does fit in.

I can't. I think we're off base. This totem pole connection is just coincidence. There is no Indian ritual making use of a severed he . . .

Unless . . .

Unless it's not the head as a head that the killer is after. Then it fits Hamatsa and the Cannibal Cult.

DeClercq looked back at the picture.

Then several seconds later he picked up the phone.

9.36 a.m.

The telephone was answered on its tenth ring.

'Allo.'

'Good morning. Did I get you out of bed.'

'Non, je suis tout juste de la douche. Attends un moment.'

DeClercq waited. In his mind he pictured his wife naked, her auburn hair and lithe body dripping water all over the floor. In the background he could hear classical music, a concerto for flute and harp. Genevieve always played Mozart in the morning.

'Okay,' she said, retrieving the phone. *'Je suis décente.'*

'The reason I called you, Genny, I've got a rather wild theory I'd like your opinion on.'

'Shoot. I'm listening.'

Once he had finished, there was silence from the other end of the phone. Then after a few moments' thought his wife slowly said: 'Has there ever been an Indian Death Cult before?'

'Not that I know of.'

'So your theory's based on Zebra?'

'Yes, that case and some others.'

'Run the Zebra theory by me again.'

'Okay, in April of 1975 there was evidence given at the trial of four Black Muslims in San Francisco that they were members of a group called the 'Death Angels'. The purpose of this cult was to start a race war by the random killing of whites. According to the chief witness for the prosecution, he had been approached in San Quentin prison by two men who asked him to teach them martial arts so they could murder Caucasians. According to a theory outlined by Mayor Alioto before the trial began, the Death Angels' organization had titles and offices to which advancement was awarded on the basis of criminal acts performed. The pattern of killing was by random street shooting or by hacking the victims to death with a machete, cleaver, or knife. Decapitation and other forms of mutilation brought special credit to the killers from the organization. In the first Zebra killing, a woman was beheaded.'

'Where's the term "Zebra" from?' Genevieve asked.

'The police radio band used in the case.'

'And you think Zodiac was a similar form of cult?'

'Yes, but he was never caught. He or they, that is.'

'Isn't it "they" if you're talking about a cult?'

'Not by my definition. A single killer may think that he's part of a group – even if the rest of the cult exists only in his head. Zodiac used to send messages to the police bearing an astrological sign and stating that when he died he'd be reborn in Paradise with all the people he had killed as his slaves.'

'Sounds like "Reverend" Jim Jones and his Guyana cult.'

'Exactly. So what do you think?'

Again there was some silence, then Genevieve said: 'I agree that the totem pole must have some form of meaning. I also agree that there could very easily be a radical fringe

138

group within the Red Power movement. The fact the heads are missing is certainly bizarre. But don't you think that cannibalism is stretching it a bit?'

'Perhaps. But then there's a precedent in the Hamatsa. It all depends on just how weird this cult or killer is.'

'Don't we have a book on that?'

'Yes, it's in the spare room bookcase. On the lower shelf.'

'The title?'

'A History of the Potlatch.'

'Hold on. I'll go and get it.'

DeClercq heard Genevieve put down the phone, and her footsteps creak a floorboard. For several minutes he sat in his office with his eyes closed imagining the scene at his home. His wife would be dressed in one of four floor-length bathrobes. She'd have it belted at the waist and as she walked the slit front would reveal glimpses of her legs.

Over the years, Robert DeClercq had certainly enjoyed the show. For in her own way Genevieve was as much an actress as Kate had been.

Then the thought of Kate brought back the scene of that leaf-strewn, wind-swept graveyard. His eyes snapped open and he shook off a sudden chill.

During the early years of his second marriage DeClercq was always touched by guilt when he remembered his first family. Not an hour seemed to pass without a thought of Kate or Jane. Particularly Janie sitting on his knee. When the Superintendent remembered Kate, often as not his mind would return to that night in New York when he met her. The month had been November, just before Thanksgiving.

DeClercq had been in New York for an extradition hearing. An NYPD homicide cop, on learning that the Canadian Corporal enjoyed a night of theatre, had offered to get him a scalped ticket for a revival play on Broadway. DeClercq had readily accepted.

The production was one of *Rosmersholme*, by Henrik Ibsen. Kate had played the lead.

Even today DeClercq could clearly recall the thrill, the tension, the erotic shiver that her acting had fired within him. She seemed to physically hold the stage and rivet his attention. Never before in all his life had he been stunned by such a feeling. It was strange and intangible. Just watching her seemed to fill his existence with meaning. He felt like a fool, sitting anonymously in that crowd and tumbling head over heels in love with this woman. What a wild, insane sensation.

Don't hold yourself too tight, was the thought that ran through his head. *For once throw caution to the wind – go backstage and see her. Whatever have you got to lose? If you get the brushoff, you're going to recover. But if you don't try it . . . My God, what an actress.*

The security guard had stopped him at the door. 'And just where do you think you're going, my friend?' the heavy set man had asked him.

'I was hoping to get backstage. Isn't this the way?'

'You got a pass to get there?'

'No.'

'Then for you this is not the way.'

It was only for a moment that DeClercq had hesitated. Then he'd reached into his pocket and flashed his Regimental Shield. 'Is this pass enough?' Then leaning forward he had whispered, 'Let's avoid a scene.'

The guard had let him through.

Well, what's a little fraud in the name of love? he pondered. He certainly had no legitimate business backstage – why ninety-nine per cent of the males in the audience that night must have fallen in love – and his shield held no authority in the USA. Yet there he was wandering the corridors, searching out the dressing rooms, fearing exposure at any moment for his amorous deceit, his heart beating in his throat while sweat dripped from his armpits, asking someone for the way and then before he knew it, knocking on the door. It had suddenly occurred to him that he'd thought of nothing to say.

'You enter at your own risk,' called a voice beyond the door. 'Take warning, I'm not dressed.'

And now here he was almost twenty-five years later, sitting at his desk and imagining another unattired wife.

Patterns, DeClercq thought. Then: *Janie, how I miss you*.

Again and again in those early days of his second marriage, the Superintendent had told himself that it was wrong and unhealthy to spend so much time in the past. Things happen. That's life. Or fate. Or God-knows-what. The living go on living. Sure they had been good times, but that part of life was over. *Besides, think of her.*

You're a lucky man, Robert DeClercq, who's acting like a fool. Few men are fortunate enough to find love once in their lives. And you've found it twice. Can't you get it through your head that any other man in your position would be down on his knees in prayer that Genevieve came along? Where would you be now had she not picked up the pieces?

But then he would think of Jane, and that toothless baby smile.

DeClercq had never seen Kate as happy as the day their daughter was born. In truth he had never been as happy himself. Then promoted to Sergeant within the RCMP, he had stood in that Montreal hospital room and watched his wife, hair matted and streaked with sweat, cradle the new-born infant lovingly in her arms. He had been overwhelmed by the sight of that shrivelled up, wrinkled prune. But a prune with such eyes.

Many years later that same image had been in his mind on a cold snowy night in December, when sitting in front of the embers of a rapidly dying fire, the wind of winter wailing along the coast of West Vancouver, Genevieve had touched his arm and crouched down to sit beside him. 'You look troubled, Robert. Tell me what's the matter.'

'Just thinking,' he had said.

'About Kate or Jane?' she inquired.

'About Kate *and* Jane, I guess.' He had poked at the fire.

'It wasn't your fault, Robert. I wish you'd remember that. I wish somehow I knew a way to lessen the hurt.'

DeClercq had looked at her with veiled sadness in his eyes. 'You do, Genny. I mean it. Every minute. Every day. I really don't know where I'd be without you. I love you and I need you – but still I feel this guilt.'

'For what? Their deaths? Your life? The hand that Fate has dealt you? Robert, you've got to learn to be easier on yourself. *It wasn't your fault!*'

'Wasn't it, Genny? I think it was. If I hadn't been a cop it never would have happened.'

'If you hadn't been a cop you'd have never got backstage. And you never would have met her. And if you hadn't met her, you would never have had the child and all the joy she gave you. It may have been a short time, but Robert, it was worth it. I know that. And you know it too. Besides, if you hadn't been a cop I'd never have met you either. Then where would I be? Can you give me an answer?'

'You wouldn't be with a man who can't forget the past.'

'I wouldn't be with you, love. And that's all that matters.' Then ever so softly – was it spoken? – she whispered to the fire: 'Oh God, I'd give my very life to bear you another child.'

'I know,' he said gently, and took her in his arms.

For a long time they sat there just looking at the embers. Red, orange, yellow sparks danced hotly before their eyes.

'Genny,' he said finally. 'This isn't fair for you.'

She turned around and looked at him, frowning, and said: 'Don't you think that I'm the one to decide what's fair for me?'

'Of course. It's just that . . .'

'It's just that you think you're using up my youth. You think, *chéri*, that I have a world of experience before me, a world that if I don't taste now, I'll live to regret later. You are deeply worried that you're using me as a crutch. You think that to be fair to me, to give me the sort of love that I need, you must forget Kate and Jane. That you can't seem to do, so you think you're unfair. Have I got it right?'

She reached out and touched his face and warmed him with her eyes. 'Believe me, Robert, it's good *for me* for you to remember them. Please try to see you and me from my point of view. I've never met a man or woman who could find total satisfaction – physical, mental, emotional – with just one other person. The odds are stacked against it: we all develop

142

in different ways. Yet all of us seem to want that. To find somebody special in a relationship or marriage. Then later we're disillusioned and we look for someone else – maybe for a sexual fling or maybe just to talk. Even those who never break away, it doesn't stop them thinking.

'Well I think I'm different.

'I was so lucky to come of age within the women's movement. I could seize a freedom that no one before me had. And seize it I did. Job. Men in numbers. And lots of self esteem.

'The job and the equality, those I'll never give up. But the men became a bummer. Indiscriminate fucking makes for a female or male slut. The benefit of my freedom was I got that out of my system. Men for me are easy, I've always been lucky that way – and maybe that's why I know in my heart that I only want one guy. That's just the way it is, Robert. And baby, I want you.'

She cast him the slightest trace of a very wicked smile.

Then without another word she slowly extricated herself from his arms. He remembered her standing up before him by the dim light of the fire, remembered thinking in earnest *Genny, I'm blind compared to you*, remembered the way she straightened her back and planted her feet apart, reaching for the top button of her blouse, pausing for one long erotic moment before she let it . . .

'I think I've found what you're talking about,' said Genevieve, excited, on the other end of the phone. 'The ritual of Hamatsa. Will you just listen to this!'

Robert DeClercq moved his notepad into place.

'It seems that just over a hundred and twenty years ago, cannibalism was general among the Kwakiutl Indians. Two fellows named Hunt and Moffat brought back first-hand accounts of the custom. Sometimes they said slaves were killed for the benefit of the Hamatsa. At other times the Hamatsa were content merely to rip mouthfuls of flesh from the chests and upper arms of their own tribesmen.

'It would appear that the Hamatsa held a special privileged position within the group. They were literally

143

licensed cannibals.

'Hunt and Moffat swear they saw the following near Prince Rupert. A Kwakiutl shot and wounded a runaway slave who collapsed near the water's edge. Immediately he was set upon by a group including Hamatsas. They watched the Kwakiutl cut the slave to pieces with knives while the Hamatsas squatted in a circle crying: 'Hap! Hap! Hap!'. According to Hunt and Moffat, who were helpless to intervene, the Indians snatched up the flesh still warm and quivering and offered it according to seniority to the members of the Cannibal Cult who were present. In memory of the episode, a rock on the beach was subsequently carved into a likeness of the mask of Baxbakualanuxsiwae, He-who-is-first-to-eat-Man-at-the-mouth-of-the-River. Baxbakualanuxsiwae – the Cannibal God – was said to live in a spirit house high up on the slopes of the Rocky Mountains where day and night blood-red smoke billowed out from the chimney of his home.

'There's then a whole list here of evidence collected from other whites who confirm the practice.

'When Hamatsas were interviewed it was noted that their teeth were rotting away. This was from filing them sharper in order to better deal with their food.

'Do you think it possible that Hamatsa is being used as a modern terrorist tactic?'

'I don't know what I think right now, but stranger things have happened,' DeClercq said.

'Don't I know it. I can think of four examples of cannibalism – or close to it – in the annals of abnormal psychology. Fish in New York. Gein in Wisconsin. Kemper in California. And maybe Nelson here in BC.'

'So maybe I'm not off base.'

'Maybe not. But I hope so. Cause if you're right this killer is restricting his diet to brains.'

'For now I'd settle for *any* Indian who popped up in the case.'

'Well,' Genevieve said, 'who knows what the future holds? Perhaps you'll only find the answer in the lair of

Baxbakualanuxsiwae himself. Maybe the truth is hidden high in the Rocky Mountains.'

10.07 a.m.

Robert DeClercq was smiling when he hung up the phone.

The Superintendent stood up and crossed over to the window. DeClercq glanced at his wristwatch, then removed his uniform jacket from the back of the chair and put it on. As he was heading for the door his eyes fell once more on the blowup of Joanna Portman's body nailed to the burial pole. His impression was that the carved Dogfish face was laughing at whoever was looking.

And in that instant he remembered another laugh many years ago. He recalled a shack in the wilderness in the northern part of Quebec, where a child lay on a cot in death, its head twisted at too sharp an angle. He had felt the knife pierce his abdomen but knew it didn't matter. All that concerned him was the fact that his hands were closing rapidly around the laughing man's neck, squeezing the very life out of him and choking, crushing, annihilating that black laugh from his throat.

Even after the man was dead, the Superintendent could hear it.

Black laughter.

FLYING PATROLS

10.15 a.m.

'Good morning. My name is Robert DeClercq. I hold the rank of Superintendent. I have been assigned command of this investigation.'

145

As he spoke, beginning slowly, getting the feel of once more addressing a task force of officers, DeClercq stood erect with his hands behind his back at the front of the room and moved his gaze from face to face connecting with the eyes. The parade room, like everything else at Headhunter Headquarters, was still under construction, and those who had been unable to find an empty folding chair sat on the top of piles of lumber or leaned against the walls. There were more than seventy officers in the room, two-thirds of them dressed in the brown serge working uniform of the Royal Canadian Mounted Police, the others in plain clothes. Approximately one fifth were women – a change which had come over the Force since DeClercq had retired. It occurred to him now that for its next edition *Men Who Wore The Tunic*, his first book, would require a change of title.

'The task assigned to this squad is not an easy one,' he began. 'It would appear, from what we know at the moment, that the object of this manhunt is a random killer – an assassin in the purest sense who kills for the love of killing.' DeClercq caught Joseph Avacomovitch's expression of agreement, a brief nod from where the Russian stood at the back of the room.

'You men and women have been specially selected to spearhead this investigation. The purpose of this, our first briefing, is to discuss the operational structure under which this squad will be working. Basically it is this.

'Effective communication is the essence of any team-work. I therefore hope that each of you will utilize every avenue of dialogue within this group without rank creating a barrier. The bulk of you have been assigned to the Central Corps or general investigative body of this dragnet. Attached to this core as adjuncts will be a Scientific Section under the control of Joseph Avacomovitch, who I am sure you all know by reputation, our own Identification Squad and our guiding brain, a Computer Command under Inspector Chan. This Computer Command will build on the program developed during the Olson investigation to integrate and enhance each bit of information gathered by our hunt. Every member of this Central Corps will receive a daily printout from Inspector Chan listing composites, suspects, and developing avenues of inquiry. At the end of each day you are invited – every one of you – to pose questions or assumptions or guesses to Computer Command. You'll have a software-enhanced answer by the following morning.

'In addition, this core group will be working in liaison with those Municipal Police Forces separate from the RCMP, and each of them will appoint a specific liaison officer. I am informed that Vancouver Police co-ordination will be through Detective Almore Flood of the Major Crimes Squad. He is here this morning.

'The overall command of this Central Corp – our general investigation – has been assigned to Inspector Jack MacDougall. He is the gentleman off to my right frowning over the misrepresentation that I just made of his rank – unaware that for the quality of his work to date on this case Ottawa has accepted my recommendation that he be promoted from Sergeant.'

A spontaneous round of applause began, and at this point DeClercq paused both to let MacDougall be congratulated and to let the implication of his promotion permeate the group.

DeClercq then moved off to his left and sat down informally on the corner of a desk. He continued his roving gaze, still connecting with the eyes.

'I think that we must all recognize that any coordinated police investigation works on a base of assumptions – these assumptions being the tentative conclusions that are drawn from the evidence at hand.

'The importance of this is that here is where our greatest danger lies.

'Let me give you an example. In November of 1980 it was commonly believed by the West Yorkshire police in England that the killer called the Yorkshire Ripper had cracked the skulls and mutilated the bodies of thirteen women. Victim No. 2 they thought was a 26-year-old prostitute named Joan Harrison killed in November 1975. There were bite marks on her body – and swabs taken from her vagina and anus indicated the presence of semen deposited by a secretor with the rare blood group B. As with all the Ripper's other victims she had been killed by a hammer-like blow to the head.

'During the course of the investigation, Assistant Chief Constable George Oldfield who was in charge of it received a number of letters signed "Jack the Ripper". Saliva on the gum flap of the third letter was analyzed as coming from a secretor of blood group B, and the letter was postmarked Sunderland in the North of England. Then in June of 1979 the police received a tape from someone claiming to be the killer taunting Oldfield for his lack of progress in tracking him down. The writing on the envelope containing the tape was the same as that on the letters; the saliva that sealed its flap was also from a secretor of blood group B. The tape was of a male voice with a Geordie accent from the North East of England.

'Based on this evidence at hand, the West Yorkshire police made certain assumptions about the killer that they were seeking. The result was that people in 11,000 households were questioned and a million-pound publicity campaign was undertaken on the slogan: "The Ripper would like you to ignore this."

'In fact, the man who was ultimately convicted of all the Ripper crimes *except that of Joan Harrison* was a Bradford truck driver with a Yorkshire accent named Peter Sutcliffe.

'The point of all this is that from the evidence at hand the West Yorkshire police appear to have made an erroneous assumption, and then working on the basis of that assumption acquired tunnel vision. And that tunnel vision may have allowed Sutcliffe to kill again, slipping through the police net until his use of a stolen licence plate finally brought him down.

'As I have said – assumptions are where our greatest danger lies.

'Now,' DeClercq said smiling and using an easy tone of voice, 'the question is, what can we do to counteract this natural human tendency from the very beginning of our manhunt?

'First, we can take as our motto: *Watch for tunnel vision!*

'Secondly, while it is fairly obvious that we are hunting for one killer or set of killers in all three cases, we can make sure that we look at each case as both separate and connected. Just in case life is throwing us some bizarre coincidence.

'And thirdly – our greatest protection – we can learn from history.'

At this point Robert DeClercq stood up and loosened his uniform tie. It was a small gesture, in many ways out of character, but he did not want his audience to feel that they were being given a lecture. He wanted them to sense instead that this was a dialogue. That they were truly a team.

'I'm sure that most of you will agree with me that it is our sense of history which is this Force's strongest asset – that because we record it in such detail, revere it, and build upon our past foundation year after year, we have constructed the most integrated policing unit the world has ever had. We deserve our reputation: it's founded on fact.

'I sometimes feel, however, that we don't look far enough in the past – that we revere the early years for our pageantry, but study the techniques of later years for skill in investigation. This squad is going to rectify that fact.

'Now if you'll bear with me a moment, I'd like to illustrate what I mean by an excursion into our past.

'In 1886 Lawrence Herchmer was appointed Commissioner of this Force and it was he who transformed us from a military organization into a civilian police force. In doing this, Herchmer's most important contribution was in setting up the patrol system. Under this system members of the Mounted Police were distributed in small detachments throughout the Northwest Territories.

149

These detachments became the operational centres of the policing system.

'Herchmer then introduced the patrol report form. This was a document to be prepared by each member as he performed his mounted patrol.

'Copies of these patrol reports from each and every detachment were then forwarded to divisional headquarters where they were assembled to give a complete and comprehensive picture of all activities within Mounted Police jurisdiction.

'Now you will see the organization that I have outlined as our Central Corps, our general investigative body, is the modern computerized parallel for this patrol system. There is nothing new in that. A similar organization was used to hunt the Yorkshire Ripper and for the Atlanta child killings.

'Commissioner Herchmer, however, was not content to stop there – and this is the part of our history that I fear, in our modern desire for centralization, we tend to forget.

'For in 1890, in order to prevent evasion of the patrol system Herchmer introduced the additional system of flying patrols. These flying patrols did not follow the regular trails of the patrol system, but instead they functioned totally on their own, independent of the main centrally-organized system. They were, if you like, the commando guerrillas of the Northwest Mounted Police.'

DeClercq paused for a moment, then said: 'In our manhunt for the Headhunter I intend to bring back the flying patrol.

'These flying patrols will be seven in number. Each patrol will consist of a male and female member.

'The flying patrols will be our third line of defence against tunnel vision. They will counteract the possibility that we might err in our assumptions – for they will work totally independent from the Central Corps of this squad which I have already outlined. These patrols will follow their own instincts, and the members who will be involved have been selected for self-starting initiative. In order to prevent the taint of a possible faulty assumption, no member in the Central Corps will discuss any aspect of the case with a flying patrol member. Each patrol will receive all facts collated by Computer Command – but without any enhanced conclusions, theories or assumptions. Liaison with the main group will be through Sergeant James Rodale. He is the man who just entered through the rear door and who, like Inspector MacDougall, is unaware that for his work to date on this investigation he has also been promoted.'

Again there was a spontaneous round of applause, but the frown on Rodale's face in no way abated. In his right hand he was carrying a brown manila envelope and he was making his way to the front of the room through the crowd.

'In closing,' DeClercq continued, 'I'd like to add three comments.

'The first is to caution all of us against creating a copy-cat killer. Any and all information going out to the media for public consumption goes through Jack MacDougall.

'The second is to tell you that any interrogation of a possible suspect will be put on videotape. These tapes will be reviewed once a week by each flying patrol. This gives us a guarantee of independent assessment, and also of female perspective. We are dealing with a killer who has a perverted passion for women. No one can know the hunter to the same degree as the hunted.

'And the third is to advise you – and I mean this – that my door is always open. As I said at the beginning, my goal is effective teamwork – and teamwork to be effective requires open communication. If something is important, or you need direction, discussion, resources, you only have to climb those stairs and knock. For let's be certain about one fact: we're working against the clock. Believe me, there is a ground-swell of panic out there in this city and all it might take is one more murder to bring out uncontrolled mass hysteria.

151

'It took the English police more than five years to catch the Yorkshire Ripper.

'It took the Atlanta police twenty-two months to arrest a suspect later convicted on two of those twenty-eight black child killings.

'It took this Force thirteen days to nail Olson for eleven murders.

'Let's get this Headhunter – and shorten our own record.'

It was as DeClercq ended the briefing that Sergeant James Rodale handed him the envelope. It was addressed to the Canadian Broadcasting Corporation, having been dropped in the mailslot of the central Post Office during the night and delivered this morning. After copying it for broadcasting, the CBC had dispatched it to the Vancouver Police Department by special courier. The envelope and contents were coated with fingerprint powder. A police Xerox copy was also enclosed.

'You'd better look at this,' Rodale said. 'Before you adjourn the meeting.'

The Superintendent opened it and removed a Polaroid print sealed in a clear plastic VPD evidence pouch, plus a note constructed from cut and paste newspaper headlines, also plastic sealed.

The Polaroid picture was of Joanna Portman's severed head stuck on a wooden pole.

The note read: *Welcome aboard, Robert. Do you think you're up to this?*

Macho/Macha

11.05 a.m.

Katherine Spann was standing at the bulletin board looking at the photograph of Joanna Portman's head when one of the men in the group with her said: 'Well this sure puts all our balls on the line.'

'And just what does it do for me?' the woman asked.

The male cop who had spoken looked her over from head to toe. 'Depends what part of your body you want to put at risk,' he said, winking in conspiracy with a couple of the men. Spann turned back to the bulletin board, ignoring the taunt.

Beside the plastic sealed photograph and note from the Headhunter MacDougall had just pinned up the duty roster. Spann scanned the list of assignments and began to hunt for her name. She found it under the list heading: *seven flying patrols*.

'Anybody here know a guy named Rick Scarlett?' she asked.

'You're looking at him,' the man said who had just given her the visual once over.

'Oh, great!' the woman said. 'Just great!'

Scarlett was tall, just under 6' 2", and in his late twenties. His hair was short and light brown with just a hint of redness, the colour the same as that of his clipped military moustache. His eyes were a muddy brown. The features of his face were clean and sharp as were the other lines of his body. His muscles were tightly-knit, and he moved with fluid motion. *Athletic* was the single word that best summed him up.

'I'll see you downstairs,' Katherine Spann said, then she turned on her heels and made for the locker room.

Behind her someone whistled.

Locker rooms – even co-ed locker rooms – are the same the whole world over. There is that universal smell of sweat. There is the certain knowledge that the fungus of athlete's foot is lurking in at least one of the corners. And – if males are present – there is sure to be a jock mentality to the level of conversation. Men in locker rooms always relate that way.

When Katherine Spann came down the stairs at 4949 Heather Street, two men and a woman were talking at the foot of the steps.

'. . . he was a bum-face all the way,' one of the men was saying.

'A bum-face? What do you mean?'

'You know, one of those guys with big fleshy round orbs for cheeks, skin stretched tight as it goes. Always got a little mouth pursed together like a twitching sphincter. Guy looks at you, ya think he's hangin a moon.'

'Do you always talk about judges this way?' the woman in the group asked.

'Always,' Ed Rabidowski said.

'Mad Dog' Rabidowski at thirty-two was a Charles Bronson type: square shoulders, over-developed muscle tone, latent violence. His face looked like a piece of rough-cut stone. His cheekbones were chiselled high with an Oriental slant, his nose chipped fine and his mouth slashed thin. He had Clark Gable ears, jet black hair, bushy black eyebrows, and a drooping black moustache. His eyes were coloured gun-barrel blue.

The Mad Dog's father had been a trapper in the Yukon and by the age of six Rabidowski was able to take the eye out of a squirrel with a .22 at 1000 yards. It was Rabidowski who had picked off the Albanian sniper in Ottawa sent from China by way of Hong Kong to assassinate Soviet Premier Kosygin on his Canadian state visit. The incident had kicked off the Mad Dog's rise to fame. Then for the last five years straight he had taken

154

the trophy for both pistol and rifle marksmanship in the RCMP annual competition. When he wore his uniform jacket, both rifle and handgun insignia – each surmounted with a crown to denote a distinguished marksman – were displayed prominently on one sleeve. At the present moment, however, Rabidowski was stripped to the waist.

'Mark my words,' the Mad Dog continued, 'a lawyer with a bum-face always goes to the bench.'

'Come on!' the woman said.

'Excuse me,' Katherine Spann said, interrupting the conversation. 'May I please get through?'

'Oh no, not another broad,' the Mad Dog sighed in disgust. 'This place is crawling with them!'

'Makes you long for the old days, don't it?' Spann said sarcastically.

'Don't it ever,' Rabidowski replied, being completely honest.

Spann let it go. Just as she had with Scarlett. For the truth of the matter was that since her initial day of training in Regina in 1974, this internal attitude had come along with the job. And that was to be expected. 1974 was the first year that the Force had recruited women: for a hundred and one years previously it had been an elite male club. Even today most men did not want to work with a female partner; for in the back of their minds they feared being caught short if there was something physical needed or there was a fire-fight. A woman just couldn't cut it. Every man knew that.

It was not, of course, as though in day-to-day police work this anti-female attitude was blatant in its manifestation; indeed most of the men bent over backwards to accommodate the women. And that, more than anything else, was the real root of the problem.

But then Rabidowski was different: his thoughts on the subject never went unspoken. 'You're Scarlett's partner, aren't you?' the Mad Dog asked of Spann. 'Do the man a favour, eh. Try not to distract him. He'll have work to do.'

As he finished speaking Rabidowski put a cigarette to his lips and lit a match with the nail of his thumb.

As the phosphorous flared Spann turned to the other woman in the group and said: 'This guy's a "matcho" man.'

The other woman grinned and asked: 'Is he always such a jerk?'

'Always,' Rick Scarlett answered. He had just come down the stairs to join the bottleneck at the bottom.

'Hi. I'm Monica Macdonald.'

'My name's Katherine Spann.'

'This is Rusty Lewis. We've been paired as partners on one of these flying patrols.'

'So have we,' Spann said. 'Me and the guy who just came down the steps.'

'My name's Rick Scarlett,' Scarlett said, shaking hands all round. 'How you doing, Mad Dog? Long time no see.'

'As well as a working cop can when he's inundated with broads.'

'"Inundated",' Spann said. 'That must be a pretty big word for someone like you.'

'I see you've met the Mad Dog,' Scarlett grinned.

'Where'd he get the nick-name?' Macdonald asked.

Katherine Spann said: 'It must be all the hot air – it makes him foam at the mouth.'

'Broads!' Rabidowski snorted.

'We used to shorten Rabidowski down to Rabid,' Scarlett said. '"Mad Dog" came from "Rabid". And believe me, he acts it.'

'I'd never have guessed.'

'Don't sell the man short,' Rick Scarlett added. 'He just might be the best marksman this Force has ever had.'

'I doubt that,' Spann said. 'I hear DeClercq was better.'

Rabidowski guffawed. 'You call a bow a marksman's weapon!'

'A crossbow,' the woman corrected. 'They say at one time he almost made runner-up to the Olympics.'

'Yeah, well crossbows went out with the Middle Ages.'

'Amazing!' Spann said to Monica Macdonald. 'The guy

knows history too.'

'When it comes to weapons, lady, I know a lot more than you.'

'Try me,' Spann said sharply.

'Don't make me laugh.'

'Hey, wait a minute,' Monica Macdonald said. 'What's this about DeClercq? You mean our Superintendent?'

'Of course,' Rick Scarlett said. 'Come on. You must know the story. The man's almost a legend.'

'*Is* a legend, I should think,' Spann corrected.

'All right. *Is* a legend.'

'Will someone fill me in?' the other woman asked. Beside the blonde woman she looked positively plain. Her hair was brown and tied back in a bun. Her eyes were brown and warm and her figure was round. She stood five inches shorter than Spann. Physically her only striking feature was her full and sensual mouth.

'Broads!' Rabidowski repeated, as if all this was to be expected. What did women know about the glory of tradition? What, indeed?

Rick Scarlett said, 'The year was 1970, a bit before our time. The Quebec October Crisis. Anyway, by then DeClercq was recognized as the best homicide man in the entire Force. In terms of success, his name was up there with Steele and Walsh and Blake. When the FLQ kidnapped Cross and Laporte and then killed the Labour Minister, DeClercq was called in. It was he who located both the Chenier and Liberation Cells.'

'How did he do that?'

'No one knows. But he had a lot of contacts in the Montreal underworld. A lot of informers. But in light of what happened subsequently he never revealed his source.'

'What happened?'

'A gang of punks got both his wife and daughter,' Katherine Spann said.

Macdonald turned to her. 'Killed them you mean?'

'Do you really not know any of this?'

'No I don't.'

'You tell her,' Spann said to Scarlett.

'Two weeks after Cross was released and the Chenier Cell went to Cuba, three men invaded DeClercq's home while he was up in Ottawa. They murdered his wife on the spot, ripped her up with a machine pistol. Then they carried off his daughter. She wasn't very old. Five or so, I think.

'At the time everyone assumed that it was an FLQ revenge operation. But in the end it turned out to be just a group of Montreal thugs caught up in the groundswell of the Quebec independence movement.

'Anyway, DeClercq, of course, was banned from the case because of personal involvement. Shelved with a leave of absence. He didn't like the orders and he didn't follow them. He went on his own and did a rogue investigation. Using the same underworld grapevine that had helped him find Cross and the murders of Laporte, he managed to discover where the gang was holding the girl. It was in a cabin out of the city in the Laurentian backwoods. DeClercq went out alone, determined to get her back.'

Monica Macdonald's eyes squinted slightly. 'And he didn't,' she said.

'No,' Scarlett stated. 'Not alive.'

Rabidowski said: 'Story is he killed five people getting into that cabin. Picked off the first guy when he came out for some wood. Got three more when they came out looking for him. Took them all down with a crossbow, if you believe it. Because it's silent I guess.

'They say he killed the last man with his hands as he was coming through the door and after the guy had stabbed him. But he didn't save his daughter. Two other punks had joined the original three, and there had been a dispute over what to do. The winning group in the argument had broken her neck that morning.'

Monica shook her head.

'So that's why DeClercq was retired,' Rick Scarlett said. 'He'd contravened orders and you know what that means.'

158

Katherine Spann added: 'There was an internal investigation into his conduct. As usual he couldn't have a lawyer and so they appointed a member to present his defence. The guy they appointed was François Chartrand.'

'The Commissioner?'

'He was an Inspector back then.'

'What happened?'

'DeClercq was never charged. He had a legal defence under protection of his family and public sympathy was on his side. Besides, the odds were five to one no matter how you cut it.'

Spann said: 'Now Chartrand is Commissioner. And Robert DeClercq is back. I wonder if he really is as good as they say.'

'Well, we're going to find out,' Rick Scarlett said.

Rabidowski nodded. There was a smirk on his face.

Spann turned on him: 'You know something, Ed? You're a first class pain in the ass. You're a mental dinosaur. Come to think of it, I know what the four of us are doing here. What's your job on this Squad?'

'Firepower,' the Mad Dog said bluntly. 'Lady, I'm a one man SWAT Squad. I'm our Emergency Response Team. Believe me, if the chips are down I'm more important than you. I won't go into detail. I'd be talking over your head.'

'Try me,' Spann said quickly – and as sharply as the last time.

'Gimme a break.'

Rabidowski walked over to his locker and removed a clean shirt from inside. He began to put it on.

Monica Macdonald glanced at Spann and picked up something in her look backed up by intuition. She said: 'What's the matter, Ed? Are you afraid to try her?'

Rabidowski turned. 'Put your money where your mouth is and it might be worth my time. Or better yet, with lips like yours I can think of somewhere else to put your mouth if your sister cop here loses.'

159

'Ten bucks,' Macdonald said.

'Who holds the pot? Who decides?'

'Not Scarlett,' Spann said. 'You're in bed together.' She sized up Rusty Lewis. 'Let's take a chance with him.'

Lewis took the money.

'Okay,' Rabidowski said. 'Let me pose a problem. We're talking firepower.'

Katherine Spann nodded.

'You got a four man Emergency Response Team and you gotta cover all the angles. We're talkin shots per second and we're aimin for accuracy. Arm it,' the Mad Dog said.

'You first,' the woman replied. 'And give me your reasons.'

Rabidowski grinned. 'Okay, long-barrels to start with. I'd give two guys pump action Remington Model 870 12 gauge shotguns. Why is obvious. We're talking scatter-force. The third guy gets a sniper's rifle, the Remington Model V for Varmint heavy barrelled Calibre .22–250. There you've got a small bullet with high velocity so that means pinpoint accuracy with a flat trajectory. No compensation needed. The last guy gets your Heckler and Koch Model HK 93 assault rifle in Calibre .223 with telescoping stock. There you've got high class German manufacturing technique – which by the way is becoming standard in this state of the art – and a roller-locking mechanism. I'd take semi- over fully-automatic. More target control.

'And finally,' Rabidowski continued, 'I'd top each guy off with a whizz of a short-barrel. Each man gets a semi-automatic Beretta Model 92 S pistol, Calibre 9 mm Parabellum with a magazine capacity of 15 rounds plus one in the chamber. Your Beretta's double action. The whole trip means *Kapow!* So top that, lady. And Lewis, hand me the cash.'

'James Bond used a Beretta,' Rick Scarlett added.

Spann almost laughed. Her mind weighed the man up and found him a couple of ounces short. 'My turn,' she said.

160

'Come on, Spann. Better minds than you or me have put that team together. Go down gracefully,' the Mad Dog said.

'Better minds than you or I are also rethinking it, Ed. For the sake of argument I'll keep the long-barrels the same. Now let's chuck the Beretta and replace it with four Ruger Model Security 6 .38 Special revolvers with either .38 Special +P ammunition or maybe .357 Magnum. I'd take the 4 inch barrel over the 2 and ¾. So we've stepped up the Smith and Wesson, and it's also double action. And it's easily field stripped.'

'Lady, you're a fool. Your Ruger's only got 6 shots compared to 16 in the Beretta. The buzz words in this exercise are "greater firepower". That means semi-automatic.'

'Look,' Spann said, 'we're also talking accuracy and reliability. If you don't hit with the first few shots what does it really matter: all four women on the team will be dead and . . .'

'Women! That'll be the day. We're talkin *action* here. Not pushin paper.'

'. . . and besides, your firepower is in the long-barrels: you're not going to meet a short-barrel firepower situation. You're going to use the pistol only if you're right against it, eh? If your semi-auto misfires and jams, well then you're fucked. If your Ruger misfires you just pull the trigger again. Your Beretta you'd have to clear and that takes precious time. So your Ruger's reliable.'

'Oh, smart broad,' Rabidowski said, raising his eyebrows and looking at Scarlett. 'Let's look at transportation. Your semi-auto's thinner and more easily concealed and holstered than your bulky cylinder. And to reload you got speed: just eject one magazine and jam in another. What about that, eh?'

'Irrelevant,' Spann said immediately. 'Have you never heard of a speed-loader for a revolver? Besides, your Beretta 92 S is fussy in what it feeds. It won't reliably take your Glaser Safety Slug. It won't take a hollow-point or

161

flat nose. It won't take either your Wadcutters or your armour piercing cartridges. With your Ruger, if it goes in the chamber, it fires. So your Beretta's got no selection of ammo. Your options are nil.'

Rabidowski went to counter this, then realized as he opened his mouth that he had run out of arguments. He blinked instead.

'And while we're at it,' Spann said, 'you're creating jeopardy. Your semi-auto will be spewing out hot casings with every shot fired. What if one of those hits the guy running beside you? A second can mean survival, and there the next guy is with a red hot cartridge down his shirt. And what about the floor? You want your whole team rollerskating on spent Beretta casings? Your Ruger hasn't got that problem. And anyway, for the sake of argument, why does your squad need sidearms at all? You're in a tactical response situation: it's the long-barrels that you'd use. But if you really want a pistol . . . yep, your Ruger is the one.'

'Amen,' Macdonald said. And then she turned to Lewis. 'Well, what's your judgment?'

Rusty Lewis was 29 years old and slightly overweight. He had drooping eyelids that made him look half-asleep. Sort of like Robert Mitchum. Above all, Rusty Lewis was fair. 'Kathy wins,' he said.

'Jesus, Mad Dog,' Scarlett exclaimed. 'The woman set you up!'

As Monica took the money she let out a thankful sigh.

'You just saved me, Kathy, from having a rabies shot.'

Everybody laughed.

Except Rabidowski.

11.56 a.m.

'I'm impressed,' Rick Scarlett said, 'with the way you handled Mad Dog.'

'Yeah sure. Nice friends you got.'

'No really, I mean it. And he's not my friend. We just

162

spent some time together in the same detachment. Where'd you get that knowledge? I certainly didn't expect it.'

Katherine Spann gave him a long, hard look. 'And just what did you expect? That I'd be reduced to tears when the subject turned to hardware? Don't be such a jerk.'

'All right. I admit it. I started out an asshole. I'm sorry. Okay? So let's change the programme. We got to work together, that's orders.'

They were both sitting in the White Spot coffee shop at Cambie and King Edward waiting to order lunch. The waitress came and they ordered burgers Triple 'O' with a side of French fries. Scarlett had coffee. Spann had tea.

When they were finished eating, Rick Scarlett said: 'Let's pose you another problem. You've got this flying patrol, see, that wants to get this Headhunter. Where does it start?'

'At the beginning,' Spann said. 'So let's hit the files.'

12.37 p.m.

Monica Macdonald and Rusty Lewis came into the White Spot just as Spann and Scarlett were leaving. They took the same table. Both ordered the Weight Watchers' platter.

'So where do we start?' Lewis asked, sipping a cup of coffee.

'The way I see it, we haven't many options.' Macdonald thought a moment. 'The Central Corps will start with local info. I say you and I abandon our country. Let's go south.'

'And do what?' Lewis asked. 'Tap the FBI?'

'Remember that baby kidnapping case several years ago? The infant out of White Rock found in Oregon? Well I was on the Force team that worked with the FBI. I even went out a few times with this Bureau guy from Seattle. He'll remember me.'

'You still keep in touch?'

'No, but he'll remember me. So I say we leave this afternoon and make for Washington State. Let's get a look at the skin list they'll have there. We'll get a jump on the other flying patrols and Central Corps and maybe we'll get lucky. Maybe we'll find an American skinner poaching in Her Majesty's far western forest.'

'Sounds good,' Lewis said. 'Do you want to drive or shall I?'

'I'll drive,' Macdonald said. 'You look far too tired.'

2.45 p.m.

Commercial Crime Section (Special 'I')
Target: Steve Rackstraw (aka 'The Fox')
Tape installed: October 31st 0900 hours. (Tipple)
Tape removed: October 31st 1130 hours. (Tipple)
u/m 'The Weasel' now known as John Lincoln Hardy.
u/m only known as 'The Wolf'.

Outgoing local call.

Weasel:	Hello.
Fox:	Hey.
Weasel:	Hoodoo.
Fox:	Hoodoo yourself.
Weasel:	(Chuckling) Hey nigger . . . Hey nigger . . . what's happening:
Fox:	Be ready . . . you know . . . It's on.
Weasel:	That's cold, man.
Fox:	I was wondering about that house youse knows. Burnaby?
Weasel:	It's cool. Everythin all moved in.
Fox:	Ah . . . that's good.
Weasel:	There were so many ladies out last night.
Fox:	Uh huh.
Weasel:	They shoot at you, no need to shoot at them . . . you know, drive them white boys wild.
Fox:	Yeah I know. Play the sucker man . . . Hey

164

Nigger, are you ready? You be gettin your hoodoo soon.

Weasel: That's good . . . cause I's hurtin.

Fox: Okay. Bye.

Weasel: Bye . . . Hey.

Fox: (Laughing) Hey hey.

3.57 p.m.

Incoming call. Long distance.

Fox: Hey hey.

Operator: I have a collect call from Mr Wolf. Will you accept the charge?

Fox: Yes I will.

Wolf: It's cooking on the 6th . . . The pot boils over at midnight.

Fox: I'm ready . . . The cous will be down there to see all you.

Wolf: Ah . . . right . . . be seein' the man then.

Fox: Okay, bye for now.

Wolf: *Au Revoir.*

4.01 p.m.

Outgoing local call.

Weasel: Yeah?

Fox: Time for a nigger hoodoo man to catch his ride an be gone. It's on for the 6th.

Weasel: All right . . . let's go.

Fox: Say hello to our Momma for me . . . you hear?

Weasel: I hear. Bye for now.

Fox: Bye. Hey hey.

HALLOWEEN

6.15 p.m.

Tonight the moon was almost full. And tonight was also Halloween.

There are those who say they don't need to look at the sky or consult an almanac to know when a full moon lurks behind the rain clouds. For they are policemen and firemen and hospital workers and bartenders and ambulance drivers. From years of experience they have learned that the nights just before full moon will bring out more violence, more uncontrolled emotion, more just plain weirdness than any other time.

It has long been known that in mental hospitals the most bizarre behaviour occurs in the twenty-four to forty-eight hours preceding the full moon. Now there is scientific theory to back this up: it is accepted as fact that the moon's weak magnetism affects the earth's metal-induced magnetic field. This is primarily true of iron. Based on this fact, a Chicago study concentrated on a single element in biological tissue. It concluded that magnetic and gravitational interaction between the earth and the moon may very well be involved in certain human physiological and psychological changes.

Halloween, of course, takes no account of science.

Halloween concerns itself with only evil forces.

And so it would this year.

At 6.15 p.m. a nun came out through the front door of the convent, past the shaded alcoves in the wood designed for contemplation, along one side of the shallow pond with its celestial reflections, and up the path to the main road where the North Vancouver bus was waiting.

Before this Halloween was over there would be another victim.

7.05 p.m.

The library was a dingy room on the main floor of the command building. Over the years it must have been used for some sort of storage, for all four walls were lined with shelves from the ground up to the ceiling. Several very large tables were scattered about the room and covering these were photostats of every available document on all three of the killings. Copies of the various photographs were in the process of reproduction, while every half hour additional material came in that had not been there before.

Scarlett and Spann sat at one of the tables working on all three files.

'When you get right down to it,' the woman whispered, 'there's really not much here.'

'I was just thinking the same.'

'This haystack will have to get bigger before we'll find the needle.'

'Yeah.'

'Want to get some supper?'

The man looked at his watch. 'Actually I was thinking that it's time for me to leave.'

'Oh, so you still go out Trick-or-Treating.'

'No, it's my mother. She hasn't been very well. She lives in the East End and the street punks scare her. My sister and I go over every Halloween.'

'Sorry. I shouldn't have been so flippant.'

Rick Scarlett shrugged as if to say, *It's what I expected.* Out loud he said: 'Where shall we go from here? We're going to have to come up with a line of investigation. This got us nowhere.'

'Let's wait for a look at the pictures. Maybe there's something in them.'

'I got a minute,' Scarlett said. 'Let's look at them now.'

'Well, we can't do that, my good man, until they arrive, now can we?'

'Let's go up and take a look at the Superintendent's wall. He said his door was open. He's not going to object.'

Three minutes later the two of them knocked on DeClercq's office door. When no one answered, Scarlett tried the handle. The door was unlocked. They entered the room and Spann switched on the lights.

As a result of the Superintendent's work during the day, the overview had exploded. Two whole walls were now covered with pinned-up pictures and reports and pages of notes. It was only a minute before Katherine Spann locked on one of the photos. She let out a low whistle then began reading the notes and reports and telexes tacked around the picture. Finally she turned to her partner and said: 'Tomorrow we go downtown early and quaff a couple of beers.'

'Great. We kick off by drinking on duty. Tell me lady, where'd you have in mind for this professional suicide?'

'Let's start with the Moonlight Arms.'

'The heart of junk city. You got class. I like your debonair style.'

'That, my good man, is where I once saw this dude. And perhaps we'll find him again.'

Rick Scarlett followed her pointing finger to one of the photographs – the picture of John Lincoln Hardy, suspected pimp of Helen Grabowski.

8.17 p.m.

The black man stormed into the apartment with his face contorted by rage. He slammed the door behind him, the wood crashing against the jamb. She heard him wrench the lock viciously and the tumblers fall into place.

'Johnnie?' she asked vaguely, getting up off the couch.

He grabbed her by the hair. He was a strong man and it took but a single jerk to throw her across the room. Colliding with a table, she knocked a lamp to the floor. The bulb shattered, spewing glass shards everywhere. Then before she could try to gain her feet, the man pounced across the space between them and with one hand seized her face. He yanked her up toward him, and suddenly she was frightened. Very frightened indeed.

'Where is it?' the man hissed, spittle hitting her skin.

'I . . . I don't know what you mean.'

'Don't you get smart with me, bitch!' It was almost a scream. 'You know exactly what I mean!'

'Please Johnnie. Let go,' she pleaded. 'You're hurting . . .'

'Shut it, or I'll cut your throat! Do you hear me?'

Her eyes opened wide in terror, her mouth opened wide to scream. But she couldn't get the sound out because he tightened his grip on her cheeks.

'Now you listen to me!' His eyelids were practically squinted shut. 'That ain't just *any* object. That ain't a piece of junk. It's my religion, woman. Now where the fuck is it?'

'Johnnie, pleeease,' she gasped through the vice-tight grip of his fingers. 'I was so sick. I tried but I, I couldn't take it. You just disappeared. You were gone so long. I thought I was gonna go cra . . .'

'Where is it?' he spat out through his clenched teeth, and then he slapped her suddenly. 'Where?' he repeated, and he hit her again. 'Where?' This time the blow with his closed fist. 'Where?' 'Where?' '*Where?*'

'Oh God, I sold it! Please, not again!'

He let her go abruptly and she crumpled to the floor. For several long moments she lay there, sobbing to catch her breath. Then she heard a dull *click* that brought a knot to her stomach, and she jerked her head up sharply to find that he had switched a blade on her. She could see the light from the ceiling fixture dancing along its steel edge.

'Okay, baby.' His eyes were tense, as though his head were hurting. 'It's time for you and me to have a little talk. I really hate to do this.'

10.19 p.m.

The rain had begun at last.

Since morning dark clouds had hovered all along the western horizon far out at sea, kept at bay by a high pressure ridge along the spine of the mountains. But now the battle had been lost. First a light drizzle, then a shower, then a full downpour had taken over. The nun was soaked to the skin before she was ten feet from the bus stop.

It didn't bother her, this rain – to her it was Heaven's touch.

She came slowly down the slope of the path that wound through the convent gardens, past the reflecting pool now pock-marked by the raindrops, past the alcoves in the Garden of Christ where she often sat in thought. She was deep in thought now. Above her the moon, one day from full, was hidden behind the storm clouds.

The nun had spent the evening with an old woman who was living out her final days in a decaying house in the East End of Vancouver. Her hands gnarled with arthritis and her eyes clouded by cataracts, she could barely take care of herself yet she steadfastly refused to be warehoused in a hospital or a rest home. That tenacity had reminded the nun of when she herself was a child, when this strong woman, her surrogate mother, had helped convince her to take the Holy Vows. It had hurt her tonight to sit in that room in that house in East Vancouver, and listen to the one whom she loved so now shake her fist at God.

So tonight especially the nun was looking forward to Mass.

It was with utter surprise that she felt the arm circle around her throat. Suddenly her breath was cut off and so was any scream. A hand seized her roughly, throwing her to the ground. The motions were swift; the person was strong; the force applied was brutal. The attacker abruptly let her go, then fell down upon her. Now a

170

gloved hand was instantly clamped over her mouth.

The eyes of the nun opened wide when she heard the material ripping. Above her she saw a flash of blood-red colour at the neck of the nylon jacket worn by her violator. The face was hidden behind a black nylon mask, the eyes leered out of two small incisions, and a third hole revealed lips pulled back in a snarl over bared white teeth. Then in utter horror she felt the hardness stab between her legs. The pressure. The entry. And realized, *Oh My Lord, this is rape!'*

In that instant she thought of the Sister who had been attacked in New York City. The other Sisters raped and killed in El Salvador. *How in the name of Mercy*, she thought, *can God let this happen!*

Then there was a glint of light on steel.

And the knife slammed through her throat.

THE JACK-O'-LANTERN

Monday, November 1st, 1.03 a.m.

Robert DeClercq had seen more of death than was healthy for any man – no matter how professionally anaesthetized his human sensibilities.

As with all men and women who deal daily with homicide, the Superintendent had been forced to take it in his stride and discover his own way to objectify this most subjective of human fears – the knowledge you're going to die. DeClercq had found it impossible to eschew all emotion. Nor was he able to develop a sense of gallows humour. In the end his mind reached a compromise with itself: reason was left to do its job hindered only by an accumulating overtone of sadness. Sadness about the loss.

171

For thirty years that technique had worked.

But it didn't work tonight.

It was the total outrage of what DeClercq saw that made the anger well up inside him.

The body of the nun lay on the ground bathed in arc light about thirty feet from the garden path. Around her the men who made murder their business went about their work, the Ident. crew flashing their photographs and sweeping the ground with humming metal detectors, the dog masters leading the German shepherds out from where the nun lay sprawled in the mud. Joseph Avacomovitch was crouched on his heels about a foot and a half from the victim, flanked on his left by Inspector MacDougall and on his right by the Superintendent. It was what had been done to the Sister that enraged Robert DeClercq.

'Same MO,' Avacomovitch said, 'in the pattern of the killing.' He pointed toward the flesh of the neck where the head had been severed. 'You can see the perpendicular stab just below the horizontal cut of decapitation. I'll want the top vertebra, Jack, once the autopsy's over.'

Inspector MacDougall nodded. He too was angry for this was the second body found within North Van jurisdiction – and North Vancouver Detachment was Mac-Dougall's home turf. He looked away to size up the progress of the ongoing search.

'She's been raped,' the Russian said, 'and slashed across the breasts.' He looked up for a second, his forehead frowned with distaste. 'The intercourse was brutal.'

'You mean with her a virgin?'

'Virgin or not, it wouldn't matter. This guy's a savage.'

'Were the clothes ripped or cut?' the Superintendent asked.

'Both. The one from the crotch to the feet is a knife slash. It was torn from the neck to her waist.'

'Was she killed here?' asked Inspector MacDougall.

'Yes. Too much blood for it to be otherwise. The rain's

172

done damage to any footprints or ground marks but it looks like she was walking down the path and dragged into the bushes. There's the sign of a struggle over near the walk.'

'Who found her?' DeClercq asked.

'Another Sister,' MacDougall answered. 'She came out to close and lock the gate. She saw the candle burning.'

'I'd like to know what a shrink would make of all this.'

Just then the almost full moon emerged through a break in the rain clouds. The crime scene turned a metallic silver as the three men stood in silence around the corpse of the nun. Each had his own thoughts about what had happened. Not one of them would pretend to even begin to comprehend the mind of the Headhunter. That they were dealing with a maniac was all that was certain. It appeared to DeClercq that the killer had either been waiting to ambush his victim or else had followed her. He had raped her and stabbed her and cut up her clothes and then had cut off her head. What nagged at his mind once again was the vertical cut to the throat. He knew that in order to catch the contractions of the body in its death throes, such a wound was common to homicidal rapists. But this was something different. This one was a monster. For not only had he cut off the nun's head and also carried off her cowl, but in its place at the top of her neck he had left a jack-o'-lantern. The face of the pumpkin had two triangles for eyes, another triangle for a nose, and a mouth which was fang-filled and shaped into a malevolent grin. A candle had been burning inside. It was the light of the candle the Sister had seen when she came out to close the gate, and though the wax had now melted away the grinning pumpkin still looked blankly down at the butchered body.

One of the corporals involved in the search came over to speak to MacDougall. His hands and uniform were covered with mud, his clothes soaked. He had just climbed out of the reflecting pool.

'Not a bloody thing,' he said. 'We've given the

grounds a once over with dogs and metal detectors. At least as far as I can tell nothing was thrown in the pond.'

'Do it again,' MacDougall said. The Corporal nodded and walked away to carry out the order.

Now DeClercq was worried. *God*, he thought, *– four bodies and not a thing to go on. That's against the odds.* Avacomovitch murmured something.

'Sorry Joseph, I didn't hear that. My mind was on something else.'

'I said I'm going to try and fingerprint the pumpkin.'

'Fingerprint it? Print a rain-washed pumpkin?'

'Yeah, I'll Krazy Glue it.'

MacDougall caught DeClercq's puzzlement and said, 'He's talking about Visuprint. You've been gone awhile, Robert.'

'I guess I have. Fill me in, Joseph.'

'Well the way I see it,' Avacomovitch said, 'all we've got to go on is the jack-o'-lantern. We know the killer brought it with him as a head-substitute. It wasn't carved here. Maybe the hairs and fibres section will turn up something on it – dust or lint from his home, chemical traces, something like that. Maybe we'll get something out of the marks made in the carving. Or maybe I can pick up the killer's prints upon it.

'A few years ago a policeman from Ontario named Paul Bourdon was using Krazy Glue to repair a photographic developing tank. After the repair was completed, Bourdon discovered that his fingerprints had appeared on the inside of the plastic tank. Subsequent experimentation revealed that the chemical in Krazy Glue – its name is cyanoacrylate – reacts with the moist residue left by a person's fingertips on any number of articles – handguns, plastic bags, porous metals – which had previously been impossible to print with existing powder and iodine fume techniques.

'In one case a robbery suspect's fingerprints were recovered from a whisky bottle discovered floating in the bilge of a stolen yacht. In another case prints were lifted from an oil-covered cashbox at the scene of a business break-in.'

'I must be going to rust,' Robert DeClercq said.

'Not your department,' the Russian replied. 'But I'd like something else.'

'What's that?' asked the Superintendent.

'Remember this morning you suggested that I take a look at the bones kicked up by the two young girls? Well I think I'd like to take a look at all four victims. I might find something in my field that a pathologist wouldn't look for.'

'Good idea.'

'That means a court order. They've already released Portman's remains to her mother. But the other three are around.' He looked once more at the nun.

'We'll apply for the order tomorrow,' the Superintendent said.

'Do you think there's anything in the fact that both the Portman woman and the nun were Catholic?' MacDougall asked. 'Maybe some sort of satanic cult. Black mass or black magic.'

'Might be,' DeClercq replied.

'I'll check it,' the Inspector said, 'but in the meantime, why don't you go home and grab some sleep? No use all of us being wasted when the panic hits later this morning. I know where to reach you if anything comes up.'

'I agree,' the scientist added.

For a moment DeClercq hesitated, then he said, 'I guess you're right.' He glanced at his wristwatch and at the sky to the east. Four hours and it would be his normal time for waking. He did feel fatigued. There was little more he could do here, and come the groundswell of terror that was sure to arrive with morning a clear mind would be important. He had set the machine in motion, so let the machine do its work.

'I'll see you later,' he said, and the other two men nodded.

DeClercq turned his back on the victim and followed

the silver path up to the gate. Outside he could see the cordon of royal blue patrol cars, and beyond that a hodge-podge of spectators and reporters. As he reached the gate flash bulbs started popping. And just as thunder follows lightning, the second he went outside he knew the questions would be coming. At the gate he turned.

Back down the path near a silver statue depicting the Crucifixion, a group of three nuns were huddled together as if seeking warmth from each other. Behind them the convent rose up like a silver mausoleum.

It had been a long time since Robert DeClercq had been a practising Catholic. In fact he had not set foot in a cathedral, except for the funeral, since the day that he had walked down that country road with his dead daughter in his arms.

What was it Christ had said? he thought. *'Blessed are those who have not seen and yet believe.' So where does that leave me? Are those men damned who have seen too much and therefore cannot accept him?*

Robert DeClercq went home.

RIOT

Dawn.

It hit like a plague, the fear that came in a wave with the morning papers. Then from mouth to mouth it spread like a virus uncontrolled throughout the city.

In a banner headline from every newsbox *The Province* informed each working citizen HEADHUNTER STRIKES AGAIN in 96-point type. The subhead screamed out NUN AS FOURTH VICTIM.

There are times when information is dispersed at

lightning speed, but only once since the end of the Second World War had it spread so fast in this city. That was the day that President Kennedy took a bullet to the head.

The panic that came along with the fear showed itself in a number of ways.

All of them edged in black.

7.00 a.m.

Artie Fripp drove down to the warehouse to count his profits. All of his staff as usual had the first of November off.

Fripp parked his Corvette behind the building in the space marked 'President' and entered the warehouse through the rear door. Weaving among the shelves of merchandise, he made for his small front office. Business this particular Halloween had been even better than expected: monster masks had sold out, make-up kits had sold out, fireworks had sold out, trick or treat candy sales were up a whopping thirty-one per cent. It looked as if Artie Fripp would once again winter in the Caribbean.

As he passed the section of his warehouse reserved for pornographic supplies – the soft-core paperbacks and sexual toys that sold so well in the winter – Fripp was smiling to himself, thinking of all the jerks who put out money for this junky titillation while he, dressed in Bermuda shorts under the tropical sun, got a real eyeful of almost-naked female flesh. *Titillation*, Fripp thought, *now that's my kind of word. Any word that starts with 'tit' is* . . .

And that was the moment that Artie Fripp, president of Get-A-Whiff Productions, stepped on a twelve-inch dildo left lying on the floor and instantly was airborne. The dildo was one of those electric types sold under the byline of 'hum a different tune'. During the party last night after work the staff had used it for their own version of that time-honoured game known as 'spin-the-

177

bottle'. Someone it seems had forgotten to put it back on the shelf.

So that was how Artie Fripp found himself flying with arms akimbo down the pornography corridor of his Burnaby warehouse, past the penis-shaped cigarette lighters sold as 'Flick My Dic', past the stacks of paperback books like *Hump Happy*, whizzing by cartons of 'Prolong Cream' and 'Lustfinger', and 'Hap-penis', zooming by a special display platform of 'Anal Intruders' complete with batteries and an additional free 'Butt Plugger', finally crashing into a four-tiered plywood shelf stocked with lifesize 'Johnnie The Bucking Stud' and 'Suzie Your Wild Teen Nympho' dolls, wrenching his back in the process.

'Oh, shit!' Fripp screamed as the pain spread out from his spine, for he had just injured the same vertebra that he had dislocated last year in Vegas while trysting with a blonde show-girl by the name of Belinda.

It took Fripp more than five minutes to drag himself to the nearest telephone, and it was just as he was about to pick up the receiver to call hospital emergency that the instrument rang. This particular telephone was reserved for his bookie so it was a single line.

Fripp grabbed it and groaned into the mouthpiece: 'Call me a doctor and get the fuck off this circuit. I might not walk again!'

'Hey, Artie, it's me. The Flashman. At Play-It-Safe Security.'

'Get me a doctor, Flashman. My sex life is in danger. Minutes count.'

'Artie, Artie, baby. No time for that. You read the morning rag. Some nun got iced. My phone's been ringing off the hook for those lipstick alarms. The ones that screech like a banshee.'

'Flashman, you prick. I'm dyin. Now get the hell off . . .'

'I'll take two thousand to start, with an option on two thousand more.'

'Flashman, you jerk . . .' But suddenly, Artie Fripp shut up. He had just remembered that the mark-up on those lipstick alarms was four hundred per cent.

'When?'

'Now!'

'Cash on the line?'

'If I get 'em right away. I just drew up an ad to run in the afternoon rag. Catch the panic before it breaks.'

'Okay,' Fripp said. 'Call me back in five minutes.'

As soon as the phone was free it rang again – then again – then again – for Artie Fripp did a sideline business in Mace, pepper squirters, and whistles.

By 11.00 a.m. all of his staff were back on the job at double pay filling an endless stream of orders. It was only then as he sat in his office smiling at the green numbers in the little window of his Japanese calculator that Fripp remembered the pain in his back and his need to see a doctor. Who knows, maybe this year he should forget the Caribbean. Go a bit further afield, like the French Riviera.

Yeah! Fripp thought as he picked up the phone. *Like the Riviera. The broads go topless there.*

8.05 a.m.

Avacomovitch was finished.

The room stank of Krazy Glue and his head was light from the chemical as he stood up, stretched, rubbed his eyes with the backs of his giant hands, and strode over to the open window to get a breath of fresh air. Outside a bird was singing.

After a few minutes of deep breathing he returned to his work-bench in the room at Headhunter Headquarters and picked up the treated pumpkin. He was pleased with himself, for the prints he had lifted were three in number and each of them was perfect.

Now if only – hope on hope – the person with those fingerprints also had a record.

9.00 a.m.

The Dragon Kung Fu Studio was located on Marine Drive in the heart of North Vancouver. It had been open for business the sum total of three days, Wednesday, Thursday and Friday at the end of the previous week. The sole proprietor and only employee was a young man of twenty-six named Bruce Wong whose greatest disappointment in life was that he had not been born Bruce Lee.

On Friday, October 29th, Wong had put an ad in the Sunday edition of the *North Shore News* to announce his grand opening.

That Monday morning when Wong arrived at his studio he had the sum total of two clients recruited the week before.

By twelve noon when the phone circuits finally overloaded and blew, he had signed up another four hundred – all of them women.

At 12.07 Bruce Wong ran next door to the barber shop to use the phone and try to rent larger space.

9.40 a.m.

'Okay,' Chan said with determination. 'Let's run it by one more time.'

The Inspector was standing at the blackboard in the parade room at Headhunter Headquarters. MacDougall was off to his left. The members of the Central Corps of the Squad were seated on the chairs.

'The first thing to know is that our Computer Command has been assigned the highest priority rating in the country for tapping the Ottawa data base. This will give us an immediate sketch of criminal activity in any part of the province or the criminal history of any particular offender.

'The second thing to know is that our civilian programmers have transferred an indexing system generated specifically for this investigation to one of the IBM machines in Ottawa. I generated this particular program myself on one of our local computers. Here's how it works.

'The program is code-named Cut-throat.

'It will provide us first of all with an index to all paper-file material. Those files contain all of our regular police information: criminal records, outstanding warrants, suspected offenders, and each and every query from each and every officer each and every day in each and every police force in this country. This is called "the blanket" and it's tied to Interpol.

'In addition – and this is important – this blanket also contains all the information collected on all known sex offenders identified during the Clifford Olson case. It has been updated to yesterday. When supplied with specific search criteria – such as the description of a person or car or registered weapon – the program generates a list of the numbers of all documents that refer to the person or vehicle or weapon that matches the description.'

'How detailed will it go?' one of the cops asked.

'The search criteria can be as specific as a person's name, date of birth, age, height, weight, sex, race, hair and eye colour, or the place where the person was last checked by police. It can contain as little information as say, just hair colour.' Chan took a moment to sip from a cup of coffee rapidly cooling on a desk top to his right. 'And finally. I am in the process of preparing an up-to-date skin list. I have culled all known possible sex offenders from our files and as soon as we get a psychological profile of the Headhunter from our psychiatric services I will computer-enhance it into a formal sweep sheet. This list will have the necessary key word to retrieve information on any offender listed in the margin.

'And that's about it, unless there are any questions. Remember, Computer Command is set up to reflect the present state of the art. Use it!'

There were no questions so MacDougall took over. 'All

right,' he said. 'You all know what happened last night and you all know what that means. You heard the Superintendent yesterday morning. So let's roll.'

Then as MacDougall was turning away to have a quiet chat with Inspector Chan, someone in the audience made a *sotto voce* comment: 'Well, I'm disappointed. After all that he didn't even say, "Let's be *real* careful out there".'

No one laughed. Most cops don't watch cop shows on TV.

10.35 a.m.

The RCMP Report Centre in Ottawa has 24,000 sets of fingerprints on file for British Columbia alone.

Sergeant James Rodale had spent the morning putting the finishing touches to DeClercq's flying patrol concept. For that reason he had come up to Computer Command in order to arrange the independent information pool which – excised of all theory, conjecture, and conclusion – would be available to these patrols. That was how he was near the communications centre as the teletype reply from Ottawa came in on Avacomovitch's fingerprint request concerning the lifts that he had obtained off the jack-o'-lantern. Out of habit Rodale glanced at the piece of paper emerging from the machine as he walked by. Then he stopped dead in his tracks.

The fingerprints on the pumpkin, Report Centre said, were a match with those on the record of one Fritz Sapperstein.

Sapperstein had a record for B and E in 1974 and an address in the Municipality of Richmond.

Richmond was Rodale's home turf.

The Sergeant tore the sheet off, leaving a copy for Avacomovitch, then checked his Smith and Wesson .38 and left Computer Command to go and find 'Mad Dog' Rabidowski.

He found him.

The good citizens of Vancouver and its many suburbs spent the overcast morning watching for more rain and waiting impatiently for the first edition of the *Sun*. When the paper finally hit the streets the over-run sold out in a matter of minutes and the good burghers got exactly what they were wanting. The murder of the nun was spread over two pages of print with an additional two pages of photos.

In addition to the facts of the case there were the usual colour stories. One of these was a barometer reading from women interviewed on the street. These were some of the comments:

'Well I don't plan to leave my house without a knife in my purse. The police say that's breaking the law, carrying a concealed weapon. Well I don't care. The Headhunter's not going to get me without one hell of a fight.'

'A nun! My God! Is any woman safe? This guy's a raving maniac. If City Council had any guts at all they'd slap a 10 p.m. curfew on every male in this city.'

'Why are people so shocked? I don't see this as so special. This Headhunter and his attacks are no more than an extreme version of the fears that most women suffer every day of their lives. I'm on a bus, eh, and I have to fend off a drunken businessman who sits too close and tries to put his arm around me. But – and every woman in the world will recognize this – I have to do it nicely so I don't cause a scene. Then once I'm off the bus a strange guy stands in my path and asks in a tough voice: 'All alone? Don't you know there's a killer around? Where do you live? I'll take you home.' And then it takes an eternity to get rid of him – nicely. Now I ask you, do we go around putting our arms around men minding their own business, insisting on accompanying them to their homes and getting nasty if they refuse? Not on your life – sorry, that was a poor choice of words!'

'I say take every sex offender – maybe every male while you're at it – and cut his fucking nuts off. Amen, sister.'

As a child Matthew Paul Pitt had been misdiagnosed as 'retarded but without psychosis'. As a result, of the twenty-eight years that the Australian had been alive, twenty-four had been spent in various mental institutions. In fact Matthew Paul Pitt had an IQ of 128, in the above-average to superior range.

Matthew Paul Pitt had a pathological hatred of his mother. She had committed suicide when the boy was four. Pitt's father placed both his sons in a foster home. He had later returned to retrieve one of the boys, and had left Pitt in another institution. Ever since, Matthew Paul Pitt had pathologically loathed his mother. For if she had not killed herself the family would not have fractured.

The actual psychological problem afflicting the man was dyslexia – a learning disorder in which the affected person sees everything backwards resulting in an inability to read or write or count. The original misdiagnosis of a disorientated and angry child had never been corrected, and therefore, trapped for twenty-four years of his life in mental institutions for the retarded, surrounded daily by persons with whom he could not communicate, Matthew Paul Pitt like an ingrown toenail had slowly turned in on himself. Ultimately, as a result of this misdiagnosis and his subsequent institutional-ization, Pitt had developed a real psychiatric disorder. Pitt was now a classic borderline personality – and it had been almost two years since Matthew Paul Pitt had escaped from a Queensland mental hospital.

By noon that Monday Monica Macdonald and Rusty Lewis knew a great deal about this man. They also had at least a rudimentary knowledge about a borderline state. The knowledge they had looked promising. Promising indeed.

Early yesterday afternoon, following DeClercq's briefing and their coffee together, the two constables had driven the 150 miles south on Highway 99 connecting at the border with Interstate 5 to take them into Seattle, Washington. In Seattle they had found the FBI building and had talked to Monica's friend. The FBI agent remembered her very well (a little *too* well, Lewis thought, judging from the grin on the American's face), and he had told them: 'From the word go you can make yourselves at home. Anything you need, just let me know.'

'Thanks, Daryl,' Macdonald said with a grin every bit as wide as his.

Uh. Huh, Lewis thought.

The two RCMP officers had spent that afternoon and a good portion of Halloween night rummaging through the FBI files on known and suspected US sex offenders. There was a great deal of information. Both Bundy and part of the alleged Hillside Strangler team – not to mention the recent Green River Killer – were alleged to have murdered repeatedly in the State of Washington. Thus a detailed and thorough profile of sex crimes had recently been compiled by the FBI. By midnight, with the aid of a computer technician, the two Canadians had composed an American skin list of sixty-seven possible cross-border sex suspects who might just fit the Headhunter's MO.

The man who sat at the top of this list was the Australian Matthew Paul Pitt.

Pitt was wanted by the FBI for questioning in a number of interstate rape/murders over the previous year and a half. In each of the killings the throat of the victim had been cut, and in two of them the head severed completely from the body. There had been one murder outside Los Angeles, California; one seven miles from Tucson, Arizona; two on the Stockton Plateau in Texas; one at a road junction near Wichita, Kansas; three twelve miles from Cheyenne, Wyoming, and two murders between Spokane and Everett, Washington. The FBI had concluded that all the murders were related.

Each crime scene was located just off the US Interstate Highway system. Each victim had had a Phillips screwdriver rammed through her nipples. One of the victims' vehicles had been pushed over a plateau, and both inside the car and among the push marks on the rear of the trunk a number of usable fingerprints had been found. Though these prints had come up negative for the United States the FBI had routinely passed them on to Interpol where a match had been obtained. The prints, the International Criminal Police Organization told the Federal Bureau of Investigation, were a match for those of a mental institution escapee from Queensland, Australia, named Matthew Paul Pitt who coincidentally had been on the loose for the duration of the US murder spree. In consequence, the FBI wanted very much to have a little talk with Mr Pitt.

'I think this guy is definitely our best bet,' Monica Macdonald said as she placed a Xerox copy of the 752-page FBI summary down on her kitchen table, beside her sleeping cat.

'So do I,' mumbled Lewis through a mouthful of bologna sandwich. As he talked a blob of French's mustard slipped out from between the pieces of whole-wheat bread to drip onto one of the Xeroxed FBI reports. He wiped it off leaving a yellow smear.

'Will you pass me that picture again?' Rusty Lewis asked, wiping his hands on a paper serviette. Macdonald rummaged through the papers spread out over the table in front of her and retrieved the photograph. She handed it to him.

Pitt, as depicted in the wire-graph, looked almost ten years older than he really was. He had jet black hair, obviously uncombed for weeks or maybe months and a scruffy growth of beard. He was dressed in a sloppy shirt, dirty and open at the throat to reveal at least twenty slash marks along either side of his neck. Though it didn't show in the photograph Lewis was certain that the man's shirt tail was hanging out of his pants. The Australian's face was bony and angular, with the gaunt stretched look of a concentration camp victim. His face had Charlie Manson eyes.

'Gives me the creeps,' Lewis said tapping the photo lightly.

'Yeah?' Macdonald replied. 'Well magnify your feelings a hundred times and you'll begin to have some grasp of his effect upon a woman.'

She was now reading from the Australian hospital records that had been forwarded to the FBI. Judging from several psychiatric documents Matthew Paul Pitt was a very confused young man.

In addition to the neck slashings that could be seen in the photo that Rusty Lewis held, Pitt had over one hundred horizontal cuts along the inner aspect of each arm, over fifty cuts on each leg. Four years ago, one of the doctors had noticed that while watching a western on television in the hospital common room Matthew Paul Pitt had obtained an erection. Asked why, he had answered: 'I like seeing blood on TV but I like my own blood better. Is it true that women have the reddest blood of all?'

Macdonald turned to several handwritten sheets found in Pitt's room after his escape and began to read.

My drems are very weerd. I hope I can remember my drem to night cause I want a gril with tits. Maybe why I can't remember my drems is because someone is maken me forget them, so I can't write them down, or its something to do with me. I got to get out of hear. It is almost like I am be in Brain Washed every time I wake-up. I just keep on sayin to myself, I am going to meet a gril with tits in my Drem or Drems tonight. I will tell you about the drem to-morrow when I wake-up. thats if I Remember it. never know I mite meet you.
Good night, Sleep tite, and don't
Let the Bed Bugs bite.
Good night.

Tits! titstitstitstitstitstitstitstits! tits! tits! TITS!

Women are just like screen doors, once they get banged a few times they loosen up.

When Monica Macdonald was finished reading she looked up at Rusty Lewis and said: 'Did you get a look at these writings by Pitt?'

'Uh. Huh.'

'Well, I'd have diagnosed him as retarded too.'

'Yeah, but those notes mean very little. Pitt's got a learning disability. So he's a case of stunted growth. His mind's got a natural intelligence even though he can't express it. No doubt that's what the shrink means about his being a complicated case.'

'I wonder how a guy like this ever got out of Australia and into the United States?'

'Who knows? Remember that guy acquitted here a few years ago on a murder charge by reason of insanity? He escaped too and made his way to the States and then into Australia. I guess it works both ways.'

'Perhaps. And I sure think he's a good candidate to be our Headhunter. Breast fixation. Severed heads. And gone, gone, gone in the mind.'

'Right, but how do we try and find him?'

'On that, I have an idea. There's a note in the FBI summary saying that after the fingerprint ID they put out an all-points pick-up poster. A highway patrolman in Washington State later saw the poster and recalled checking this fellow for hitch-hiking about a week before. He went back to the area and found a bush camp in the woods about thirty feet in from the road. It had been abandoned, he thought. Then he heard the noise of breaking branches some way off and went to investigate. Pitt must have seen him coming and made a run for it. He wasn't caught. When the patrolman re-checked the camp he found a lot of utensils, which later revealed Pitt's fingerprints, a tent and a knapsack.'

'That fits the tattered tent where those little girls found the bones.'

'Right. Anyway, in the knapsack he found several hits of acid, some hash and some speed. And also seventy-seven matchbooks.'

'The man must smoke a lot of hash to need that many matches!' Lewis said with a grin.

'Every one of the matchbooks advertised a different American strip joint.'

'Are you suggesting that we start spending our time hanging out in strip clubs watching women disrobe?'

'Rusty Lewis, shame on you. I got your number. You know, that's the first time since I met you that you've looked wide awake? And yes, that's exactly what I'm suggesting.'

'You're on,' Lewis said.

12.47 p.m.

'We got troubles, Mr Schmidt.'

'Yeah? What kinda troubles?'

'Three women just barged in without stopping to buy tickets.'

'I'll be right out,' Schmidt said, and he slammed down the intercom receiver. As he pushed away from his desk he thought, *We ain't got no troubles like these twats are gonna have*.

Kurt Schmidt was in no mood to have another problem. He was sick and tired of problems. Every week he had problems with Canada Customs just trying to get a few measly skin flicks across the border from LA. Every month he had problems when the Vice Squad came sniffing around just to hassle him: they couldn't get an obscenity conviction on softcore in this city with a jury of Mennonite ministers. Yesterday he had finally managed to smoke a little of the old in/out footage past the Provincial Censor – a raunchy little New York private eye flick called *Hot Dames On Cold Slabs* – and thought maybe for one day he'd get away from problems, problems, problems, and now this. *Well, a few cheapskate cunts are gonna learn not to mess with* this *theatre manager*.

Schmidt came storming through the door from his cubbyhole office. 'Where are they?' he yelled.

189

The lobby of the Silver Screen Theatre was deserted except for Doris, his platinum blonde ticket seller, who was now quite agitated and frantically pointing at the door of the viewing auditorium from beyond which a lot of shouts and obscenities were now issuing. 'They're in there,' she said.

Schmidt quickly traversed the lobby and tore open the door. Then he stopped in disbelief.

With their faces chalked white and wearing fedoras pulled down to shade their eyes, three women were standing in the main aisle of the theatre heaving objects at the screen. The objects were splattering bursts of colour all over the celluloid image of *Hot Dames On Cold Slabs*. The objects were egg shells filled with oil-based paint. 'That screen's worth a thousand bucks!' Schmidt screamed as three more bursts exploded, then he realized that it was not his patrons who were shouting and swearing – it was the intruding women.

Schmidt grabbed the nearest female by the arm and yanked her around, hissing 'You cheap snatch, I'll . . .'

He stopped dead when the straight razor slashed across his belly, slicing his jacket, his shirt, and nicking the flab that covered his intestines.

Then he stood there, frozen in disbelief, as the women backed out through the door.

12.52 p.m.

Rabidowski pulled the unmarked RCMP ghost car over beside a drainage ditch and switched off the engine. Then he and Rodale climbed out. Around them harvested fields stretched for acres, most of the crops recently cut and the rich brown earth ploughed under. On the edges of the fields they could see the jerry-built condominiums encroaching on farmland. The only thing holding them back was the down-turn in the economy.

One hundred feet down the pot-holed road stood the produce outlet. Ying's Market consisted of an old shed open on one side to face the roadway. It was crammed with bin upon bin and shelf upon shelf of freshly-harvested fruit and vegetables. There were several customers in the shed, each with a basket on their arm, each poking and squeezing the produce. A man wearing a leather apron was standing beside a barrel of MacIntosh apples. The two policemen approached him.

'Police,' Rabidowski said, flashing the tin.

The man looked up with a wary smile and said, 'What can I do for you, gentlemen?'

Rabidowski moved off to the man's left and un-buttoned his jacket. Both he and Rodale were in plain clothes. Though the Sergeant had never worked with the Mad Dog before he knew him by reputation: word was that for action Rabidowski was the man.

'We're looking for Fritz Sapperstein,' Rodale said. 'We understand he works here.'

A look of some concern came over the man's face. He glanced at Rabidowski, then nodded and said: 'That's me. Is something the matter? I've been clean for years.'

'Mr Sapperstein,' Rodale said, 'I won't beat around the bush. A woman was killed last night and her head was cut off. In its place someone left behind a pumpkin. That pumpkin's got your fingerprints all over it. We want to know why?'

Sapperstein blinked. Then he looked from Rodale to Rabidowski and down at the visible gun. Finally he let out a deep breath to dissipate his tension and said: 'Can I show you something? It's just out that back door.'

Rodale nodded. 'But take it easy,' he said.

When the three men reached the doorway Rabidowski stopped Sapperstein by lightly gripping his arm. Rodale walked past them and took a look outside. All he could see was a field that stretched for five hundred feet partially filled with pumpkins.

'We plant 'em near the shed cause those mothers are so heavy. Within the last ten days we harvested nine-tenths of the crop. I picked a lot myself. I must have sold a thousand. You are aware that yesterday was Halloween?'

Rodale looked at Rabidowski who let go of Sapperstein's arm.

The man with the apron tried a weak grin. 'You give me someone's description,' he said, 'and chances are better than ten to one that a person matching what you say purchased one of our pumpkins. I didn't kill anyone.'

Rabidowski took his hand off the butt of his gun.

2.11 p.m.

There are no mounted Mounties in the City of Vancouver. The only mounted officers are with the VPD.

That afternoon when the call came through from Downtown, Sergeant Scott Barthelme was sitting in his office in Stanley Park. Just down the hall were the stables and today the office smells of ink and fresh paper were overpowered by the earthy aroma of straw and manure. Except for the occasional munching of feed and shifting of hooves the stables were quiet. Bandit, the black and white stable cat, had tired of leaping around the bales of straw pretending to look for mice. He was now stretched out on the office window sill.

Sergeant Barthelme listened to what Downtown had to say, then he hung up the phone and groaned.

Sergeant Barthelme did not in the least like what he had been told. For the Sergeant had been around long enough to remember only too well the public drubbing that the VPD had taken over their actions against certain pot-smoking hippies who had crowded Maple Tree Square in 1971.

Sergeant Barthelme remembered only too well the day of the Gastown Riot.

3.46 p.m.

The demonstration had started out disorganized but

peaceful. It was disorganized largely because the crowd that slowly congealed in Robson Square was assembling spontaneously. It was true that in the earlier hours of the morning a loose coalition of feminist groups had met and by early afternoon were well on their way to setting up audio equipment on the back steps of the old courthouse, but the audience that finally collected was really nothing more than passersby through the square, most of them working women returning from lunch who began to realize that this issue was a little more important to them than punctuality at the office. By 3.09 there were more than 7,000 people in the square.

Several women carried printed posters that read *Women Unite Against Violence Against Women, Every Man Is A Potential Rapist*, or, no beating around the bush, *You Can't Rape A .38*.

At 3.11 p.m. two women in their forties, both wearing tight blue jeans with knee-high leather boots, one sporting blue-dyed hair, hung a mural painted on cloth between two columns of Francis Rattenbury's old courthouse. The mural depicted a man with a physique like Arnold Schwartzenegger's, all rippling muscles, rock-hard torso, but without a head. Down in the lower left-hand corner of the mural was a reproduction of the Queen of Hearts from Disney's animated version of *Alice In Wonderland*. From the mouth of the Queen, in scarlet letters two feet high and enclosed in a dialogue bubble, were the words: OFF WITH HIS HEAD!

By 3.15 p.m. the women collected in the square had started to chant the phrase.

Now if only this were a perfect world that's how matters would have remained. A ragged but peaceful citizen's group exercising its legal right of assembly.

But this is not a perfect world.

And perhaps that's why fate intervened and allowed two things to happen. Both coincidence.

The first coincidence lay in the fact that at this very same moment, some ten miles away in a suburban sports stadium, a group of 10,000 unemployed men, 99% of them drunk, had gathered to watch the Annual Blue Collar Soccer Convention. By now the playoffs were over and this was the final game. At this precise moment it was half-time, and for some reason some wag who had read the morning papers began to yell his own chant that went something like this: *'Headhunter four. Women zero! Headhunter four. Women zero!'*

Within minutes the bleachers were filled with men who were filled with booze who then filled their lungs with air and picked up the chant:

'Headhunter four! Women zero! Headhunter four! Women zero!'

The media on this day just happened to be broadcasting live from the game to those fans who got drunk too early and never got out the door. In the background of the broadcast a listener could hear the chant. And such a listener was a woman named Joan Thistlethwaite who at that moment was caught in the massive traffic jam to the right of Robson Square and who happened to tell one of the feminist organizers of the rally who passed by her driver's window about the content of the broadcast and what its message was.

Within one minute the woman had returned to the steps of the old courthouse, had seized the microphone from an octogenarian who had been part of the original Suffragette Movement, and had told the crowd. The crowd was not pleased. And to show its displeasure the group began to shout out a chant of retort. *'Kill the Pigs! Kill the Pigs! Kill the Pigs!'*

It is likely, however, that even at 3.46 that afternoon disaster might have been averted. For the group in Robson Square, despite all the animosity now finding verbal vent, was still under control. And it very well might have stayed that way if only by a second coincidence Fernand Zirpoli had not decided to work the crowd.

Zirpoli was a small greasy man with crooked teeth and

a fringe of straggly Einstein hair surrounding his balding pate. As a young man Zirpoli had misspent his youth in Rome by watching the gigolos cruise around those tourist spots most adored by North American women who had come to the Eternal City with stars in their eyes, softly sighing as the Latin lovers pinched their bottoms and any other soft parts of their bodies. Often Zirpoli looked back on those days with fond memory, wishing to God that he had never emigrated to Canada. Women here just did not seem to crave the same hot-blooded male attention. Zirpoli already had seven Criminal Code convictions for indecent assault on a female.

Unfortunately for him, he'd never make number eight.

His usual technique, the one with both the best results *and* the best defence if needed, was to find a tightly packed group of women and then to slowly move among them toward some imaginary destination, rubbing this breast or that buttock. Most of all, Zirpoli liked redheads. Particularly redheads in sweaters, just like that redhead standing over there.

Zirpoli was smitten.

He stepped back a pace or two – a very difficult manoeuvre given the number of people now cramming Robson Square – and approached her from behind. With force he bumped into her back, a squeaky-voiced 'oops, sorry,' escaping from his lips as both his hands circled her front to close on the mounds of her breasts. The woman lost her balance and pitched forward, her buttocks rubbing the man's groin as she went down on one knee.

'*Kill the pigs! Kill the pigs!*' The crowd took up the chant again.

Zirpoli didn't notice. He was in ecstasy, his penis hard in his pants, his hands refusing to let go of the redhead in his grasp – refusing, that is, until the woman next to the two of them, who had had too much to drink at lunch and was caught up in the mood of the moment, bent down and removed her high-heeled shoe, also a difficult manoeuvre given the pack of the crowd, and screaming out 'Kill the pigs!' herself, drove the spiked heel full force into Zirpoli's left eye.

His scream literally seemed to shatter the brittle autumn air.

As blood in a spurt mixed with ocular fluid fountained out from his mangled face, the Italian was mobbed and clawed and kicked even after he was dead.

An impact seemed to radiate out from the point of violence to the very edge of the crowd. Push turned to shove as people craned to see what was going on.

Then all hell appeared to break loose as order disintegrated.

And that was the moment that Sergeant Scott Barthelme ordered his Vancouver Police Mounted Squad in full riot gear to charge the crowd.

The squad hit the square at a gallop.

Within seconds the centre and heart of the city was filled with cries of agony, the clatter of horse-hooves on stone, shouts and obscene hollers, and the sound of wood on bone.

One woman, screaming 'No more violence!', pulled a policeman from his horse and kicked him in the groin. Four seconds later a riot club took out all her front teeth.

It was not until 4.30 p.m. that the Battle of Robson Square ended. And even then the police were kept busy galloping up and down the stairs of the open concourse, flushing out the remnants of those women not in hospital, in jail, or dispersed and fleeing throughout the city.

5.20 p.m.

They say that a man with virility problems will often reach for a gun.

If this is true then recent statistics tell us quite a lot. For in 1980 the comparative figures for handgun deaths within a number of countries were as follows: Japan, 48;

Great Britain, 8; Canada, 52; Israel, 58; Sweden, 21; West Germany, 42; United States, 10,728.

Even taking account of population differences the conclusion is quite obvious: either the American male is in desperate need of psycho-sexual therapy. Or something is very, very wrong with US laws on gun control.

The two women who left Vancouver for Seattle late that morning were counting on the latter conclusion as being the correct answer. At 5.20 that same afternoon they stopped at the Douglas Border Crossing to re-enter Canada. As a matter of routine Canada Customs searches every fiftieth car. Theirs was number fifty. So that was how, both in the trunk and under the back seat, a rather surprised Customs Officer found fifty-two loaded Smith and Wesson .38s purchased that day in Seattle.

As the slogan goes: *You can't rape a .38.*

Hoodoo

5.46 p.m.

It was Corporal William Tipple of Commercial Crime who first made the connection: in fact were it not for Tipple the left hand might never have known what the right hand was doing.

The Corporal was not the sort of man that the Royal Canadian Mounted Police would portray on a recruiting poster. He was five foot ten with a slight build, a pock-marked complexion, and an ever present dusting of dandruff on the padded shoulders of his checkered sports jacket. Though the collar of the shirt he wore was a little frayed and dirty, and though there was also grime

197

under his fingernails, the man made up for his short-comings by his boundless energy and an effervescent disposition. Tipple had spent the past five years as an electronic surveillance specialist in Commercial Crime Section, but he missed being in harness. Tipple was the sort of member who enjoyed wearing a uniform, *passé* though that may be.

Late that Monday afternoon the Corporal had come to Headhunter Headquarters to get a feel of the action. He had no other reason to be there. It was just that Tipple was proud to be a Member of the Royal Mounted and liked to feel that he was a part of all that was going on. So late that Monday afternoon Tipple walked into the library.

The library was jammed.

There were men and women everywhere, members in and out of uniform sitting at tables, leaning on walls, some even squatting on the floor reading. Tipple was elated. He was thriving on the activity. Wishing to feel a part of it, he moved about from table to table.

At the photograph table the Corporal paused and gave it a little attention. There were prints coming and going and moving about the surface, photos being passed from hand to hand with the occasional comment, pictures of bodies and pictures of heads and pictures of murder locations, snapshots of women, a shot of a nurse decked out in her graduation garb, mug-shots in full-face and profile of hundreds of men, most with dark hints of fetishism and obsession in their eyes.

The man beside him was holding a photo in each of his large hands. In his left was a picture of a woman's head stuck on the end of a pole; and in his right the same face staring out from a mug-shot.

'It's like a jigsaw puzzle, eh?' William Tipple said.

The man turned to look at him without a smile on his face.

'I'm Bill Tipple,' the Corporal said, introducing himself. 'Commercial Crime Section.'

'Al Flood,' the man replied, 'VPD Major Crimes.'

Ah, Tipple thought to himself, *so they're working this one too*. He was a wee bit hurt. For here was a Vancouver City bull as an outsider on the inside, while he – Bill Tipple of the RCMP – was an insider out in the cold. That wasn't right.

'Looks like a bargain basement sale at the Hudson's Bay Company, eh?' the Corporal said jovially, nodding at all the others.

Flood merely shook his head and turned back to his picture.

Yeah, well same to you, buddy, Bill Tipple thought. Then he too began to rummage about the table. It seemed to him that pictures of heads and bodies were now at a premium. Someone threw down a photo of a black man and reached for something else. Tipple picked it up. Someone grabbed for an Ident. enlargement of marks on a neck vertebra and revealed underneath a second photo of the woman in Flood's right hand. It was also a mugshot, but a different type of one. Tipple picked that up also.

'Here,' he said turning to Flood and handing him the picture. 'Another piece for your puzzle.'

'Thanks,' the Vancouver Detective said, reaching out with nicotine-stained fingers. There was a puffiness under his eyes.

Looks like a cynic, Tipple thought.

Flood added: 'This one's from our own VPD mugbooks downtown.' He wagged the photograph which he held in his right hand. 'The woman's name is Grabowski, she's up for heroin possession. The shot that you just gave me is from the files of the New Orleans PD. I believe the black dude in that surveillance photo in your hand is also linked to her. And to New Orleans.'

At the words 'New Orleans' Tipple almost jumped as if he'd been jabbed in the ribs. 'Can I see that again?' he asked, indicating Grabowski's NOPD picture. Flood gave it to him.

For a minute or two the RCMP Corporal examined the two American photographs, front and back. The names of the persons depicted were printed on the reverse side of the shots. Then Tipple put both pictures in his left hand and dug his notebook out of his jacket pocket with his right. Flipping over several pages, he stopped and nodded. 'Well I'll be damned,' he said. 'Will you take a look at this.'

Flood looked at the notebook and at a name written on the page. Tipple held out the photograph of the black man and indicated the name printed on the back. Both names were the same.

John Lincoln Hardy.

9.45 p.m.

It was while Robert DeClercq was pinning the wiretap transcripts from Commercial Crime up on the corkboard beside the photo of John Lincoln Hardy that he noticed his hands were shaking. *Lack of sleep*, he thought. It had been an exhausting day.

After leaving the scene of the nun's murder he had gone directly home and tried to get some sleep. But sleep wouldn't come. For no matter how hard he had tried to clear his mind of all its nagging thoughts, he could not shake off the sense of tension and urgency that the latest murder had caused. The killings were coming so quickly that the city was bound to explode. And now explode it had.

After obtaining the body release order early in the afternoon, the Superintendent had spent half an hour arranging to have the CPR train with Joanna Portman's body intercepted along the line and her remains rerouted. Then he had left the courthouse and driven out to UBC. Next to the University Hospital, in the Department of Psychiatry building, he had found the office of Dr George Ruryk where a secretary was waiting.

DeClercq had reached the point in the investigation

where he thought it advisable to obtain a psychological profile based on the information that they now had on the Headhunter. He knew as well as anyone that this was a very long bow to draw, that there are as many psychological profiles as there are people on this earth. Being married to a psychologist, however, he had also learned that a disease of the mind might strike any one of those individuals at any time, and that if it did, depending upon the mental illness, that person would show certain recognizable symptoms. There was always the chance that observed symptoms might lead them to the killer.

It was a weak straw to clutch at, sure.

But a straw nonetheless.

'I hope your back is strong,' Ruryk's secretary had said. She had pointed to a box filled with books off to the right of the office door. 'George marked the relevant parts with bookmarks but said you might want the rest of the volume in order to get your bearings. Otherwise we would have Xeroxed. I understand you're to leave him a synopsis of the investigation.'

DeClercq walked over and placed it on her desk.

'He'll pick it up after his evening lecture,' the secretary said.

'Would you tell him that I'll expect him tomorrow any time after nine?'

'Right. Does he know how to get there?'

'Genevieve's my wife. I believe he's been over before.'

'Oh, right,' the woman repeated, and then DeClercq had left.

Once back at Headhunter Headquarters, the Superintendent had asked Inspector MacDougall if he could round him up a sandwich and following that had sat down and unpacked the box of books.

By the time that MacDougall had entered the office later that night with the wiretap transcripts just sent over by Tipple of Commercial Crime, Robert DeClercq was struggling just to keep his eyes focused. He welcomed the break.

'We might have some good news,' the Inspector said. He handed the wiretaps to the Superintendent. 'We just got a printout from Headquarters in Ottawa. Interpol might have traced the identity of the bones. A German national named Liese Greiner left Switzerland eight months ago for a camping trip in North America. She never returned, and hasn't been heard from since early August. She was by herself. Six years ago she was badly injured in a car accident and suffered a number of bone fractures. Interpol sent the X-rays. Joseph is going over to the morgue to compare them with the North Van skeleton.'

'Good,' DeClercq said. 'Anything else come up?'

'The autopsy on the nun proved negative for sperm. Perhaps our man was interrupted by the Sister going up the path to close the gate.'

'Probably not. She'd have seen him lighting the pumpkin.'

'A Corporal named Tipple at Commercial Crime thinks he's got Grabowski's pimp on some of his wiretaps. The target is a guy named Steve Rackstraw who calls himself the Fox. Land fraud. Corporate rip-offs. That sort of thing. Evidently an unknown male known as the "Weasel" started turning up on the tapes. Tipple later pegged him as John Lincoln Hardy. He's a cousin of Rackstraw. There's also another guy known as the "Wolf" floating around on the taps. He's Rackstraw's brother. Tipple culled out some of the calls and sent them over. You've got them in your hand.'

'How's Chan coming along with the computer enhancement?'

'One or two more days and he'll have the sweep sheet ready. He wants the psych profile in order to feed it in.'

'He'll have it tomorrow. I'm reading up on it now.'

'Right,' MacDougall said. 'I'll leave you to what you're doing.' He left the room.

Ten minutes later the Superintendent had just completed pinning the wiretap transcripts from Commercial

Crime up on the corkboard wall when MacDougall once more knocked at the open door. DeClercq turned around and saw the envelope that the Inspector held in his hand. His heart lurched. In his other hand MacDougall was carrying a portable tape-recorder.

'Another one?' DeClercq asked, a flatness to his voice.

'The nun,' MacDougall answered. He held out the manila folder.

Inside the Superintendent found a Memorex tape and a Polaroid photograph. The picture was of another head slammed on the end of a pole, same white background, nothing more, the head of the nun still wearing a black, white-banded cowl. A wave of nausea spread through DeClercq's stomach at the sight of the rolled-back eyes. A thin trickle of blood seeped from the corner of one of them.

'It was left in Christ Church Cathedral under one of the pews. No one saw it placed there,' Jack MacDougall said. 'I've had it dusted. No prints, except the Father here.'

Beyond the door DeClercq could see a Roman Catholic priest, his face etched with a troubled look of deep concern. 'Play it, Jack,' he said.

The Inspector set the recorder up on the Superintendent's desk. Both men listened.

They heard a guitar, party chatter, whistling in the background, and then words:

The police walked in for Jimmy Jazz
I said, he ain't here but he sure went past
Oh you're looking for Jimmy Jazz

'Good God,' MacDougall whispered.

. . . cut off his ears and chop off his head
Police come looking for Jimmy Jazz . . .

'Who the hell is that,' DeClercq asked in astonishment. The Inspector shrugged. 'Damned if I know,' he said. 'Well let's find out fast.'

So go look all around, you can try your luck brother
And see what you found
But I guarantee you that it ain't your day
Chop! Chop!

Tuesday, November 2nd, 1.12 a.m.

'Rock music!' Scarlett exclaimed.

'Headquarters!' Spann replied.

The two of them looked at each other in total disbelief. It was now after 1.00 a.m. on a weekday morning, the empty hours of the day, a time when a cop might expect to find the squad room proceeding at half-speed, perhaps the occasional sound of a typewriter pounding or small talk among the members on night patrol, but certainly not the time or place for rock and roll to assail his or her astonished ears. This was just *too* much.

They had spent the afternoon and the entire evening on a pub-crawl of Vancouver's skid road beer parlours hoping to find John Lincoln Hardy or the Indian who might have contact with him. They were both dressed in grubby clothes, jeans and soiled T-shirts, Scarlett with the stubble of one day's beard shadowing his face. Over the past thirteen hours they had watched more scores of junk and grass and speed and acid and coke and angel dust go down than went through the courts in a year. They had seen the gypsy switch pulled more times than they could count. And they had overheard more blow jobs and around the worlds and just plain straight lays negotiated than went on at an accountants' convention – and that was saying a lot. They had felt the insidious sleaze of each successive hangout soil their expectations, but by the end of the day they had not seen hide nor hair of either hunted man.

Now they had called it a night.

They had driven back to Headhunter Headquarters, had parked the unmarked squadcar outside the building, and had hauled their tired behinds up the front walk, through the doors, and come upon a rock and roll party in progress. Punk rock blared from the speakers:

Don't you bother me, not any more
I can't take this tale, oh no more
It's all around, Jimmy Jazz

J – A – Zee Zee J – A – Zed Zed Zee Zee . . .

The youth who sat directly in front of the speakers was maybe eighteen years old and a throw-back to the fifties. He was dressed in black jeans, black winklepicker shoes, and a black leather jacket with several silver chains adorning it. His hair was greased and swept up in a duck-tail. Scarlett looked for the rat-tail comb sticking out of his back pocket. Sure enough, it was there.

Around him, the other listeners were not quite so cool. Several of them were wearing the RCMP uniform, DeClercq and MacDougall excluded, and all had a short military cut to their hair. They all looked straight, while the bopper looked stoned. The bopper had the floor.

'The name of the cut is *Jimmy Jazz*. The name of the group is The Clash. Third cut. Side one. Off the double, *London Calling*. Great disc,' he said.

'When was it put out?' Robert DeClercq asked.

'1979. Epic Records.'

MacDougall asked: 'What's Jimmy Jazz?'

'I've no idea,' the youth said, shaking his head. 'Dope, I guess. Isn't that what you guys are usually looking for?'

'Not this time,' the Inspector replied. 'Where can we get the album?'

'Any record store. The Clash are very big time. If you want I'll lend you the copy we got at the radio station.'

'Please,' DeClercq said. 'And I'd like it tonight.'

Scarlett and Spann skirted one side of the group of music lovers and made their way to the second floor. The reason that they had come into the building was to take another look at the corkboard visual. As they reached the top of the stairs Rick Scarlett said: 'Punk rock, huh! Puke rock's more like it!'

'Well I happen to like The Clash,' Katherine Spann said.

'You would,' the man replied.

The woman cocked her head to one side and slightly raised one eyebrow. 'Chances are you don't even know where the band is from, you're so narrow-minded.'

'Don't put money on it, Kathy. I'm not Rabidowski. The Clash came out of England along with the Sex Pistols. Part of the first wave of new wave music.'

'My my!' the woman said. 'And I thought you were stupid.'

The first thing they saw on entering DeClercq's office were the books scattered everywhere. They each picked up a volume and looked at the title. One was *Murder For Sex* and the other *Psychopathia Sexualis*.

'You know why he's reading this stuff?' Rick Scarlett asked.

''Cause he's Jung at heart,' Spann replied.

All three walls of cork were now covered with information and in some areas the reports now overlapped. Spann immediately saw the pinned-up wiretap transcripts and crossed to them. She flipped through the pages while Scarlett read over her shoulder. When she was finished she walked to the bank of windows and stared out at the street, thinking.

Scarlett walked up behind her.

'I wonder what they're talking about in those wiretaps,' she asked. 'What's a *hoodoo*?'

'So now who's stupid?' the male Constable said. 'Seems your education is lacking when it comes to geography. "Hoodoos" are eroded pinnacles of rock that stick up out of the ground. The Indians used to believe that spirits lived in such sandstone towers. There are some of them in the Deadman Valley of BC – but most jut up out of the Alberta foothills of the Rockies.'

'Well now I know,' Spann said.

But that told them nothing.

THE SPLINTER

5.15 a.m.

Robert DeClercq was up before dawn. He climbed out of bed and padded into the kitchen to put on a pot of coffee, then while it was dripping went into the spare bedroom to dress warmly for the weather. Returning to the kitchen to pour himself a cup, he carried the steaming mug into the greenhouse and out through its back door down to the edge of the sea. It was dark outside and the air was brittle with the sharp chill of late autumn. He sat down in the driftwood chair, the sundial on his left, and began to think. The sea was wild this morning, spitting forth its spray. The Superintendent ignored it.

What bothered him more than anything else was the attitude of this killer. There had been psychotics and psychopaths before who had taunted the police – Jack the Ripper and Zodiac were two notorious examples – but never quite on this level. For this was almost *personal*. No sooner had the squad been formed and had it been reported by the press that he was in command, than the Headhunter had sought him out and paired off for a fight. *Why?* DeClercq wondered. *There's some special reason. What is it?*

At the moment he had no idea.

It bothered him in the same way that the pose of the last two bodies nagged at his mind, and the feeling of pose he got from the Polaroids of the heads. There was something going on here that didn't meet the eye. The Headhunter wanted something more than the thrill that came from the killings. DeClercq was sure of that.

So what's the missing motive?
I don't know.

For a long time he sat there contemplating this problem and a host of other ones. Eventually the sun came up and burst upon the onyx waters, highlighting the crest of each raging Pacific wave. A cormorant swooped out of the sky and knifed cleanly into the sea, diving for something unseen beneath the chilling surface. When it came up, its bill was empty.

The Superintendent stood up.

During the motion it occurred to him that from this very driftwood chair he could see the sites of all four murder scenes, or at least where the bodies were found. The thought didn't please him: it was like another taunt. Off to his right the Point Atkinson Lighthouse winked.

Slowly DeClercq climbed the path back up to the house. Once inside he stripped off his clothes now wet with spray, dressed again and took a second coffee back out to the greenhouse. There he picked up Lazarfeld's *Woman's Experience of the Male* and turned to the marked section.

For the next two hours DeClercq read, diving for something unseen beneath the chilling surface.

Outside, pale sunshine beat down upon the words etched in a circle around the sundial's edge. The words said: *The time is later than you think.*

5.20 a.m.

Avacomovitch felt like a ghoul.

His frame of mind no doubt came from the fact that he was standing alone in the centre of one of the autopsy rooms at Lions Gate Hospital surrounded by a couple of bodies, each at a different stage of putrefaction and decay. But that wasn't all of it: he had done this before.

More than anything else, however, Avacomovitch's frame of mind came from the time of day.

For never before, with the black of night outside the windows closing in on him, with the stillness of a

208

deserted laboratory surrounding him, had the scientist worked alone in a room among the rotting dead. The stench was nauseating so he wore a chlorophyll mask on his face. In one hand he held a magnifying glass and in the other hand a scalpel. And it didn't help matters that in the four hours that he had been here, two new residents had been wheeled down from the hospital, toe-tagged, and tucked into drawers. This place gave him the creeps.

From somewhere something unknown sighed, and the air conditioning groaned.

A water tap was dripping.

Far off in another wing was the soft sound of laughter.

The scalpel scraped on bone.

Turning to the bones from the hillside, he pushed the corpse of the nun aside.

It was necessary for Avacomovitch to work at this time of the morning in order to gain access to the lab; come dawn the pathology section of the hospital would be reclaimed by the living.

Earlier he had been to Richmond General Hospital to examine the remains of Helen Grabowski. He had found nothing there.

The body of Joanna Portman was still in the process of being returned. The scientist half expected it to be carried into the morgue by Messieurs Burke and Hare.

Compared to Dr Kahil Singh, Avacomovitch had taken the North Van remains in reverse order: least to most ugly. He had X-rayed the corpse of the nun to find any metal fragments, and then had used ultrasound equipment to scan the soft body tissue for non-metallic particles. As far as he could tell from analyzing the screen pattern, the sound waves that were penetrating the flesh were bouncing back from nothing but bone.

That left the hillside skeleton.

For half an hour Joseph Avacomovitch traced the pattern of injury recorded on the skeleton and compared what he found to the X-rays of Liese Greiner sent by

Interpol. The match proved almost identical. There were several cracks in the femurs of both legs and a break in the fibula and tibia of the left one; the part of the ilium on the left side had been fractured as had the left humerus. There was a crack in the left ulna although the radius hadn't broken.

It was while Avacomovitch was running his magnifying glass over the bones comparing and charting these fractures that he happened to also notice a hairline crack in the pubis. The pubis is the bone which forms the lower front of the pelvis. And it was in this particular fracture that the scientist found the splinter.

The splinter was miniscule and dull black in colour.

The fracture in which it was lodged was not on the X-rays sent by Interpol.

That of course meant little: it could have been caused when the bones were kicked up by the little girl.

Is it from the sole of a shoe? Avacomovitch wondered. *Perhaps a piece of bark? Or picked up in the moving to the hospital morgue?*

Whatever it was it was all that the scientist found that morning.

When the first pathologist came on duty with the light of dawn, the Russian asked him for a small glass plate and a pair of tweezers in order to prepare a slide.

PSYCHO

9.30 a.m.

'Did you enjoy the reading?' Dr Ruryk asked.

'It was informative,' DeClercq replied. 'But pretty heavy going.'

The psychiatrist nodded. 'How shall we handle this?'

'If you have no objection, I'd like to make a tape. It will be on file in the squad room for those who want to listen and benefit from your views. Nothing formal, just a general discussion with free association.'

'Sounds okay to me,' Dr Ruryk said. 'Let's roll.'

Dr George Ruryk was a man of advancing years and growing reputation. DeClercq's wife Genevieve spoke highly of his ability and was rather amazed that the police had made so little use of his knowledge in the past. She had persuaded her husband not to make the same mistake. That more than any other reason – for DeClercq valued his wife's opinion – was why the Superintendent now found himself sitting in the wicker chair opposite the psychiatrist as filtered sunlight streamed into the greenhouse and brought the colour of the roses vibrantly alive. Ruryk wore round wire-rim glasses and a Vandyke goatee that made him look like Freud. As DeClercq picked up the microphone he thought *Why is it that psychiatrists all have beards? What have they got to hide?*

He punched on the tape recorder.

'This tape,' DeClercq said, placing the microphone down on the corner of the desk between them, 'concerns the Headhunter case. With me is Dr George Ruryk of the Department of Psychiatry at the University of British Columbia. The purpose of our meeting is to discuss a possible psychological profile of the killer whom we seek. I wish to re-caution you strongly, however, on the danger of tunnel vision. What comes out of this discussion may parallel reality or be entirely off base. Dr Ruryk?'

'First let me say that I must agree completely with your warning. A number of years ago the man dubbed the "Boston Strangler" reduced that city to a state of terror. At one point during the hunt for him a panel of experts composed of psychiatrists, psychologists, social workers, criminologists and policemen was convened. This panel decided that the murderer they were seeking,

211

without a doubt, would be a schizoid, unmarried, latent homosexual with a disturbed psychosexual life and suppressed mother fantasies. When he was eventually apprehended Albert DeSalvo turned out to be a happily married man with two children. So I reiterate your caution.

'Having said that, however,' the psychiatrist continued, 'I do believe that we can postulate several possible theories about the Headhunter's thinking. I also believe that one at least will eventually prove true. Let us begin though with a general orientation.'

As he spoke the doctor reached into the pocket of his tweed jacket, complete with leather patches at the elbows, and removed a smoking apparatus befitting Sherlock Holmes and a package of tobacco. For at least a minute, between sentences, the professor performed his igniting ritual, and when at last great billows of sweet blue smoke twisted about the room, the Superintendent inwardly sighed and thought *I wish you'd think of the plants*.

'Psychiatry basically recognizes three major types of mental abnormality,' Ruryk stated. 'Psychosis. Neurosis. And Character Disorder.

'Of these, the psychotic – the one who suffers from a psychosis – is the most disturbed. He or she would correspond to the layman's term "crazy". The distinguishing feature or symptom of psychosis is that there has been a loss of touch with reality: in other words, because of the pressure of the illness, the psychotic has replaced some important aspect of the real everyday world with a creation of his or her own deranged mind. Here are a few examples. At issue in the recent Yorkshire Ripper trial was whether or not Peter Sutcliffe, while standing in a grave that he was digging as a cemetery labourer, actually heard a voice which he interpreted as God informing him that it was his mission to rid the world of prostitutes. David Berkowitz – New York's "Son of Sam" – evidently conversed with his neighbour's talking

212

dog before killing six people with a .44 calibre pistol.

'The neuroses – that is the second main branch of mental illness – are somewhat different, and for the case in question probably irrelevant.

'Of more importance from our point of view, however, is the third major class of mental aberration – namely character disorder. For it is here that we find the psychopath or sociopath with his or her case history of unbelievable horror.

'In character disorder, rather than a break with reality, there is more what I would call a *compromise* with reality. Over the course of his or her life a person affected by this disease, instead of developing some symptom such as an hallucination or obsession, develops a change in character structure that systematically alters his or her way of interacting with reality.

'Often this is the failure to develop a normal moral sense, an inability to distinguish between right and wrong. The person affected is still in touch with reality, it's just that he or she does whatever he or she wishes for whatever reason with no concern whatsoever for anyone else's feelings. Sadists often fit this mould – and that's why begging, beseeching and imploring have no effect upon them.'

'Will you expand on psychopathy?' Robert DeClercq asked.

'Certainly,' Ruryk said. 'For this is the area in which we find the vast majority of mass murderers.

'Psychopaths may be divided into two important subcategories.

'The first of these is the *under-controlled aggressive psychopath*. This is the type of individual who does not have the constraints on behaviour necessary in society. Such a person will frequently be involved in acts of aggression and will be well-known to the police because of a number of previous charges or convictions for violence. I put Clifford Olson in this category.

'Far more dangerous and elusive, however, is the

second sub-category – the *over-controlled aggressive psycho-path*. For this type of man has many constraints issuing that govern his behaviour. He is often a rather meticulous, rigid, obsessional individual. At times of stress, however, this man is unable to control the aggressive urges that lie buried deep within his personality, and at such times violent behaviour can occur. It is as though a safety valve has blown or a volcano erupted. Then once the pressure has been released this type of psychopath immediately returns to his normal self.

'You can see why this type of killer is extremely diffi-cult to locate, for the factors which cause such outbursts will vary with each individual: what will upset one man will not perturb another. I put Bundy in this category.

'The most important point, however, is this: both the deeply repressed psychotic and the over-controlled aggressive psychopath may appear perfectly normal on the surface as they go about their daily lives.

'Hunting either one is like searching for the proverbial needle in a haystack.'

There was a lull for a moment in the conversation and then Robert DeClercq said: 'Doctor, in the readings that you have provided me there is mention of "the Imposter". I wonder if you would expand on that term within the present context?'

"The imposter" as we call him is a relatively rare but dramatic form of psychopathic personality. He is relatively common in cases of psychosis. The Imposter is one who is bound neither by society's sanctions, nor by a sense of his own identity. The Imposter assumes the role and status of any part that he might wish to play. In many respects his entire life is the wearing of a mask.

'The danger of The Imposter is that people around him relate to the mask and not to his psychopathic per-sonality which is doubly removed – removed once because he is over-controlled, and twice because even his over-controlled identity is hidden behind the mask. As the Chinese say in a proverb: "Fish see the worm, not the hook".'

'That means, does it not,' DeClercq said slowly, 'that the person responsible for the Headhunter killings may for all intents and purposes be as indistinguishable as the man who lives next door?'

'It means,' said Dr Ruryk, 'that the Headhunter might very well *be* the man next door. In fact, the man next door may be the Headhunter and not even know it himself. You see, this is the sort of situation that occurs in documented cases of split personality. It would be possible for our killer to have created "an Imposter" within his mind and then to have psychologically assumed the role of "the Imposter" and subconsciously buried and forgotten the personality that created him. This is precisely the situation that Stevenson was writing about in *The Strange Case of Dr Jekyll and Mr Hyde*, except that in that story the process was externalized, whereas we are talking about transactions totally contained within the human mind. In such a case should the killer want out he merely assumes the body of the Imposter but shuts down the Imposter's artificial awareness until he – the unrecognized psychopathic personality – slips back into hiding once again. At that point the awareness of the Imposter will reactivate and know nothing about what has happened. He – the Imposter – then walks outside and you and I spend a few boring minutes watching him water his lawn.'

DeClercq asked: 'Is mental abnormality genetically inherited?'

'We don't know,' Ruryk replied cautiously. 'It is definitely passed on from one generation to the next. But that could be by genetics or by socialization.'

DeClercq: 'Now might I ask you, doctor, for your general impression of the killer whom we seek?'

'To answer that,' Ruryk said, 'I'll ask another question: "Why have the heads gone missing?" That to me is the mystery. And I can think of four possible answers:

'Each head is removed to impede identification of the victim.

'Each head is removed to satisfy cannibalistic desires on the part of the killer toward that section of the female body.

'Each head is collected for some reason as a trophy of the killing.

'Each head is removed because the killer has a fetish for female hair.

'Let's take them one by one.

'Does the Headhunter take the head to prevent victim identification? This I doubt. Though it is not without precedent – indeed Peter Sutcliffe, the Yorkshire Ripper, contemplated this very act concerning his sixth victim, Jean Jordan – I would expect the killer to have cut off the fingers too. In a frenzy of murder he might forget this second act concerning the first body, but not the subsequent ones. So that to my mind leaves us with one of the three perversions.

'Does the Headhunter take the head in a cannibalistic craving? Very possibly so.

'I note, Superintendent, in one of your reports the possible theory that the killer or killers may be members of a cannibalistic cult. You refer to the Zebra killings and you mention the local Kwakiutl Indians and their history in that direction. I can think of a few even more blatant examples.

'Take for example the crimes of the man upon whose murders are loosely based two motion pictures – Hitchcock's *Psycho* and the cult film – *The Texas Chainsaw Massacre*.

'Ed Gein was a farmer in Plainfield, Wisconsin. According to psychiatric reports his mother had been a religious fanatic who exerted a strong overbearing influence on her son.

'After her death it is believed that Gein had read of the sex change undertaken by Christine Jorgensen and wished himself to become a woman – to become his mother.

'At first a grave robber, he later took to murdering women.

216

'In a shed next to his large farmhouse Gein would skin each corpse and then study his dissected trophies. He began to don the skins that he removed and wear them for hours draped over his own body so as to experience a bizarre thrill in thinking himself a woman.

'*Psycho* is based on this premise. *The Texas Chainsaw Massacre*, however, is concerned with another aspect.

'After Gein was arrested the local Sheriff went to the farmhouse. There he found a woman's body with its head cut off, hanging upside down from the ceiling of the shed. Scattered around the main house, the Sheriff located a number of Ed Gein's trophies: there were bracelets made of human skin, four female noses in a cup on the kitchen table, a pair of human lips on a string dangling from a windowsill, two human shin bones, strips of human skin used to brace four chairs, a tom-tom made from a coffee can with human skin stretched over both the top and bottom, a pair of leggings made from the skin of several women, the skin from a female torso converted into a vest, nine death masks made from skinned female faces mounted on the walls, ten heads belonging to women sawed off above the eyebrows to open up their brain vaults, another head converted into a soup bowl, and a purse that Gein had made with handles of human skin.

'A further search revealed that the refrigerator was stocked with frozen human organs and that a human heart was in a frying pan on the stove. By the Sheriff's estimate, the various body pieces discovered would add up to fifteen women. Of course no one knows how many more Gein had consumed over the years.

'In December of 1957 – after admitting to graverobbing, intercourse with the bodies and cannibalizing the remains – Gein was committed for life to an institution for the criminally insane where, I believe, he resides today.

'I could go on and on with the cases of modern cannibals,' the psychiatrist said. 'The public is either not aware – or soon forgets – just how common a practice it is.

217

'The point is,' Ruryk said, 'that every jurisdiction has similar cannibal cases. That's why I say that this very well might be the reason why the Headhunter cuts off heads. And if it is the reason, I'll venture he's eating the brains.'

At this juncture they took a break while DeClercq turned over the tape. Ruryk packed and poked his pipe and then he continued.

'Does the Headhunter take the head to collect it as a trophy? Well this I think is also a distinct possibility.

'Again we have the case of Ed Gein: nine skinned female faces were found mounted like masks on the walls of his farmhouse. Though the animal is human, the psychology at work here is that of the big game hunter. The trophy above the mantel.

'And finally: Does the Headhunter take the head because he has a fetish for female hair? Again very likely.

'In one of your reports, Superintendent, you have noted that the first three victims all had long black hair. To my mind the killing of the nun might also fit this pattern, for in that case her black cowl is a symbolic representation. What one must realize is that a fetishist is a person preoccupied with symbol.

'The psychological link between sex and hair goes back a very long way.

'Prostitutes, of course, have used this knowledge for centuries; a large per centage of them keep a selection of wigs to meet the psychological needs of their various clients.

'A problem arises, however, when a mania develops.

'In a case of mania we find that the affected person's mind has upset or lost its natural connection with reality. An obsession has taken over resulting in the collecting of or concentration upon some concrete object which the mind links to sex.

'Hair is a prime example. Take the case of John Reginald Halliday Christie, a sexual psychopath who committed eight murders of women between 1940 and 1953.

'Before disposing of the bodies he would shave off the pubic hair and store it in a tobacco tin. Later when his fetish overtook him, he would gloat over the tin of hair, masturbating as he did so.'

At this point Dr Ruryk glanced around for an ashtray. DeClercq handed him an empty flower pot.

'So,' Ruryk began again, 'where does all this leave us?

'I believe back at the question which to my way of thinking is at the centre of this case: "Why have the heads gone missing?" That is our real mystery – and the key to the Headhunter's illness. Answer that question and you will be well along the road to revealing his identity. For you see everything else in this case revolves around those heads. Not only the fact that the heads have gone missing, but also the fact that in the later crimes the killer has gone to great risk to leave a head substitute.

'This attention-seeking is typical for a psychopath. Such a person believes himself superior to and better than everybody else. He doesn't make mistakes, and if he does he blames it on another. In effect this killer is saying: "I can do no wrong. You have not caught me on four occasions. See what you can do now."

'So believe me, Superintendent, centre on the heads.'

For a moment Ruryk turned away from the microphone and looked out over the ocean beyond the glass of the greenhouse. With a swoop a cormorant took a dive at the water. Ruryk watched the bird awhile, then brought his attention back.

'I believe,' the psychiatrist said, 'that we are now able to return to your original question. You asked me for my general impression of the killer whom you seek.

'Most likely he is a sexual psychopath with one of those three perversions concerning his victims' heads – cannibalism, trophy hunting or hair fetishism.

'Less likely he is a psychotic with one of the same three perversions.

'And then there is one more *very* rare possibility.'

'What's that?' DeClercq asked with a bare trace of a frown.

Ruryk met his eyes and said: 'There's the off-chance, Superintendent, that what we have here is the most dangerous of men. For it is possible that the Headhunter is a psychiatric crossover. He may just be a psychopathic sadist with psychotic overtones.'

That afternoon when Genevieve DeClercq arrived home she found her husband sitting by himself down by the edge of the sea. Across the water clouds were boiling above the city of Vancouver.

'A penny for your thoughts,' she said, crouching down beside him.

For several long seconds Robert DeClercq was silent. Then he said: 'I was just thinking how life affects the very young. And how those young grow up to become an effect on life.'

Out on the water a cormorant was swimming with a fish clamped in its bill.

THE PRICE OF YOUR SKULL

11.50 a.m.

That morning as Dr George Ruryk was driving out Chancellor Boulevard from the University of British Columbia on his way to meet Robert DeClercq, Spann and Scarlett were driving in. Earlier they had tried to contact Corporal William Tipple at Commercial Crime in order to get a lead on John Lincoln Hardy but it was Tipple's day off. The member who answered the phone told Spann that the Corporal had gone hiking in the

North Shore mountains and wouldn't be back till tomorrow.

They had decided late last night to follow the trail of DeClercq. What was the use of a manhunt if you didn't know your quarry? Therefore, they had spent the morning reading psychology texts.

'Okay,' Katherine Spann said. 'I've read enough. I think I'll recognize this guy if we bump into him in the dark. Let's sweep the pubs again.'

'Why not wait for Tipple? It'll save us some time.'

'Why give the collar away? Besides what else do we have to do?'

'All right,' Scarlett said, 'but give me another minute. I'm at a juicy part.' The book he was reading was Wilson: *The Origins Of The Sexual Impulse*.

'I'll meet you upstairs by the card catalogue. I need some air.'

Spann left Scarlett buried several stories underground. Climbing the stairs to the stacks she passed row upon row of old texts housed in sunken levels, the only sound was that of the compressors and convectors pumping oxygen into the subterranean space.

Ten minutes later when Scarlett emerged he found Spann standing at the catalogue studying a card. 'You'd better look at this,' she said as he came up beside her. She pointed to the card. It read: HOODOO. *See* VOODOO.

Two minutes later they were back in the stacks searching out a volume called *Voodoo and Hoodoo: Their Practice Today*. Scarlett only had to scan a few paragraphs before he began to feel like a fool:

'Detectives smashed a grave-robbing ring early today as they rounded up the last of five suspects accused of stealing the skulls of long-dead women. The macabre loot was worth an estimated $1000 on the occult market, and was headed for voodoo rites, detectives said. There was no connection made between the grave robbery and a grisly discovery in a Bronx apartment yesterday. Maintenance men who entered an empty apartment found an altar, a human skull, a goat's skull, dried blood and feathers apparently used in voodoo rites. An investigation was ordered. *New York Post*, November 18, 1977'

Spann looked up and said: 'I think we now know "what's happenin" with that "nigger hoodoo man".'

'Yeah,' Scarlett said sheepishly. 'And it sure the hell isn't limestone pillars between the Rocky Mountains and the prairies.'

9.00 p.m.

That night they sat together at the water's edge, huddled against the chill of the dark, combining the heat of their bodies as the world slowly turned toward winter. Waves lapped against the shore and to the east a Hunter's Moon hung in the sky like a moist overripe piece of fruit, half its surface shining in purple twilight, the other half obscured by clouds. Occasionally a dead leaf would flutter down to the ground.

Later they built a fire in the living room and both took off their clothes, but when they tried to make love DeClercq couldn't get an erection. When they finally gave up he noticed once again that both his hands were shaking. Closing his eyes, he took a deep breath and whispered 'Oh my God.'

Genevieve sat up. 'Roll over on your stomach,' she softly said to him. She began to deep rub his back. As her fingers moved she could sense the stress built up in him. 'Relax, just relax,' she said.

She moved down to massage his feet, the most important part of the human structure when it comes to relaxation.

'Will you listen to me, Robert, or have you shut me out? I won't let you close up on me, not without a fight. Hey, relax, relax, I can feel that foot tensing up. Can you hear me, Robert? Is anyone home in there?'

'I hear you, Genny,' he said, his voice buried in a sigh.

'Good, then let's talk it out.' She began to work on his legs. 'Robert DeClercq, I've told you before – you hold yourself too tight. You cling to the values of a time that has gone forever. Then you wonder why life never seems to work. The value of a man's word as the currency of friendship; help your neighbour; the compact of love. I think at long last you're beginning to doubt that your values have any place. You're a throwback to another time and you're beginning to feel very old.'

'And it's starting to show, isn't it Genny?'

'Starting to . . .? Oh, you mean our missing erection, and you'll note I said "*our*". So what am I to do? Is this such a major problem that I should run naked from the house to find some young buck stud who'll do sexual service? You're only fifty-five, man. Believe me, I'll squeeze a lot more fun out of you yet.'

Her hands massaged his lower back.

'Just because you're under a monumental amount of tension, and just because you're burning the candle at both ends to try and catch this killer – and, love, we did drink wine with dinner – then if suddenly we find on this occasion that a hard-on is not instantly forthcoming, don't sell me short and think that *I* think that *you* have a problem. You're the only man I ever met who honestly holds my sexual satisfaction as more important than his own. *Chéri*, I'm with you to the end.'

Her hands moved up to his shoulders.

She then said: 'Tell me what's bothering you.'

'He's laughing at me, Genny – and perhaps he has reason to be.'

'Robert, it's common knowledge that the insane laugh without reason. This is so unlike you. I thought you were the one who believed that order and precision could always meet the match of chaos.'

'Maybe once, but not now.'

'Believe me, Robert, if you still weren't Number One they'd never have brought you back. In fact, what with your reading in tactics you're more equipped for this

223

investigation than you were in the past. Just trust your knowledge and use it. Put it into practice and I'll bet it sees you through.'

From out of nowhere DeClercq said: 'Genny, I'm having nightmares. Actually one nightmare, over and over again.'

'So tell me,' she said.

The dream is all in silver.

He can see a silver room beyond the door, a room of silver walls with silver windows and a mist of silver vapour rising up from the floor. Even the sound of the sobbing has a metallic tone about it. And the silver blade of the silver knife is silver-cold in his stomach.

A tree beyond the window is stripped and bare of leaves.

Now his hands are closing about a neck and his fingers are pushing in, crushing the muscles and the veins and the pipes that feed life to this man's brain. The man's silver eyes seem to bulge out of their sockets. Suddenly with a pop they fall out on the floor. But it doesn't stop him squeezing. Now the tongue of the man is slithering out of his silver mouth like an eel dropping down from a hole in a rock five feet up from the ocean floor.

Silver, all in silver. Silver sobbing electric in the air.

Then abruptly there is colour in this monochromatic dream, for the face of the man whom he holds in his hands has now turned livid blue. He opens his grip to let the dead man drop to the floor.

Janie, he whispers. Janie. For it is her sobbing in this room.

Turning toward the sound he sees a silver figure shrouded in mist lying on a bed. He crosses the floor; he opens his arms; he holds her against his chest. Then he screams in anguish at the source of the sobbing sound. For the surface of the cut that has taken her head is flat and silver-smooth. The sobs are coming from an open tube sticking out of her throat.

Screaming, he tears the room apart.

But he doesn't find her head.

'Robert,' Genevieve asked, 'what does the dream mean to you?'

He thought for a moment, then said: 'That I'll never find those heads.'

'You're wrong. It means that you are afraid that you'll never find those heads. Not that you'll never find them. You see the difference, don't you?'

DeClercq forced a smile. 'Genny, they never caught Jack the Ripper. Nor Zodiac in San Francisco. Nor the Axe Man of New Orleans. The Thames Nude Killer was never found. Nor the murderer of the Black Dahlia. Nor the . . .'

'So what,' Genevieve said, almost spitting out her words. 'None of those killers ever went up against the RCMP.'

The force of her exclamation stopped him in midsentence.

'Steele. Walsh. McIllree. Get it through your head. I've read your book. I know where you're coming from and so does most of the world. Men who wore the tunic: it's time to believe the myth. For all your doubts about modern times they still produce some wisdom.' Then she softened. 'Don't you think it's time you took a lesson from Obee Wan Kenobe?'

'And what's that?' DeClercq asked frowning, for he rarely went to the movies.

'Let the Force be with you,' she said – and DeClercq actually laughed.

For even he understood. Such is the grapevine of culture.

She waited until he was asleep, knowing that she had soothed him and made him forget his work for awhile, then she curled herself in against the warmth of his body and let the void take her too. She fell asleep smiling.

At 3.00 a.m. Robert DeClercq woke up in a sweat. For the dream had come again.

He lay on his back for several minutes listening to his wife's even breathing, then he slipped out of bed and out of the room and dressed to go down to the sea.

Next morning Genevieve DeClercq found her husband

225

in the greenhouse with a pistol in his hand. The revolver was almost one hundred years old, a six shot Enfield Calibre .476.

The Superintendent didn't tell his wife about the nightmare.

VOODOO

9.15 p.m.

That evening Katherine Spann arrived home to find a cockroach in her kitchen.

Actually three cockroaches.

After she and Scarlett had left the University library late that afternoon they had driven downtown once again to look for the Indian and John Lincoln Hardy. When they had found neither one by 9.00 p.m. they had agreed to call it a day. With Scarlett at the wheel of the unmarked Ford the two Constables had driven along Fir Street under a half-hidden moon, the dull silver glow of the moonlight shimmering on the pavement, then had crossed 16th to enter Shaughnessy where the car slowly picked its way among the shadows of the trees. A wind was coming up from the direction of the sea so the light-ghosts were moving. Scarlett pulled the cruiser into the curb and Katherine Spann climbed out.

'Pleasant reading,' he said as she closed the door. Then the car drove away.

For a moment Spann stood on the curb listening to the autumn wind moan in the boulevard trees, then re-moving a ring of keys from her pocket, she unlocked the gate at the servants' entrance and entered the yard of the mansion. Tonight the grounds were aromatic with the smell of decaying autumn leaves, and as she walked toward the groundkeeper's house those same leaves crunched beneath her feet like cellophane candy-wrappers. Having closed the gate on squeaking hinges she had locked the city outside.

The groundkeeper's house stood in the shadows this side of Sussex Manor. As she approached it, her hands shoved deep in her pockets, both library books on voodoo clamped firmly under one arm, Spann could hear the chill November wind skating under the eaves of the mansion. The sound was like a thin scream escaping from an aged mouth lost somewhere in the darkness. Mixed with that noise she could also feel the gathering storm as it rattled through the old gutters and down-spouts, scraping with it the rusty leaves that clawed at the metal.

Altogether it was a night fit to follow Halloween. The type of autumn night that Katherine Spann enjoyed. Eerie. Weird. Mysterious. A night to curl up at home.

With her windbreaker still zipped up under her chin to keep out the creeping cold, she came in through the back door of the groundkeeper's house and switched on the overhead light. And that was when she saw it, smack-dab in the middle of her kitchen floor.

Like all cockroaches this bug had a flat shiny body, six hairy legs, and a pair of long feelers that waved above a head hidden beneath a plate of armour. The insect was nibbling at a spot of goo caked to the linoleum floor. But the moment the light lit up the room it began to move. And though the roach moved quickly, Katherine Spann was quicker. She caught the ugly insect over near the sink.

Crunchhh! With a heavy stomp the woman squashed both the external skeleton and internal pulp underneath the heel of her boot.

It was as she was cleaning the mess from her foot that she saw the other two insects. There were two more shiny roaches in front of the garbage container. With two

227

successive stomps she managed to get them also. *Ughh*, she thought.

At first Spann's reaction was to blame the age of the building: *When you live in Edwardian premises, kiddo, what do you expect?*

Katherine Spann had made up her mind to go out and buy some Raid, in fact she had opened the back door to venture forth with that purpose, when a realization slipped in and tugged at her brain. She stopped in her tracks, turned, and looked about the kitchen. The problem was not, it would appear, the advancing age of the building. The problem was her.

It's strange, Spann thought, *the way that blindness can strike you in degree. It can shut out all the lights at once or just put blinders on*. For there was not a clean plate or coffee cup in the entire kitchen. The sink was over-flowing with dirty dishes, most still caked with the remnants of meals she could not remember eating. How long had it been since she had scrubbed the floor? One month? Two months? No, it was probably half a year. Suddenly she could smell the stink of garbage in the room: why had she not noticed it on entering this evening?

Spann closed the back door and walked from the kitchen into the living room. It was in no better shape.

The closet was just to the right inside the front door of the building. On entering the room she could see that it was empty, just a metal rod hung with skeletal wire hangers. The clothes that once had hung there were scattered about the place. Every stick of furniture was now buried beneath her discarded clothing. There were turtleneck sweaters and parts of her uniforms strewn about the floor. In one corner lay a pile of high-heeled pumps, loafers and running shoes. There were dressing gowns and socks and skirts and under-pants here and there. There were blouses and T-shirts and overcoats hither, thither, and yon. One of her bras was hanging limply off a table surface; it reminded her of those Dali clocks, surreal and warped and melting. Not one picture upon the walls hung on the horizontal.

Sure you hate housework, kiddo, but this is ridiculous!

It occurred to her now as she stood in the room letting the mild shock sink in, that perhaps this mess was no more than the external manifestation of just how hard she had been working. While training in Regina on how to go underground, Spann had had an instructor who put the art like this: 'And you women, you gotta pretend that you're nothin' but scummy sluts. No combin' your hair. No washin' your bods. No ironin' your clothes. When your pits are gettin high as a kite, you're ready for the jungle. That's the way of survival.'

This was sound advice, Spann had learned her first day on the skids. She had followed it and had survived among those who hated narcs. Perhaps she'd followed it too well.

The problem, as she now saw it, was that she had not come all the way back: she had jumped from her undercover posting right to the Headhunter Squad, donning her uniform without also taking the time to clean up and change her act. There had not been time for mundane affairs like housework and doing the laundry, *And come on girl, be honest, that's the way you like it. Housekeeping is the shits!*

Tonight it took Katherine Spann almost two hours to get her home in order. Finally at 11.30 p.m. she put on her jacket and opened the door to take out the garbage. All six bags of it.

Outside the wind was howling like a banshee on a drunk. Across the pockmarked face of the moon, now high and full and yellow, rafts of cloud were sweeping by on the river of the storm. Suddenly Spann felt a chill worm its way down her spine, like a freezing finger that slowly touched each vertebra. She turned on instinct and looked back at the windows of Sussex Manor. For lately the eldest of the sisters who lived there – the one without hair or teeth – had taken to sitting up late at night behind the upper left-hand window. Several times Spann had seen her there in ghostly silhouette. Tonight, however, all she could see of the two-storied house were the three high-pointed gables and the massive stone turret bulging off to one side.

The woman crossed the yard to the gardener's shed and dug out the two-handled axe.

For the next fifteen minutes Katherine Spann chopped up alder rounds, then having lathered up a sweat she carried the wood, quartered and split, back into her house. She lit a blazing fire in the antique cast-iron hearth. Entering the bathroom she stripped off her clothes and turned the shower on. For ten minutes she stood in the tub with her eyes closed, languishing and relaxing beneath the sharp needles of hot water. When she climbed out, refreshed, Spann towelled herself dry with a rough brisk rub and put on a pair of blue pyjamas, a maroon velour bathrobe and fuzzy sheepskin slippers. Then she towelled her hair dry one more time and shuffled out to stand by the fire.

The flames of the hearth were licking and snarling within the bricked-up cage, every so often emitting a crack like a circus master's whip.

Her world now in order and everything clean, Spann picked up a voodoo book. Then she curled up in an easy chair off to the right of the fire, cracked the cover of the Huxley volume and slowly began to read.

The roots of voodoo twist among the myths and tribes of Africa. That much she knew. What she was about to find out was just how developed and widespread that root system was.

It was now midnight.

Outside the autumn wind continued to scream in the trees.

11.32 p.m.

In an article dated September 26th 1979, the Toronto *Globe And Mail* informed its readers that sometime in the previous week about 800 French paratroopers and marine commandos had flown into the Central African Republic to stage a bloodless coup to end the rule of Emperor Jean Bedel Bokassa. The Emperor had subsequently gone into exile on the Ivory Coast. When David Dacko, the new President of the Republic, held his first press conference he told the international journalists gathered in Bangui that 'pieces of human flesh have been found in the refrigerators in Bokassa's Colongo villa.'

Old habits die hard, Rick Scarlett thought – and he put down the book. The newspaper clipping was Scotch-taped inside its front cover.

For over an hour the policeman had been reading about how prevalent the practice of voodoo was – and is – in Africa, particularly when it overlaps with cannibalism and human sacrifice. The number of cases was startling.

In the early fifties it had surfaced dramatically among the Kikuyu tribesmen of East Africa. That was when the Mau Mau took on the British in Kenya.

As the initiate climbed the Mau Mau ladder, the oath and rituals performed increased in bestiality. One of the pledges required that whenever an initiate to the society murdered a European, he had to cut off the head and extract the eyeballs and drink the fluid from them.

In a postscript to the volume that Scarlett had been reading it was stated that in order to intensify the atmosphere of these oath-taking ceremonies, they were usually accompanied by sexual orgies and perversions involving animals. Rams or dogs or sheep were used, or whatever was available. It was said that the authenticated reports were so disgusting that they were not available for general study. They could, however, be consulted on the premises of the Colonial or Commonwealth Relations Office Library.

Although the British had crushed the Mau Mau in 1956, the same type of structure had arisen again with the Zebra killings in San Francisco. Was it now arising here?

For the last quarter hour Rick Scarlett had found that

he had trouble in concentrating. That was the reason he had finally put down the book.

After dropping Katherine Spann off earlier in the evening, he'd returned to the Headquarters building up on Heather Street. He was hoping to find Rabidowski or other suitable male company, for the truth was that Rick Scarlett felt like a horse's ass.

Right from the start he had somehow felt that this woman had taken effective control of their flying patrol. It worried him that the good ideas seemed to come from her. As a boy on the prairies he had spent a number of years in Alberta. Scarlett's father had been a regular member of the RCMP posted to 'K' Division. Many a day the boy had spent with his dad up around those sandstone pillars where men like Sam Steele and Wilfred Blake had once maintained the law. When the word "hoodoo" had shown on the taps, a connection to the Rocky Mountains had instantly linked in his mind.

Oh God, Scarlett thought. *Do you think she's gloating right now? Why did this have to happen to me immediately after De-Clercq gives us a warning on tunnel vision?*

Up at Headhunter Headquarters Scarlett had not found Rabidowski. What he had found was a group of constables sitting around a tape recorder listening to a lecture by a guy named Dr George Ruryk. Hoping for something to one-up Spann, Scarlett had joined the crowd. He had left when one of the other cops had turned to him and asked: 'Don't you think hearing this ruins your independence? I thought you were part of a flying patrol?'

Tonight as he had inserted his key into the lock of his apartment door Scarlett had wondered what Katherine Spann would be like in bed. Hot, he suspected.

It was now just after 11.30 and he was thinking that same thought.

Scarlett got up and walked over to the living room window to see if Miss Torso was dancing tonight. The window of the apartment across the street was dark and the curtains were drawn.

With a sigh Scarlett went to put on his strip and go for a run in the park.

Wednesday, November 3rd, 12.31 a.m.

From an upper floor window of Sussex Manor the old woman looked down at the groundkeeper's house in the yard. Framed in one window by firelight she could see Katherine Spann reading.

In the development of voodoo, the most important feature was the way the original African beliefs and practices were combined with Catholicism. For just as the Roman Catholic Church has a pantheon of its God and saints, so the slaves who came to the New World had a religious pantheon of their own. Thus a form of the Catholic religion became at once acceptable to these transplants from Africa.

A typical slave religious altar might bare a statue that was flanked by coloured oleographs of St Peter, St George, and St Patrick. To the African these figures represented the *Loa Legba*, the god who guarded the way to the world beyond; *Ogoun*, warrior god to the Dahomey; and *Damballah*, god of the snake. Under this altar the slaves would place bottles of rum or whisky, alternating them with cloth-covered bundles and white porcelain pots which were used to house their *loa* and the spirits of the dead. These spirits eventually came to be called by the African word *zombi*.

Among the slaves carried off to America there were voodoo priests, medicine men and sorcerers. It was these priests who connected the African pantheon with the Roman Catholic religion of the New World. It was the sorcerers – who in Africa had thrived during times of war and destruction – who now found their position enhanced by the confusion and disorientation rampant among the slaves. It was not long before the sorcerer rose in power and totally absorbed the profession of the priest. And out of this blurring came to flourish the practice known as voodoo.

The appeal of voodoo was basic and it spread very fast: for only by voodoo practice could the African slaves strike back at the hated white man.

After the slave uprisings in Haiti and the formation of an independent black republic in 1804, thousands of French fled the island, taking with them as many of their African slaves as possible. Ten thousand of these refugees ended up in New Orleans. With them came the practice of voodoo.

Soon there were wild group dances in that city's Congo Square. Both serpent worship and the drinking of blood were a common phenomenon. Rituals were performed around trees in St Tammany Parish. When the backlash came in the form of waves of anti-voodoo sentiment, this practice of the black arts merely went under ground. As before it was disguised as the Roman Catholic religion.

What is not common knowledge however, is that from the very beginning of the organized use of voodoo in New Orleans, whites could be found among the secret cultists.

In August of 1850 several white women were among those arrested for dancing nude in a bloody voodoo ritual.

12.45 a.m.

Every great city, no matter what size, has by definition at least one major park. For there must be some place where its citizens can escape from the hustle. London has Hyde Park. New York has Central Park. Paris has the Bois de Boulogne. Vancouver has Stanley Park.

Scarlett was beginning to open up for the final stretch. He was running the Seawall clockwise around the perimeter of the park, with seven miles behind him and less than a mile to go. Pumping his arms and breathing hard he came around Hallelujah Point, passing the Brockton Point totem poles on the right and closing the distance between him and Deadman's Island ahead.

The moon was now at Scarlett's back and as he jogged his moonshadow stretched out longer and longer on the ground in front of him. Suddenly a second shadow split off from it like some weak Gemini twin, this sub-shadow caused by the moon's reflection off the waters of the harbour. To his right the Douglas firs were swaying. Leaves the colour of dried blood were slipping their hold on the maple branches and tumbling like falling acrobats to be crushed under his feet. The tide was out and the mud at the base of the Seawall was glistening like a quicksilver flow. Then, without warning, a veil of cloud slipped across the face of the moon. The wind turned cold. All light was gone. And the rain came once more.

By the time Rick Scarlett returned to his apartment in the West End he was soaked to the skin.

Shucking his clothes off on the bathroom floor he turned on the shower. Once under the piping hot spray he let himself relax. He found that the run had cleared his mind and he brought his thoughts once more around to the investigation in progress. Theories came into focus.

The way Scarlett saw things at the moment there were mainly three active and pregnant possibilities.

The first of these was the theory that the Headhunter was a psychopathic killer acting on his own. The strength of this theory was in the fact that it was the simplest explanation. It gained credence from the number of similar cases that had surfaced in so many other cities over recent years, Clifford Olson's rampage being merely a local example. Also, Vancouver is one weird town. Most seaports are: ask any cop or criminal lawyer. Here, however, there were not only the usual drifters and perverts who float in each day with the tide, but this town is also the foremost North American gateway for the import and traffic of heroin. And that means a lot of burnt-out freakos come here to tap the source.

The second theory – more subtle – arose out of Superintendent DeClercq's tape on psychology. For it had struck Scarlett while listening to Dr Ruryk's examples, that if these crimes arose from psychosis, from some madman with a hole in his brain, then the Headhunter quite literally could be any man in this city. He could be a homicidal rapist, living a life of surface normalcy, going about his legitimate daily business and all the while keeping a watch for his next female victim. In fact if you accept what Ruryk said about the Imposter, the killer might not even know that he himself was the Headhunter. Taken to its extreme that could even mean that one of the other guys on the Headhunter Squad could be the killer for whom all of them were searching. A madman hunting himself and not even knowing it.

The final theory was the one that he and Kathy now seemed to be onto. This theory was that the Headhunter was actually a cult. A voodoo cult? A cannibal cult? A cult of North American Indians? Perhaps it was an active form of mass psychosis. For Scarlett had read earlier today about a psychiatric concept known as *folie à deux*. That was where insanity starts with one person and then by close association passes from that individual to another. The 'Reverend' Jim Jones' Guyana cult might be explained in this way. Perhaps there was a voodoo cult active in Vancouver, with Hardy a lone psychopath using it as a blind. Anything was possible. The history of murder showed that.

As Rick Scarlett stepped out of the shower he put these thoughts aside. He wiped off the steamed-up mirror and stood examining his body. This was one of his favourite pastimes. He was proud of the fact that he could not find the slightest sign of fat, just a firm sheath of tight muscles, his shoulders strong, his stomach and pectorals flat, his thighs well-developed. And he was well-hung.

Yep, Scarlett thought smiling. *If I were a woman I'd cream myself over a man like that*.

He did a few muscle flexes, watching himself in the mirror, and then an image of Kathy without her clothes intruded into his mind.

Damn her, Scarlett thought. *I must take back control*.

And with that concern in his mind, he dismissed his several theories about the Headhunter investigation.

It was as Rick Scarlett walked out of the bathroom that a light came on in the windows of the apartment across the street. His heart jumped. Swiftly he killed his own lights. Then he went into the bedroom to retrieve his binoculars.

A few years ago when Scarlett had first rented this apartment he had a view of Stanley Park. But that view had not lasted long. Within the year a developer had built on the land next door and this new structure contained residences stacked up as tall as his own building. Scarlett had been thoroughly pissed off until Miss Torso moved in.

Scarlett had never met her. But he had called her Miss Torso since last seeing Jimmy Stewart in Hitchcock's movie *Rear Window*. Miss Torso was a dancer who practised regularly late at night. She was blonde. She was young. She had a stunning figure. And lately she had taken to dancing in the nude.

It had not always been that way. When she first moved in, the lady used to pirouette about in a rainbow of different coloured Danskins. During that first summer she had switched to a bikini. And then one very hot August night she had shed that too. The next day Scarlett had gone out and bought his binoculars.

Of late it had occurred to him that perhaps Miss Torso knew that he was watching. *Perhaps she's a show-off*, he thought. *Aren't we all*. Scarlett was not a modest individual within his own home: and if he could see her, surely she could see him. Why else would she dance naked within the full view of all those other apartments? Mind you, it was true that she danced very late at night.

Scarlett wanted to wander over and ask her the reason why. But that might kill the golden goose and make her pull the curtains.

So, as always, tonight he sat down behind his darkened window and peered across the road. He adjusted the binoculars to get the proper focus. Then he held them in his left hand, keeping his other hand free.

If you want to show it, woman, he thought, *I'll oblige you and look.*

Miss Torso appeared on stage.

LOOKING FOR JACK THE LAD

12.55 a.m.

Monica Macdonald had seen more than enough.

For the past two days she and Rusty Lewis had been moving from one strip-club to another across the map of the city. She found the trip a bore. There had once been a time when Macdonald had seriously considered a career in art, and to that end she had studied Fine Arts in college. Even today she was still proficient at the charcoal-sketching of nudes. But that was the human body in its classic form. This was something different.

It was almost 1.00 a.m. but Phantoms was going strong.

Macdonald and Lewis were both dressed in civilian clothes and they were sitting at a small table ten feet from the raised dancefloor. Both were sipping beers. The woman up on the stage in front of them was not wearing civilian clothes. She was maybe eighteen years of age and had long black hair. All she had on were satin-covered, high-heeled, ankle-strapped pumps and a sequined G-string. Her breasts were bare.

There were several speakers situated about the club and two above the stage, all of them playing canned soft rock – Olivia Newton-John growling about wanting to get physical.

While Macdonald and Lewis scanned the customers' faces looking for Matthew Paul Pitt or any of the other illustrious members in their memorized Rogues' Gallery, the stripper danced to the edge of the stage and squatted down in front of a solitary British sailor dressed in Navy blues. Spreading her legs wide, she pulled aside the G-string to expose herself completely. There were catcalls around the room. As the sailor stared at her genitals with his Adam's apple bobbing the woman licked her lips. The sailor reached for a pair of glasses to get a better look, but the moment he put them on the stripper removed them from his nose. She began to wipe them slowly across her exposed crotch, pursing her lips and pouting an expression of innocence. Then she replaced the spectacles on the sailor's face and arched her back like a gymnast. Supporting her weight with her arms and her feet, she began thrusting her pelvis toward the man's face, pumping and rocking her hips as he continued to stare wide-eyed.

The hooting and laughing and whistling rose as the crowd in the room went wild. Then one drunk shouted above the din: 'Hey, lady, I'll sniff your bicycle seat anytime!'

Monica Macdonald sighed. *How does any woman end up in a place like this?* she thought.

'Seen enough?' Macdonald asked, leaning over to Lewis. Rusty Lewis nodded. He knocked back the rest of his beer, then the two of them left the table just as the woman on the stage ripped off the G-string.

Monica Macdonald liked to think that hers was an open mind. So she had started out on this strip-club crawl with a clinical attitude. Not once in her life had she had a Lesbian experience, unless of course you counted the time that her Uncle Harold while babysitting had tried to get both her and her fourteen-year-old sister into bed at once. At the age of eleven (even then destined to be a cop) Monica had turned Uncle Harold in to her mother. After that Uncle Harold stopped coming for Christmas dinner.

After watching thirty-two strippers expose themselves, Monica Macdonald was now convinced irrevocably that her DC had no AC to trot along beside it. So to keep from getting bored on this trip she had turned her attention to Lewis.

The man was entertaining.

For to start with, it was hard to believe that any man in his late twenties could possibly be this shy. When the first stripper had exposed her crotch Rusty Lewis had blushed as scarlet as his red serge dress uniform.

'Is that why they call you Rusty?' Monica had chided.

Lewis had turned a deeper scarlet and averted his eyes from the woman.

To be honest, Rusty Lewis was a rather pleasant change. Most of the men within the Force were closer in their attitude towards women to the views of Rabidowski and Scarlett. Most males liked both the authority and the power that came with the uniform. In the RCMP a shy man was a bit of a rarity.

'Let's check the barman,' Macdonald said, 'then let's get out of here.'

The liquor supply in Phantoms English Pub was thirty feet from the dance-floor. The barman was out of Yorkshire by way of London, large and beefy with a bulbous, red-veined nose. As they approached the counter he looked them up and down and said: 'I'm betting you two are fuzz.'

Lewis flashed the Regimental Shield.

Fishing out the picture of Matthew Paul Pitt, Macdonald placed it on the counter. 'Seen this one?' she asked.

The Englishman glanced at the photograph, then looked up. 'You looking for Jack the Lad?' he inquired.

'Just routine.'

'Coppers don't do nothing that's just routine, my lass.'

'Have you seen him?'

'Nope,' the barman said. 'But I seen a lot just like him.'

Macdonald looked at Lewis, and then back at the giant.

'You're looking for Jack, right? Jackie, our Head-hunter?'

'You're correct,' Monica said. 'We're looking for him.'

'And you're checking out the dirty-raincoat brigade, eh? The lads who come into the pub just for the show. Cause if there's an orifice up there, these fellers'll be hanging on to the rail looking up into it. Well, there's lots of them here tonight but I ain't seen this bloke.'

The Yorkshireman tapped the picture then gave it back to Macdonald.

'If I was you, lass,' the barman said, 'I think I'd keep right on looking. Don't stop here. And don't stop with that picture.'

'Why's that?' Macdonald asked.

'Coz there's three dozen lads what come into this pub alone have the eyes or the mouth to do what this Jack's done.'

THE ENFIELD

7.45 a.m.

'Robert, what in the world are you doing?'

Genevieve DeClercq stood in the doorway to the greenhouse and stared at the revolver in her husband's hand. The Superintendent looked up, then held up the Enfield.

'You mean this?' he asked. 'I was just taking a breather and reading about Wilfred Blake. This gun was his service revolver. It was found in the snow of the Rockies after he disappeared.'

Genevieve understood. She glanced at the library table and the open volume upon it. The book was *Men Who*

Wore The Tunic. She knew then that her husband was searching for anything that would give him the strength to go on. *Did he sleep at all?* she wondered.

'Reinforcements?' she asked.

'I guess,' he said, and he gave her the weakest of smiles. His face looked drawn and tired.

'I'm afraid I've got a faculty conference this morning. The Deanship is coming open and the infighting is fierce. Will you be here for dinner? It's my turn to cook.'

'I don't think so, Genny. Tomorrow is the sweep. I'll be down at Headquarters until everything is ready. You'll see me when I get here.'

Tomorrow is your birthday, too, DeClercq's wife thought. She turned to go, then stopped in mid-stride and glanced back at the policeman. 'Do me a favour? Please,' she said. 'Take it easy on yourself.'

'I will,' he assured her. But his voice lacked conviction.

Genevieve paused in the doorway as if she had something else to say, but in the end she said nothing and simply left the room. Several minutes later he heard her car drive away.

Alone in the greenhouse once again, Robert DeClercq stood listening to the rain on the glass roof. *Thump . . . thump . . . thump:* it sounded to him like the formal drum tattoo one hears at an RCMP funeral. He put Blake's Enfield down on the table and walked over to the greenhouse door to stare out at the angry sea. All the world before him stretched out dull and grey.

He thought about the Inspector. What sort of man had Blake really been? What had driven him on? No other member in the Force had left behind him such a strange, strange legacy. For within the formal version of history, the one which the RCMP records revealed, the Inspector was simply the finest detective that the Mounted Police had ever produced. His quota for stunning arrests had never been duplicated. It was said that his style of fighting in the British Army before joining the Force was awe-inspiring. The man literally knew no fear. His Victoria

242

Cross had been recommended by the Queen herself.

Still, there had been rumours.

When DeClercq was doing research for *Men Who Wore The Tunic*, he had taken it upon himself to interview all the old timers yet living from those early days of the Force. A number of them went back as far as the Royal Northwest Mounted Police.

Officially, within a few short years of joining the Force, Wilfred Blake had set himself up above all others as a first-class troubleshooter. The man's tracking ability was legendary, supposedly learned both in the Far East and from the North American Indians. If a task seemed impossible, it was assigned to Blake. For somehow he always came back with his man.

The rumours were born out of the fact that so many came back dead.

According to some, Commissioner Herchmer thought the Inspector's methods excessive. That was the reason that Wilfred Blake never rose in rank. Others, however, said that was because the Inspector enjoyed his position. Blake was just not the sort of man to ever abandon the hunt. He turned down promotion in order to stay exclusively in the field.

Whatever the rumours, DeClercq soon learned that they died with the mess hall chatter. For the Inspector's official service record had not one black mark upon it. Citation of Merit upon Citation of Merit continued in an unbroken succession. Most surprising, perhaps, was the recorded fact that in any given year toward the end of his service, Wilfred Blake spent eleven months out on the trail by himself. He never took a partner.

The brass of the Force at that time put it down to dedication.

Dedication, DeClercq now thought. *What would Wilfred Blake do if he were here to take on the Headhunter?*

He'd do whatever was necessary. Just like you're going to do.

DeClercq turned away from the door and once again picked up the Enfield. He could still see the flecks of rust caused by the time it had spent in the snow.

Yes, you do what you have to do, he thought, then he sat down at the table.

Inspector Chan had completed his computer-enhanced list of sex offenders, feeding in the psychological profile obtained from Dr Ruryk. The list presently contained every pervert within the province over the past thirty years. A second list of names covered those from across the rest of the country.

Tomorrow the Headhunter Squad would go out to sweep the streets of those offenders. Each one who could be found would either be questioned then and there or arrested for interrogation. The old British Columbia Penitentiary in New Westminster was now vacant and slated for eventual demolition. By Order-In-Council the federal government in Ottawa had placed the building at DeClercq's disposal.

Canada had a brand-new Constitution and a brand-new Charter of Rights. The Superintendent did not like the idea of abrogating such freedoms. But if that's what it took to catch the killer, that's what he would do.

Tomorrow, the Superintendent knew, his investigation would step over the line of the law.

But he also knew with the mood in this town, politically no one could stop him.

FOLLOW THAT MAN

12.17 p.m.

Corporal William Tipple was elated.

He had just returned from an overnight hike in the local North Shore mountains to find a message requesting that he call either Rick Scarlett or Katherine Spann at Headhunter Headquarters concerning John Lincoln Hardy. There was an even more important message, however, from Inspector Jack MacDougall ordering him to suspend whatever Commercial Crime investigation he was presently embarked upon and immediately prepare a complete set of wiretap transcripts on Steve Rackstraw. And then to top it off, a follow-up request had come from Sergeant Rodale on behalf of Scarlett and Spann asking for those same taps.

Tipple began surveillance of Rackstraw because of possible land transaction scams. Soon the case had expanded to include alleged music industry kickbacks and perhaps a prostitution ring. But that was all pretty dry stuff compared to a homicidal nut loose in a terrified city. Now fate it seems had intervened to steer the course of his investigation toward the Headhunter murders.

Corporal William Tipple was elated because he too was involved.

He had his foot in the door.

12.42 p.m.

Junk recognizes no holidays, no break in the daily routine. For in the world of the junkie life is measured out in eyedroppers full of heroin solution. To the body cells of the junkie life is but a continual pulse of shrinking and growing and shrinking again, the never-ending cycle of shot-need for every shot-completed. Junk is a prison guard: junk controls the cells.

Per capita Vancouver has the highest percentage of junkies in all of North America.

Not so many years ago the wise ones who sit on Vancouver City Council decided to close off Granville Street, the town's main drag, and turn it into a mall. A solid concrete mall stretching for many blocks.

Now the city fathers and mothers have never been known for their musical taste, and five'll get you ten that none of them listen to the Rolling Stones. For it is rumoured that they prefer instead the sort of classical sound that one can hear played again and again and again in any highrise elevator. Of course if only they had listened to *Exile On Main Street* they might have understood a bit about the junkie's frame of mind when it comes to environment. And if they had really listened, well then they'd never have built that mall. And Vancouver would not now have for its main thoroughfare a slab of concrete with down its centre a single weaving buslane just about as straight as the snakes that curve down the inner aspect of every junkie's elbow.

Vancouver can thank its Council for creating an instant slum.

The RCMP ghost car came slowly down the mall.

From the window on the passenger's side Katherine Spànn peered out through a light grey mist of rain to probe the face in each doorway.

She dismissed the woman with deep-sea eyes who seemed to stare out vaguely as if through a murky medium that she carried around with her.

She turned from the boy who jerked about like a marionette on a string, his slack jaw making him look like a ventriloquist's dummy.

She let the man go who was dressed in women's clothing and whose fleshless hips twitched as if to say, 'You should see me in the nude.'

She cast aside the peripheral dopers, the ones high on angel dust or benzedrine or knocked out of their skulls on goofballs.

She paid no attention to the fellow who staggered out of an alley with his face jerking at intervals like dead flesh coming alive, who fell down like some galvanized corpse with a toothless mouth pursed to give the impression that it had been sewn together with thread, his limp arm flopping in the gutter while a drop of blood bubbled up at the crease of his inner elbow.

For she had no interest in any of the regular junktown

people today. Today she was searching for either the Indian or John Lincoln Hardy.

'Nothing here,' Spann said. 'Let's go back to Gastown.'

It was as the ghost car entered Gastown's Maple Tree Square that afternoon – with its quaint narrow alleys and antique restaurants and liberal lawyers' offices – that Katherine Spann yelled suddenly: 'Turn right, Rick! It's him!'

The Indian was running before they were even out of the car.

He had been walking on the north side of the square about five feet away from Gassy Jack's statue when the screech of tyres on pavement told him: 'Run, you fucker, run.'

He ran.

By the time Rick Scarlett's feet hit the cobblestone pavement the Indian was climbing a wire-mesh fence at the end of Carrall Street and making for the water. The fence was eight feet high and it separated the City of Vancouver from the CPR lands that ran along the harbour. For one brief moment the cop caught a glimpse of the Indian outlined against the snowy ski-fields of Grouse Mountain across the Inlet, then the man vaulted the fence and dropped like a cat to make his way in leaps and bounds across the rain-slick railway tracks. Fifteen feet behind him, Scarlett hit the wire fence at the exact same moment as Spann.

They both scrambled and clawed with hands and feet to swing up and over the top. As he crested the barrier, Scarlett's uniform caught on a wire barb and ripped from his crotch to his knee. He ignored the fact and was running the second his shoes touched the ground.

'Watch out for the train!' Spann yelled, as she too completed the leap. She had just seen the Indian ahead of them throw himself under a boxcar.

Not a second later, with an ear-splitting slam, a CPR diesel engine hit the car next to the boxcar as it shunted the rolling stock together. With the grate of steel on steel the boxcar lurched forward. Luckily for him, the Indian was lying parallel to the tracks.

The instant the cars slowed down enough, the fugitive – seeing a break – rolled out between the moving front and back wheels of one of the boxcars to gain the other side. His left leg missed being pulverized by a distance of one foot. Then he was up and running.

Scarlett grabbed the ladder of a tanker and swung himself onboard. Within five seconds he had climbed up to the loading spout. It took one more second to slip over the top of the cylindrical tank. Then less than a second to let go and drop down to the ground.

He landed ten feet down the track from where he had climbed on.

His right foot slipped on the gore of a seagull squashed by one of the trains and he fell down on his face.

In the meantime Spann – playing it safe – had run to the right and around behind the shunting CPR engine. There was another train beyond but it was standing still. Twenty-five feet off to her left she saw Scarlett down on the ground.

On the far side of the second train lay a road that ran parallel to the harbour. It was the woman's guess that the Indian had made for it, turned left, and was now running west toward the CPR station. To turn right would take him into the hands of the National Harbours Board Police.

By the time Rick Scarlett had caught his breath and was struggling up to one knee, Spann had scaled the side of the second train and dropped down on the ground beyond. She ran across an old cobble road to a four-foot gravel bank. As she crested the embankment the peaks of the North Shore Mountains loomed up in front of her. Today the summits were cloaked with cloud and rain pockmarked the choppy purple waters below. She turned to her left and began to head for the office buildings of the city core that jut up out of the ground a quarter-mile away. The fleet-footed Indian was already half way there.

Spann picked up the chase.

The driver of the CPR engine was mildly surprised when Rick Scarlett burst into his cab. Were it not for the uniform he would have reached for a wrench. Milt Molesworth was getting on in age but he still had a memory like a trap. Back in the 1950s he had seen the very same situation that he was now living on TV in the programme *Follow That Man*. He truly expected this tattered Mountie to throw out one arm and shout those words.

Scarlett disappointed him.

'Let's move! Fast!' he yelled, pointing toward the station.

Molesworth replied, 'You're the boss,' as he reached for the throttle. After thirty-five years of shunting box-cars it was nice to have some action.

With a lurch, the engine moved forward.

As the diesel ran parallel to the stationary train on the right, Scarlett craned his neck for a look between each join of the cars. At one point he saw Katherine Spann running and wildly pumping her arms. Through the gap at another connection he saw tugboats chugging out of the harbour as the Seabus came in to dock. Then at yet a third point he caught a glimpse of the Indian frantically pulling at a door. The door was on the lowest level of the Seabus terminal and it was obviously locked.

'Stop this thing!' Scarlett ordered as the Indian once more took off running.

'You're the boss,' Milt said, and he jammed on the brake.

With a hump and then a hiss the engine stopped moving.

Scarlett jumped down and picked up on the chase. As he came around the western end of the stationary train, the wind and rain off the water slammed into his face. Katherine Spann shot by in front of him. To his left the

Indian was running beneath the rampway that led up to Burrard Street, to the Marine Building, and to the ritzy Vancouver Club. A man at the club window stared out with a bemused look as he sipped his Beefeater gin.

Just as Spann was about to collar the fugitive man, he threw himself into an opening under the ramp where wooden pilings rose out of the sea to give the structure support. As Scarlett ran up the Indian was starting to shinny along a crossbeam soaked with creosote.

'Damn!' Spann said as her grip closed on empty air. Then she crawled in after him.

It was dark under the ramp. For here was a murky claustrophobic space where water dripped down from holes worn in the asphalt above and the sea slapped angrily against the barnacle-encrusted old wooden pilings below. The air stank of rotting fish and sea salt and creosote oil carried up on the ocean spray tossed off by the lurching waves. From several of the crossbeams water rats sniffed at the intruders and blinked their seedy eyes. Both the Indian and Katherine Spann inched slowly forward. There was seven feet between them.

Ahead of the fugitive there was a second opening. Through it he could see the pier that jutted out into the sea. That opening and freedom was only five feet away. Then four. Then three. Then two. Then Rick Scarlett jumped down from the ramp above to land on the pier and stick his right hand through the opening.

'Police,' Scarlett said quietly from behind the gun in his fist.

In resignation, the Indian stopped creeping along the beam.

Spann closed the gap between them and reached out to grasp his foot. Suddenly a violent kick knocked her hand away. Then with a shove the cornered man pushed himself off from his perch and tumbled down into the water. The splash from his body hitting the sea drenched the woman above.

250

'Damn!' Spann said again, filling her lungs with air and plunging in after him.

Up on the pier Rick Scarlett stood and waited for both heads to surface. It was certainly not his intention to join these midday swimmers, preferring instead to wait up top where it was high and dry. Then abruptly it occurred to him that Spann would make the collar. That she would get first credit if something big came out of this. *Good God!* Scarlett thought. *She'd one-up me again.*

'Damn!' the man said aloud, then he too crawled in under the pier and tumbled into the water.

His timing was perfect. For no sooner had the Indian surfaced to get a breath of air than Scarlett landed squarely on him with his uniform boots. The Indian went back under. Crushed between the descending cop and the slope of the submerged shore he crumpled into a ball and choked out the last of his oxygen. By the time that he surfaced again, he was sputtering, wheezing and gasping. The man was in no condition to fight as they dragged him out of the water.

Scarlett snapped on the cuffs as Spann frisked him down.

'Jesus, Blondie!' the Indian exclaimed, recognizing the woman. 'I never made you for a narc!'

'It's a world of deceit,' Spann said, and she tugged off one of his boots. When she turned it upside down a red balloon fell out.

'You dropped something,' she said, holding out the heroin bundle.

'I never seen it before. You must have planted it on me.'

Scarlett unsnapped a button at the man's right wrist and yanked his shirtsleeve up to the elbow. The needle tracks exposed were more than seven inches long. The veins had long since disappeared, retreating down toward the bone to escape the incessant probe of a needle.

'I want a lawyer,' the Indian said. And then he started to shiver.

'I want information,' Katherine Spann said in reply.

As she spoke she watched the handcuffed man. His pupils were not pinned so he hadn't recently fixed. His body was beginning to move in jerks as if his clothes were made of poison ivy. She knew that the feel of water on skin was unpleasant to an addict, that this was why junkies were reluctant to take a bath. The Indian's nose was starting to run and he was beginning to sweat despite the chill in the air. She concluded that the man's junk-clock was running down. And that soon it would stop.

All cops know that addicts have a fear of time. For time leaves them jerking with no place to go. The only escape from external time is another stab of the needle.

Now all we do is wait, she thought, shivering herself.

'I'm freezing,' Scarlett said. 'Let's take this guy downtown.'

The Indian shivered and shook, his spasms slipping out of control. 'Oh, my skin,' he whispered.

Spann nonchalantly took a look at her watch, wondering in her mind if the water had ruined it. 'I'm waiting,' she said.

'F-f-f-fuck you!' But no sooner had the man spoken than a stomach cramp doubled him up.

'Make it easy for yourself. First tell us your name.'

The Indian said nothing.

'Tell me what I want and I promise I'll let you fix.'

'Y-y-yeah sure,' the man said. 'It's a w-w-world of fuckin' deceit.'

'I mean it,' Spann said, dangling the bundle before his nose.

The Indian jerked his head away and looked her in the eye. 'W-w-what do you want?' he asked, the withdrawal taking hold.

'Where do we find John Lincoln Hardy, that black dude that I saw you score from?'

'Go on!' the man said, trying to spit on the ground but his throat was just too dry.

252

'Tell us now or tell us later. We can wait it out.'

'Lemme fix now, cunt, if you're so fuckin' honest.'

Rick Scarlett lashed out to grab the man by the hair, but Spann was able to intercept and knock aside his hand. 'No Mutt and Jeff,' she said, scowling at her partner. Scarlett merely grunted, then he dropped his arm.

'Look!' the woman said sharply, turning back to the Indian. 'You don't have much choice here, so let's not screw around. You're wanted on three held warrants out of that undercover operation, all for trafficking. In addition we've now got you cold nuts on possession of junk for the purpose. And then to top it off, the state of your condition tells me that you need a fix. I think you just scored that bundle from Hardy and we got to you before you cranked yourself and farmed the rest of it out.

'Now, don't take me for stupid. If your idea of a good afternoon is writhing around on a jail cell floor while your guts to try to squirm out your mouth, be my guest. I don't care. We'll get Hardy all the same. If you talk all it does is save us time.

'So here's the deal. I know Hardy's your pusher, and I know you know how to find him. I can't do anything about the warrants from the undercover trip. They're already in the courts. But I will forget this beef. And I will let you fix. So there's the choice. Take it or leave it. A fix for John Lincoln Hardy.'

Out on the water a float plane droned across the harbour. The Indian winced as another contraction closed its violent fingers around the entrails in his belly. The drone died away as the seaplane banked and made for Vancouver Island.

'Take all the time you want,' Spann said and she opened the knot in the plastic balloon and shook out a Number 5 gelatin capsule. She pulled the pink half from the white half and tapped each rounded end to release the powder within. It blew away in the wind before it hit the ground.

She shook out another cap and emptied it also. Then another, while the Indian watched in horror.

'Where's Hardy?' Spann asked. The powder blew away.

A fourth cap lay in her hand before the junkie broke.

'Ah, fuck, Blondie! Don't be such an a-a-asshole. I don't know where he is! Gimme a fuckin fix!'

'What's your name?'

'J-j-joe Winalagilis.'

'Where's your outfit, Joe?'

'In a pouch in my other b-b-boot.'

'Take the cuff off one arm, Rick, and chain his other wrist to you.'

Scarlett did not look happy but he did as she suggested. The woman pulled off the second boot as the Indian sat on the ground. She turned it over and an outfit with a burnt spoon fell into her hand.

'Come on,' Spann said. 'Let's find some place to try and strike a deal.'

Single file, the three of them left the pier, Winalagilis stumbling and all three shivering. They made their way past the CPR Ferry dock, past the rows of container trucks down to where there was a tongue of rubble and rock and boom logs that stuck out into the sea. Alongside the mini-peninsula there was a small wooden dock. Moored to the dock with its prow pointing out at Stanley Park beyond the oil barges dotting the harbour was a sailboat swaying and rocking on purple-green water. From this dock they could just make out the Brockton Point totem poles half hidden within the Park's trees.

Winalagilis first, the three of them climbed onboard the boat.

Still soaking wet, they hunkered down in the stern where they were gone from the eyes of the city. Katherine Spann removed a cap from the balloon and emptied it into the spoon.

'I take two,' Winalagilis said.

She opened another one. It was still raining, so the rain

254

provided the water. The Indian had a lighter in his pocket which he took out. While Scarlett shielded the flame, the woman cooked up the mixture. The junk dissolved and she sucked it into the needle.

'Use my headband,' Winalagilis said, so she tied it around his arm. Then she tapped his skin continuously trying to raise a vein. The task was almost impossible. They were cowering down near the bone.

'Okay,' Spann said. 'This is the deal. In return for this jab you tell me all you know about Hardy. Agreed?'

The Indian shivered and nodded. 'Hit me, Blondie! Hit me!' he hissed with excitement in his breath.

Spann slid the needle in. Dark red blood spurted back into the outfit. 'Let it go!' Winalagilis ordered. But Spann didn't press the plunger.

The Indian blinked. 'What the fuck you doin?'

The woman looked him in the eye. 'Just so we're straight,' she said. 'You come clean on Hardy, and every one forgets this. You lie or fuck up, and we put out on the street that you were the rat. That should have you killed even before you're out of jail. Agreed?'

'Christ yes,' Winalagilis choked.

Spann let the headband go and squirted in the mix.

As the morphine blast hit him in waves, Joe Winalagilis relaxed. A long exhalation escaped from his lips, contentment lighting his face. He closed his eyes and kept them closed for several exhilarating minutes. When he finally opened them once again they were covered with glass.

'Okay,' Spann said. 'Where's John Lincoln Hardy?'

'Huh?'

'Hardy? Your pusher? Where is he?'

'I don't know,' Winalagilis said, his head going into a nod as he smiled from far, far away.

Scarlett looked at Spann and his eyes said, *You blew it*. What puzzled the woman was the feeling she got that this was what he secretly wanted.

'Where do you meet him to score the stuff?' Spann's voice was screwed up tighter.

255

'Huh? Oh . . . him.' A pause. 'He comes to me.'

'Where?' the woman demanded.

'Wherever he finds me . . . Blondie.'

'Look Joe, I'm warning you. I won't be played for a fool. You've got to have some meeting place where you score junk from him. Where is it?'

'You don't understand.'

'I understand that a deal is a deal.'

'You're making a mistake.'

'Cough up, my man, if you know what's good for you.'

'Your mistake is, Blondie, thinkin' he's pushin to me.'

Spann glanced at Scarlett as the fact sunk in.

'Truth is, it's *me* pushin to *him*,' the Kwakiutl said.

3.10 p.m.

The Japanese steam bath was Scarlett's idea.

By the time the two RCMP constables had returned Joe Winalagilis to the abandoned patrol car and transported him the two blocks to the Vancouver City Jail, all three of them were freezing cold and shivering out of control. The guard at the booking desk on the third floor took one look at them with a gambler's eye then turned to his partner and said: 'Five bucks says at least two of these three come down with pneumonia.' His partner checked them over and refused to take the bet.

A few minutes later while riding down in the elevator that would take them to the alley out back of 312 Main, Scarlett nudged Spann and said: 'How 'bout a steam?'

'What do you mean?'

'Look, by the time we get you to your place and me to mine, we could both be freezer material. Just a block from here there's an old Japanese steam bath with separate and private rooms. If you're not hung up on modesty, we can get warm and send our clothes out for a dry. If you are hung up, then drop me off and you go down with the ship.'

Katherine Spann shivered once more and said: 'Let's go.'

Fifteen minutes later Rick Scarlett was sitting alone in a

small, very old, pipe-lined room. With a towel wrapped around his waist, he slouched listening to the hiss of water vapour as he waited with anticipation for Spann to come in through the door.

On checking in they had paid a young Japanese to take their soggy uniforms to a local one-hour laundry, and then Spann had disappeared into the bathroom. Scarlett now occupied himself by imagining Katherine taking off her clothes.

His mind had her down to her panties when the door swung open. Scarlett nonchalantly counted the number of tiles on the floor.

He did not look up as the woman took two steps into the steam room and then stopped in order to adjust her lungs to the vapour. She had tied a towel around her waist in a Polynesian style. She stood near the door breathing in shallow breaths, her chest slowly rising and falling as she stretched her spine and her muscles. When she finally climbed onto the wooden bench and sat back against the wall, Scarlett looked up for no more than three seconds and muttered, 'Not bad, eh?'

'Not bad,' she said as he looked back down at the floor.

The next time Scarlett turned back, Spann had closed her eyes and was revelling in the warmth. Slowly he looked her over from head to toe. Then he stopped at her breasts.

That's the nicest pair of headlights I've ever seen, he thought.

Spann didn't open her eyes. She was lost somewhere in a world of warmth and relaxation. The man turned his attention to the towel around her waist. The steam and the sweat from her pores were making it stick to and outline her body. He stifled an almost irresistible urge to reach out and rip off the towel, and instead he bent forward to lean his arms on his thighs to hide his growing erection.

Yessiree, Rick Scarlett thought. *Do I want a piece of that.*

Now all he had to do was bide his time.

Soon the moment would come.

THE BIRTHDAY PRESENT

4.45 p.m.

It was a quarter to five by the time that Scarlett and Spann returned to Headquarters. The place was alive with activity as the Royal Canadian Mounted Police prepared for next day's roundup. There were computer printouts everywhere, sweep sheets being distributed, each with a mugshot photo attached for each suspect and a key word to open the software circuits printed at the side. Bulletin boards around the parade room were pinned with lists of assignments. As Scarlett went to check on the role that the two of them would be playing, Spann found the nearest free telephone and dialled Corporal Tipple at Commercial Crime. This time she made contact.

'You're a hard man to get hold of, sir. My name's Katherine Spann.'

'Good,' Tipple said. 'I've been waiting for your call. You working the Hardy angle?'

'Yes.'

'And you want to see the transcripts?'

'Very much so.'

'Okay. How about tomorrow morning before you go out on the sweep? I've been reassigned to your squad and right now I'm in the process of putting the Damballah ones together. I'll have 'em for tomorrow.'

'Damballah?' Spann asked, knowing the word had a voodoo connection.

'Damballah Enterprises. That's Rackstraw's holding company. You'll see what I mean tomorrow.'

'When and where shall we meet?'

'Roll call's set for 7.00 a.m. So how 'bout 6.15? In the parade room?'

'We'll be there.'

'Right. Bring your reading glasses. These guys are very busy dudes.'

11.56 p.m.

'Is it lonely up at the top, Robert?' Avacomovitch asked.

'Oh hello, Joseph,' DeClercq said, turning from the window. 'I was just turning tomorrow over in my mind.'

'Okay if I interrupt?'

'Of course. I'd like the company.'

It was closing on midnight and the room was filled with shadows cast off by the desk lamp. The surface of the desk was piled high with computer sheets and projections, police files and copious notes in DeClercq's even hand. On the edge of the desk closest to Avacomovitch a space had been reserved for a picture in a silver frame. It had not been there the last time that the scientist was in here. The Russian picked it up and looked at the woman in the photo.

'She has very intelligent eyes,' he said, 'set in a beautiful face.'

'Yes, doesn't she,' the Superintendent replied. 'I'm a lucky man.'

There was something in his voice that arrested Avacomovitch's attention. For more than half a minute he took a long close look at the man. DeClercq did not look well. There were now heavy bags under his eyes and lines of tension radiating out to the edge of his face. Though he tried hard to mask it there was also a nervous tic to his mouth. It appeared as though he had been robbed of sleep and left utterly exhausted. He looked as if the weight of the investigation upon his shoulders might buckle his legs at any moment. But strangely, more than anything else, it was a sense of irony that the Russian picked up from this man.

His heart went out to DeClercq.

Carefully, Avacomovitch replaced the photograph on

the edge of the desk. He turned it so that the woman could watch DeClercq when he sat in his chair. He thought: *In the currency of friendship there is only a single test. Will your friend be at your side if you should ever need him?*

'May I be blunt?'

'By all means do.'

'You're too hard on yourself.'

'Funny. That's the same thing Genevieve said this morning.'

'I think you're taking too much on your shoulders. I want this guy as much as you, you know?'

'I believe you do.'

'So share the burden. Spread the load around. The Headhunter is taunting you because you're the figure-head among his adversaries. It builds him up by having a rival equal to himself. It could be anyone, sitting in your chair.

'The trouble is, I think, you take it personally. Don't you see that lets him get to you? And that's just what he wants. If this were chess, he's making you play the defensive game.'

'Perhaps.'

'Robert, please understand. When the Headhunter throws barbs at you, he spikes me too. I'm a policeman also, albeit the civilian kind. This Force means a lot to me, just as it does to you. *You* mean a lot to me, you're one of my few friends. Remember all those years ago when I was totally adrift? I burned every bridge by defecting and there I was alone. Isolated. Well you helped me though, helped me assimilate. Robert, I owe you a debt. Hell, I owe myself a debt. And I want to pay it off. So let me work this with you. And I mean really work it. I want half the load.'

For several minutes the Superintendent said nothing. It was obvious he was moved. Finally he walked over and put his hand on the other man's shoulder and pointed at the corkboard. The operations visual now covered every bit of wallspace with many overlaps.

'Okay, Joseph. You're on. What do you suggest we do?'

Avacomovitch smiled.

'First, two things,' he said, 'to help us tighten the net. One: let's request every distributor of Polaroid film in this city and the outskirts get the name from identification of customers making a purchase. If anyone balks, they take a description and call the Headhunter Squad.'

'Good idea. And the second.'

'I give you a birthday present, and you tell me what you think.'

DeClercq's brow rose. He looked at his watch and saw it was after twelve. *What a memory*, he thought.

'Come on,' Avacomovitch said. 'I've got it down in the lab.'

The Superintendent followed him down the stairs to the makeshift laboratory. Except for a light on the Russian's desk, the room was now in darkness. The light was shining on a large bifocal microscope and a note-covered pad beside it.

'Take a look,' the scientist said. 'Happy birthday.'

When DeClercq looked down the barrel of the instrument and adjusted it into focus, what was magnified before his eyes was a dull black sliver. Behind him Avacomovitch said, 'When I examined the bones of Liese Greiner kicked up by that little girl, I found that lodged in a hairline fracture in her front pubic bone. It could have been debris from the area and of no forensic value. But it's not. It's foreign to the scene and has some sort of significance, though what I have no idea. It took me quite a while to get it identified.'

'What is it?' DeClercq asked.

'A splinter of ebony.'

261

DAMBALLAH

Thursday, November 4th, 7.45 a.m.

'I don't think he looks well,' Monica Macdonald said.

'Who, DeClercq?'

'Yeah.'

'I guess the pressure's getting to him,' Katherine Spann replied.

Rick Scarlett said: 'What do you think he meant when he said to keep an eye peeled today for anything made of ebony. And why does he insist on knowing personally?'

'Beats me. Maybe it's got something to do with his fear of tunnel vision. Keep us all in the dark so we don't over-look a thing.'

'Personally,' Tipple said, 'I thought he went a little overboard on the concept of duty.'

'Perhaps,' Rusty Lewis said. 'But don't you get the feeling that man really means it when he says we have a sacred trust to "Maintain the Right".'

'I don't know,' the Corporal said slowly. 'This whole idea of a sweep is on pretty shaky ground. If we score with one of these guys, the lawyers will have a field day. Mark my words that Charter of Rights is going to make it as hard for us up here as the cops have it in the States.'

'Maybe the right he's talking about isn't – legal right,' Lewis replied. 'Maybe it's moral right.'

'Anyway,' Monica Macdonald said, 'DeClercq moved me this morning. I say we get the job done.'

'I agree,' Lewis said. 'He moved me too.'

Macdonald opened the door and they both turned up their collars and walked out in the pouring rain. Tipple, Spann, and Scarlett were left standing in the front hall at Headhunter Headquarters.

'May I see those taps again?' Katherine Spann asked. The Corporal passed the transcripts to her. As the woman leafed through the pages reading them one more time, Scarlett looked out at the rain and asked: 'How do you suggest we go about finding Hardy?'

'Don't know,' Tipple replied. 'I've never seen the guy. He just shows up on the tapes every now and then. Rackstraw's been my quarry, not Hardy.'

'Strange no one seems to know the telephone is tapped.'

'If you saw the set-up, you'd understand why.'

Scarlett was silent for a minute. Beyond the door the skies were sodden and grey with the afterbirth of one storm while a new wave of thunderclouds shoved in from the sea. Still the rain came down.

'What about the cousin?' he asked. 'Where do we look for him?'

'I think you should leave his studio alone so he doesn't wise to the tap.'

'Studio?'

'Yeah, the man is involved in the music business. Runs it under a holding company called Damballah Enterprises Ltd.'

'Damballah is the snake god in voodoo.'

'I know. Why don't you try to find him tonight down at the London Calling. That's a club on Pender.'

Tipple fished into his pocket and removed a small telephone pole poster. There were rips in all four corners where staples had once secured it. It read:

Save Yourself For Thursday Night, November 4th, 1982
LIVE IN CONCERT FROM ENGLAND
RAW-T
With Special Guests
VOODOO CHILE
Save Your Soles!
The London Calling Ballroom,
742 West Pender Street.

'Why do you think he'll be there?' Rick Scarlett asked.

'Voodoo Chile's his band,' Tipple said in reply.

Katherine Spann had folded the corner on one of the transcript pages. Once she had perused all the rest she turned back to that one. She held it out to Tipple.

'This tap is long distance, Bill. Where's it coming from?'

'Let's see,' Tipple said. He took the transcript from her and read:

Incoming call. Long distance.

Fox:	Hey hey.
Operator:	I have a collect call from Mr Wolf. Will you accept the charge?
Fox:	Yes I will.
Wolf:	It's cooking on the 6th . . . The pot boils over at midnight.
Fox:	I'm ready . . . The cous will be down there to see all you.
Wolf:	Ah . . . Right . . . be seein' the man then.
Fox:	Okay, bye for now.
Wolf:	*Au Revoir*.

Finished reading, Tipple looked up and said: 'That call's from New Orleans.'

THE SWEEP

8.36 a.m.

They hit the pornographer's first.

Rick Scarlett entered the sex shop on Granville Street close to the Granville Bridge wearing a raincoat over his uniform and with his soaked head bare. The store was already open to catch the early morning crowd – or at least that was the front. Walking swiftly up to the counter the policeman skipped his eyes around the shop, taking in the shelves of skin mags and books all sealed in plastic wrappers, then he leaned forward over a display case of artificial vaginas and Suck-U-Lators and asked for something in rubber.

The man behind the counter was in his late forties, a thick-set balding individual with a fat savage face and wet, sneering lips. His eyes held the look of someone preoccupied with thoughts of sex every waking hour. Scarlett was quite sure that he dreamt about it too. As the cop spoke, the man looked up from a book titled *The Variations of Anal Intercourse* and taking in the raincoat sized him up for a flasher. In that opinion the man was correct.

With a flourish, Rick Scarlett flipped open the outer garment to reveal his uniform beneath.

'Oh shit!' the man behind the counter said, and his eyelids snapped wide like blinds released and flapping over windows. His left hand reached out for a button on the wall, but before the fingers could get there Scarlett seized hold of his wrist.

'No alarm,' the cop warned, 'or you're in big, *big* trouble.'

As the fat man dropped his arm, Katherine Spann came in through the front door. She ran across to where an entrance gave access to the girlie peep-show booths in the rear of the shop and pulled back the curtain. Behind there were six booths lined along one wall. Two sets of men's feet showed below the hinged half-door on one of the cubicles. Beyond the booths was another door set into the wall. The woman tried it and found it locked.

Moving swiftly across the corridor, she braced herself with her back to the opposite wall. Pushing off with both hands, Spann propelled herself across the passageway, raising her right leg to connect with the door just above its lock and handle, her left leg keeping up the momentum. The door burst inward amidst a shower of splinters.

Inside the room two men were sitting on a bench against the left wall. One of the men was a 'bomber pilot', his head now up in the clouds and exploding with chemical flak. His body was in a slouch and his jaw hung slackly open, his fingers caressing a pair of little girl's panties. The other man was Kurt Schmidt, who was also the manager of the Silver Screen Theatre. Schmidt's abdomen was still bandaged from where the feminist had slashed it with the razor. As the door crashed in Schmidt was in the process of focusing a 35 mm Pentax camera.

To the left and right of both men, banks of high-powered lights shone down upon a raised dais to the right of the door. Two children now stood on that platform. One was a young girl no more than nine or ten who was dressed in a tiny black lace corset and wearing miniature nylon stockings. Her crotch was bare and her face was painted with the heavy makeup of a whore. The other was a young boy the same age as the girl. He was naked except for a fedora on his head and a plastic Thompson submachine gun in his hands. The boy's genitals had been rouged red.

'Jesus, no!' Schmidt exclaimed as Spann came hurtling into the room. He reacted immediately, wrenching the back of the camera open to expose and ruin the film. Then he turned to run. Reaching out with one hand the woman grabbed him by the arm, but Schmidt jerked free. He swung back his left hand to punch her in the nose just as Rick Scarlett came flying through the door.

It had taken several seconds for the bomber pilot to come out of his haze. He was very stoned and only now beginning to realize that this was a raid. It was as the spaceman was struggling to gain his feet and get up off the bench that Scarlett pulled his .38 and aimed it at Schmidt's head.

'Freeze! Police!' Scarlett yelled.

And both men froze.

10.50 a.m.

Macdonald and Lewis were not prepared for the man who answered the door. Dexter Flesch did not look remotely like his mugshot, but then the police picture was over eight years old.

To start with, the Constables were surprised to find that a D. Flesch still resided at the West End apartment address recorded in the police file. In 1974 the man they were now seeking had pleaded guilty to eleven counts of indecent assault on a female. He had served one year in prison with a two-year probation order on release requiring him to see a psychiatrist at least twice a month. The psychiatric condition was because his MO had been a little peculiar.

On May the 10th of 1974, Dexter Flesch – wearing a white smock with a stethoscope around his neck – had entered the gymnasium of a local high school while a class of Grade 12 girls was having Physical Education. The man had flashed a printed College of Physicians and Surgeons card at the instructress and had then taken the woman aside for a *sotto voce* talk. The truth was, Flesch told her, that he had been sent by the School Board to check on an outbreak of . . . well, to put it simply . . . of crabs among the graduating class. It seemed that these genital parasites (and here Flesch lowered his voice even more) were emanating from a young lady in this very class. Did the instructress have any idea – all in the *strictest* of confidence, of course – just who the carrier might be?

Yes, the instructress had told Flesch, there were one or two girls who she suspected of having hinges on their heels.

'Then let's take a look,' Dexter Flesch had said.

The man had set up a temporary clinic in the Phys. Ed. teacher's office and had asked that the girls be brought to

267

him one at a time, starting with the most promiscuous, in order that he might examine them to isolate the carrier. The instructress had been more than pleased to oblige.

It was unfortunate, however, that the cause of personal hygiene was not to prevail that day. For as luck would have it the school nurse had come down to the gym to fill out a report on an injury incurred that morning during an earlier class. She found Dexter Flesch lowering the gym shorts of his twelfth victim.

In a way Flesch was lucky. A few more seconds and by gum he might have been subsequently facing a twelfth count of indecent assault.

That was eight years ago. The D. Flesch who answered the door today was a very different man. On seeing him Lewis looked at Macdonald and Macdonald looked right back. Neither one of the cops was prepared for this. *It's a mixed up world*, Rusty Lewis thought.

'Yes,' Flesch said in a voice as soft as corn silk. 'What is it you want?'

'We'd like to talk to Dexter Flesch,' Monica Macdonald said, frowning.

The person who stood before them in the open doorway had eyes like a cat and every few seconds he licked the lips of his feral mouth like a kitten licking cream. His hair was red, exploding from his head to cascade down about his shoulders in ringlets of fire. The makeup that covered his features was almost a work of art. In a rough estimate, Monica Macdonald calculated that it would have taken him over two hours to apply.

The man's figure was a perfect hour glass and he knew just how to show it off. He wore a black French push-up peek-a-boo bra over his small pert breasts and a black sheer blouse over that. The suit that encased the rest of his frame was sewn from white linen, definitely hand-tailored. His nails were red; his boots were snakeskin; his only jewellery was two gold hoop earrings and a bracelet of gold fashioned to look like a snake that twisted around his left arm. To be honest with himself, Rusty Lewis thought that this man was perhaps the most beautiful woman that he had ever seen. The only female who even came close was a lawyer by the name of Lorelei Ashe who had once made a complete fool out of Lewis in the witness stand. But Ashe didn't have these eyes.

Please God, don't give me a hard-on, Lewis thought with a smile.

Flesch said: 'I'm afraid that Dexter is no more. He's gone away forever.'

'Where has he gone?' Monica Macdonald asked.

'Just gone,' Flesch said with a vacant fly-away wave of one hand.

'Which are you, Miss Flesch?' the woman asked softly. 'Transvestite or transexual?'

The man who was now a woman gave her a sloe look. 'I've had the nip and tuck,' he said.

'Do you mind if we come in?' Rusty Lewis asked.

'Yes, I'm afraid I do. I'm just on my way to work and I'm late already.'

'Where do you work? What do you do?' Macdonald asked.

'I teach women makeup art at a modelling studio. I transform frumpy housewives. Now if you'll please excuse me?'

'Miss Flesch, I'm afraid we can't. We're with the Squad investigating the Headhunter killings,' Lewis said.

Flesch blinked. 'I-I don't understand,' he said. 'What has that to do with me?'

'Can you account for your whereabouts in the last three weeks?' Monica Macdonald asked.

'My what! My what! You think I . . . You're crazy, sister!'

'I'm not your sister, Miss Flesch. And I want a straight answer. Where have you been for the last . . .'

Suddenly the cat-eyes widened as Flesch took one step back and tried to slam the apartment door. Lewis stuck out his foot in time to prevent it closing. With one hand he pushed the door back open sharply.

'You . . . you . . . you . . . PIGS!' Flesch screamed shrilly, his voice turning very high pitched.

'Take it easy,' Macdonald said. 'Don't let . . .'

'STAY AWAY FROM ME, YOU . . . YOU FUCKING PIGS.' Now there was a hysterical look growing in the transexual's eyes. 'JUST WHO THE FUCK DO YOU THINK YOU ARE, CALLING ME . . . ME! – . . . A RAPIST!'

'Nobody called you a rapist!' Lewis said, raising his own voice.

'LEAVE ME ALONE! JUST GET THE FUCK OUT OF HERE!'

'Calm down!' ordered Lewis, but before either Constable could make a move to restrain him, Flesch whirled on his spiked heels and leapt up on a glass table in the entrance hall of the apartment. The tiny sole on one of the heels must have worn away for an abrupt sound of metal scraping glass took a shred from Macdonald's nerves. Then her momentary shudder turned to awe as Flesch wrenched his belt free and dropped both slacks and panties.

Monica Macdonald found it hard to believe that here she was, standing in this man's residence, confronting this woman who was the man they sought, her eyes now staring at a set of female genitalia as anatomically perfect as any of the vulvas that she had seen bared on all those strip-show stages. She thought: *We're all cut off at birth with a knife and left at the mercy of strangers*. Perhaps Dexter Flesch had once had the same thought, but had taken it literally.

'DON'T YOU COPS UNDERSTAND! CAN'T YOU FUCKERS SEE!' Flesch shrieked, his face turning purple with rage. 'I'M NOT A RAPIST! I'M A LESBIAN!'

Then the outburst was over. Without another word Flesch crumpled down onto the glass surface of the table and rolled onto the floor. Then he started to weep.

A few minutes later Monica Macdonald took hold of his arm and gently helped him to his feet. By then the art of makeup on Flesch's face was streaked and smeared and running.

12.20 p.m.

The call for assistance was clocked in at just after noon. Scarlett and Spann were a mile away, having just come out of a dilapidated two-storey walkup on East Broadway where they had failed to find a six-time convicted pederast. They caught the squeal on their patrol car radio the second they climbed in. Less than fifteen minutes later they were at the scene.

When their car had skidded to a stop on the rain-drenched pavement, Monica Macdonald left a doorway and came running through the storm up to the driver's side. Scarlett rolled down the window and a wet spray blew in.

'There might be a rumble,' the woman said. 'We're waiting on Rabidowski.'

'Where's the clubhouse?' Scarlett asked.

'Around the corner and down a block. Rusty's got it covered.'

'How did it come down?' As Scarlett spoke Katherine Spann drew her .38 from its Sam Browne and checked the action. She snapped the cylinder shut with a sharp flick of her wrist.

Monica Macdonald said: 'We were looking for a biker by the name of Whip O'Brian. Guy's out here from Alberta. Back home in Edmonton he strikes the colours of The Barbarians, but lately Special E says he's been riding bike with the Iron Skulls. He's got connections through a brother.'

'He's got a record?' Spann asked.

'O'Brian did seven, five, and one a few years back in Calgary for rape, buggery and bestiality. The guy's a speed freak. Some woman ripped him on an amphetamine deal so he got even by attacking both her and her invalid brother. The two of them had a dog. Believe me, this man's dangerous. He's not all there.'

'Is he inside the clubhouse?'

'Yep, with about ten other bikers. Maybe more. Rusty

271

and I were casing the place when this group of guys on hogs came blasting out of the rain. They had a woman with them and they dragged her inside. She didn't look happy at all. Word from Special E is that the Skulls are taking strikers. I peg her for a mama to be used in the initiation.'

'A gang bang?' Scarlett asked.

'That's my bet,' Monica said. 'Today. Right now.'

'Damn. Where's Rabidowski?'

Just as he spoke a police van came wheeling out of the rain. The Mad Dog was at the wheel. As three large men with Remington pump shotguns and semi-automatic rifles climbed out from the back of the vehicle, Spann noticed a V of steel welded to the front bumper. It looked like a battering ram.

Rabidowski rolled down the window. 'Who can give directions?'

'I can,' Macdonald said.

'Okay, you and Scarlett come with me. Spann, you take these guys in the cruiser and follow right behind. The moment I take down the door everyone goes in. Got it? Let's roll.'

As Katherine Spann took the driver's seat, one ERT man climbed in front with her and the other two took the back, each one jamming his door open with a metal flashlight. The rear doors of a cruiser cannot be opened from inside.

'Hang on,' the woman said, and the four of them were moving.

Up ahead, Rabidowski took the corner in a skid and then fishtailed down the street. As Spann gained on him the van began a wide arc that led to the clubhouse door. Suddenly motorcycle hogs were flying in every direction and the brick frame dwelling where the Iron Skulls ruled loomed up out of the storm. The sound of the hit was deafening.

At just the last moment Mad Dog Rabidowski stepped on the brakes to hold back their momentum. The ram welded to the front of the van slammed the heavy-bolted door and threw it careening open. The police vehicle was seven feet down the entrance corridor and two feet into the meeting room before it screeched to a halt. The Mad Dog slid it into reverse and pressed the accelerator. Tyres spinning the vehicle came flying back outside just as the SWAT Team jumped out of the cruiser followed quickly by Spann. The woman's Smith and Wesson was gripped in her hand.

'Come on!' Rabidowski shouted, grabbing a Heckler and Koch from the seat and swinging open the door. Macdonald and Scarlett tumbled out. Then they all went running in.

The clubhouse was pandemonium.

In the centre of the large room there was an eight foot high representation of a human skull made from welded and riveted iron plates. The room itself was in darkness, the only light cast by several Bosch headlamps which shone forward out of the eye sockets of the skull. The jaws of the Death Head were open and the teeth of the mouth, which were actually iron plates, bit down on the fuel tank of a 750 cc Harley Davidson that was half emerged from the throat.

The woman was tied facing the skull with each of her wrists roped to one of the prongs of the handlebars. Her clothes had been ripped down the centre of her back and were now hanging off her in tatters. Standing behind her with one hand gripping her hair and the other clutching her waist was a man whose face was scarred by a dozen old criss-cross knife slashes. His hair was dirty and hung down in matted hanks, his body was naked except for a jean jacket with the sleeves torn off and a crest on the back which screamed FEAR THE BARBARIANS. His skin, in the light of the headlamps, shone with motorcycle grease and the man had an erection.

Not five seconds ago – before the police assault vehicle had taken down the door – almost thirty bikers had been seated on chairs drinking beer and watching the performance. These men had upper chests of ripcord muscle from years of pumping iron, and bellies bloated by floods of ale that now strained at their jackets. All of them had tattoos.

One second after the door came in not a man remained in his seat. For now they were running and diving for weapons and turning to meet the threat. Most were armed with baseball bats and pipes and axes and chains. The first biker to reach Rabidowski was armed with a tyre iron. With one hand he reached out to grab the cop as the other arm raised high in the air to crack the iron down on his skull. The Mad Dog judo chopped him once and dropped the man to the ground. Then he pointed the Heckler and Koch up toward the ceiling and pulled off a rapid burst. Casings spewed out on the floor amid the sound of a US Fourth of July.

As chunks of wood fell down from the roof and the rain came dripping in, Rick Scarlett for the second time that day shouted: 'Freeze! Police!'

And once again, luckily, everybody froze.

EBONY

10.12 p.m.

When they got to the London Calling, now in plain clothes, they walked into the fifties.

The London Calling Ballroom had transformed itself over several decades. Built before the Second World War it had swayed to the big band era, then later it had jitter-bugged, jived and Motowned up to the days of psychedelics. In the late sixties the club had been known as the Synapse Circus, and during the reign of President

Nixon had been the home of Dare To Be Great. Now it was back to rocking with your English rock 'n' roll. English rock, that is, in the classic American style.

They had missed Voodoo Chile.

When they entered the club the lights were on and several roadies up on stage were dismantling equipment. The job was half completed. What caught the attention of both officers immediately was a trellis structure above the stage that held the lights and some of the speakers. The trellis was covered right and left with almost fifty voodoo masks.

'Want a beer?' Scarlett asked, looking for a table.

'Sure,' Spann said. 'This place makes me want to smoke in the school washroom and neck at the drive-in with James Dean.'

'How about me?'

'Nope. You're not Marlon Brando.'

'Don't be cruel,' Scarlett said with his finest Presley sneer.

Two men were leaving a table so Spann quickly grabbed it. She sat down on one of the wooden chairs and slowly took in the club. A majority of the men had haircuts with short back and sides. Quiffs were slicked back with Brylcreem and Wildroot Oil. Some wore zoot-suits with padded shoulders and thin, thin ties.

As the speakers cut in with a canned *Rebel Rouser* Spann surveyed the women.

There were those trying to look like Brenda Lee in red satin dresses with crinolines showing all leg and no breast. Others had close-cropped hair dyed every hue and shade – blue, orange, yellow, purple, chartreuse – while their bodies were hidden beneath men's shirts with the shirt-tail hanging out. There were paste-skinned girls in mini-skirts with black-circle slut-lined eyes. There were women with bobbysocks and ponytails, most of them smoking cigarettes holding their fingers on top and their thumbs underneath, one or two with a steady's ring on a chain around the neck.

'Jesus,' Scarlett muttered, returning with the beer. 'You should see the bar. It makes you want to thumb your nose and cruise for chicks and try to cop a feel. There's nothing but muscle and mouth. There's a toilet on top of the counter filled to the brim with match-books and I saw this one dude chewing on a toothpick and practising through-the-teeth spitting. What a mad-house.'

'What's this?' Spann said after tasting her mug of beer.

'They've got English draught on tap, warm and flat as it should be. The place even honours English pounds.'

As the woman placed the mug down on the table she saw that its wooden surface was carved. Back in the sixties some freak had written in a fine classic script: 'People are strange, but people are nice.' More recently someone had scratched over it: 'Fuck you and your mother.'

'The door to the left,' Scarlett said. 'That must be the place.'

Spann looked back to the stage. By now one roadie had collected all the voodoo masks and placed them in several cartons. He had carried the boxes one by one off to the left of the platform. As the woman watched she saw him knock on a door to the left of the stage. When it opened she caught a brief glimpse of a tall black man wearing a yellow suit. The roadie took in the boxes, then left, and a guard came out of the room to stand in front of the door.

'That cat looks like Rackstraw. He fits Tipple's description.'

'Let's wait till the second act comes on and they kill the lights. Then let's pay a visit,' Rick Scarlett said. He wiped some beer foam off his mouth with the back of his hand.

While they waited out the intermission and the roadies set up equipment, Scarlett busied himself by trying to place what was coming out of the speakers. Most of the old ones he recognized – Carl Perkins and Johnny Horton and Gene Vincent and Eddie Cochran. Most of the new ones he did not. It was during a souped-up version of *Up the Lazy River* that a woman at the next table offered a joint to Spann.

'No thanks,' Katherine said. 'I'm already flyin'.'

'Suit yourself,' the woman replied, and she shrugged her shoulders vaguely.

Spann said: 'We missed the first act. Were they any good?'

'You like voodoo rockabilly? The Cramps? That sorta thing?'

'Some,' the cop said.

'Then you might like Voodoo Chile. They use two drummers and a standup bass. Not my cup of . . .'

The lights were killed suddenly and she cut off the sentence. Around the club people began to stomp their feet. There was hooting. There was yelling. There was whistling. Then a single spotlight lit up a high-school blackboard up on the stage. Scrawled in chalk across its surface were the words: 'Erase the Blackboard Jungle!'

An announcer's voice cut in. 'Tonight, live from London, England by way of the USA. May we have a warm Vancouver welcome for the one and only . . . RAW-T!'

With the shout that delivered his last word, a man's arm burst out of the dark onstage and into the stab of the spotlight where – before anyone could cover their ears – four blackpainted fingernails scraped across the surface of the blackboard. The amplified screech that followed shredded a nerve or two. A microphone nearby magnified the noise about seven trillion times. As Scarlett gritted his teeth and Spann's neck-hairs stood on end, the lights onstage exploded and a born-again Buddy Holly ripped into *There's Good Rockin' Tonight*.

'Let's go!' Scarlett shouted.

They abandoned their beer and the table and made for the far left wall.

As they approached the door to the left of the stage, Spann began to play the drunk and leaned on Scarlett's shoulder. As soon as she was within distance the woman fell into the arms of the guard. For a second or two the man took a peek down her neckline and in that moment of distraction Scarlett dashed for the door. With a crash he swung it open – and interrupted a party.

In the centre of the small room a black man and a white man were leaning over a tabletop mirror covered with chopped cocaine. As one man took a snort from a spoon, Scarlett said: 'It's the police.' Involuntarily, in surprise, the man inhaled the powder into his lungs by mistake, and abruptly began choking and coughing and wheezing. The cocaine on the tabletop rose like a cloud into the air.

'Hey, what's this shit?' Yellow Suit said as Spann also moved in through the door.

He snapped a glance at the worried guard who came running in behind her. Turning, the woman kneed the man in the groin and dropped him to his knees. As she kicked the door shut RAW-T was just beginning the Big Bopper's *Chantilly Lace*.

'Let's all take it easy,' Scarlett said calmly, 'so no one else gets hurt.'

Apart from the two cops there were six black men in the room along with the single white. All the blacks wore leather jackets and had their hair straightened, swept back in pompadours like Little Richard. The white looked like an extra from *Rebel Without A Cause*. Yellow Suit didn't fit in. He was standing over near a bench along which several voodoo masks were set out. The blank faces of the masks seemed to stare up at him as if waiting in anticipation for the confrontation that was coming. There were guitars and drums scattered everywhere.

'What do you want?' Yellow Suit asked as cocaine settled like snow throughout the room.

'We're looking for John Lincoln Hardy.' Scarlett took out his shield.

'Well, he ain't here. That's obvious.'

'Who are you?'

278

Yellow Suit paused a moment, then said: 'Rackstraw. Steve Rackstraw.'

'Who's he?' Scarlett asked, indicating the coughing man.

'Ask him.'

'I said, who is he? And I expect an answer.'

'One of the drummers,' Rackstraw said. 'Didn't you catch the show?'

'Where's Hardy?'

'I've no idea. I'm not the man's keeper.'

'Would you rather talk about the dope?'

Rackstraw didn't answer.

'Kathy, how much stuff do you think is floating about the room?'

'Perhaps an ounce and a half.'

'That's PPT, Rackstraw. And trafficking's the big one.'

'You got nothin' on me, man. I'm leaving to call a lawyer.'

'The coke's in the room. You're in the room. That's enough for me. You can make your call downtown.'

'That ain't sufficient evidence.'

'You tell that to the judge.'

For several seconds the man stood still, contemplating his position. Rackstraw wore his hair in a tight Afro and sported rings on every finger. His cafe-au-lait complexion contrasted with the suit. It was hand-tailored and pulled in at the waist. Beneath the concern that showed in his eyes he had a pencil-thin moustache tailored to his lip.

'Okay,' Rackstraw said finally. 'Can you and I talk in private?'

'Where?' Scarlett asked.

The man indicated a washroom off to the right. They left the room. Once inside the toilet, the black man closed the door and the white man leaned on the wall. Rick Scarlett waited.

'What do you want Johnnie for? You know the man's my cousin?'

'I know,' the policeman said.

'So what's goin' down?' Rackstraw sat on the edge of the sink with one foot on the floor.

'One of his girlfriends got herself iced by a psychotic killer. We're trying to trace her movements. We think Hardy was her pimp. Perhaps he lined up a john.'

'I see. You open to a suggestion?'

'Try me,' Scarlett said.

'Okay. You leave me alone, and the boys alone, and I'll put you in touch with Hardy. But it'll take a couple of days.'

'Where is he now?'

'Not till we got a deal.'

The policeman thought a moment. In effect this was the exact same trip as Winalagilis and his fix. Same game, different players.

'All right,' Scarlett said, 'here's what I can do. We'll take the two on the mirror plus the stash of cocaine. You we let go. You produce Hardy and we'll reconsider the charge. If not we pick you up.'

'Come on, man. Have a bit o' heart. I own these niggers and honky, lock stock and barrel. Next month we start a tour of over forty cities. They gotta practise. They can't be in the can.' The man reached into his pocket and pulled out a tour schedule. 'Here, look at this. Even John my cousin ain't worth a forty-city circuit. How am I gonna welch if you know where I am?'

Scarlett glanced at the paper. 'Okay, a compromise. No arrests now but we take the powder. And I want a ransom. Give me one of those masks.'

Rackstraw frowned. He was puzzled by the suggestion. 'You don't know what you're askin,' he said. 'Those masks are antiques. Each one is more than a hundred years old.'

'Good. Then I'll take two. You see, my man, I want to check if you got customs clearance. Those masks are not from here.'

'I don't need customs clearance. They're antiques.'

'That means you don't pay duty. They still got to clear.'
Rackstraw sighed.

'Where's Hardy?'

'LA.'

'What for?'

'Scoutin' a record deal.'

'When's he back?'

'Don't know. Depends how long it takes.'

'Okay, you produce Hardy and we kill the charges and give you back the masks. You don't produce Hardy and we drag both you and your band off stage on a warrant. A deal?'

'Shit,' Rackstraw said. 'Yeah, it's a deal.'

The two men left the washroom and returned to the larger room. Scarlett and Spann took down the names of all those present and as best they could collected up the scattered powder. Scarlett then found an empty box and walked along the row of masks set out on the bench. He stopped beside a black Demon's Face with a curled protruding tongue. As he picked it up, the voodoo mask slipped from his fingers and tumbled toward the floor. Scarlett managed to catch it just before it smashed.

'Jesus!' Rackstraw shouted. 'Can't you be more careful? That's my people's culture. And that ain't just any wood.'

I know, Rick Scarlett thought. *It's carved ebony*.

WOLF AT THE DOOR

Friday, November 5th. 12.22 a.m.

Robert DeClercq arrived home late to find Genevieve sound asleep. For a long while he stood in the door to

281

their bedroom listening to his wife's shallow breathing and watching her chest rise and fall in the wedge of light cast in from the hall. His shadow lay across her like a strange man in their bed.

How long has it been, he asked himself, *since we did nothing but that? Just lie in bed together, relaxing or making love or whispering small talk?* It seemed to him like years.

In a wave, suddenly, exhaustion overwhelmed him and in that moment he truly wished that he had never gone back to the Force. He wished that she were awake now and that they could make love unhindered by time and pressure. He wished that the case were over and this weight were off his shoulders. He wished his book on World War I were waiting in the greenhouse. He wished . . . well, he wished . . . *Well, if wishes were horses then beggars would ride*, he thought as he turned away.

The Superintendent walked down the hall and over to the front door. Before leaving the Headquarters building he had packed several briefcases full of the pertinent documents in the case, his intention being to set up another overview at home. He had long known that his best insights came in the hours before dawn and he had reached the point where mentally he had to draw on every asset just to keep on going. The first briefcase he picked up seemed ten times as heavy as when he had carried it down the driveway. His head ached and his back was stiff and his legs were full of lead.

Robert DeClercq had spent the entire day analyzing the results of the sweep. With each new arrest there were reports, computer projections and videotape interrogations to be reviewed. As the day wore on he had begun to get depressed just from the number of weirdos there were out there walking the streets. Had it always been that bad – or were more people snapping lately?

Leave it alone till tomorrow, he thought, and then it occurred to him that tomorrow had already become today.

As he took the briefcase out into the greenhouse and

placed it on his desk he wondered if someone would find another victim tonight. He wondered if he would get yet another call.

It was while he was unpacking the contents of the case that his eyes fell upon a note that he had made about haematomania. He picked up the piece of paper. Until today the Superintendent had never known that there actually was a medical condition akin to vampirism. The incidents were rare, but they were well recorded. John George Haigh confessed to eight murders in 1949 stating that he took a wineglassful of blood from the neck of each victim and drank it.

Was that it? he asked himself. *Did the Headhunter suffer from haematomania? And if so might there not be a record of it somewhere? Perhaps a minor incident? Something someone had noticed?*

His eyes fell upon the books.

For there were now five volumes standing at the corner of his desk which had not been there that morning. Each book was bound in rich tooled leather with gilt worked into the hide. All five were held upright by two bronze bookends, one of a very fat man.

DeClercq removed one of the volumes and looked at the spine. It read: *The Very Best Of Nero Wolfe.*

He opened the cover to the title page. On one side there was a colour plate of the great detective himself, sitting in his own greenhouse surrounded by hundreds of orchids, waiting no doubt for Archie Goodwin to return. Across from this in black ink and a fine hand his wife had written: 'To the Greatest Detective Of Them All. I love you. Genevieve.'

The Superintendent smiled. Then he remembered what she had said to him early yesterday morning. *Do me a favour? Please. Take it easy on yourself.*

'All right,' he whispered. 'I'll try to do that for you.'

He walked out of the greenhouse door and into the living room. In spite of his tiredness, DeClercq knew that he was just too wound up to sleep. That he had to calm down first.

In the record rack he looked for something very light by Chopin. Withdrawing a disc, he placed it on the stereo, turned the volume very low, and sat down between the speakers.

Fifteen minutes, he told himself, *and then I'll go to bed*.

Three minutes later he fell asleep sitting in the chair.

12.55 a.m.

Some days you're lucky, some days you're not. Life just plays it that way.

It was twenty minutes to one by the time that Monica Macdonald and Rusty Lewis returned to the Headquarters building to retrieve their personal vehicles. Most of the afternoon they had spent booking in bikers charged out of the Iron Skulls scramble. Following that they had turned once more to their sweep sheet pickup list and gone back out on the street. Between 5.00 p.m. and midnight they had collared six more skinners. By half-past twelve, exhausted, they were ready to call it quits.

'Let's meet back here at eight,' Rusty Lewis said.

'Fine,' Macdonald agreed.

She climbed into her Honda Civic and pulled out of the lot.

Tonight she was simply too tired for highway driving, so she chose the long but quieter route home. It happened to take her by the Pussycat Club. A neon sign outside blinked: 'Our Girls Bare All.'

Monica Macdonald did not intend to stop.

At the moment her mind was a jumble of visions, the foremost of which was her eiderdown bed and soft, soft pillow. The image of Robert DeClercq, however, was also in her thoughts, for Monica could not forget how beaten down he had looked that morning. Yet even in adversity the man rose to the occasion and what he had said about duty had stirred something within her. *Your duty is maintain the right, no matter what the cost*, her weary mind told her now.

So Monica Macdonald pulled to the side of the road.

She found a pair of jeans and an old sweater among the clutter in the back seat of her car and changed out of uniform in the shadow of a doorway. Then she ran through the rain across the street and in through the door of the Pussycat Club.

'It's not ladies' night,' the burly doorman said. 'We bring the cock out Thursday night at seven.'

'Thanks,' Monica said. 'But I'll look anyway.'

'Suit yourself, lady. But it's pretty rough in there.'

She came through the door to find a naked stripper on her knees in front of a table of men. The men were all wide-eyed and staring between her legs. The woman was smoking a cigarette with her vagina.

It's too late for this, Macdonald thought – then her heart took a lurch.

For there in the front row of men was Matthew Paul Pitt.

SPECIAL O

7.45 a.m.

Robert DeClercq climbed the stairs that morning to find five people waiting outside his office door. They were all sitting on a bench along the opposite wall of the corridor. Four of the five were squad members, while the other was a civilian. He took the civilian first.

DeClercq felt better for a good night's sleep in which his nightmare had not come again. He was ready once more to tackle the sweep and whip it into shape. He had told himself that perhaps today the break would come in the case. But either way it mattered not: when you've got a job to do, you roll up your sleeves and do it. Wisdom ought to tell you, nothing does like doing.

'My name's DeClercq,' the man said. 'I command this investigation.'

'I'm Enid Portman. Joanna Portman's mother.'

A jolt hit the Superintendent. *How am I so stupid!* he thought, for there on the wall just behind this woman was the picture of her daughter's head stuck on the end of a pole. *What the hell am I doing bringing the public into this room?* DeClercq was angry with himself. How would he correct this?

'I apologize for the mixup with your daughter's . . . with your daughter,' he said. 'I realize how that must upset you.'

Mrs Enid Portman was about fifty-five years old. She was very thin and her hair was already white. She did not look in good health. Her eyes were sad and it was obvious that she had cried a lot.

Any policeman will tell you that the toughest part of his job is informing the next-of-kin that a wife, a husband, a child, a relative will not be coming home. It never gets any easier, and every case is different. Sometimes a mother will not say a word, just silently walk into the kitchen and plug in the kettle for tea. Another time a wife will break into hysterical laughter and shout: 'Why that bugger! It's about time.' Yet another occasion a father will attack you for bringing the news and have to be subdued. Every cop knows that a death close to home can bring forth any emotion: silence, a scream, sorrow, tears, hysteria, violence. What do you tell a widow who has lost her only child? That she'll remarry and have a baby and be happy once again? *Not at fifty-five you don't*, Robert DeClercq thought.

'Will she be cut up again?' Mrs Portman asked.

'Yes. There'll be another autopsy.'

'Is that my daughter's picture on the wall beside me?'

DeClercq's gut turned. 'Yes,' he said. 'I'm sorry. Perhaps we ought to . . .'

'It's all right, Superintendent. I'm not going to twist around. And I'm not going to cry. I've done enough of that to last me a lifetime. I was very angry at you people when my daughter's body was snatched off the train. But I'm not angry any more. In fact I want you to have her remains if it will help you find her killer.'

DeClercq found his throat dry when he tried to swallow.

'You see,' Mrs Portman continued, 'I hope that one day very soon I can lay my whole daughter to rest. And I'll never be able to do that unless you find her head.'

'We'll find her,' the man said.

The woman looked up, holding back her tears. 'There's something else,' she said. 'I believe my daughter had a boyfriend that no one knew about. She never mentioned it, and I never met the man. I think you should check it out.'

'We will,' DeClercq said quietly. 'But what makes you think that?'

'A mother knows,' she said.

The Superintendent used the intercom to call Inspector MacDougall. 'Would you give us a statement?' he asked her.

'Certainly,' she said. 'You're French, aren't you?' she added. 'Are you a Catholic?'

'Yes,' DeClercq lied.

'So was I. Tell me, Superintendent, has your faith ever been shaken?'

'My daughter and wife were kidnapped and murdered twelve years ago.'

The woman slowly nodded. 'My father and my husband both died in a boating accident. For ten years I've run a Mission on skid road in Regina. I used to think God must be sad, looking down and seeing all that religion and so little Christianity. Do you know what I mean? Religion is just talking. The Christian work is doing.'

Just then MacDougall entered the room and Mrs Portman stood up.

287

'Well I don't believe that anymore,' the sad woman said. 'I no longer believe there is a God.'

Neither do I, DeClercq thought, and he watched her walk out through the door.

While the Superintendent was talking to Mrs Portman, Rabidowski and Scarlett and Lewis and Spann sat outside and brainstormed the case. Both flying patrols had staked out their course and were not afraid of pollution. Each told the other what they were doing and Rabidowski filled in the theories going around the main corps. Monica Macdonald was conspicuously absent. Dead beat, she was still out on the street following Matthew Paul Pitt.

When DeClercq finally ushered them in, the first thing he saw was the mask. Scarlett was holding the ebony carving gripped underneath one arm.

Thirty minutes later DeClercq sat back and digested what he had been told. He did not think much of Rabidowski's theory concerning the motorcycle club. While it was entirely possible that the rape murders were part of an initiation – several gangs throughout North America were known to demand a killing before a striker was admitted – and while the decapitations did fit in with the motif 'Iron Skulls', DeClercq had been told that Special E Section had a spy within the gang. If that sort of trip were going down the RCMP would know.

Matthew Paul Pitt, on the other hand, was a very promising lead. The man was mentally ill; he was in the area now and could have been for the duration of the Headhunter killings; the US murders fitted. The real problem with the Australian was lack of evidence. They could bring him in like the others for questioning at the Pen, but gut reaction told DeClercq to play him another way. Give the man a little line and he might just lead them to a stash of heads. Was it worth the risk?

DeClercq looked at Rusty Lewis who was sitting beside

Rabidowski. It was hard to believe that two men doing the same job could be so radically different, but then the Superintendent had chosen his team to cover every contingency. Balance was his buzz word. So whereas the Mad Dog was a superb marksman and a well-known rabble-rouser, Lewis was filled to the brim with steady common sense. If Lewis thought a suspect fit then the man was worth a hard look.

'Where's this fellow Pitt now?' the Superintendent asked.

'I don't know, sir, but I do know my partner is on his tail. I got a call from her in the middle of the night saying that she had spotted the guy in a place called the Pussycat Club. We've been trying to find him for a couple of days.'

DeClercq glanced down at the twelve page report sitting on his desk.

'Your outline convinces me. We'll call out Special O.'

Then DeClercq turned to Spann and Scarlett. For the briefest of moments as he looked at the woman he found a strange thought intrude into his mind. *Might Janie have grown up to be like this?* he wondered. For DeClercq had hand-picked this woman for the squad on the strength of her service record. She had distinguished herself by the cool way that she had handled her assignment in Iran. In addition, a number of other cases had shown she could take care of herself. There was something in this woman that given time would drive her up the ranks. DeClercq recognized the quality: he had had it once himself.

Rick Scarlett, on the other hand, was a different matter. He was just a little too sure of himself and that was dangerous in a cop: it made you tend to overlook things and unbending in compromise. On balance, however, the man did have a reputation for never giving up, and DeClercq knew that if a situation got really rough Scarlett would hold up morale. A good leader must know that a team has different parts.

At this moment the Superintendent was of the belief that Hardy was the best lead of all. Starting with nothing but a picture, Spann and Scarlett had connected him to Grabowski, the Moonlight Arms, and in some way the traffic of heroin; followed his footsteps through Tipple's wiretaps and made the hoodoo/voodoo connection; linked the voodoo element to a traffic in human skulls; found an ebony object perhaps in some way associated with Avacomovitch's finding of the splinter (though how he had no idea); and now were on to some sort of ritual or other act joined to New Orleans.

Not bad when you put it together, for two Constables working alone.

'I wish I could go with you,' the Superintendent said.

'Sir?' Spann frowned.

'My forefathers were Cajuns who lived in the bayous of Terrebonne. Even my father lived down there for a while.'

Rick Scarlett's face began to flush with excitement.

'That is what you came up here for, isn't it? In order to get my permission?'

'Yes, sir,' Spann said.

'Well, you've got it. You two may go to New Orleans.'

11.20 a.m.

It was Special O – short for Special Observation – that ended the rampage of murder by Clifford Robert Olson.

Like the SAS and the SBS in Great Britain, Special O has its secrets. Most Canadians in fact are not even aware that such a team exists – and Special O likes it that way. The ten men who make up its core group are experts in police surveillance. For these men terms like front tail, side tail, three-car plan, and flood pattern have rather special meaning. The techniques they employ were refined and tested by British, American, and Israeli Intelligence – but of course the men at Special O have come up with a few of their own. Their daily stock in trade includes computers, 'homers', satellite bounces, infra-red cameras and gyroscopically-mounted binoculars. It is not uncommon for this team to send as many as one hundred disguised Members after a single suspect, and more if they think he needs it.

At 11.20 that morning Special O relieved a very tired Monica Macdonald and took up the tail of Matthew Paul Pitt.

Except for the RCMP itself, nobody knew they were there.

THE QUEEN

New Orleans, Louisiana
Saturday, November 6th, 3.45 p.m.

'Ever been to New Orleans?' Katherine Spann asked.

'Just once, with my dad,' Scarlett replied. 'But that was long ago.'

They had caught a flight on Air Canada to Seattle, con-necting there with an Eastern Airlines run down the Mississippi by way of Atlanta, Georgia. Looking out the window now as the aircraft began its final descent on to Moisant Field, Scarlett saw a landscape not unlike a huge lily pond. Almost half the land area of this city was located under water, and what kept the river from claim-ing the rest was a series of levées and pumping stations that diverted the seepage first into canals and then into Lake Pontchartrain.

The two men who met them inside the International Airport were different in the extreme. The Caucasian was named Luke Wentworth and he was from the FBI. Went-worth was wearing a light blue pinstripe suit that prob-ably cost in excess of a thousand dollars. His face was made up of sharp acute angles with a long thin jaw; his hair was short and brown and he was wearing those silver reflecting glasses that prevent others from seeing your eyes. For some reason Spann connected him with Paul Newman or Steve McQueen.

The black man, on the other hand, reminded her vaguely of a young Martin Luther King. His name was John Jefferson, Jr and he was with the NOPD. 'Welcome to N' Orleans,' he said. His voice was like warm iron and he held out his hand.

The two Canadians nodded, and they shook hands with both men.

'I hear it rains a lot back where you come from,' Luke Wentworth said.

'It does,' Spann agreed.

'Too bad,' the FBI man said. 'I hate rain.'

The moment they left the airport Scarlett and Spann broke into a sweat. The day was clear and bright, the air hot and humid with a heavy oppressiveness. Scarlett noticed a sheen of sweat on Wentworth's upper lip and that his throat had turned slightly pink. Jefferson, however, remained as cool as cool could be.

As they drove into the city Scarlett observed: 'The heat must really get to people. You seem to have a lot of cemeteries.'

'This is nothing,' Jefferson said. 'There are more than thirty of them up ahead in town. You'll find that N' Orleans cemeteries are more akin to cities of the dead than they are to graveyards. Most of all, the tombs are above ground because of the river seepage. In this town, believe me, it's hard to dig a dry hole. In the old days the colonials used to have architects design their graves. Many of the tombs look like narrow residences with rounded roofs and eaves. That's particularly true of St Louis Number 1. It dates from the 1740s.'

'Is that where Marie Laveau is buried?' Katherine Spann asked.

'Probably,' Jefferson replied, 'but there are those who

say she's in an unmarked oven in St Louis Number 2. You'll find red brick-dust cross marks in both places. The real site of her grave is certainly open to question.'

'Who's Marie Laveau?' Rick Scarlett asked.

'Hey,' Jefferson said, turning from the steering wheel and casting him a friendly frown, 'I thought you two were interested in voodoo. That's what the telex said.'

'We are,' Spann replied with a tone of exasperation. 'Don't mind my friend. He's just along to carry the bags.'

Scarlett's face went red as he glared at the woman.

'Marie Laveau,' Jefferson said, 'is the name of New Orleans' great mulatto Voodoo Queen.'

'Voodoo!' Wentworth said with a snort. 'What a crock of shit.' This was his first comment since they left the airport. During the trip he had busied himself by staring out the window at the Louisiana countryside. He obviously found babysitting visitors a bore.

'Well,' John Jefferson, Jr said, ignoring the man from the FBI. 'If voodoo is the subject, then I'm your man. What do you want to know?'

'What's the practice like today?' Spann asked.

'Pretty watered down and far removed from its roots. Some say, however, that a few pure cults still exist. And of course Haiti's still going strong.'

'Is there anything to it, John? You know what I mean?' This question by the woman surprised Rick Scarlett. Even Luke Wentworth turned his attention into the car.

'Let's put it this way,' John Jefferson said. 'I was raised in Philadelphia, okay? But I had this cousin who grew up in a small Mississippi town. I went to visit him one summer when I was eight or nine. It didn't take me too long to learn that within that community there were several hoodoo doctors and root workers on call. They looked like everyone else, but they sure had a lot of visitors. Especially on weekends there would be this steady stream of cars with out-of-state licence plates pulling up to their doors.

'My grandmother lived in that town and some days a

root doctor would sit with her up on the porch. My cousin and I'd be playing on the wooden steps below. You could tell when they were discussing a topic we weren't supposed to hear – cause 'mammy would lean over and spit on both of us.

'Even my old man, who was well-educated by standards set for blacks back then, respected those Southern beliefs.'

Just ahead and to the right Spann could see the colossal Louisiana Superdome, a flying saucer come to earth.

'Haiti is real weird,' John Jefferson continued. 'At a crossroads late one night I actually saw two men, back-to-back like Siamese twins, one dressed in white, the other in black, just going round and round. Voodoo permeates the place like some religion of fear. The sorcerers – *zobops*, they're called – are organized in groups a bit like masons. They go out late in the evening, supposedly summoned by a drum that beats louder the further away it is. At crossroads they hold their ceremonies and that's where they make the *zombi*. The Haitians say if you see an empty car drive by then you know *zobops* are in it.'

Wentworth took out a handkerchief and proceeded to blow his nose.

'On one of the Hardy wiretaps someone makes the statement ". . . the zombi walks". Can you hazard a guess what it means?'

'Sure, but it's a long shot,' Jefferson replied.

'Go on and shoot, my friend.'

'Along comes one of these groups at night and it stops at a crossroads. In a ritual where blood is shed one of the members of the group calls out to the *zombi*, then digs him out of the ground.

'I don't suppose that you believe in the Undead any more than I do, so – '

'I don't,' Katherine Spann said, casting a mock glance of paranoia over each of her shoulders, then grinning at Jefferson.

' – here is how they do it. Before the man who will become a *zombi* "dies" he is fed a poison. It is usually *curare*. The poisoned man is then buried on the same day. It's a hot country, remember? The next night the *zobops* drive out to the graveyard crossroads in order to bring him "alive". Once he is summoned out of the ground, the *zombi* is given a drug to counteract the poison. When under the effect of *curare*, a man looks like he is dead. Under the antidote he becomes a catatonic, sort of like Frankenstein's monster. The *zombi* is then put in handcuffs and leg irons to stop him running away – and lo and behold, the *zobop* has himself a slave.

'What better slave can there be than a dead man who follows your orders?'

'Is this what you Mounties do when you're tired of getting your man?' Luke Wentworth asked. 'Go out and hunt *zombis*? Great police work that.'

Spann thought: *This guy's a first class pain in the ass.*

'In Haiti,' she asked, 'did you ever hear of a *zombi* actually killing anyone?'

'I've been told they hack up several victims a year. But remember that *zombis* are catatonics: they have no adventures of their own. They must be urged on by a master to perform whatever deed they do. The *zobop* then waits safely for the *zombi's* return. Usually the *zombi* must bring back something to show that the job has been done.'

'Interesting,' Spann said.

'Tomorrow you tourists will want to drive out to Chalmette National Park,' Luke Wentworth said. 'It's just east of here.'

'What's there?' Scarlett asked.

'That's the site of the famous Battle of New Orleans. That's where General Andy Jackson *royally* fucked the Redcoats right in the ass.'

'Luke,' Jefferson said, turning to the man. 'Why don't you take your brilliant wit an shove it where the sun don't shine.'

Grinning Luke Wentworth readjusted his shades.

'Anyway,' Jefferson said. 'Haiti's where it's at. And of course that's where the woman's from.'

'Who?'

'Our latest Voodoo Queen.'

'I don't get it,' Spann said, puzzled by the comment.

'I don't either,' Rick Scarlett added.

So for the second time during the trip, John Jefferson, Jr turned away from the steering wheel and glanced into the back seat. 'This man you're looking for,' he said. 'This John Lincoln Hardy. He was raised in the USA but his family's not from here. His step-mother arrived Stateside about three years ago from Haiti. Word along the grapevine says she's our new Voodoo Queen. I thought you two knew all this, what with the telex and all?'

'We didn't,' Katherine Spann said.

Cops like hardware, the gadgets of the trade.

Of course now that they use computers, cops like software too.

The New Orleans Police Department was not to be outdone. Tonight they had laid on some Yankee technology – or Confederate if you prefer – to show the two Canadians the present state of the art.

'You got a pair of wheels each. Don't wreck 'em,' Ernie Hodge said. 'The electric teeth you'll find under the dash. The teeth are already sucked on to each eyeball frequency, so don't fiddle with 'em. Each bloodworm car's got an eyeball up its ass. If more than one fish swims out, make sure you're sucked onto *his* wavelength or you're gonna lose him. You both got that?'

'Got it,' Spann said.

'Ditto,' Scarlett replied.

Ernie Hodge had four chins and a face that Mad Dog Rabidowski would stamp with his beloved label: *bum*. When Hodge spoke – and he only talked in cop jargon – a ripple would start at his mouth and spread out from chin to chin. While shaking hands he had told Rick Scarlett that Steiger got the role in *In The Heat Of The Night* because he had turned it down. The Canadian almost believed him. He also believed that Hodge's ancestors had spent their sunny days whipping backs to make their slaves work hard before them cotton balls got rotten. For as Hodge put it: 'We all like John Jefferson, Jr. That man is one smart coon.'

Ernie Hodge, however, was also a skilled cop.

'Okay,' the American said. 'Let's set out the rules. Neither of you is heeled, right? We don't want US citizens stoppin' Canadian lead.

'Two: no collars and no one hits the pit without us doin the job. That should go without sayin'. A hummer down here can get a cop up to his ears in hot water. Her ears too,' he said glancing at Spann. 'I'll bet our laws on false arrest are a fuck of a lot tighter than yours.

'An' three: You both be careful. Down home you're not – and this is a Southern State. Bloodworm puts a chill on you, you'll both get a footbath an' end up cold meat for the sharks.

'If a fish takes you out to the country, watch out for the fuzzy bears. We got our own county mounties down here an' they hoard their jurisdiction. Also come mornin' the NOPD will have several eyes-in-the-sky. Choppers spark up busy air, so don't use the radio unless you have to. Either of you got questions?'

'Yeah,' Rick Scarlett said with a smile. 'What *can* we do?'

'Hell, boy, you can sit stake-out. All by yourself.'

'In case you don't know it,' Wentworth said. 'That's the shitty job.'

Ernie Hodge frowned. He obviously did not like this fellow either.

'Okay,' Spann said. 'Where's John Lincoln Hardy?'

They were standing in a vacant lot near the Mississippi River. Behind them was a levée and in front of them stretched what looked like a large black slum. The throb of music from distant bars hung in the humid air as insistent and elusive as the smell of night-scented flowers.

'Four blocks down river you'll see Jefferson in a car. Across the street from him an' down half a block again,' Hodge said, 'you'll see a drugstore. There'll be four cars parked out front, the ones with the bumper-bugs. Hardy's inside the building with several other people. An' believe me that's the weirdest drugstore you ever saw.'

'Maybe not,' Spann said, climbing into one of the cars. 'Up in our cold city, we got a Chinatown.'

She drove away.

'I'm surprised they left us alone without a shadow,' Rick Scarlett said.

'That's the FBI,' Katherine Spann replied. 'They want to ensure a free hand when they do a tail in Canada.'

'Think that's why Ernie Hodge is so jumpy?'

'Sure. If something screws up, it happens in his jurisdiction.'

'What do you think of our boy, Cool Hand Luke?'

'The man's an asshole,' she said.

'Did you see the way he's had his piece tailored into the suit? Probably a Beretta or some exotic rod like that.'

'Just like James Bond, eh?' Katherine Spann said, smiling wryly.

'I wonder where the FBI gets a prick like that?'

'Who knows?' Spann replied. 'The guy's so scuzzy I'll bet he spends his time off peeking in his neighbours' windows watching women undress.'

Rick Scarlett blinked. 'Want a sandwich?' he asked.

It was still hot. They had bought themselves large bottles of orange juice and were now staked out between two garages across the street from the drugstore which backed onto the river. In this neighbourhood one of the houses actually had mud walls and a corrugated iron roof. Its door had broken at the hinge and was lying aslant the doorway. Five doors down an old man was sitting on a verandah in a squeaky rocking chair sniffing the scent of tobacco flowers' as the darkness closed in. Occasionally there was the crack of a nut bursting as it fell down from a tree.

The drugstore sat between two small cemeteries. Within each graveyard there was the odd wrought-iron mausoleum, but mainly they were filled with white-washed tombstones. The drugstore building leaned crookedly, the shutters askew at the windows. A light was burning inside beyond the open door.

Leaving Spann, Rick Scarlett walked down the street to an all-night cash-and-carry. A sign over the counter warned: *Because of food stamp regulations, there will be no drinking in front of the store.* He purchased two po'-boy sandwiches, each one made from a French loaf; shrimp with mayonnaise and chowchow for Spann, an oyster loaf for himself. He bought himself a paper cup of coffee which he sipped as he walked back. The coffee tasted of chicory.

Spann was watching the drugstore through a pair of binoculars when he returned to the stake-out. After a while she passed them to him in exchange for the sandwich. He also took a look.

The pharmacy was dirty and broken down, the paint on its counter worn to the wood and grimed with decades of use. Behind the counter was an unglazed cupboard framing several sooty boxes and old hunks of root.

There were several people in the drugstore, most of them female. Two old women dressed in white lolled on the floor in front of the counter. They were smoking cigarettes and scratching their heads while at the same time running small cloth-covered bundles through arthritic fingers. These bundles had been removed from a small altar built into the base of the counter. Within the altar Scarlett could make out oleographs of St Peter, St George, and St Patrick surrounding a statue. Beneath the pictures but above the floor were bottles of rum and vermouth and whisky alternating with white porcelain pots. Then a weird old woman dressed in white sat down to join the others. She appeared to be holding her head in her hands.

Just then two other figures walked into the light beyond the doorway. One was a wizened old woman of at least seventy-five. She was wearing a faded print housedress and a pair of black laced shoes. Her thinning grey hair was pulled back into a small bun at the nape of her neck. Her cheekbones jutted out over a toothless mouth. Walking behind the drugstore counter she pointed up to seven drums, four of them painted green, that hung by a rope from the ceiling. Then she indicated a bull whip hanging on the wall.

The second figure, a man, began to take the seven drums down.

'That's our boy,' Scarlett said, for the man was John Lincoln Hardy.

Spann looked at her watch. 'You remember the telephone tap said "The pot boils over at midnight"? Whatever's going to happen, we don't have long to wait.'

All four cars moved out at 11.00 p.m.

Scarlett and Spann counted seventeen people – fifteen blacks and two whites, all but five of them women – come out of the drugstore single file and climb into the vehicles. In a line the automobiles drove off, following the river.

'Let's take both cars,' Rick Scarlett said. 'If the group splits up we can fork the tail.'

Once they were underway, each officer switched on the electric teeth underneath the dashboard. The electronic homing devices were just what Hodge had said – the latest and the best. Each device had a small screen that glowed a soft red colour, imprinted upon which was a map of this section of New Orleans. As each vehicle moved, the map changed, following the route.

There were now four small lights blinking in unison on both computer screens. Scarlett and Spann could actually watch the drugstore vehicles as they moved across the electronic grid. A digital display at the side calculated the distance between each police car and the homing devices.

Out to the suburbs, then out of the town, then deep into the countryside, Rick Scarlett and Katherine Spann stalked John Lincoln Hardy.

In Terrebonne, the home of the Cajuns, the demarcation line between what is liquid and what is earth is vague and always changing. The bayou streams weave a sort of lacework out of the land, curving and twisting and then curling back on their own curves to split and resplit again. Lose your way in such terrain and you could be lost forever. For here, hemmed in by decay and dripping trees, crowded by grass and sedge and palmetto, totally without a foothold on firm ground, terror can come quickly – followed just as quickly by death. Terrebonne sucks its victims into a grave of mud and buries them alive.

Beneath the light of the moon tonight, Scarlett and Spann followed John Lincoln Hardy deep into bayou country.

After the town of Houma and just east of Humphreys, the four cars from the drugstore left the highway and turned south onto a road made out of potholes. The potholes were filled with water, each one like a well.

At first there were several bayou shanties standing three and four deep on either side of the road, the air around them awash with a stench of fish, excrement, sweat, ashes, garbage, dogs, and mud. Beside these hovels grew mango trees with their plump and heavy fruit hanging from long green navel cords. But after a distance of several miles the shanties disappeared. Now the moon shone down on the procession of cars and the air hummed gently with distant noise and the sound of crickets and frogs.

Scarlett and Spann dropped back to give their quarry some room. Both Constables switched from head to parking lights. Soon they doused the lights altogether and let the moon show the way, the teeth as their guide. Then twenty minutes later, the four blinking lights on each computer screen ceased moving across the map. Wherever they were, it seemed they had arrived.

It had been at least ten miles since they had last passed a sign of habitation. It was in fact questionable whether or not the road on which they were driving continued to exist.

Scarlett and Spann pulled off to the right and drove in behind some trees and bushes. The place where they finally stopped the cars could not be seen from the road. Spann was just switching off the engine of her vehicle when Scarlett came running up to the open driver's window.

'Come on, let's move, or we're going to lose them,' he said. He pointed off to the left. Through the trees she could just make out several flickering torches. Spann climbed out of the car.

By the time they were back to the road again the torchlight had disappeared. Crouched low in case there was a guard they both moved swiftly toward the four cars parked up ahead. They found no sentry and turned off into the woods. By now the torches were gone from sight, swallowed by murky vapour. Within minutes the two cops were splashing through cypress woods where grasping roots and malignant hanging nooses of Spanish moss beset them. A few seconds later they were both up to their thighs in smelly water. Then up to their waists. Their chests. Their necks – when Katherine Spann found herself wondering if this part of Louisiana was known for its amphibious snakes.

'What the hell is that?' asked Scarlett, stopping dead in the water.

The woman beside him strained her eyes and was surprised to see a pile of dank stones jutting up out of the murky bayou fifteen feet in front of them. It looked like a fragment of some rotting man-made monument built among these malformed trees then flooded by the waters of the swamp. Beyond the stones and up on the ground which was bathed in silver moonlight, Spann could see a miserable huddle of huts. In front of them several bones hung from moss-covered gallows.

It was at this moment that the first sound of drums came throbbing through the trees, the *thump . . . thump . . . thump* of an insistent and malevolent tom-tom beat.

'We found them,' Scarlett whispered. 'Let's go take a look.'

Sunday, November 7th, 12.07 a.m.

Crouched low and then down on their stomachs, Spann and Scarlett closed the gap. First they skirted the un-inhabited huts, crawling out of the water and sticking to patches of shadow as they followed the voodoo drumming into the trees. Each time the beating stopped they picked up on a monotonous soul-chilling chant that droned through the muggy air. Several harrowing screams erupted, raising the hackles on each cop's neck. They left the shelter of the trees and came upon a natural glade within the swamp where a grassy island, almost clear of vegetation and washed in splinters of moonlight, humped out of the bayou. At once they could see that the island was a graveyard – perhaps an ancient cemetery for runaway Southern slaves – for from one end to the other crooked tombstones stuck up from the ground like rotting lower teeth.

For the next twenty minutes neither Spann nor Scarlett would speak a word. They lay submerged in mud on the fringe of the foetid waterway that circled the island and watched.

Near the centre of this graveyard, seven naked figures – one of them white – were bellowing and braying and writhing around a raging ring-shaped bonfire. An occasional rift in the high curtain of flame revealed a gnarled cypress tree that stood at the heart of the blaze. Surrounding both the dancers and the fire like a circle of Stonehenge rocks was another concentric ring of several wooden scaffolds. These gibbets were similar to those in front of the uninhabited huts but from each of these hung the still-twitching corpse of a freshly-slaughtered goat. One of the goats was still alive for the air was rife with its screams, while beneath each scaffold the ground was littered with hundreds of skulls. The dancers were moving counter-clockwise in between the ring of gibbets and the fire.

The goat stopped screaming and died.

Then suddenly someone with an almost disembodied voice cried out the word 'DAMBALLAH!' and the chorus of dancers in return chanted *'L'argent, ce sang!'*

A man with a snake curled around his neck burst through the ring of flame.

Thump . . . thump . . . thump . . . the drums began again.

Scarlett tapped Spann on her mud-covered shoulder and nodded off to the left.

Twenty feet from the bonfire stood a squat, square mausoleum. It was the only structure on the island and it was made from stone that shone an eerie irradiant white under the light of the moon. The fire-glow licked one side and turned it red.

Sitting around this charnel house were several knots of people. Four drummers in one group off to the right were thrashing the top of a single drum. Within a second huddle, four women – each one wearing an ebony mask carved with the face of the Devil – sat on the ground facing the tomb, their hands busily stroking and working red cloth bags as if they were rosaries. Up on top of the white stone mausoleum, with her legs crossed and her eyes closed, with one wrinkled arm and pointing finger outstretched toward the man with the snake, sat the old woman in the faded housedress who Rick Scarlett had seen earlier through binoculars inside the drugstore.

John Lincoln Hardy, a bone in one hand, lurked behind this woman.

Thump . . . thump . . . thump, the drumming picked up in pace.

It was the sight of the snake, to Rick Scarlett's mind, that really set things off. First the drummers on the *assotor* frantically began setting up a shifting structure of counterpoint beats. But as soon as the writhing figures began to adopt the beat, each drummer abruptly abandoned the *assotor* and reached for a separate drum. Three started thrashing tom-toms, the fourth an iron *ogan*. Fragmented now, the musicians slapped out monologues while the dancers around the fire followed them into frenzy.

Thump, thump . . . thump, thump . . . thump, thump . . . slap . . .

The man with the snake – 'Damballah!' – approached the tomb – 'Damballah!' – and the old hag on top stood up.

'Dam' – *thump* – 'Ba' – *thump* – 'Llah!'

Thump, thump . . .

Reaching down the old woman grabbed the hem of the housedress and pulled it up to her neck. Moonlight rippled across the wrinkles of her belly and her drooping pouches of fat.

The old woman spread her legs.

Thump, thump . . .

Her feet were planted firmly a yard apart on the top of the white stone tomb.

Thump, thump . . .

Her head was thrown back, swinging, her arms stretched up to grab the moon.

Thump . . .

She thrust forward her crotch.

Black-grey hair, twisted and tangled, climbed halfway up the old woman's abdomen, spreading out like creeping vines from between her legs.

Jesus! Rick Scarlett thought as the man with the snake

eased the head of the reptile up toward the old hag standing on the tomb.

The masked women went wild.

'Dam-ba-llah! Dam-ba-llah!' they began to chant.

John Lincoln Hardy retrieved a skull from the ground and started to beat on its cranium with the large bone in his hand. The old woman leaned back like a limbo dancer and lowered herself to the tomb. She was now lying with her shoulders two inches off the stone, her skirt still raised, both feet doubled back under her to support the weight of her body, the snout of the snake firmly nestled up into her sex. She began to undulate her hips to the pounding of the drums. And as she rolled and heaved and humped spasmodically, the four masked women on the ground stood up and stripped off their clothes. Then they too began to rock to the rhythm of the drums, naked save for the masks which continued to cover their faces.

Spann closed her eyes when the man let the reptile go.

When she opened them once again, the snake had slithered up over the old woman's abdomen and between her withered breasts. Now Spann could see that the reptile was over six feet long, for its head was wrapped in a coil around the woman's neck while its slippery skin still slid across her groin. The old crone's voice was moaning out: *'Bande, Damballah, bande!'*

Then the man who had released the snake began to shake out of control. Though his steps were sedate to begin with, he abruptly gathered himself into a whirl, gyrating about on one foot, then breaking away with a stagger amid flailing arms.

This stagger was more a leap than it was anything else, a violent forward-reaching movement as though he were falling into space and could only avoid calamity by falling yet once more – so at the last moment he recovered himself and whirled about once again.

Then his face became a staring blank, every muscle collapsing. Suddenly he stopped moving. His body went rigid. And at that moment one of the masked women broke away from her group, dancing slowly toward him. She rolled up his trouser legs and bound a green handkerchief about his waist and draped a red cloth across his chest and up over his right shoulder. Then she placed a machete in his hand and he started to shake again.

Thump, thump . . . thump, thump . . . thump . . . thump . . . thump . . .

Her body still thrashing wildly, the old woman up on top of the tomb cried out wildly in a strangled shriek of orgasm.

Then John Lincoln Hardy dropped the skull and reached out with the bone in his hand. For a split second Rick Scarlett detected a bright glint of light near one of the knobbed ends of the bone, but quickly it was gone. Hardy looped the piece of skeleton under the belly of the snake and removed the reptile from the stomach of the woman. He placed it in a bag.

Beside him, Rick Scarlett heard Katherine Spann breathe a low whispered sigh of relief.

Afraid of snakes? the male cop thought. *Believe me, woman, one day soon have I got a snake for you.*

Then from the ring of bonfire dancers a moan rose up through the night.

With a look of desperate bewilderment on her face, one woman broke away from the group. She began to whirl herself in a private fury toward the mausoleum. She flailed around and around, crying and choking, turning once, then twice, then a third and fourth time with ever increasing abandonment until her face was twisted in agony and her hand clutched at her head. As the white darkness of a voodoo seizure set in like a rush throughout her body, she slapped her forehead and the nape of her neck in an effort to ward off possession.

Behind her the ring of dancers hopped closer to the fire. One dangled a foot into the flames, while another waved a hand ecstatically among them.

From the group of drummers one man stood up and walked over to the possessed woman, still carrying his tom-tom. He began beating sound at her in a series of vicious slaps. The woman collapsed with a wild cry striking her head on the ground. In a snarl her lips pulled back from clenched white teeth. Her body began to convulse and the drummer went wild.

As he attacked her with his frenzied pounding, the man looked as though he would burst the drumskin in his effort.

The woman was now shaking her head from side to side, silently screaming, *No! No! No!* to every throb, but it wasn't any use. For she was learning that nowhere are drums played quite the way that they are in voodoo. The spirit was perched on her neck and whispering secrets in her ear.

John Lincoln Hardy, with the bone still in one hand and a bottle in the other, ran over to the woman. He took a swig of rum, spraying it over his face and rubbing it into his hair. He took another swig and spewed this mouthful over the woman. Then he struck her four times on the head.

The woman stopped convulsing.

The drummer ceased to beat.

The old woman on top of the tomb sat up and looked at Hardy.

Hardy hit the possessed one again and then pushed her softly toward the man who held the machete. He was standing near the mausoleum.

Both Spann and Scarlett tensed. Something was going to happen.

With one hand still to her head, her jaw now working under her hollow face, the woman-possessed slouched toward the man who held the knife. There was something untouchable about her, as though she really wasn't present. Enigmatically she mumbled to herself, her voice slurring the words until they were meaningless. At the tomb she stopped to bend over and kiss its stone. She groped in her hair and tied knots in it until the old hag who still sat on top whispered something down to her.

The woman nodded, flicked her tongue like a snake.

Then turned slowly and began to approach once more the man who held the knife. She was swinging her hips from side to side and flouncing her breasts as she walked. Stopping directly in front of him, she mocked the man with her body. She placed her arms around his neck and hung there provocatively. She rubbed her body against him until he slapped her to the ground. Then laughing aloud she knelt at his feet and began clawing the earth. The man struck her four blows with the side of the machete, knocking her onto her back. She tried to rise but he struck her again, even harder this time. The woman merely laughed. She went to rise again, but the man put the point of the machete to her belly and forced her back down to the ground. In a jeering manner he smeared the blade over her breasts and arms. *He must have cut her,* Spann thought, for the woman let out a cry –

And that was when the clutching hand burst up out of the earth.

The second time the woman shrieked, Scarlett jerked involuntarily. The grasping fingers of the *zombi* were now entangled in her hair.

Clods of earth began to erupt as the buried man tried to break out of his prison under the ground.

The woman's head was being yanked back and forth as a hole opened in the earth and the man with the machete carved an X across her trembling stomach.

The old crone smiled.

Then one by one, the naked women with the red cloth bags removed the masks from their faces and placed them at the feet of the Voodoo Queen. For each mask delivered the matriarch gave to her subject a small hoodoo doll. Pins stuck out of each doll, glinting in the moonlight.

Thump . . . thump . . . thump . . .

The drums began again.

Then the *zombi* came out of the ground.

First the earth broke away from around him in large

309

chunks and clods. Then his head popped up all smeared with mud, his eyeballs vacant and bulging and dull, his voice groaning out broken noises from deep down in his throat. He bit the screaming woman and tossed her to one side.

By now the old women with the red cloth bags had joined the dancers around the fire. The air was filled with booms and rattles and whistles and chants and passionate wails and whines. As their skeletal, wrinkled, empty-breasted bodies began to shiver to the drums, the old women worked the dolls with their hands, jabbing them with the pins.

John Lincoln Hardy, bone still in hand, walked to one end of the tomb. A hinge squealed as he pulled open a stone door. With his free arm he reached inside.

The *zombi* was out of the ground.

He stood in the moonlight, motionless, his arms held limply out from the sides of his body.

Gyrating abruptly on one foot, the man with the machete strode grandiosely over to the fire dancers. A few of them were now slapping their necks out of time with the drums. Still dancing, the group surrounded him – and even the woman who the *zombi* had bitten ran to join the crowd. Then the man with the knife whirled savagely and sliced out at the air, missing the dancers by inches as each powerful stroke came down.

John Lincoln Hardy walked over and cut the carcass of a goat down from one of the gibbets. To do this it appeared to Scarlett that Hardy used the end of the bone still clutched in his hand. Then a moment later he saw the attachment screwed into one knobbed end. It was a razor-sharp sickle about four inches in length. Like a silver eye, the steel winked in the moonlight.

Hardy returned to the tomb once more, and this time when he reached in, pulled out a wooden crate on rollers. From this crate he dragged another goat by the horns.

As Hardy struggled to get the animal over to the scaffold, the *zobop* with the machete knocked each dancer to the ground. They lay in a circle like hour strokes around the edge of a clock, each naked body on its back with its feet to the gallows pole.

Finished, the *zobop* joined Hardy. Together they dragged the goat, bleating and struggling, between two of the supine figures. Then hoisting the animal up, they hung it by its horns. The goat was left thrashing about, fear riveting each eye.

Hardy passed the bone with the sickle attachment to the *zobop* and returned to the tomb. After a nod from the old woman he began to collect the masks, stuffing each one carefully into a large black bag. Spann wondered if that was the same bag as the one for Damballah the Snake. The thought, however, was snapped off when she heard the unearthly gibberish of an animal unhinged by pain.

Her eyes jerked to the gallows.

The *zobop* had handed the *zombi* the bone with the sickle on the end. The *zombi's* arms were red. The sharp silver crescent of the sickle was streaked with dripping blood. The *zombi* – once given the weapon and the order – had staggered over to the hanging goat and ripped its belly open. A mass of raw viscera had tumbled out of the gaping wound. The thin legs of the animal were now jerking and quivering, kicking the grey cords of intestine that dangled down to the ground. The goat turned on the scaffold as the moon shone down.

Even at a distance, Scarlett and Spann could see into the red maw of the cleaved belly where glossy tubular glands and bulgy membranes slid about, the entrails still palpitating. The screams of the animal were now climbing to a terrible pitch. It was like a wild cry that burst up and out until something in the tortured throat tore, and the wail trailed away to the hiss of a hoarse whisper.

The *zombi* reached into the cavity and pulled out the animal's guts. Then slowly the Undead creature began to drape the ropes of steaming intestine across the up-turned faces of the voodoo dancers circled on the ground around the scaffold.

'Damballah,' someone whispered, barely audibly.

Rick Scarlett felt light-headed. Nearby a fly buzzed, its sound a little too loud.

The goat jerked and died.

As the stretched-out dancers covered with gore now began to writhe in ecstasy, the two cops turned and looked toward the tomb.

Only then did they realize that John Lincoln Hardy had disappeared. With the bag over one shoulder, he had been swallowed into the grave of night like a stone sucked into quicksand.

Rick Scarlett tapped Katherine Spann on the shoulder.

'Let's get the fuck out of here,' he whispered into her ear.

Less than a minute later, they too were gone.

10.35 a.m.

Banks of cloud swept north from the Gulf and the tropics. When the ball of the storm finally cracked open, a white flash of wavering light filled the horizon, showing up each leaf, each twig, each bough on the trees in stark black relief. An emphatic crash of thunder followed shortly after. As the storm drew closer to Moisant Field each lightning blitz was yellower than the last, each volley of thunder succeeding it at shorter intervals. Ultimately the brilliance and the noise met in one consumate explosion right above their heads – and the rain came down, making the hood of the police car rumble like a roll of military drums. For Scarlett and Spann the downpour made them both feel right at home.

Ten minutes later the rain stopped and Ernie Hodge, head ducked, lumbered out through the Air Express door of the cargo building.

The sudden calm was deceiving, however. For no sooner had the NOPD detective opened the rear door of the car than a wind almost tore it off its hinges. High above, the trees sighed and swayed and moaned.

'Je-sus Ke-rist!' Hodge exclaimed, yanking the handle shut. 'What are we in for anyway, some sort o' typhoon?'

The rain began again.

'Why don't you fly anyway?' Luke Wentworth said. He sounded like he meant it.

'What's the situation?' Spann asked of Hodge.

'They're booked in, all right. Same flight as you guys, if the plane flies. Once you get to Seattle, they take a different route. They're not going to Vancouver.'

'Where are they being shipped?'

'Spokane, Washington. According to the bill of lading.'

The woman looked at Scarlett; Scarlett shrugged his shoulders.

'You're sure that's the package?'

'Says right on it: voodoo masks. Just how many shipments like that do you think they got on board? Of course it's the package.'

'Okay,' Spann said.

'If you think there's drugs hidden in them masks, why don't we scoop it right here? Drugs in a case smell as high as a bayou outhouse.'

'No way,' the woman said. 'This is not a drug bust. It's a murder investigation. The masks stay put. Right, Luke?'

Wentworth didn't turn from looking out the window. He was still wearing his glasses though it was dark as sin outside. 'It's your case,' he said. And then the wind died down.

John Jefferson said: 'You two had better get into the terminal. Otherwise the masks will fly and we'll still be yakking.'

He put the car in gear and they all drove away. Ten minutes later they pulled up in front of the entrance to Eastern Airlines. They shook hands all round, just as they did on arriving. Then the two Canadians climbed out into a dying rain.

Just before she closed the door Spann turned to Wentworth. 'Does it always rain like this down here?' she asked the FBI man.

'Sometimes,' Wentworth said, not turning from the window.

'Too bad,' Spann said. 'I hate rain.'

The last thing she saw as she closed the door was John Jefferson Jr smiling.

THE RITUAL OF BLOOD

Wednesday, November 10th, 10.25 a.m.

He could feel the pressure building. And he did not feel well at all.

Since 4.45 in the morning DeClercq had been working at breakneck speed. His greenhouse at home was now littered with books and files and a videotape machine. He had spent the hours before dawn reviewing every memo, interview, police report, picture and note of importance. Around him his roses were dying. Those which bloomed in the autumn – Erfurt and Eternal Flame and Ferdinand Pichard and Golden Wings – were showing the signs of neglect in their petals scattered about the floor.

At six he had left the house and driven down to Headquarters. The past hour and a half had been spent on the phone. First he had heard from Victoria where the A-G was calmly wondering, 'Just what the fuck's going on?' The Mayor of Vancouver had called to say that she was sick and tired of questions and henceforth would be directing all press inquiries to him. Then Chartrand had phoned from Ottawa to see how he was doing. It seems the Opposition in the House of Commons had been giving the Government a rather rough time, so the

Minister responsible was putting pressure on him.

'Men and equipment, Robert. Requisition whatever you need.'

The work and the politics, however, were not what was bothering him. For though he was careful not to vocalize his fear, DeClercq was almost certain that soon the Headhunter would strike again. If his previous pattern set the pace he had already waited too long. The thought terrified the Superintendent no matter how calm he tried to be. For if a riot had followed the last killing, what would come this time. *Go on, admit it,* his mind said. *You're afraid of another taunt!*

Robert DeClercq sat at his desk and opened another file.

The case was turning bad. To start with the sweep and its aftermath had become a paper chase. Not one of the sex offenders picked up had in any way panned out. Matthew Paul Pitt was still their best suspect, yet Special O after several days had nothing to report. Pitt spent each day and every night front row centre in the strip clubs. During the day he slept in the bushes of Stanley Park.

Equally disturbing, John Lincoln Hardy had disappeared. It had been two days since Spann and Scarlett had returned from New Orleans. DeClercq had read their report on the voodoo ceremony and the follow-up memos again and again. The squad knew that Hardy had returned to Canada by a flight from the USA into Calgary, Alberta. They knew that the parcel of masks had gone to Spokane, Washington. But Hardy had somehow slipped away and vanished into thin air. Now all they could do was wait.

DeClercq was almost tempted to throw the entire investigation on to the cases of Pitt and Hardy. In other words to make the same mistake that the British had over the alleged Yorkshire Ripper tape. But he resisted the temptation, knowing full well that it was born out of desperation.

God! DeClercq thought. *Why did I ever take on this case?*

Then he remembered Janie. Why, oh why, he asked himself, was she always in his mind? At least when he was writing, the more he went into history the more he forgot the past.

He pushed the thought aside violently and tried to concentrate on the case. When he made a note he noticed that his handwriting was degenerating. That his hands were shaking. Suddenly he felt very tired. He shook himself sharply and looked at the corkboard.

Then he opened a drawer and dug to the back where he had hidden his prescription for Benzedrine. He took another one.

11.41 a.m.

'Damn,' Rick Scarlett said. 'What a colossal fuck up.'

He knew it had been a mistake and that it was a big one.

They figured the voodoo cult in New Orleans was centred around the Haitian matriarch, her two sons and their cousin. One of her sons was Rackstraw, now living in Vancouver; the other was the *zobop* who controlled the ceremony. John Lincoln Hardy, the cousin, was the white sheep of the family.

The voodoo cult in New Orleans was run to make some money. Like that of Marie Laveau so many years ago, it was based in the slums of the city where the most converts would be found. The group sold tricks and spells and dolls and operated the drugstore. Who knows, perhaps they had a chain of pharmacies all across the States.

As with all long-founded religions, there was a core of fanatics waiting for the Messiah. Now she had come from Haiti and they had gathered around. In exchange for the ceremonies to satisfy their blood-lust, the old crones supplied the voodoo masks which had probably been in their families for several generations.

The Wolf had remained in New Orleans to oversee the cult, but Rackstraw – the Fox, as he was known on the taps – had decided to set out on his own and for some reason chose Vancouver. Perhaps black competition was too tight in the States. Perhaps because his scams were doing well.

Rackstraw was into corporate fraud, land deceit, music industry kickbacks, and now the traffic of cocaine. The cocaine was hidden in the masks and brought across the border. The drug was removed and dealt in Vancouver while the empty masks were recycled in the Voodoo Chile performance. Part of the drug sale profits no doubt went back south of the border and into the hands of the *zobop* and Mama.

It was the theory of Spann and Scarlett that John Lincoln Hardy, the Weasel, had been making his living in New Orleans off the profits of prostitution. The taps seemed to show that he held his girls by a combination of drug addiction and a pervading fear of his 'hoodoo'.

As Spann said: 'After what we saw in New Orleans, that man could keep *me* in line too!'

Hardy had now for some reason also arrived in Vancouver. Perhaps Mama had sent him to learn a thing or two from her son. From what they could tell, when Hardy hit town he was living the role of a lowlife, so perhaps Mama was out to kick her nephew out of a skid. Perhaps he'd been fucking-up.

So Hardy hits town and takes a room down near skid road. With him he's also brought Helen Grabowski aka Patricia Ann Palitti. She's peddling her ass for money while he gets his trip together. 'No doubt,' Spann had theorized, 'he starts the girls on coke and then adulterates it with junk. Once he's got their noses hooked he jabs them in the mainline. The first thing he did on hitting the city was seek out a connection to get junk for his whore. In the end the man he finds is Joe Winalagilis, our Indian. Hardy connects with his cousin and soon he's on the way up. Rackstraw puts him to work as his cocaine go-between.'

Meanwhile, however, unknown to the cousins, Tipple out of Commercial Crime was into his investigation.

So the flying patrol gets on to Hardy and . . .

'Damn! We had to lose him!' Rick Scarlett exclaimed.

'You know,' Spann said, 'if we're right and Hardy is a skinner using this voodoo trip as a blind, or even if the murders are part of the ritual itself, we're going to look awfully silly if another body shows up. People are going to ask why.'

'Do you think he takes the heads in order to traffic in the skulls? Do you think that's his reason?'

'Who knows?' the woman said. 'Perhaps he just wants to fuck them and kill them and takes the skulls as a sideline. Maybe he's into some personal ritual of his own. Maybe the bones go Stateside and into the voodoo market. Or maybe the bones end up on the ground out on that bayou island. Anything's possible.'

'Okay, let's say Grabowski crosses him and becomes his second victim. Perhaps he has no need for her once he connects with Rackstraw. Perhaps he's pissed off cause she gets herself busted and raises his profile in town. She's an alien working the streets and that's bound to draw him heat. So assume all that, what about the bones in North Vancouver? What about Liese Greiner?'

'Maybe he was up here once before trying to find Rackstraw and didn't make a connection. Perhaps he killed her then. Or maybe Rackstraw did it and they're in this together. Like the allegation about a Hillside Strangler team.'

'And maybe killing is now in his blood and he's unable to stop it. Damn! What a colossal bummer. Why did we have to lose him?'

'Because we played this tail too loose, that's why. We should have bugged those masks. We should have followed Hardy instead of counting on him to call Rackstraw when he returned. We should have had the FBI stake out that air freight office in Spokane to see if someone picked up the masks. We should have done a lot of things which stupidly we didn't. We shouldn't have been so smug.'

'I wonder where those masks are now?'

'Maybe they're crossing the border hidden in amongst a museum consignment.'

'Maybe they're being trucked in through the wilds of the Rocky Mountains.'

'Wherever they are they were picked up and we lost them in Spokane.'

'So what are we going to do?'

'Let's have a talk with Tipple,' Katherine Spann suggested.

'I'd rather go find Rackstraw. He knows where Hardy is. They're his masks and the stuff is his cocaine.'

'What good would that do? It would only tip him off. He didn't talk last time. He won't talk now.'

Rick Scarlett smiled and looked her straight in the eye. 'You don't know me, Kathy. I won't be played for a fool. The next time we see Rackstraw, believe me, I'll *make* him talk.'

'I do believe you're serious. Let's find Tipple.'

Ottawa, Ontario, 5.30 p.m.

At half past five on that dark afternoon Commissioner François Chartrand left his office at RCMP Head-quarters. As usual he strolled slowly along the crowded streets of the capital, watching the civil servants queue up for buses as ambassadors in long long black limousines swept by. It was the time of day that Chartrand savoured, so when he reached the parliament buildings he found himself an empty bench on the con-course out front and sat down to relax. Lighting another Gauloises, he inhaled the smoke in deep.

Before leaving his office that afternoon the Com-missioner had received yet another call from Edward Fitzgerald. The Minister was phoning to tell him that the Opposition in the Commons would not let the matter die;

319

they wanted to know exactly what was being done to ensure that the Headhunter was caught before he struck again. The Solicitor General was jumpy. 'François,' he had said, 'I tell you we cannot afford another killing. Not one more.'

This particular call had not disturbed Chartrand greatly: it was all a part of the job. There were those who thought the Commissioner no more than a figurehead, a man put out to semi-retirement as Commander of the Force. All one had to do, they said, was sit behind a large desk with so many levels strung out below that every problem was resolved before it reached the door. But Chartrand knew different.

To François Chartrand his job was one of awesome responsibility. For as he saw it he was one man assigned the duty of protecting an entire nation. In Canada if something went wrong it was *his* responsibility. And something was very wrong now.

Chartrand was bothered by his last call to Robert DeClercq.

There was nothing to put his finger on, other than perhaps a certain tone that came through in the Superintendent's voice, but the Commissioner was far too shrewd a leader not to know that every man at war has a breaking point. It was fair to say that the Force was now facing a challenge far out on its western flank that was quite unlike any war that it had ever fought before. The difference was that public hysteria was mounting at a mathematical rate. Chartrand was receiving reports. He knew that incidents of violence involving women in Vancouver were exploding in number, mostly over-reaction to minor situations. People were frightened. That fear was building every day the killer wasn't caught. And every day the pressure on DeClercq screwed up a notch.

Chartrand was worried that Robert DeClercq might be near that breaking point.

It had happened to the man who led the hunt for the

Yorkshire Ripper. It could easily happen in Vancouver.

What am I doing in Ottawa? the Commissioner asked himself. *The true place of a General is with his men in the field.*

Then Chartrand reached for a cigarette and knew he had made up his mind.

Tomorrow he'd go to Vancouver, tomorrow he'd meet with DeClercq. It was time to troop the colours. And to bring out the uniform.

Vancouver, British Columbia
Thursday, November 11th, 3.45 a.m.

'*Sparky.*'

'Shut up! Go away! Fuckin' leave me alone!'

'*Sparky, now really, is that the way you talk to your mother?*'

'You're dead! Get lost! I know you can't be here!'

'*Sparky, I'm waiting for you. Come down and stroke my hair.*'

'No!'

'*Soft, soft, so soft — and how long and black it is. Black, black, black, child. Black as the time of night.*'

'Mother, why must you torment me? Why won't you leave me alone!'

'*Because I love you, Sparky.*'

'No you don't. You make me do awful things.'

'*Sparky, how can we have pleasure — unless we also have pain?*'

'Well, I won't do what you ask!'

'*You'll do anything I say.*'

'No I won't.'

'*Yes you will.*'

'No I won't.'

'*Then I'll tell.*'

Silence.

'*It makes no difference to me, Sparky. I'm well-hidden away. It's you who they'll cage like an animal. And you'll have no one to talk to. They'll all think you're weird.*'

'I'll find someone else.'

'Bullshit, Sparky. You know that isn't possible. I've fixed you so that I will be the only lover you ever have.'

'I hate you, Mother! You hear that? I hate, hate, hate . . . AUUGGHH!'

'Now will you do what I say?'

'Oh, please, no, no, no. Don't do that a . . . AUUGGHH!'

'Child, that one's just to make sure.'

'Oh, please, please, please, it hurts too much. Don't do that again.'

'Then come, child, come. Let's hear your footsteps on the stairs.'

'I'm coming. I'm coming. I'm coming.'

'Oh Sparky. Please. What are those tears. Come downstairs and stroke my hair and let's feel good together. Tell me you love me, child.'

'I do. I mean it. I love you, Mommy. Mommy, you fucking cunt!'

No, Sir, that thing in the Mask was never Dr Jekyll

5.43 a.m.

By the time the sun came up that morning Natasha Wilkes was ready and waiting. With a cup of coffee in her hand, she watched from the cabin window as the orange rim of the solar crescent broke through the horizon. Then she buttoned up her parka, picked up her gloves, and walked outside into the mountain air.

Her cross-country skis were still leaning against the north wall of the log chalet where she had placed them the night before, but now they were coated with frost.

For several minutes she worked at cleaning them off, then she stood up straight and stretched, her eyes scanning far down Seymour Mountain to the waking city below. *Poor schmucks*, Natasha thought, *just another working day*. Then she recalled that it was Remembrance Day and that no one would be at labour. The thought pissed her off. That meant people on the slopes.

At twenty-seven Natasha Wilkes was already established as the city's foremost movie critic. She held Fine Arts degrees from both London and New York. She went to work on an average day at four o'clock, sat in a theatre for a couple of hours watching films, then went home to write her column and pack it in by ten. And if landing that job wasn't good enough, yesterday she had sold her first romantic novel.

Natasha Wilkes felt elated. Life was going well for her.

After using blue Swix wax on her Silva skis, she snapped the skis on to her feet. Though it was only November, already the mountain was covered with snow and was building up a good base – and that meant a super ski year. She pulled her toque down over her ears, fluffed her black hair on her shoulders, then gripping a bamboo pole in each gloved hand set off down the trail. *At least for a while*, she thought, *I should have the mountain to myself*.

By 6.25 that morning she had worked up a very good sweat. Natasha Wilkes was now standing on a small precipice about fifteen feet upslope from the Seymour River. The water below was rushing with run-off, crystal clear and cold. Unhooking her pack and removing a thermos, the woman poured herself some hot chocolate.

At first she did not see the skier who had just come around a bend in the trail ahead. The steam was rising thick from her cup and the sight of Vancouver stretched out below was commanding her attention. When she did see the figure approaching her it was with a tinge of resentment. For when Natasha Wilkes skied in the mountains, she liked to be alone. Now there was a crowd.

The skier had first come into view thirty feet from Natasha. At fifteen feet Natasha noticed that the figure was all bundled up and wearing a fullface mask. That seemed a little strange to her, for the season was not mid-winter. And besides this was cross-country, not downhill. All she could see was a break for the mouth and two small holes for the eyes.

When the skier was seven yards away, Wilkes drained her cup.

At five yards distance she screwed the lid on the thermos.

At three she stashed the container back in her pack and went to zip it up.

Then she noticed that the tips of both pairs of skis were finger-locked together, yet still this person didn't make the slightest move to stop.

Asshole, Natasha Wilkes thought as they were face to face, then she went to open her mouth and say, 'Why don't you watch what you're doing?' but before she could get the words from her throat, the karate chop cut her down.

By the time that the woman stopped tumbling she was just three feet from the river.

Still dazed, her mind didn't register the knife cutting away the front of her pants.

11.10 a.m.

'Full dress parade!' Rick Scarlett exclaimed. 'What the hell is that for?'

'Maybe cause it's Remembrance Day and the Force lost men in the wars. Or maybe it's cause the Commissioner is flying in this morning,' William Tipple said.

'Just great,' Spann said. 'As if we've nothing else to do.'

They were now sitting in the White Spot with a second cup of coffee. Finally they had connected, for yesterday when Scarlett and Spann had tried to find Tipple they

324

had once again been told the man was out of town. He had been up in Kelowna giving evidence at a trial.

'We've lost Hardy,' Scarlett said abruptly.

'Join the club,' the Corporal said. 'We've lost track of Rackstraw.'

'You're joking?'

'We tailed him out to Airport South where it seems he had rented a plane. The guy's got a private licence and he took off into the sky. It was an aircraft with pontoons.'

'Where do you think he was going?'

'I have no idea.'

'So what do we do now?' Katherine Spann asked.

Tipple shrugged his shoulders. 'Keep our stake-out warm I guess and wait till they show up. Nothing else we can do.'

'Sure there is,' Scarlett said. 'We can all go twiddle our thumbs at a full dress fucking parade. You know, sometimes I wonder. Really, I do.'

11.15 a.m.

Robert DeClercq was frightened. For the dream had come again.

Last night he had lain on his back for hours and marvelled at the bursts of colour exploding upon the ceiling which he knew in reality were not there. It was just the amphetamines.

At 2.00 a.m. he told himself that he was through with the drugs.

At 3.00 a.m. he had risen to take an Atavin in the hope that it would bring him sleep.

At 3.45 a.m. at last he had started to slip away.

And that was when he had begun to dream about that house in the woods.

Instantly he had woken up and had broken out in a sweat.

The rest of the night was spent staring up at the ceiling.

At one point just before dawn he had thought he heard

a voice from over on Genevieve's side of the bed. 'You've lost it,' the voice had whispered. But when he looked over all he could see was his wife sleeping peacefully. *Just let it pass*, he had told himself. *You're hallucinating.*

At 5.00 a.m. he had sat up and had spent half an hour just watching Genevieve at rest. Her hair was spread out across her pillow like willow-wisps in a breeze. 'Do you know how much I love you?' he had whispered in her ear. And then he had climbed out of bed.

At 5.55 a.m. he had left the house to start another day.

Now he stood on the airport ramp and viewed the flight come in.

The Commissioner had arrived.

1984

3.02 p.m.

Though cops themselves, even Spann and Scarlett were surprised by the size of the room. Who would have suspected that the Force had this many ears?

Just before three they had parked their patrol car in the lot behind 1200 West 73rd and had walked to the entrance door of Vancouver RCMP Headquarters. With identification tags pinned to their chests they had taken the elevator up to Commercial Crime where Tipple was waiting for them. As the door slid open both cops saw a smile on the Corporal's face. 'Tail's back on the donkey,' Tipple said.

The three of them walked down a long corridor, the Commercial Crime member in the lead, and stopped outside a door. On the door some wag had pinned up a hand-printed sign that read: 'Don't be too astonished, ye who enter here. Just beyond this point is 1984.' Tipple turned the knob and ushered both of them inside.

There were more than 500 tape recorders stored inside the room. Spann and Scarlett were astonished.

About a quarter of the machines had take-up reels that were turning, while every few seconds a few would stop and others would begin to revolve. It took them a moment to realize that what they were looking at was only *half* the recorders present, for each master machine had a slave machine positioned on the shelf behind it.

'Listen to this,' Tipple said, as he walked over to one of the Uhers and placed his finger on play. 'Rackstraw flew in a while ago and went straight to his studio. He started phoning in a rush.'

The Corporal indicated two sets of headphones hooked up to the recorder and the Constables put them on. As with most bugging devices used by the RCMP, the Uhers work on voltage. The machine sits dormant and shut off when the tapped phone is not in use. If the receiver is lifted there is a change in the electrical current running through the line. This change sets off the recorder and its reels begin to spin. Each recording set has a master machine to make an original tape plus a secondary slave machine that produces a working copy. Tipple punched the play button on one of the slave machines.

Spann and Scarlett both listened as the connection went through.

'Your number please,' an operator asked.

A voice that they knew was Rackstraw's responded to the question.

'Where's he calling?' Katherine Spann asked, removing one of the headphones from her ear.

'New Orleans,' Tipple said.

'Hey, what's happenin?' New Orleans asked. It sounded like the *zobop* from the ritual, otherwise known as The Wolf.

'It's me.'

327

'Yes, you?'

'They're not where they're s'posed to be.'

For several moments there was a long pregnant pause on the line. Then Rackstraw added: 'Either it's a ripoff or Weasel's bin scooped.'

'Keep cool,' New Orleans said.

'Same mountain. Same lake. I mean you can see the friggin' border just to the north. I tell ya I checked the cache and they just ain't there.'

'Easy. Things can happen. He may not be the coldest man but he does know how to survive. Give the Weasel time and he'll come through.'

'Man, I got people waitin'!'

'Give him one more day.'

'I can't wait no one more . . .'

'You'll wait!' New Orleans said sharply. 'The man is *family!*'

And then the line went dead. Scarlett and Spann could still hear Rackstraw's heavy breathing. Once he hung up too, they removed the headphones from their ears.

Spann said to Tipple: 'Well, you found your half, and even *he* can't find ours.'

'How come he talks so freely?' Rick Scarlett asked. 'I mean, we rousted the man once, so he must know something's afoot.'

'Cause he thinks he's smart,' the Corporal replied. 'He's got phones at home and at his recording studio. Those phones he knows might be tapped. Next door to his music place is a small nondescript building that houses an Austrian import house. The buildings look separate, but they share the same basement. The phone in the storeroom of the import house is the one he uses.'

'How'd you find that out?'

'Easy,' Tipple said. 'We got bugs in the walls as well. It was my idea to put a listening device in the basement too. Crooks always seem to think it safer when they talk underground. In this case there's no cellar talk, but what there is is all these sounds of a door being opened and closed. Actually two doors: one of 'em squeaks. We went in there one night and invisibly tossed the place. We found a passage hidden secret-like behind a movable shelf of stereo speakers. It was the hinge on the shelf that squeaked.'

'Not bad,' Scarlett said.

'Nah, just dumb.' Tipple turned from the two of them and pointed across the room. 'See those twenty Uhers there? Now that's what I call a system. That's a crook with class, though he's a dumb one too.'

'Who's he? Chinese tong? Black Hand? Something like that?'

'Nope,' Tipple said. 'Just a smart-ass lawyer.'

It was at that moment that the master recorder hooked onto Rackstraw's phone clicked and began to revolve. Then abruptly it stopped.

'Change his mind?' Spann asked.

'No, that's an incoming call. They got this system, see. The procedure is that someone phoning in lets it ring twice and then hangs up. The initial call sets off a warning light in the mixing-board panel of Rackstraw's studio. It tells our friend the Fox that there's a call coming in and to get his ass next door. The guy on the other end of the line knows to try once more in five minutes or so. By that time Rackstraw's in the basement next door and ready to pick up the receiver.'

Tipple flipped a toggle switch that activated two speakers overhead, and then they waited. Sure enough, five minutes later the Uher began to revolve again. They could hear the trill of the phone as it rang and then Rackstraw picking it up.

'I'm here,' the Fox said, his voice trapped in one of the speakers.

'It's me,' a second voice stated. John Lincoln Hardy.

'You're hot!'

'Don't I fuckin' know it! The guy who picked the package up in Spokane was *followed*, man! I just grabbed it an' ran like hell an' lost 'em in the mountains. I tell you, man, I fear them dudes was the FBI!'

So that's it, Spann thought. *Wentworth tried to screw us.*

Obviously Hardy had left Calgary on his return from New Orleans and immediately crossed the border back into the States. He was supposed to connect with the mule who picked the masks up in Spokane. Hardy would then take the package and hide it in a cache near a lake in the mountains just south of the borderline. His job done, the Weasel would cross legitimately back into Canada, leaving Rackstraw to fly in the pontoon plane and pick the package up. All this trouble was Wentworth's fault because he wanted an exporting bust.

Play it by the rules, Spann thought, *and this is what you get.*

'Don't you dare come roun' here,' Rackstraw said with conviction.

'I know. I know. I know.'

'Now I mean it, man. No matter what, don't you come roun' here. You know where to go.'

'Huh, huh,' John Lincoln Hardy said, and the Uher once more shut down.

CRACK IN THE WALL

3.30 p.m.

Where do *you* go when you're worried, when you need some time to think?

François Chartrand was worried, so he put on his coat, left the Westin Bayshore hotel by the back door and walked along the Seawall beside Coal Harbour until he reached Stanley Park.

As the Commissioner strolled through the afternoon chill, his collar turned up at the neck, he breathed in great lungfuls of air, exhaling slowly, slowly and willing himself to relax. When he reached the entrance to the park he saw an old man fishing off the dock near the rowing club. Two lovers were smoking a joint as they played with their reflections in a small pool left by the rain. Two old people, a man and a woman, were hunched together over a checker-board on the ground. Leaves fell constantly from the trees and he could hear the sounds of the zoo.

Eventually Chartrand found a bench by the penguin pit. The walk had cleansed his mind, so he ambled over and sat down to think.

He was worried about DeClercq and felt guilty about him.

For there was no doubt in his mind now that it had been a very foolish move on his part to have brought the Superintendent back. He cursed himself for not having realized that the fissures created by the man's past were just too deep to have healed over even with twelve years. The fact that DeClercq was in torment was written all over his face, the way that his flesh hung from his bones.

So what am I going to do?

Pull Robert from the command and destroy his self-esteem?

Let him go on and allow this madman to slowly shred him to pieces?

He had to do something, that was for sure, to try and relieve the pressure. For Chartrand had spent his whole life working with men at the line of combat. He knew all the signs, and he could see them building.

DeClercq was on that combat line. And Robert DeClercq was cracking.

4.15 p.m.

It was MacDougall's idea to draw lots to see who would go and who would stay.

The North Vancouver Detachment of the Royal

Canadian Mounted Police was filled to overflowing with men and women all bedecked in their red serge uniforms.

The men wore heavy scarlet tunics with stiff choker collars, Stetson hats, breeches, white lanyards, Sam Browne belts, and riding boots and spurs.

The women wore the tunic, turtle neck sweaters and long blue skirts. They all wore gloves. Some had stitched to their sleeves the insignia of appointment: rough riders and dog masters and bandsmen and lancers of the musical ride. Some wore the crown and firearm badges that set apart the distinguished marksmen. All wore the regimental badge of the RCMP.

It was no secret that Jack MacDougall was damn proud of the Force. It was also no secret that he expected every other Member under his command to feel exactly the same way. That was why he had ordered them to attend a dress rehearsal before proceeding from North Vancouver Detachment to the Parade.

'All right,' MacDougall said. 'Those who are going, polish your brass and form into groups of five. Those who are staying, hold the fort, and luck be with you next time.'

They were just about to leave for their cars when a very excited dispatcher came running in from the radio room.

'Bad news, Inspector,' the man said. 'We got another one.'

For a moment MacDougall hesitated, stunned, then he recovered himself and said: 'You mean here? In our jurisdiction?'

'Looks like it. Number three. Up on Seymour Mountain. Found about forty-five minutes ago by two cross-country skiers.'

Good God! MacDougall thought. *Not here! Not again!*

Then he held up his hand for silence among the Members gathered around him.

'Okay, let's roll,' he said.

4.18 p.m.

'My, my,' Genevieve stated, leaning against the door-jamb. 'Now I see why women used to go for a uniform.'

DeClercq turned from the mirror and gave her a wan smile. He was dressed in the blue serge of an RCMP Superintendent. 'At the present rate of recruitment,' he said, 'we'll soon have more women in uniform than we do men.'

'Well don't you turn the tables and fall for a woman dressed in red serge.'

'I won't,' he said as the telephone rang.

Together they moved to the living room where DeClercq picked up the receiver.

As she watched him listen, Genevieve saw her husband's face fall apart and his spirit disintegrate. She saw him swallow dryly and his shoulders actually slump. Instinctively she comprehended the news coming over the line. *Oh no, not another one. Please don't do this to him.*

DeClercq put down the phone. 'Don't wait up,' he said.

4.53 p.m.

By the time Chartrand reached the murder scene it was swarming with uniformed Members. For a moment even he was surprised – all those years in the Force and here was his first red serge investigation. *It certainly gives one a sense of history*, he thought as he walked over to the body.

Robert DeClercq looked up from where he was squatting on his knees.

'It's a bad one,' he said.

It wasn't that Inspector Jack MacDougall was any more hardened than the others, it was just that for him the outrage of the crime had no sexual element. When he looked down at Natasha Wilkes all he saw was the violence.

The woman lay spread-eagled on her back in the snow a yard from the bank of the river. On her feet were a pair of cross-country skis. Her legs were spread apart, the left boot four feet from its partner. The back half of each ski had been rammed vertically into the snow. The clothes on the lower half of the corpse had been ripped to shreds with a knife. Her pubic hair was matted with ice and blood. There was a long slash across her breasts, rending her jacket open. A great deal of blood had stained the snow, particularly in a wide pool circling out from the throat. Rivulets of red were still seeping into the Seymour River where they washed toward the sea. The head was missing.

As MacDougall watched Avacomovitch pick up what had replaced the skull, he thought: *DeClercq does not look well.*

BUT IF YOU MEAN, WAS IT MR HYDE? – WHY, YES I THINK IT WAS!

4.55 p.m.

Joseph Avacomovitch pulled on a pair of surgical gloves before he picked up the mug. It was sitting in the centre of the pool of blood that had pumped out through the severed arteries and veins of Natasha Wilkes' throat. Careful not to smudge any latent prints, the scientist stood up and held it out.

The beer mug was the size of a large grapefruit and made from fine bone china. The porcelain had been fashioned into the face of W. C. Fields – that hard-drinking, misanthropic braggart with the big bulbous nose.

Across this nose was pasted one word clipped from a newspaper. The word was: *Robert*.

As Avacomovitch slowly revolved the mug in his gloved hand, Chartrand, DeClercq and MacDougall saw that its ceramic base was etched with an inscription: *Never give a sucker an even break*.

4.56 p.m.

Inspector Jack MacDougall broke the silence among them. 'It's your command, Robert. Let's have the orders. My men are ready to move.'

The Superintendent turned to him with anger in his eyes. When he spoke it was through teeth that were clenched with rage.

'Jack, I want divers in this river and I want every inch of it covered for a mile both up and down stream.

'I want a cordon with a diameter of 500 yards, no, make that 1000, around this body and every ounce of snow sifted with a sieve.

'I want dog masters from around the mainland out here as soon as possible. Put a quarter of the dogs on search lost, a quarter on search small, and the other half on command to search large. They cover every square inch of this mountain until we know there's nothing here.

'I want a hands and knees search of every road for tyre tracks and then a police dog follow-up. This killer arrived and left somehow and I want to know his route.

'I want choppers over this mountainside armed with infrared. The slightest change in temperature I want thoroughly investigated.

'I want a house-to-house with every cabin inspected, every owner interviewed.

'I want this woman identified *now* and I want her whereabouts traced. Have every person from the sweep re-interviewed as to exactly where they've been since she was last seen alive and do a computer match for any possible connection.

'Get out a media blanket calling for public information.

'As soon as the autopsy is completed, set up a funeral and spread the time and place around. Have a squad outside the service to photograph secretly whoever comes and goes. Have every motor vehicle licence recorded for a quarter mile around.

'I want a running log computer enhanced hourly from Chan.

'I want *every* traffic ticket given out on the North Shore within the last twenty-four hours examined.

'Have someone contact the British cops on the Ripper Squad, the Atlanta task force, and the guys who got Son of Sam and pick their brains for any technique we're missing. If one of them wants to help, buy the man a ticket.

'I want the Attorney General called and a $100,000 reward posted by tonight.

'Get a couple of psychics here and see what they have to say.'

DeClercq then turned to Chartrand. 'François,' he said, 'I want triple the manpower.'

'You got it,' the Commissioner replied.

5.12 p.m.

'I think you'd better look at this,' a voice from up above said.

Avacomovitch turned from the body of Natasha Wilkes and glanced back up the hill. Corporal Murray Quinn of North Van Ident. Section and a dog master named Ingersoll were crouched down on their haunches about half-way up the slope that led to the cross-country ski trail. They were squatting alongside the route where the woman had tumbled down. Ingersoll was rewarding his German shepherd, King.

The sense of smell of a German shepherd is a hundred times stronger than man's. A dog can detect odours that otherwise go unnoticed. A police dog is trained to always work into the wind. A dog will pick up any scent foreign to an area. A police dog works for only one reason and that is its master's praise. In the present case King was one of the more senior veterans of the seventy RCMP dog teams in Canada. Once told to search up the hill it had taken him less than ten seconds to find the three threads.

'What is it?' Avacomovitch asked as he came plodding through the snow.

'The dog's found these,' Ingersoll said, interpreting the animal's actions and pointing to the broken branch of a bush growing out of the side of the hill. He turned a flashlight on it, for dusk was rapidly coming down.

Avacomovitch crouched near the snow, removing a clean laboratory envelope from his coat pocket as he did so. With a pair of tweezers he removed the three ripped threads from the bramble bush. After he stood back up, he held out the envelope to Ingersoll and Quinn.

The pouch now contained two black threads.

And a third one, scarlet red.

Friday, November 12th, 6.30 a.m.

They had worked right through the night.

Robert DeClercq felt as though his body was half numb and his mind was rapidly shrinking down inside a small protective shell that hoarded what was left of his reason. He moved about Headquarters restlessly, checking and rechecking each and every aspect of the investigation, yet nothing seemed to be in perspective.

In one room a wall was papered with graphs and maps. There was a chart for the ages of the victims; there was a chart for their heights and weights; there was even a chart which showed the temperature at the time that each victim had last been seen alive.

In another room a police artist was working with a psychic. There were a number of sketches of the psychic's impressions already tacked up on the walls.

Every computer terminal was in use, with several officers lined up waiting for time.

Two men from BC Tel were hooking up fifty more telephones.

At Headquarters paper was mounting up. The days and days and days of repetitive, tedious work processing an endless flow of data – indexing, filing, and cross-filing – was threatening to drown the building. To DeClercq it seemed as though each detail within the mass was mocking him personally, challenging his weary mind to fit the pieces together.

But still he worked on.

At 7.23 a.m. a report came in that a burglar caught in the act overnight by two women had been beaten to death with a fireplace poker and shovel. Both women were over sixty.

At 9.17 that morning Coquitlam Detachment arrested a gang of seven 'slasher' girls who had spent the past ten hours ripping up the faces of six men – blinding two – with knives and the sharpened spikes of high-heeled shoes.

Then at 10.05 a.m. women began to mount a vigil.

Within an hour there were more than three hundred people standing outside the Headquarters building holding lighted candles. Before another hour had passed, that number had doubled.

Still those inside worked on.

6.07 p.m.

Commissioner François Chartrand found DeClercq sitting in his office staring at the corkboard overview. Softly, he closed the door. Chartrand took a seat across from the Superintendent. He lit a cigarette.

'We've known each other a long time, Robert, so I'm going to be blunt with you. I have spent a night and a day reviewing your investigation. I have not found one thing that I would do differently, but I have discovered a number of techniques that would never have crossed my mind. You've mounted as fine a manhunt as I have ever encountered.

'Now Robert, I think you know that I have loved nothing else in life quite like I love this Force. I literally grow and thrive off our tradition. And I miss being in the harness.

'That's why I've come out here. Not to check up on you, not because of political pressure, but because I want to be an active part of this undertaking. Robert, this is what we're about – this Force, you and me.

'To tell you the truth, it feels damn good to be back. So look upon me as fresh reinforcements and let's work this one together. And the first thing that I suggest we do, is have you get some rest. Let me hold matters here at the fort and you take tomorrow off.'

DeClercq shook his head. 'I'm all right,' he said.

'Robert, please, as a friend, just do as I say. Don't make me have to order you not to come in tomorrow.'

6.35 p.m.

The Superintendent left Headhunter Headquarters by one of the side doors. As he walked outside he noticed a knot of riot police hidden within an alcove out of sight of the crowd. They looked edgy.

For a moment as DeClercq climbed into his car he surveyed the size of the crowd. There were now more than three thousand candles burning out on the street.

As DeClercq drove away he thought to himself: *Come tomorrow morning they'll be calling for my head.*

LIGHT IN THE GREENHOUSE

6.45 p.m.

They went home disappointed.

As Rusty Lewis accelerated to enter the 401 Freeway, Monica Macdonald said: 'You live near here, don't you?'

'Yeah, just off Willingdon.'

'If you've got booze at your place I wouldn't mind a drink.'

'I've got booze,' he said.

Five minutes later they climbed the stairs that led to his apartment. Once inside, Lewis brought out a bottle of Canadian Club and a litre of 7-Up. He mixed them both a strong one.

As with nearly everyone else on the squad they had worked right through the night and then through the day. When the written report had finally come in from Special O stating that Matthew Paul Pitt had been under the eyeball of at least ten Members during the period when Natasha Wilkes had been killed, the two Constables knew it was time to call it quits. When Lewis had offered to drive her home, she'd accepted. They both needed company.

'You know, Rusty, I was so sure that the Headhunter was Pitt.' With a sigh of released frustration, Macdonald put her drink down on the small kitchen table.

'If it's any consolation, so was I,' the man said. 'Sometimes you win. Sometimes you lose. We'll be a winner next time.'

'Yeah, sure,' the woman said. Then she knocked back a stiff swallow of rye which burnt her throat going down. 'Would you believe that I once made a choice between going to Art School and joining up with the Force. I had

340

plans to open my own interior design studio. It was going to be called *The Finishing Touch*. What do you think of that?'

'Sounds sexy,' Lewis said.

The woman laughed. 'That's nothing,' Macdonald said. 'My original idea was to call it *Monica's Interiors*.'

At that Rusty smiled. 'My ultimate reason for joining the Force was to be in the musical ride. I still plan to get there. Besides, we put forth a good try and I think you're a good cop.'

'May I ask you a question?'

'Fire away,' he said.

'Instead of as a cop, what do you think of me as a woman?'

Rusty Lewis blinked. 'You're just like one of the guys,' he said, then added, 'I'm only kidding.'

'How would you like to find out?'

The man blinked again.

'Are you hungry?' Monica asked. 'I'm offering to buy you dinner. Ply you with a little wine – not too much – and let you think it over. We'll go somewhere ritzy.'

'I'm hungry,' Lewis said.

'Good, let's go,' the woman said, rising from the table. 'But understand one thing, my man. I'm going to spend some money on you, so you'd better come across later.'

And then she gave him a wink and added: 'Ever since I've been dating, that's been a rule of the game.'

7.05 p.m.

'Okay, let's make a decision,' Bill Tipple said. 'Should we call in Special O?'

'My vote's no,' Rick Scarlett said.

'Me too,' Spann agreed.

'Why?' the Corporal asked.

'In a nutshell,' Scarlett said, 'because I want to be promoted. I think we're on to something big, cause I think Hardy's the Headhunter. Whoever makes the collar, his career is laughing.'

'Or *her* career,' Spann added.

'Look, Bill,' Scarlett said. 'You know as well as I do that this Force has got too many chiefs and not enough Indians. Quite frankly, I have no wish to remain a Constable for the next ten years. I want up the ranks. This case is the best crack I've had at making a quantum leap. I'm sure Rackstraw is going to lead us to Hardy. Why should Special O get the credit for our investigation? I say let's do the round-the-clock ourselves.'

'Here, here,' Tipple said laughing. 'My sentiments exactly. Just testing you out. A future Sergeant should do that, before an issue's settled.'

'Yes, *sir*,' Spann said – and then all three of them laughed.

They were sitting in a windowless black van parked on the street half a block away from Rackstraw's recording studio. Although the telephone bugs from the building were channelled into West 73rd Headquarters, the listening devices in the walls had been channelled into this van. In the rear of the truck behind them, several Uher machines stood idle and waiting. As they sipped their lukewarm coffee out of styrofoam cups, one of the tape recorders cut in by voice activation and its reels began to revolve.

They all three picked up headphones and listened to what was being said.

7.31 p.m.

Tonight Genevieve had a faculty dinner, so Robert DeClercq arrived home to an empty, lonely house. The first thing he did was pour himself a straight, stiff drink of Scotch. It was the first hard liquor that he had had for eight-and-a-half years. It seared his throat going down, but it calmed him and that's what he wanted. He took the drink through the greenhouse and walked down to the sea.

Tonight storm clouds were blowing in quickly, surging

and exploding like nuclear bombs across the Straits of Georgia. He sat down in the driftwood chair and took another belt of Black Label.

You're all washed up, he thought.

For a while he slouched there wondering how Genevieve would enjoy living with a failure. A man who had no future and who was twenty years older than she was. It hurt him to think of all the effort that she had put into trying to patch this Humpty Dumpty together again, only to find it worthless. And then he thought of Jane.

Oh why did you have to die, Janie? he asked. Then took another drink.

It was more than an hour before DeClercq climbed back up to the house. He walked through the greenhouse – still cluttered with all his dying plants and the multitude of papers and reports on the Headhunter case – then he went into the living room and turned the stereo on. He poured another drink.

With the glass in one hand he searched among their albums until he found the recording of Wilhelm Kempff playing Beethoven's *Fifth Piano Concerto*. He placed the disc on the turntable and cranked the volume up loud, then he crossed to the centre of the room and stood directly between the speakers. As he slammed back another hit of Scotch the first chords of 'The Emperor' shook the walls of the room. An involuntary shiver wormed its way down his spine. Then he closed his eyes and let the music take him away.

When the first movement was finished, DeClercq came to himself to find that he had one of his fists clenched and that his lips were repeating again and again: 'This is *not* going to break me!'

For a moment he was embarrassed. Then as the slow second movement began, he unclenched his fist, took the record off, and walked back out to the greenhouse.

Robert DeClercq sat down at his desk and surrounded by darkness beyond the glass went back to work.

10.25 p.m.

Genevieve DeClercq was very concerned and had no idea what to do. She was afraid for her husband, afraid for herself, afraid she was going to lose him. The easiest task in the world for her was to make men fall in love, yet she knew in her heart that Robert was not someone she could replace. Where would she find another man to give her the freedom that he did? Where would she find someone to love her the same way he had – unselfishly, gently, roughly, thinking only of her? Before him her life had been a litany of men who said the same dull things as they manoeuvred her into bed, each one eventually smothering her with that pillow called possession.

And besides, Robert had values. These days a man with values was very hard to find. Unless the value was *him*.

Early that afternoon she had made up her mind to shock her husband. Genevieve could not recall who had first made the statement 'a woman's greatest weapon is man's imagination', but she did know that the human body is programmed so that at the moment of orgasm each and every problem haunting the mind is transcended. It may not be much but Robert needed every escape he could get. So Genevieve had dyed her hair black and tonight, with a little of that knowledge that separates the English from the French, she was determined that Robert DeClercq would take another woman to bed.

This evening Genevieve planned to set her husband's fantasies free.

It was with that in mind that she slipped the key in the lock and opened the front door. It was still in her mind up to the moment that she found the Superintendent in the greenhouse passed out over his desk. He had knocked over a glass of Scotch and it had smashed all over the floor.

'Oh, Robert,' she said in a whisper, and then she saw the tears. They were running down her husband's face,

344

secretly escaping while his body was asleep.

It took Genevieve ten minutes to get Robert into bed. He was too exhausted to wake up, and he was too big a man for her to carry to the bedroom. In the end she went into the guest room and brought out a roll-away cot. This she wheeled into the greenhouse, made up beside the desk, and then pulled her husband across it. Soon he was sound asleep on the other side of the room.

Finished, the woman went out to the kitchen and put on the kettle to boil. Once she had dripped a strong pot of coffee she poured a steaming cup of it and walked back into the greenhouse. There she sat down at the desk.

Genevieve was not a woman to give up without a fight.

At 10.56 she looked at her watch, then she picked up the nearest Headhunter file and flipped open its cover.

And that's where she started to read.

Saturday, November 13th, dawn.

The sun came up next morning at exactly 5.57 a.m.

As it broke the horizon and day burst forth, the greenhouse light was still burning.

RED SERGE

9.30 a.m.

Silver. All in silver.

His legs feel heavy, so very heavy as if they are forged from lead, while he tries to move fast, has to move fast to close the gap, to find Jane, to wrench his frightened daughter free from the kidnappers' grasp. It is with mounting anxiety that he looks down to find out what is slowing his progress, with shock that he dis-

covers that both his feet seem to have taken root in the ground. 'No!' DeClercq cries out. Then a panic grips him and he drops the crossbow and he grabs one leg in an attempt to tear it free from the forest floor. His leg refuses to budge. He tries the other one, tugging at it with both hands and using all his strength. It begins to break free. The earth lets go of the roots, lets go of his foot, lets go with a groan as each tiny filament clings for life to the soil of the –

'Daddyyyy!' A stark shrill scream shatters the autumn air.

'Let go of me!' DeClercq cries out to the silver trees around him.

Frantic now he tries to run, tries to free his other leg, tries to reach the silver cabin from which that scream is coming. His heart is now straining in his chest and pains from overexertion are running up and down his left arm. He can feel the tension in his temples and in the cords of his neck.

'Daddyyyyy!' This time it's longer, the scream suspended in the air.

'Don't leave me, Princess,' DeClercq cries out. 'I'm coming! For God's sake I'm coming!'

Then his legs are free and he is moving forward, dragging half the forest floor with him, closing the gap, the door before him, the clods of earth breaking away from his feet as the roots rustle like snakes in the autumn leaves around him, past the body with the crossbow bolt jutting out of its eye, up the steps and across the porch and swinging the door open wide, the knife now piercing his stomach, the blood now flowing down his abdomen and legs, his hands now closing tightly around the throat of this man in his path as the eyes, the tongue, the killing fades and the body drops to the floor.

'I'm over here, Daddy,' Janie cries. 'I'm hiding in the corner.'

So he whirls about in the silver room, searching the monochromatic space, desperately trying to find her.

'Princess! Janie! Where are you?' he cries, and at that very moment he sees her eyes in shadow in the corner.

'Oh thank God!' he says aloud, running to her and taking her small body in his arms, a body that now shrinks, getting thinner and thinner until it becomes a pole.

346

In utter horror DeClercq steps back and looks at those innocent eyes. For Janie's head is stuck on the end of a stake.

'I knew you'd come, Daddy,' she says, and then she begins to cry.

He awoke in a sweat to find himself on a roll-away cot in the greenhouse. For a moment he was disoriented, then he sat up with a start. He looked at his watch and saw that it was 9.30 in the morning.

'Genevieve,' he said aloud as he climbed out of bed.

He searched the entire house for his wife.

But Genevieve was gone.

9.45 a.m.

The value of fibre forensics stems from a theory that is known as Locard's Exchange Principle. Postulated by a French criminologist half a century ago, this theory states that a person passing through a room will unknowingly deposit something there and take something away. British researchers have subsequently found that most of the hundreds of loose fibres on a person's clothing are shed and replaced every four hours.

Until recently chemists could look at a fibre with seven different types of microscope and bombard it with neutrons, X-rays, and fluorescent light. They could measure its density, weight, melting point, solubility, and patterns of refracting light. When they finished they could tell whether or not it was permanent-press and the shape of its molecules – but they could not state that the fibre came positively from a particular piece of material.

Avacomovitch had changed that.

For his theory was based on identifying a fibre according to how it *ages*. Under the scientist's technique, a laser light scattering was used to study the molecular changes in a fibre as it becomes worn. Though two men may buy a similar shirt made from identical fabric, after those shirts are worn a while they will be very different. Body oils, perspiration salts, exposure to sunlight, whether laundered in hot or cold water: all these factors will alter a fibre. Although such knowledge is not crucial for synthetic materials – here specific characteristics can be measured by size, shape, chemical composition, and by looking at the arrangement of additives – it is essential for natural fibres. Without the Avacomovitch laser scatter technique, cotton threads from a Mississippi mill are hard to distinguish from those produced in Georgia. A laser scatter, however, gives each fibre a unique characterization. So unique in fact that it's like a fingerprint.

Joseph Avacomovitch had worked right through the night. By 9.45 that morning he had determined that the two black threads from the bramble bush were synthetic nylon fibres from a fairly new water-repellent garment. The red fibre, however, was natural and he suspected that it was a twilled worsted or woollen material. To take his assessment further he would need some laser equipment. He had arranged for access to such machinery later on in the day. It was time to take a break.

That morning as Joseph Avacomovitch left the RCMP laboratory a thought picked at his mind.

For that red thread looked a lot like the colour of red serge. Red serge is the fabric used to make the RCMP scarlet tunic.

POLITICS

10.45 a.m.

He recognized her at once.

For though her hair was now black instead of auburn

348

and she was with another man, a woman like Genevieve DeClercq does not slip from the mind. The moment that she walked into the restaurant, Joseph Avacomovitch looked up from his meal and instantly connected her with the photograph on the corner of the Superintendent's desk. He watched them take a table on the far side of the room.

On leaving the laboratory the Russian had suddenly felt hungry. It had been at least twelve hours since his last meal – and besides he wanted to think. What was concerning him was the fear there had been a screw-up. He was worried that perhaps one of the several dozen Members at the site of Natasha Wilkes' killing had broken the cardinal rule about preserving a crime scene and had snagged his or her red serge tunic while tracing the route that the body had tumbled by climbing up to the trail. With time of the essence Avacomovitch did not relish wasting hours analyzing a red herring.

At the back of his mind, however, he had another thought: *What if the killer did leave the thread? And what if it is red serge?*

The restaurant was crowded. Avacomovitch had never dined here before, but DeClercq had mentioned to him once that it served the best eggs in town. As the scientist enjoyed a good omelette he had decided to give it a try. It was as he was finishing off his meal that Genevieve and the other man came through the door.

For a while the Russian toyed with the idea of crossing the room to their table and introducing himself. He nodded to the waiter and motioned for the cheque. Then he sat there unnoticed, watching Genevieve. She was without a doubt one of the most vivacious and animated women that he had ever encountered. Occasionally as she talked with the man, perhaps to emphasize a point, she would reach across the table top and touch him lightly on the arm. At the moment the waiter came to take their order she crossed her legs and a slit in her long skirt parted. Avacomovitch caught himself eyeing the sweep of her leg and thigh.

Once more he thought of his friend DeClercq and turned his gaze away. In that moment he made two very quick decisions. One was that he would not tell the Superintendent of this encounter. DeClercq had problems already. And the other was that he would not walk across this room. For what bothered him in what he saw was not so much Genevieve: it was the man whom she was with. The Russian knew in the back of his mind that he had seen the fellow before, though just where he could not place. What he could put in perspective, however, was the look in this man's eyes.

He's in love with her, Avacomovitch thought. Then he paid for the meal and left.

3.02 p.m.

Politics, Chartrand thought with disgust as he hung up the telephone. *All for expediency*.

The Commissioner had taken the call from the Solicitor General, Edward Fitzgerald, in DeClercq's office at Headhunter Headquarters. The Opposition, it seemed, had been roasting the Government once more about the lack of progress in the Vancouver case. It had not helped matters any when both the CBC and CTV television networks had shown footage on the news of several thousand candle-carrying citizens holding a vigil outside this very building all through the night. The Prime Minister himself had told Fitzgerald to make the call.

'Look, François,' the Solicitor General had said, 'we're not playing tiddlywinks. This situation's explosive. Something *must* be done.'

'Edward, I have been right through DeClercq's investigation. Believe me this Force is doing everything in its power to bring this to an end.'

'I'm well aware of that, François. I'm not talking about what goes on beneath the surface. I'm talking about *public* consumption. A bone to throw to the masses. Keep them quiet a while.'

'What sort of bone do you mean?'

'I'm beginning to get reports about this fellow DeClercq.'

'What sort of reports?'

'Lawyers are screaming all over the place about their clients' rights being trampled under this so-called sweep. Some people are also saying that the man does not look well. François, a man who doesn't look fit can't go before the cameras. And if he's not good media what use is he to us? We're selling confidence here, plain and simple.'

'Edward, I'm not selling anything. I'm trying to catch a killer. DeClercq's the best we've got.'

'So he still works the case. Put someone else in charge.'

'I can't do that.'

'Well, I'm afraid you'll have to.'

For a moment there was a silence on the phone. 'What does that mean, Edward?'

'It means that something must be seen to be done. That we must look like we're going forward.'

'And what are you suggesting?'

'That you personally take charge.'

Again there was silence. Chartrand looked out the window at the hospital across the street. He reached for a cigarette. Finally he stated: 'Do I have any choice?'

'Just in the timing.'

'Then give me at least a day and a half to get matters organized.'

'Too long. The case is just too hot.'

'One day then. There's a lot to do before the press comes down.'

'All right. One day. But not a second longer.'

'One day. But Edward . . .'

'Sorry, François. But that's the way it goes. This fellow DeClercq. The PM wants him pulled.'

After Chartrand hung up the telephone he lit the cigarette. And as he did so he thought: *Robert, old friend. I do hope you're relaxing. One day is all you've got.*

3.20 p.m.

DeClercq had neither shaved nor had he eaten.

He walked over to the liquor cabinet and opened one of the doors. Most of the bottles that it contained were nearly full, a testimonial to how little he and Genevieve drank. At the back of the bottom shelf there was a bottle of Camus Napoléon Cognac. He removed the bottle and found a glass and then went down to the sea.

Drink in hand he sat there, thinking of his daughter.

3.35 p.m.

'Still nothing?' Scarlett asked.

'Nothing,' Tipple said.

The van was parked so that its rear doors could not be seen from the recording studio half a block down the street. Scarlett had come down a side street that met 12th Avenue in a T. When he climbed into the rear of the truck he saw Katherine Spann asleep on a cot behind the driver's seat.

'What gives with Rackstraw?' Scarlett asked.

Just then a tall black man about thirty years of age walked out the front door of the studio. Tipple picked up some binoculars from the dash. As he watched, the man stopped on the pavement in front of the building, put one index finger to his left nostril to breath in sharply a couple of times, then walked to a blue Corvette and drove away.

'They were in there all night recording, and then half of the day. You should have heard the racket,' the Corporal said.

'Who's in there now?'

'Just Rackstraw, I guess.' Tipple punched a button and flicked a toggle switch. A speaker in the van cut in and Spann stirred on the cot. They could hear the sound of someone humming to himself.

'How does the bug transmit?' Scarlett asked.

'Radio wave hook-up. All the room bugs feed into a

352

small transmitter attached to the left side of the building and buried behind an evergreen bush. It's protected from the rain by the eaves above.'

As he spoke it had suddenly started to pour, the force of the drops hitting the roof of the van, rapidly building up sound. Water ran in rivulets, then streams, then a steady sheet across the tarmac of 12th Avenue.

Scarlett said: 'Why don't you go home and catch some shut-eye, Bill? I'll take it from here.'

Tipple nodded. 'Anything important and I want to know. Make sure I'm in for the kill.'

'For sure,' the other man said, and the Corporal moved to the back. He opened the rear doors of the van and jumped out onto the street.

4.45 p.m.

'Fuck this noise,' Rick Scarlett said.

He removed his Smith and Wesson .38 from its holster and flipped open the cylinder. He checked the action, and that it was loaded, then snapped it shut. They were both now sitting in the front of the van.

'What's eating you?' Katherine Spann asked.

'I don't like farting around. And I don't like being conned.'

'So spit it out,' she said.

'Look, I know Hardy's the Headhunter and so do you. Rackstraw knows where he is. Yet while we sit around here with our thumbs stuck up our asses waiting for Rackstraw to lead us to Hardy, Hardy could be out there somewhere hacking off a head. Okay, I played it your way and we got in touch with Tipple. Now I'm going to play it mine.'

'Meaning what?'

'Meaning make that fucker talk.'

'Uh. Uh,' Spann said. 'That could be professional suicide.'

'Hardy's screwed us. Rackstraw's screwed us. Went-

353

worth's screwed us. And I've had enough.'

'Rick, we're both frustrated. But you know what Chartrand said after the McDonald Report came down? What you're suggesting could cost us our job. Plus a criminal charge as well.'

'If you can't take the heat, woman, stay out of the kitchen. You stay here.'

Scarlett climbed out into the rain and began to cross the street.

Katherine Spann followed.

4.48 p.m.

No sooner had Genevieve closed the door than she remembered the seminar. She walked to the phone in the living room and dialled the number of the student who was to host it. No one was home.

Earlier that afternoon, Genevieve DeClercq had decided to cancel this evening's class and had made up her mind to spend the time with her husband. Dead-tired from her night without sleep she had nevertheless spent the afternoon down at the public library reading up on police techniques in criminal investigation. This knowledge had now been combined with what she had learned at brunch this morning, and the woman felt ready to discuss the case with Robert. *Bounce*, she thought with a weak smile, *that's what they call it*. Bounce is cop vernacular for a brainstorm session.

But Robert was not at home.

A little surprised and a little worried the woman searched the greenhouse and the rest of their home. She noticed that nothing had been changed or moved since this morning: all the files on the Headhunter case were just as she had left them.

Good, she thought, *that means Robert has not been working. Thank God he's taken a rest*.

Her concern was heightened, however, by the fact that there was no note. He always left her a message if he was going out. Then she remembered that his car was parked at the top of the driveway, so he couldn't have gone very far. Eventually she crossed through the greenhouse and, with her shoulders hunched against the rain, went down to the sea.

But Robert wasn't there.

And neither was their boat.

4.52 p.m.

Rick Scarlett reached behind the evergreen bush and found the radio transmitter. He flicked the switch on the side that cut the power off. Then he returned to where Spann was standing and the two of them moved toward the studio door.

With what Rick Scarlett had in mind, Big Brother should not be listening.

And definitely not recording.

.38

4.59 p.m.

Steve Rackstraw was sitting in front of a mixing board with a large pair of headphones over his ears, humming inaudibly to himself. Around him there were lights and dials and recording-level meters. The studio itself was not very large. One side was reserved for technicians, the other half for musicians. A booth in the far corner set the drummer off by himself.

Right now – except for Rackstraw – the studio was empty. Not aware that Spann and Scarlett had jimmied the front door with a piece of celluloid, he removed a small silver coke-spoon shaped like a bone from his pocket and dipped it into a glassine envelope filled with white powder. Scarlett waited till the man had finished his snort before he stepped out into the open.

Rackstraw dropped the coke-spoon the second he saw the man. He ripped the headphones from his head.

'Well if it isn't Sergeant Preston and his sidekick, Dickless Tracy. You got a warrant?' he asked, recovering quickly.

'No,' Scarlett said.

'Then get the hell outa here, before I call my lawyer.'

Scarlett crossed over to the man and seized the glassine envelope. 'You were going to produce Hardy,' he said.

'Get out.'

'Where is he?'

'Get out, I said.'

'Blow it out your ass!'

Rackstraw reached for a telephone, but stopped the moment that Scarlett put the .38 to his head. The spreading effect of the cocaine helped him visualize a third eye in his face.

'Get up!' Scarlett ordered.

'Hey, man. Take it easy. What sort of shit is this?'

'Get up,' Scarlett repeated, and with his other hand he jerked the man to his feet. 'Now downstairs.'

'Just keep cool,' Rackstraw said, his voice beginning to falter and paranoia in his eyes. The sour smell of fear was starting to seep from his pores. His glance darted to Spann as if for an explanation. 'Why downstairs? What are you planning to do?'

'If you don't get moving,' Scarlett said, 'I'm going to ventilate your head right here and now. Move!'

'Better do as he says,' Spann said with a shrug. Her eyes never left Scarlett, nor his finger on the trigger.

'But why downstairs?' the man asked again.

'So the shots won't be heard.'

As Rackstraw's mouth dropped open in disbelief, Scarlett struck out with the pistol and hit one of his front

356

teeth. With a crack the enamel shattered. The man's lip split and blood began to fill his mouth. 'Are you crazy?' he shrieked.

As Scarlett cocked the pistol, Rackstraw moved toward the door. The two cops watched him open it and followed him downstairs. Spann was very concerned. She was about to speak when Scarlett turned around and said: 'Cover this asshole.'

For a moment she hesitated, then took out her revolver. She stood on the bottom step and held the gun on Rackstraw. It was dark in the cellar, only the light from one bare bulb casting long black shadows out to the walls of the basement. Scarlett tapped the bulb to start it swinging, then opened the cylinder of his Smith and Wesson and pumped all six bullets out into his palm. Holding the empty pistol out, he said to Rackstraw: 'Take it.'

The man shook his head. 'Look, I don't know where Hardy is. I swear to . . .'

Scarlett kneed him in the groin, sinking him to the floor.

'Take it!'

'No!'

Spann cocked her pistol, the snap of the hammer audible all around the room. When Scarlett reached out for her gun, Rackstraw took the empty pistol as if to head him off.

'Now look at the serial number,' he ordered.

Still doubled over from the blow to his groin, the frightened man moved the gun in his hand to look for the stamp on the metal when Scarlett lashed out suddenly and wrenched the .38 from his grip. A shiver of fright, surprise, and the spread of the coke rattled through Rackstraw's body. One by one Scarlett put the bullets back in his gun.

'Oh, Jesus. All right. Hardy's in LA. I'll give you the address. It's . . .'

'Too late,' Scarlett said, and he reached out with his left

hand and grabbed the man by his shirt. With his right thumb he cocked the pistol, then placed the steel of the muzzle directly between Rackstraw's eyes.

Like a puppet show, shadows danced about the cellar. Outside they could hear the rush of the water and two of the basement walls were cracked so rain trickled in. It pooled on the floor.

'You said you'd find Hardy,' Scarlett said, 'and then you went and fucked me. Nobody does that. We know about the drugs coming in and the voodoo in New Orleans. We know Helen Grabowski was killed by Hardy, and so were all the others. We don't have Hardy, but we've got you. So try this for a theory.

'The US police arrested two cousins for the Hillside Strangler's rampage in Los Angeles. And now that's happened here.

'We can prove you're tied to Hardy and that Hardy is the killer. We think you killed them too. A joint sexual crime.

'We just came here to speak to you and suddenly you jumped me. Guilt I suppose. We fought for my gun which you tried to seize and in the struggle I killed you. Your prints on the metal will show that for a fact. Everyone will say the cocaine pushed you over the line. My partner here and I will be the heroes of the day. You won't be around to refute us.

'Now run for the door behind you and see how far you get.'

With a shove Rick Scarlett pushed Rackstraw away.

As he raised the pistol to aim and shoot, Spann cried out: 'No, don't.'

'Back off!' the male cop hissed.

'Oh, Jesus, no, don't shoot, don't shoot,' the man on the floor screamed. 'Hardy's in town. Hardy's in town. I'll tell you where he is!'

'Where?' Scarlett asked.

And Rackstraw told him.

Five minutes later the three of them walked out into the rain.

As the handcuffed man was climbing into the rear of the van, Rick Scarlett stopped him and whispered in his ear: 'We're going to put you somewhere until we check this out. You fuck me around and I'll be coming for your balls. Then I'm going to kill you.'

Rackstraw believed him.

FAR FROM THE SHORE

5.13 p.m.

The thread was red serge, just as he had suspected.

But what did the other fact mean?

Avacomovitch had finished with the laser scatter technique. It had been two days since he had slept and his body cried out for sleep. His mind had begun to blur. Though he needed to talk to Robert DeClercq, that would have to wait. Perhaps he'd understand it all after a night of rest. Tomorrow might bring perspective.

If that's red serge, the scientist thought, *from an RCMP tunic, then the tunic that that thread comes from is more than fifty years old*.

Avacomovitch went home.

5.21 p.m.

She saw the boat approaching, hugging the jagged shore.

She stood alone on the miniature dock, waiting for him in the rain.

5.22 p.m.

'Do you want to get the warrant or the tools?' Rick Scarlett asked.

'The tools,' the woman replied.

'Okay, drop me off at Headquarters and you take Rackstraw out to the Pen and have him put on ice. I want him totally isolated and incommunicado. Have them book him for now on PPT cocaine. I'll phone Tipple and have him do a stake-out till we arrive. I'll get the warrant and meet you there sharp at ten. Got it?'

'Got it,' she said.

After Spann had dropped him off Scarlett smiled to himself. *Yes*, he thought smugly, *I'm taking back control. That's how it ought to be.*'

He went inside and phoned Bill Tipple at home.

'Hello,' the Corporal answered, his voice thick with sleep.

'It's Rick, Bill. Get up. We've found John Lincoln Hardy.'

'You mean you got him in your hands?'

'No, but we know where he is.'

'Then let's get a warrant.'

'I'm just about to do that. Will you go watch the place till we get there at ten?'

'Give me the address.'

Scarlett gave it to him.

'How'd you find him?' Tipple asked.

'Rackstraw told me.'

'Oh, I see,' the Corporal said. 'Well just don't tell me why he told you. I don't want to know.'

They both hung up.

5.27 p.m.

Robert DeClercq had been drinking.

As he climbed out of the small boat with his wife helping him on to the dock, the man tripped on a loose board and fell down on his hands and knees. The empty bottle of Camus cognac which he had in one hand rolled over to stop at Genevieve's feet. She crouched down to look at both the bottle and her husband.

'Robert DeClercq, I do believe you're drunk,' she said.

'Was drunk, Genny. Now I'm just high.'

She picked up the bottle. 'Well, at least it's a high-class binge.'

DeClercq sat down on the dock in the pouring rain and looked out across the sea. All he could see was grey, the downpour like a curtain.

'Let's go up to the house,' she said, 'and settle in for the night. I want to talk to you about your case.'

'Screw the case,' DeClercq said. 'I've got the day off.'

Genevieve stared at him in wonder. She had never before seen him this way.

'Don't you have a seminar tonight?' the Superintendent asked.

'I'm going to cancel it.'

'Why?'

'To be at home with you.'

'Well, I wish you wouldn't.' The man turned to look at her. 'Would you do that for me? Would you please go to that class?'

'Will you tell me why?'

DeClercq looked at the bottle in her hand and then looked away, once more out to sea.

'Well, Genny, do you recall telling me I hold myself too tight. Well that tightness is my cell, it's the dungeon of my guilt.

'This afternoon I took the boat and that bottle and just drifted along the coast, measuring the distance to shore. It's been a long time since I've done that – shared my own company with a bottle. And I'm finally thinking things out.

'If it hadn't turned dark I wouldn't be back yet because I still have some distance to go. But if I get just a bit more time to myself, just some more time to examine this dungeon of mine and how I built it, then I believe I'll find a way out.'

She didn't say anything at first, but watched this man she loved so much just sitting in the pouring rain. He had his legs curled up and his chin on his knees and his arms wrapped around his shins. Finally she sighed a long sigh and said: 'How long do you want?'

'Will you give me till twelve o'clock?'

'Yes,' Genevieve said.

6.55 p.m.

'What time is the seminar?' he asked.

'7.30,' she said.

'Where is it?'

'In North Vancouver. Just off the Upper Levels Highway.'

'What's it about?'

'I haven't decided yet.' Then Genevieve's eyes fell upon the open book on the living room coffee table. She walked over and picked up Albert Camus' *The Fall*. 'Do you mind if I take this?' she asked. 'I'll find a topic in here.'

'By all means,' DeClercq said. 'Perhaps you should look at I, I, I – the extension of the self. Or at The Little-ease – the dungeon of man's guilt.'

For a moment Genevieve watched him with sadness in her eyes. Again she wished with all her heart that she could give him a child. For she knew that when Janie had died, a part of Robert had died with her too. Sometimes just the fact that she would never have a son or daughter affected her as well. It was almost as though the future could hold no hope, as though without the innocence of childhood the cancer of experience would eat up all that ever had been.

Genevieve crossed to the liquor cabinet and removed an unopened bottle of port. Five minutes later with bottle and book in hand she left by the front door.

With one last look at her husband she thought, *What a time for Robert to meet his daughter's ghost.*

7.06 p.m.

She came out of the house and into the downpour, the

rain pounding against her umbrella and the wind that blew through the high trees threatening to turn it inside out. As she climbed the driveway up to where her TR 7 was parked beside Robert's Citroen the tarmac beneath her feet had become a rushing river. About her branches tossed wildly in the storm as the lights from the front porch of the house threw convulsing shadows across the wooded lot. Reaching the car she unlocked it, climbed in, put the book on the dash and wedged the bottle of port between the bucket seats, then she started the engine, and pulled out onto Marine Drive.

Fifty feet down the road there was another car parked at the curb. It pulled out behind her and followed at a distance.

Sparky was at the wheel.

THE FALL

7.07 p.m.

Once Robert DeClercq heard the car pull away he went to the liquor cabinet and removed a bottle of Scotch. He took the cap off the top and swallowed a slug straight. Within seconds he could feel the liquor ignite the lining of his stomach, the glow of its heat radiating out to the rest of his body.

After a minute he put the bottle down and crossed over to a bookcase against one of the walls. From a lower drawer that he had not opened for several years he removed a picture that was lying face down.

The photograph was of a little girl, maybe four years old, sitting in a pile of maple leaves coloured gold and amber and red and orange and brown. She was laughing, her blonde hair in curls thrown back to catch the glint of the sun.

DeClercq carried the picture over to a table and set it against a lamp. Then he pulled a chair across to face it, retrieved the open bottle of Scotch, and sat down to stare at the photo.

From the liquor bottle he took another slug.

Then with words so soft that they seemed to tiptoe around the room, he touched the picture lightly and said: 'Princess, this is your father. I want to talk to you.'

8.03 p.m.

The cutlass was two feet long. It was similar to the sort of machete used for hacking sugar cane, except for one difference. Down the back of the knife, along the spine opposite the razor-sharp cutting edge, ran a rounded ridge jutting out to both sides. Close to the handle and clamped loosely like fingers around and under both sides of this ridge was a sliding six-ounce weight. When the cutlass was swung in a wide arc, the weight would slip down to the end of the blade to increase the centrifugal force of the blow by arithmetical proportions.

One cut from the knife in Sparky's hand would slice a head clean away.

From the shadows beside the driveway and hidden behind a tree, Sparky could watch the front of the house into which Genevieve DeClercq had disappeared. Already the driveway was filled with cars. The TR 7 was eight feet away. The rain had died down to a drizzle, almost a mist hanging in the air.

Sparky settled down to wait and pass the time with talk.

For there was talk in Sparky's mind.

Lots of talk with Mother.

8.16 p.m.

Joseph Avacomovitch was too tired to sleep. For a while he

had watched the lights on English Bay from the window of his room in the Sylvia Hotel, then he had plugged in his Chess Challenger computer and set up a board.

Avacomovitch moved the black queen to put the white king in check.

8.31 p.m.

The woman emerged from the front of the house and approached the TR 7.

Sparky moved back in the shadows and watched her come up the driveway, knife in hand.

The rain had now stopped and her black hair was blowing wildly in the wind, whipping strands about her face and shoulders and high into the air. She was thinking about Camus. *I, I, I*, the woman thought, nodding to herself. *If no man or woman is innocent, then no man or woman may judge others from a standpoint of righteousness.*

When she reached the car she inserted a key into the driver's door, opened it and bent in to retrieve the bottle of port from between the bucket seats. The sucking sound of her rubber soles on the tarmac made her once more think: *I, I, I.*

As the woman eased her body back out of the car and began to straighten up, Sparky left the shadows of the trees and crossed the distance between them.

As the woman turned the knife began its sweeping diagonal descent, the whickering sound of the blade lost in the wind among the trees.

Then suddenly her world was turning over and over and over again, her vision spinning madly until with an abrupt jar her horizontal slammed to a halt on the perpendicular.

Oh God! she thought, *I see my body!* For there on the ground not ten feet away her headless form had hit the tarmac, spurting blood in all directions as it twitched in the death-throe spasms.

I've lost my head! her mind screamed with terror, but no sound came from her lips.

Then her eyes saw feet and legs approaching, a human figure walking toward her on the horizontal, crouching, reaching down, one gloved hand gripping a blood-stained cutlass, the other entangling its fingers within her hair, as her mind thought *I, I, I, I,* and then died because the oxygen in the blood within her severed head had all of a sudden run out.

Sparky picked up the head, bagged it, and ran off into the mist.

9.03 p.m.

Not ten minutes after the report of the killing came into Headhunter Headquarters the Prime Minister called. Chartrand picked up the receiver in DeClercq's office and thought: *So we have a spy in our midst.*

'Chartrand?'

'Yes, sir.'

'The Solicitor General is with me. In fifteen minutes we're telling the Commons that you have personally assumed command of the Headhunter investigation.'

'Yes, sir.'

'This man DeClercq, the one in charge. I want him pulled right now.'

'Yes, sir,' Chartrand sighed.

I'm sorry, Robert, he thought.

9.06 p.m.

It was the final turn of the screw. No sooner had Robert DeClercq put down the phone than he grabbed the instrument violently and heaved it across the room. The telephone line was wrenched out of the wall. In the process the remains of the bottle of Scotch smashed all over the floor.

There was another killing and he was sacked: that was

all he knew. He didn't care where. He didn't care who. *I don't give a damn*, he thought.

Then he began to settle down. 'Yes, I do give a damn,' he said aloud. He wanted another drink. *You're smashed already*, he thought. Then his eyes struck the photograph.

Weaving, he walked across the living room and picked up the picture. His eyes watered as he looked at the little girl, so very, very long ago, laughing in the leaves.

Then he slumped into the chair.

'Can you hear me, Princess?' he said to the photo. 'This time believe me. Daddy's coming for you.'

He went to get his gun.

FIREFIGHT

9.11 p.m.

The call came through on the radio of every Headhunter Squad patrol car.

'Spann. Scarlett. This is Tipple. Our boy just came home. He's carrying something in a bag and he's just gone into the shack. Here's how to get here.'

No sooner had Tipple finished giving the address directions and signed off than he came on again.

'Spann. Scarlett. It's me again. Hardy's just come back out. He's going to his car and from what I can see in this light, he hasn't got the bag. I'm on his tail. And this time no one gets lost.'

Monica Macdonald was down with the flu and, therefore, Rusty Lewis was on patrol alone. He was driving along the Upper Levels Highway in North Vancouver when he heard the broadcast.

Something's up, he thought.

Ed Rabidowski was less than a quarter mile from the murder scene when he picked up Tipple's reports.

With a frown of puzzlement on his face, he turned up the radio volume.

9.47 p.m.

Inspector Mac Fleetwood (no relation to the pop group; in fact he loathed rock music) was standing near the water cooler in the bull pen of Major Crimes when a constable who manned the front desk at 312 Main came up with an envelope.

'This was just dropped off,' the wide-eyed man said. 'There's a taxi driver downstairs says he went into McDonald's to get a coffee and when he returned to his car that was on the seat. He has no idea who left it.'

Fleetwood glanced at the envelope which was labelled *For the police*. It had been opened.

He dumped the contents onto a desk and out fell a roll of film and a note pieced together with newspaper clippings. The note said: SAY UNCLE ROBERT HAVEN'T YOU HAD ENOUGH? PS YOU DEVELOP THIS ONE.

'Hey, Al,' Fleetwood called to the man across the room. 'It's the Headhunter again.'

Detective Al Flood rose quickly from his desk and ran across the bull pen.

10.02 p.m.

'Where are you, Tipple?' Rick Scarlett said into the microphone of his radio patrol car. He was parked behind Katherine Spann's vehicle on a small dirt road up on Grouse Mountain. Spread out before his eyes, down below, were the jewels of the city. At least a million of them, some of them in motion.

Spann was standing outside the door. She listened to the reply through the open window.

'We're coming across the Lion's Gate Bridge. I think he's coming home.'

'Where's he been?'

'To the record studio, but he just drove by. He didn't stop. He must be looking for Rackstraw.'

'Maybe checking for his car. The Fox told him on the phone not to go near the place.'

'Well then Weasel doesn't listen. What are you going to do?'

'Enter the place. I got the warrant.'

'You better do it fast, Rick, if Hardy's coming home.'

'Yeah. And listen, I've got a walkie-talkie, so for Christ sake keep us informed. I want to know if Hardy's coming in the door.'

'You'll know,' Tipple said, and they both signed off.

'Okay,' Scarlett said to Spann. 'Let's get the tools.'

The woman moved forward to her car and removed a large box from the trunk. Both cars were one hundred yards past the shack and well hidden by bushes. When Hardy arrived, he wouldn't see the cars. But if he did drive on Tipple was on his tail.

'Pretty run down,' Katherine Spann said, 'for a ski chalet.'

'I don't think it's been used for that for at least a dozen years.'

They were skirting along one side of the structure to enter it from the back. The building was made of rotting boards with one window in each side. It was heated by a wood stove, if the pipe they passed by was an accurate indication. The place did not have electricity. It looked like an abandoned hermit's shack.

Once they were hidden around back, the woman opened the tool box and shone a flashlight inside. Scarlett selected a crowbar and began to jimmy the win-

369

dow but it slid up easily. 'This place has probably already been B & Ed a hundred times by cold-assed skiers,' he said. He put his hand up. 'Yeah, I can feel other jimmy marks. Give me a boost.'

Spann locked her fingers together and made them into a step. Scarlett grabbed hold of the sill with both hands, put one foot into her palms and hoisted himself inside. Leaning back out through the window he grasped Katherine Spann by the wrist and hauled her through the opening.

'Okay, let's spread out. You stay here and do this room, I'll do the one in front.'

The woman nodded as Tipple's voice came over the walkie-talkie clipped to Scarlett's belt. 'We're starting up the mountain. We're less than ten minutes away.'

The male cop crossed to a closed door and entered the front room. Spann remained behind. Four minutes later, Scarlett was down on his hands and knees working his way clockwise around the walls when the woman called out to him: 'Hey, Rick. You better come here.' The man went back to the rear.

As he came through the door, Spann was sitting on the floor boards with four voodoo masks at her feet. He saw she had found two planks nailed together that swivelled on a hinge. The small door now stood open revealing a hole in the floor. Katherine Spann had pried one mask apart and powder had spilled in her lap. As he watched she wet her index finger and dipped it into the mess, then she raised her hand to her lips and touched the end of her tongue.

'Is it coke?' Scarlett asked.

'Eureka,' she said. 'The tip of my tongue's frozen solid.'

'How much is in the mask?'

'At least eight ounces.'

'We're five away.' It was Tipple's voice. 'You better make it snappy.'

'You keep going here. I'll keep going out front.'

Quickly Scarlett rushed back out the door and began to tap the floor. And then he saw the blood. There was one small drop of it off to his right. Reaching out he touched it and found that it was fresh.

'We're three away. Maybe less. Hardy's driving fast.'

Scarlett rapidly tapped the floor around the drop of blood in an ever-widening circle. He pushed at each and every join of the boards. He still had the crowbar so he began to poke and pry. Then two of the floorboards gave.

'Rick, I can see the place. I'm going to have to drop back cause Hardy's pulling up outside.'

'Kathy!' Scarlett whispered sharply. 'Get in here quick!'

As he turned the volume of the radio down, she came up beside him crawling on hands and knees. 'Look,' he said, and swivelled open the boards. They both heard the car pull up outside. Both had killed their lights.

Reaching into the hole in the floor Rick Scarlett could feel two plastic bags hanging from nails in the underside of the planks. The shack was built up on stilts because of the mountain runoff. Both bags would have been hanging above the ground but as the supports were boarded around, well hidden from sight.

Scarlett removed the first of the bags and tossed it quickly to Spann. At that moment beyond the window there was a flash of firelight. Footsteps approached the front door.

Katherine Spann reached inside and removed four half-pound plastic bags of cocaine.

A key slipped into the lock of the front door. Orange light danced at the window.

Scarlett pulled out the second bag and reached for his gun. The .38 just cleared leather as Hardy opened the door.

'Freeze!' Scarlett ordered. 'We're the police!'

In shock the man in the doorway stopped in his tracks. He held a coal-oil lamp out in his right hand, the light of the flame that licked within the glass chimney cavorting about the blank walls of the room.

Hardy looked at the .38 in Rick Scarlett's hand.

He glanced at Katherine Spann and his eyes took in the bags of cocaine.

'So you found the blow,' he said.

'We found more than that,' Scarlett replied. 'Now put down the lamp. Easy. On the floor.'

Hardy followed the order. Then as he was straightening up Scarlett put his gun on the floor, reached into the second bag, and from it removed a Bowie knife and a Polaroid camera wrapped in another plastic bag. The knife was a foot long, with a shallow crescent dipping from the back of the blade down to form a point. Except for a tiny nick in the steel, the cutting edge was honed sharp.

Hardy shook his head. 'I never seen them things before,' he said, looking straight at Scarlett.

'Then how 'bout this,' the cop said. And he reached back into the bag and by the hair pulled out a human head.

'Jesus!' Hardy exclaimed.

His mouth dropped open and with a wild panic his eyes flicked from the head to the hole in the floor, from Rick Scarlett to Katherine Spann. Then he savagely kicked the lamp.

Spinning and spewing its oil which became a pinwheel of squirting flame, the lamp flew across the room in Rick Scarlett's direction. With a scream the man covered his face and the severed head dropped to the floor. It rolled toward Katherine Spann who was trying to draw her gun.

With a *whoosh* the floor ignited along with Scarlett's arm. 'I'm on fire!' the cop screamed, madly beating his flaming arm against his chest trying to fan out the blaze. At last in desperation he threw himself on to the floor, landing on top of both his gun and his arm where the floorboards had yet to ignite. His body smothered the fire.

Hardy lunged for the Bowie knife now lying on the

floor. Clutching it in one hand he took a swipe at Spann. Throwing herself away from him, the woman went sprawling back on the floorboards. With a crack she hit her head.

Scarlett was scrambling to his feet when Hardy swung again. This time the knife connected, slashing through the uniform and opening the flesh of the policeman's arm from the elbow to the wrist. Scarlett went down on his knees and Hardy was upon him.

'Don't!' Tipple yelled from the door, reaching for his gun but knowing he wouldn't make it in time.

With a full-arm slash, John Lincoln Hardy went for Rick Scarlett's throat just as Katherine Spann fired. She was now up on her knees. Her gun was in both hands.

The explosion was shocking within the small confines of the room.

As the muzzle flashed the first bullet struck Hardy's neck blowing out an exit wound the size of a golfball. The force of the slug sent him spinning and the knife slash missed by inches. Then Katherine Spann fired again and Hardy's head erupted. The lead took him just behind the left ear, ripping through his brain to blow out the front of his forehead in a shower of blood and gristle and bone. A third shot from the .38 hit him in the spine. His body crashed to the floor.

'Rick, grab the light stuff and get outside,' Tipple ordered, as he came leaping through the flames. 'Spann, get that head and the drugs and get the knife from that man. I'll take the body.'

One minute later they were all outside as the fire consumed the cabin. Like a beacon, those flames on the mountainside could be seen for miles. Twenty minutes later the skies opened up and poured down to extinguish the embers.

In this city, it often rains.

SUICIDE

Robert DeClercq had both cleaned and oiled his gun, then set it down on the desk in the greenhouse. Over the past hour and a half he had tidied up all the Headhunter files, taking them out and stacking them beside the front door entrance. That completed, he had written a long note to Commissioner François Chartrand outlining a few final thoughts on the course of the investigation, developing further one or two theories before he had signed off the letter by wishing the man good luck. He had written a note to Genevieve and tacked it to the greenhouse door.

The greenhouse was attached to the wall that made up the south side of the building. Though there were windows in the left half of the wall looking over the ocean, the right half that abutted the greenhouse was solid wood planking. A large oak door gave access, but other than that there was no other way to look into the glass outbuilding.

In the note to his wife Robert DeClercq had asked her to try and forgive him. He did not explain his actions, for she would understand. He simply said that he loved her, that he considered her the most unselfish individual that he had ever met, and he thanked her for the joy of their time together.

'I've gone to find Janie,' he said in closing, 'so please don't open the door. Just call the police and know that I have escaped from my dungeon.'

As a final act of preparation, Robert DeClercq had brushed down his blue serge uniform and hung it on a hanger beside the files at the door. He had crossed to the liquor cabinet and consumed two swallows of brandy straight. Then picking up Janie's picture he had gone into the greenhouse.

He was just locking the door when he heard the noise that made him stop.

For someone had just come in through the front door.

When he looked back out into the living room, the Superintendent saw Genevieve running toward him. She had her arms outstretched and she was crying out through tears: 'Oh, Robert, it was awful. Linda's been . . .'

And that was when he pushed her.

His hand connected with her chest, stopping her in her rush of anguish and suddenly sending her flying in the opposite direction.

'Goodbye, Genny,' he said.

And he slammed the greenhouse door.

Genevieve looked up in wild amazement from where she was sprawled on the floor. She could not believe this was happening. What was going on?

First Linda, her student, had been killed after offering to go up to the car and retrieve the bottle of port.

Then the police had been called by some fellow out walking his dog and before she knew it the house was swarming with dozens of police.

For an hour and a half she had tried to call home, only to hear from the operator that the line was out of order.

And now she had finally gotten away, had kindly been driven home by Joseph Avacomovitch who had asked to come in but who she had told she needed some time alone with her husband, and now this!

What is going on? she thought. *I do not believe this night!*

And then she saw it all. The room struck like a chime.

The telephone lying smashed against one wall.

The bottle of Scotch broken and spilled on the floor.

The files stacked beside the door and the hung-up uniform.

And then her eyes grew wide with terror as she came to realize that the uniform holster was open and its pistol was missing. *He's going to kill himself*, she thought –and then she started for the greenhouse door, knowing abruptly that it was a solid barrier of wood totally sealing him off, knowing also in that instant that in order to get to him she had to go right around the house. She knew that it was impossible for her to make it in time, but all the same that she had to give it a try. She scrambled in horror for the front door, fingers clawing at the wood, fingers slipping on the metal handle, wrenching it open wildly and running straight into another wall that was Joseph Avacomovitch.

'Where's Robert?' the scientist asked. 'It's all over the air. Tipple, Scarlett and Spann have brought the Head-hunter . . .'

'He's in the greenhouse!' Genevieve screamed, frantically trying to push the Russian aside and pointing at the door. 'He's going to shoot himself!'

Then she squeezed between the man and the door-frame and ran off outside.

Avacomovitch was moving.

He was coming across the living room floor and heading toward the door. He began to lead with his body, cutting the distance rapidly, lowering and coiling into a crouch, his left shoulder coming out to the fore as his head tucked into his chest, his right foot firm on the floor as he pushed off with all his strength, unwinding, hurtling, until finally at 6' 4" and 285 pounds, like a human battering ram, he hit the door.

The wood never stood a chance.

With a fierce crack of protest it buckled right down the middle, the lock ripping free in a shower of splinters as both the hinges gave. Breaking free, the door crashed into the greenhouse. Followed by the man.

Robert DeClercq jammed the pistol barrel into his open

mouth and bit down on the steel. The muzzle touched his palate, pointing at his brain.

Amid the tumble of shelves and potted plants, with dirt flying everywhere, the Russian somersaulted across the floor until, one foot smashing through the glass, his body came to a halt.

DeClercq's thumb snapped back the hammer as his finger closed on the trigger.

'Don't do it, Robert! You got him! A flying patrol brought him down!' Avacomovitch yelled.

And he didn't pull the trigger.

There was an awkward moment while Robert DeClercq sat at his desk with the pistol still in his mouth, looking down at Avacomovitch stretched out on the floor. Then slowly he took the gun barrel out and placed the .38 down on the leather.

'What are you doing here, Joseph?' was all he could think to say.

'I've come for that party, Robert. Don't you remember?'

The Superintendent nodded.

And that was when, beyond the greenhouse wall and standing out in the rain, Robert DeClercq saw his wife's face and hands pressed against the glass. For a moment he looked at one of his own hands, the one that had pushed her away, then he got up from the desk chair and moved toward the door.

As he reached out to undo the lock he saw Genevieve waiting outside. He watched her face in the windowpane and the streaks running down from both eyes and he wondered briefly if they were tears or just the rain on the glass.

COP A FEEL

Seattle, Washington.
Saturday, December 4th, 10.02 p.m.

'Apart from making Corporal, what was the best part of
the case for you?' Katherine Spann asked.

Rick Scarlett smiled. 'When the Prime Minister – not
fifteen minutes after telling the House of Commons that
DeClercq had been pulled from the investigation – had to
go back in and inform them that the Superintendent had
brought the Headhunter down. The man looked like
such a fool.'

Both Corporals laughed.

As they had been promoted, this trip was a
celebration. Bill Tipple – now a Sergeant – had been
asked to come along, but he had begged off saying that
Commercial Crime was hot on the tail of something big
and he could not desert at the moment. 'By the time you
two return,' he'd said, 'I'll probably be an Inspector.' The
way things turned out, Rick Scarlett was pleased, for
now they were alone.

The restaurant was a part of Pike Place Market, serving
French cuisine at sky-rocket prices. For a few extra bucks
under the table the Maitre d' (Parisian, of course) had
seated them by a window where the view out over Elliott
Bay was positively breathtaking. They were dining up on
the second floor of a building constructed on stilts so that
it jutted out over the edge of a bluff. Before the sun had
set 'the mountains really had been out,' as the people of
Seattle say. But now all that could be seen were the lights
of the boats bobbing out on the water beyond the candle
flame reflected in the glass. They had just finished dessert
and a third bottle of wine.

'I wonder what he did with them, Kathy?' Rick Scarlett asked. His words were slightly slurred. He had consumed most of the alcohol.

'With what?' the woman replied.

'With the severed heads.'

'I have no idea. And I doubt we'll ever know.'

'Yeah,' Scarlett said, then they both fell silent.

He motioned to a waiter and, when the man came over, ordered two Courvoisier. As he turned back, once again – inadvertently – Scarlett looked her up and down. Spann was wearing a black dress cut low in the front and a simple string of pearls. Her hair was swept up on both sides of her head and pinned back. Scarlett's throat was dry by the time the cognac arrived.

'You know,' Spann said slowly, swirling the liquid around in the snifter and glancing out through the window, 'the thing I like most about the States is that the people are so overt. I mean sure there's a lot of shit in this country too, but the Americans are not afraid to bring it to the surface. I believe that takes guts: they're a lot more honest than we are.'

'Perhaps,' Scarlett said, and he looked down her cleavage.

Fifteen minutes later the bill arrived. Though Scarlett insisted on paying for the meal, Katherine Spann declined. 'Not my style,' she said. So they split it down the middle and then went outside.

Immediately the aromas of Pike Place Market assailed their senses of smell: the meat, the fish, the spice shops, the bakeries and the delis. Lingering above all these was the pungent sea-salt air, blowing up Puget Sound and tugging at their clothes. Just outside the restaurant Rick Scarlett tripped and fell. Spann broke his catapult motion and said: 'You've had too much to drink.'

'No way,' the man said, regaining balance. She looked at her watch.

'We better make for Sea-Tac,' Katherine Spann said. 'Let's hail a taxi or we're going to miss our plane.'

Scarlett didn't move. Instead he grabbed her by the arm. They were standing at the top of a wooden staircase that led to the street below. Stretched out before them was the black of Elliott Bay.

'I guess this must really be something for you, eh?'

'What do you mean?' Spann said. 'Do you always talk in riddles?'

'I mean what with you being a woman, and making Corporal and all. That's quite an achievement. You're one of the first.'

The woman shook her head as if in disappointment. 'Rick,' she said quietly, 'I'm the same age as you. I've been a cop just as long as you have. And you made Corporal too. What does being a woman have to do with this promotion?'

Scarlett shrugged his shoulders. 'You know what I mean?'

'No, Rick. I don't.'

'Look, Kathy. My father was a member of this Force back on the prairies. For as long as I can remember I have wanted to be in the RCMP. That's how *I* come to be here.'

'So? I come to be here because . . .'

'Because of feminism and the liberation of women. It's written all over you.'

'Oh, is that so?'

'You bet. You thrive on besting men within a domain that has been traditionally male. For you it's a challenge, and I admire that.'

'Is that how you see it?'

'Yes, and so should you. If you don't recognize that you're just being blind.'

'And just who am I talking to? Is this Rick Scarlett speaking? Or is it two bottles of Chateauneuf du Pape?'

'I'm not drunk.'

'I think you are.'

'Come on, Kathy, admit it. Be honest with yourself. Deep down inside you're just like the rest of us. You want power. And you like to get ahead. There's nothing wrong with that.'

'Come on, Rick, let's . . .'

'And you like to get fucked.'

Katherine Spann frowned and took a step away from him.

'Don't look so shocked. It's not against the law.'

Again the woman shook her head. 'Let's catch that plane.'

'Let's not, Kathy. Let's stay here and have a little fun. Believe me, it'll be worth it. I'll make sure of that.'

'Come on, Romeo. Let's go home.'

Scarlett gripped her tighter. He had yet to let go of her arm. 'Don't treat me like I'm some little kid.'

'Then quit acting like one. And let go of me.'

Scarlett dropped his arm as anger came into his eyes. 'Aren't we the cold one? Tell me woman, just what does a guy have to do to get somewhere with you?'

'Shut it down, Rick. I've had a good time. Let's not spoil it.'

'Answer me! What's the matter? Don't you like men?'

'Rick,' she said slowly, beginning to clench her teeth. 'I work with you and you're a part of the job. I like you as a partner, but we can't be anything else. Can't you see that?'

'Don't be absurd. What does that matter? I won't tell anyone else.'

'That's not the point.'

'The point is, Kathy, that I am crazy about you. I have been ever since I first saw you standing at that bulletin board checking the assignments. You dominate my thoughts.'

'I said shut it down, Rick. I want to catch that plane. Are you coming or not?'

'You listen to me!' Scarlett almost shouted. 'Don't you turn your back on me. I won't have it! For two months now I've kept my feelings to myself. Business is business and I'm a professional too. Fine. Okay. But now the case

381

is over. The squad is disbanded. We'll be reposted and that's the end of that. But that doesn't alter the way I feel. Nothing can change that. I *want* you Kathy! You drive me out of my mind!'

'I'm leaving, Rick,' she said. And Spann turned to go.

'Fuck you!' the man yelled. 'Don't hold your cunt so tight!' And with that he reached out with his good arm – the one without the stitches – and grabbed her breast.

Katherine Spann seized his hand, pried her body free of his grip and pushed him away. 'Do that again and I'll slug you,' she said. Her right hand balled in a fist. 'Now leave me alone. I don't fuck cops. That's incest, you ass!'

Rick Scarlett's face grew livid with drunken rage.

'You bitch!' he shouted. 'You tight-ass bitch! It's all a game to you, isn't it? All a fuckin game! You dress up in the uniform and hold your back erect, masking it as protocol while you show off your tits! And look at you tonight! You hypocrite! Cut it any lower and that dress would show your snatch!'

'You child,' Spann said, and she turned on her heels and left him ranting in the night.

She took the steps three at a time to gain the road below. As luck would have it there was a cab waiting at the bottom. Twenty minutes later she was at the Sea-Tac Airport with very few minutes to spare. She was the last passenger to board the final flight to Vancouver that night.

It was only as the DC-9 gained altitude and the water dropped away that she finally began to relax and let the tension unwind.

Oh hell, Spann thought, closing her eyes. *Why is it that just when things begin to go right, someone has to spoil it?*

Now she'd have to watch Scarlett.

PART THREE

What's up, Doc?

No, it was not funny; it was rather pathetic; he was so representative of all the past victims of the great Joke. But it is by folly alone that the world moves, and so it is a respectable thing upon the whole. And besides, he was what one could call a good man.

Joseph Conrad.

ONE MIND'S I

Vancouver, British Columbia.

October

> Rain. Rain. Rain.
> Pain. Pain. Pain.
>
> It feels like a ghost
> Come back
> To haunt me once again.
>
> Slow days. No gain.
>
> I don't think I'm up to this!

I spent the night in her old chair sitting next to a shuttered window.

Now that my mother's in the ground I really must sell her house. Outside, an October wind in barren trees moaned so mournfully.

I just sat there most of the night, staring at the pictures.
While the pictures lay on her tabletop.
Staring back at me.

OBSESSIONS – It is not uncommon for neurotics to develop a special concern about some danger or problem. If these exaggerated concerns become very intense they are called obsessions. For example it may be necessary for a person to climb out of bed countless times a night to check the gas valves on the stove. Or like Howard Hughes, someone may be so concerned about the slightest contact with dirt that he is compelled to wash his hands constantly or to become a recluse. Neurotic obsessions are thought to conceal some wish that is often either of a destructive or sexual nature. This wish is usually quite obscure in most obsessions and hidden in symbolic distortion.

What do I know about *death?* Well, let me see.

I know that the true way of defining the end of life is as 'a state where time no longer exists'. Time needs activity by which to measure it, so without activity there can be no time.

'I know that the human obsession with death is called *thanatophilia*. And I know that a person who fears death in an abnormal sense is termed a *thanatophobe*.

If the shoe fits wear it.

Father. Brother.
Mother. Son.
Starting over: how many times?
Is not *will* the very core of character?
Is the rudder of the ego not a person's *will?*
All the past and all the future,
Do they not determine the now?

The course of Life surely depends upon the deftness of the helmsman. So, sail away!

I must remember to pick up my suits from One Hour Martinizing.

Also I need more Gillette Atra blades.

Is it just my imagination or do they really put the sharp razor blades in the first and last position with duller ones inbetween?

I dreamt about you last night, Cathy – about the accident. When I awoke I found I had my pillow grasped tightly in my arms.

Again I saw the gravesite, but I couldn't go near the grave. It was raining and all the mourners were standing under black umbrellas. Your mother was crying and I wanted to hold her, but somehow I couldn't join in. I stood at the periphery of the graveyard getting soaking wet. I was the only one present without protection from the rain.

God, sometimes I get so lonely.

So fucking tired of life.

I felt like that this evening so I spent some time in the sky. You should have seen Jupiter! So magnificent and alive with cloud activity. With a camera-shot through my telescope I caught Saturn at a good angle for the rings. Tomorrow night after shift I think I'll develop and blow up the film. Maybe I'll put a picture up on the bedroom wall. I could use the company.

When you're tired – alone – and afraid of the future, what else can you do? Maybe see a shrink!

Am I having an anxiety attack or is anxiety attacking me?

Tonight is Halloween.

I lay the pictures – there are three pictures now! – out on the developing table beside my photo enlarger. I had just finished blowing up the shots taken in the sky. I found my hands were shaking and my body had goose-flesh crawling. It took me more than an hour to overcome the urge. But I did it. Once again I managed to keep my MONSTER! in its cage.

Next time I might not be lucky.

Next time I might not win.

I fear that next time I might just blow those three pictures up.

God save me from that.

November

Well, I saw Dr George Ruryk today and this is what he told me.

First of all ask yourself: where do my thoughts come from?

We've all heard of complexes. 'Stop treating the child that way, you're going to give him a complex.' 'That man suffers from an inferiority complex.' 'I tell you the guy is weird. He's got some sort of Oedipus complex.' 'She's got this Electra complex. She wants to fuck her father.'

So what is a complex?

A complex is a group of ideas that dominate your thoughts and colour your experiences. You come to see everything in relation to those ideas. If you're in love, for example, the slightest thing, like just a whiff of perfume, will bring immediately to mind all the ideas and feelings that make up your 'love complex'.

A complex is to psychology what Force is to physics.

But here comes the rub!

What happens if a particular complex is for some reason totally out of harmony with the rest of the conscious mind? Perhaps its ideas are unbearably painful. Perhaps it is of a sexual nature incompatible with the person's rigid views and principles.

What happens is that a conflict arises – a struggle commences and ensues between the rebel complex in question and the rest of the personality.

Perhaps the complex can be modified by the mind so that it is no longer incompatible with the rest of the personality.

Perhaps the mind can weigh the merits of each opponent and consciously choose to abandon one in favour of the other.

Or perhaps this is impossible and there must be a fight to the finish.

If there must be a fight then the common method used by the human mind is the sledge hammer of repression.

In using repression conflict is avoided by banishing one of the opponents to the cellar of the mind. From there the exile is no longer allowed to achieve normal expression, and the victor of the fight is left in control of the field of consciousness.

But here, Dr Ruryk said, comes the second rub!

Though the complex is shut up downstairs in the dark and denied its normal function, it is not annihilated. It continues to exist within the deeper layers of the mind, festering, while prevented from rising to the surface by the constant resistance of the guard at the door, namely the mind's force of repression.

Have you ever put tarmac on a driveway before the winter snows set in?

Well if you have – and if you failed to kill every last living seed on the ground before doing so – come spring the tarmac will crack and up through its surface will sprout a small plant shoot.

Same with the human mind.

But in a much more devious way.

For a repressed complex can only influence the conscious mind indirectly. This is because of the 'censure' guard standing watch at the cellar door. It must slip out in disguise.

The uglier the monster, the more circuitous its route.

So, Dr Ruryk said, back to your inquiry about an obsession with death.

Assume something has happened which has caused remorse in a person's mind. Perhaps you know such an individual?

(Yes, I think I do.)

Now say this remorse is painful to that person's mind. Perhaps it's guilt over a death. To deal with this upset to equilibrium the complex related to this remorse is repressed by the conscious mind. But that complex still needs to express itself. So how does it manifest?

Sometimes the mind uses symbolism to express these repressed and dissociated ideas: here you have the man who thinks that he is Napoleon. The man with the delusion.

Sometimes the mind uses the device which we call projection. Here the repressed complex is no longer regarded by the personality as being part of its own self.

The complex has been projected onto another person – and thus conflict is avoided.

If the complex is projected onto a real person, then a delusion of persecution by that individual may result. And in self-defence the patient may try to kill that other person.

If the complex is projected onto an imaginary person, or one who is long since dead, then the repressed set of ideas appears as an hallucination. The patient sees ghosts. Or hears commanding voices telling him what to do. Perhaps a voice from Hell.

What you must realize, Dr Ruryk said, is that any one of our instinctive drives may give rise to a conflict in the mind.

Freud said that most cases of repression arise from the instinct of sex.

Perhaps he was right.

But right or not, the fact remains that the origin of a mental aberration is not to be found in any disturbance within the mechanics of the mind.

It is to be found in the material from life fed into the brain of any particular human being.

Therefore to answer the question of whether or not you yourself may go insane, ask yourself: *Do I have monsters lurking in the cellar of my mind?*

But there's a final rub!

For if you do they've been repressed, and you won't even know they're there until they break out of the dungeon.

That's what Dr Ruryk said when I saw him early today.

He suggested that if I was interested in pursuing the matter further I might wish to sit in on a psychology seminar given by one of his former students. He told me her name is Genevieve.

I might just do that and find out where it leads.

Of course I didn't tell Dr Ruryk about my problem with the heads.

Complex is to psychology what Force is to physics. Let's see where this goes. Eh, whadda ya say?

1954.

That would have been the year.

I remember my father standing at the drugstore counter with his change in one hand and whisky on his breath, talking to Mr Thorson. I was walking toward the rear of the pharmacy where the comic racks were kept. It was the first Tuesday in the month so the new *Blackhawk* would be in. I remember I never made it to those racks.

To reach the comic stands at the rear of Thorson's Drug Store you had to pass a long shelf filled with adult magazines. *Life* and *Look* and *Ellery Queen* and *Saturday Evening Post*. The head was waiting for me buried in among these books.

The head was on the cover of a pulp magazine, *Real Man's Adventure*. As I recall, those words were printed in red, the same colour as the blood which dripped from the neck, from the eyes, and from the nose of that head stuck on a pole. Between the shreds of skin that hung down from the hacked-off skull you could just make out a trace of neck vertebra peeking through. But most of all what I remember is the eyes. Rolled back into their sockets, just a slivered moon of pupil showing beneath each eyelid, both eyes definitely staring right at me. I was seven years old.

For at that moment a very strange thing happened, and I was no longer in that store. It was as though I had been sucked right off my feet and transported through the door of that magazine cover. I recall clearly sitting in the front of that dugout canoe facing the Great White Hunter who was crouched in the stern. His khaki jacket was soaked with sweat and plastered to his chest. I remember bullets sewn into loops across the front of the jacket. I could see a St Christopher's medal around the tense muscle cords in his neck. He wore a safari hat with a leopard skin band pushed back from his forehead. His index finger was on the trigger of the Remington in his hands.

And I knew we were surrounded.

There was a circle of severed heads ringed around our boat, each head stuck on the end of a pole fixed to the front of a dugout. The dugouts were manned by South American Jivaro Indians (I know that now), all conspiring to close off any chance of an escape. The Indians all had bronze skin and long black hair. Their bodies were naked except for breechclouts covering their loins. Each man was armed: a few with spears that were decorated with hanks of human hair, others with long hollow blowpipe tubes resting on lower lips, most with machetes three feet long with the sun glinting off sharp edges spattered with blood and gore.

Then something bumped our dugout and a hand touched my shoulder.

I could have died of fright.

For there was this grip trying to steady my trembling body before a blade swooped my head away.

'Easy son,' a voice said. 'Just turn and look at me.'

Though I tried to do as it said, I couldn't – that picture would not set me free.

Then I saw another hand reach over me to turn the copy of *Real Man's Adventure* face down on the stack of magazines below.

'There,' my father said, squatting down on bended knees. 'Out of sight, out of mind. That picture bothers you?'

'No,' I remember saying, now back in the store. I was shaking my head from side to side.

'Well it bothers *me*,' my father said. 'That's what it's meant to do. It's like your comic *Tales From The Crypt* but a little more realistic. Don't be afraid of fear, son. We all have to conquer it someday – one way or another. Now go on and pick out a comic. Your mother's got supper waiting.'

I did what he said.

Then with his arm on my shoulder, the two of us left the store. But I do remember one final look back at that stack of magazines.

On the back cover of *Real Man's Adventure*, Charles Atlas was flexing his biceps and asking: *Would you like to look like me?*

The plane went missing that December as my father was flying to Toronto. He had managed to stop his drinking long enough to land a job and was on his way back east for some sort of business upgrading.

For two months I spent every day sitting by the front door waiting for him to return.

It was the second week in February before they found the wreck of the aircraft. It had smashed to pieces on a Rocky Mountain peak. I cried for several days.

The second head was waiting for me on the first Tuesday in March.

My eyes must have seen it at once but neglected to tell my brain, for I distinctly heard the sound of a snake slither across the drugstore floor. I recall my sweat bursting from every pore as if I were in steaming tropical heat. And I know my mind was shrieking: *I GOT TO GET OUT OF HERE!*

This head was worse than the others.

For there he was again, my friend, the Great White Hunter in his sweat-stained khaki safari jacket. Only this time he was in the background, standing, Remington ready, in the door of a grass hut. You could see him between the Jivaro's legs which made up the picture's foreground. The cover focused on an Indian's loins from his waist down to his knees. That was all that you could see of him as he walked away from the hunter. Except, of course, for his hands.

His left hand held the machete dripping blood and gore.

His right hand held a leather thong attached to both ends of a needle. This needle was made of slivered bone about ten inches long. It had been rammed through one eardrum of the head until it had passed through the brain and out of the other ear. The head itself took up a good one-third of the page. Trickles of blood ran down from the corner of each eye. The eyes had rolled up in the head, one of them nothing but white road-mapped with red veins. The other revealed just the barest hint of a pupil.

I tried to turn away. But I couldn't. I tried to run. But I couldn't. I tried to shut my own eyes. But I couldn't.

'Please, father,' I whispered. 'Turn that picture away.' My hope was that he'd stop it like he had that time before.

'What's going on here? You're talking to yourself.'

'It's back, Dad. It's back. Make it go away.'

A hand fell onto my shoulder, giving it a shake.

'Are you all right, son?' the voice of the druggist asked.

And that was when I knew for sure that no matter how much I needed him my father would never be there again.

I guess I panicked.

For a moment there I looked again at the cover and thought that this time I saw my father's eyes staring out at me from that chopped head strung on a string. His pale grey eyes shone faintly through the flesh of those rolled back whites.

Then I broke away from the druggist and made a dash for the door. With glass shattering and exploding in razor-sharp shards around me, I ran right through the pane set into the metal doorframe.

Outside it was raining. That's usual for this city.

I was more than a block away from the store and still running through the downpour when I realized I was cut. Both my hands were slashed and gouged and smeared with blood. I stopped running abruptly and sat down on the ground beside a puddle rippled with raindrops. For maybe half an hour I sat there thinking about my father trapped inside that hacked-off head, watching the water distort my reflection and wash my blood away.

Four days later I knew something was wrong.

At Vancouver General Hospital a doctor had put forty-seven stitches into my hands. My mother was upset as hell and equally pissed off. Paying for the door had cost her fifty bucks that we could ill afford; my father because of his drinking had let his insurance premiums lapse. But more than that, the thought of her son with his hands paralyzed because of severed nerves and tendons had cost her several nights' sleep. And she had desperately needed that rest. It had only been a few weeks since they had found the wreckage of the plane and I know she was struggling against odds to hold up a strong front for the sake of me and my brother.

I never told her about the head on the front of the magazine. At eight years old I was now the man in this family. Men like Charles Atlas weren't afraid of magazine covers.

She was the best type of mother. She didn't pry.

The only punishment I got was that four days after the accident she sent me to the drugstore to buy replacement bandages for my injured hands. Like most mothers she saw me off with words something like this: 'I hope this trip reinforces the lesson you should have learned. You know you could have been killed.'

I bypassed the drugstore with the piece of plywood set into its door – in fact I never went there again – and walked six blocks down from Victoria Drive till I came to a Rexall Pharmacy. Through its glass door I could see shelves of medicine, Band-Aids, candy, toys, and that the bald-headed druggist was passing a youth a package that seemed to embarrass him. There was a young teenage girl about the same age as the youth waiting expectantly outside the store.

I first knew something was wrong when I couldn't get through the door.

It was science fiction come true: I was held off by some sort of force field.

Holding both arms out before me I tried to will my hands to press the metal bar that stretched across the door. But my arms refused to move. It was weird and I felt frightened.

The girl outside noticed I was in difficulty and she came sauntering over, peeking shyly into the store as she did so. 'Must hurt, eh?' she said, looking at my bandaged hands and pushing open the door to help me.

'Yeah, it does,' I said, and I tried to step forward. But now my foot refused to move. It was as if the sole of my penny-loafer was glued to the concrete. I tried to move a second time, and then the fear really set in.

Something's wrong with me, I thought. *I can't get into the store!*

Just then the youth rushed out through the door, pushing me aside. 'I got 'em,' he said excitedly. 'An' these ones are lubricated.'

'Jeez, Tim,' the girl said, her face becoming bright pink, 'you hit that little kid.'

'Oh, yeah. Sorry kid.' He gave me a disdainful look. Then noticing my hands he said: 'You need some help?'

'Would you buy me some bandages?' I asked. 'While I wait out here?'

He looked at me queerly but did as I requested. A few minutes later as he walked away with his girl I heard him say, 'You know there's somethin odd with that kid.'

And he was right.

I knew it too.

It wasn't long before my friends were privy to the secret. When one in their midst is unable to go into a confectionary to buy Double Bubble gum and has to tell his compatriots what comic books to buy him while he waits outside the drugstore, eight-year-olds cotton on fast to the fact that something's queer. Eight-year-olds also have this need to set the world a-right.

I suppose that's why Jimbo made the mistake.

You see, we had gone to the Busy Bee Market one fine April afternoon – Corry and Jimbo and I – to buy ourselves each a pop. I was hooked on cream soda at the time, and hoping to find a bottle of white stuff, not the usual red kind. The woman who ran the Busy Bee was a woman who knew her pop. And just for me she kept her eyes peeled for a case of white each time the delivery truck came around.

I know I should have been wary – what with it being April Fool's Day and all – but the morning was bright with sunshine and my bandages had just come off for good. Much to my mother's surprise, my fingers weren't paralyzed.

Anyway, we reached the store and I gave Jimbo my dime.

'The white kind, right?' Jimbo asked as Corry opened the door.

'Yeah,' I said, totally unsuspecting. Out of the corner of my eye I could see the magazine rack. I was turning a little more to the left to put the rack out of sight at my rear when they pulled the trick.

'April Fool!' Jimbo said and he pushed me through the door.

I have never felt such panic: it literally closed my throat so I couldn't get any air. My heart was leaping about in my chest as I scrambled to get back outside. But they were both blocking the door. Jimbo was laughing and chortling and Corry was slapping his sides.

That's when I broke Jimbo's nose.

I recall wildly swinging my arm in a pitcher's circle and giving him the old one-two. I popped him square in the middle of his face and heard the small bone crack. Jimbo

dropped like a sack of onions down onto his knees. Corry
had stopped laughing but was still blocking the door.
With a flying tackle I hit him in the chest and with one
hand clawed at his eyes. I distinctly remember shouting
'Lemme out! Lemme out!' as I pounded him again and
again.

'Stop it!' Corry yelled. 'You're hurt . . .' (I hit him)
'Stop it, you're hurting me!'

Both of us were now thrashing as we stumbled back
out through the door.

Then once outside, I stopped.

When I got home that night it was my brother who
opened the door.

He took one look at me all bashed up, and then he
began to cry.

Different guy, my brother. Then only five years old.
Why'd he have to go and die?

It was later that month that I developed a fear of blood.

I recall my mother in the kitchen chopping vegetables.
I was at the table drawing my own comic book. It was
about a superhero I called 'The Butcheress'. She wore
these blue tights and a purple cape shaped a bit like
Batman's. She was armed with that most sensible of
weapons for today's superhero – a giant meat cleaver. I
was getting very good at drawing her breasts.

Plop . . . plop . . . plop . . .

I could hear the sound of the vegetables landing on the
chopping board. Heads would make a sound like that
when they dropped from the guillotine.

Plop . . . plop . . . plop . . .

Then my mother cried out in pain and ran out of the
kitchen, holding her hand. The knife was on the cutting-
board with its tip stained crimson.

I ran into the bathroom after her and saw her blood all

over the floor. There was the whoosh of tapwater flowing which seemed to magnify and grow into the hoarse roar of a waterfall. The room began to wobble. 'Will you get me a Band-Aid?' my mother asked as the bathroom walls swayed, as the sound of the water faded in and out, as the tiles of the floor came up to meet me and slam against the side of my head.

I came to to find myself cradled in her arms.

She was crying (we all seemed to cry a lot that spring) and she was holding me against her, while one hand gripped her other palm still trying to stop the flow of blood as she coaxed me back to consciousness.

I loved you, Mom.

That night I awoke in my room all alone in the dark. I could hear whispering.

When I looked around there was nothing but black, black, black.

And then I saw a point of light up in the corner off to my left where two walls met the ceiling. It was this light that was whispering as it slowly, ever so slowly, began to spin in a circle. Imagine a tiny point of light on the tip of a pinwheel blade and you'll know what I mean. Round and round and round it went in an ever-widening circle. Spinning as it cork-screwed down toward me.

I remember pulling the bedcovers up to the bridge of my nose.

Then I waited, transfixed and watching, until the point of light was half way across the space separating it from me.

That was when I saw the face.

It was this little wee miniature face circling slowly round and round, shining with eerie light.

Its features were those of the Great White Hunter and he was whispering at me: 'Watch out! Watch out! Watch out! I'm going to take her too.'

I never got back to sleep that night, not until dawn came peeking in with the light of the following morning.

It was Jimbo who found the solution. I'll give him credit for that. The opportunity to find it had cost him a broken nose.

'Okay, here's what we do,' Jimbo said confidently. 'I go in and scout the place and find the magazine rack. Then I came out and tell you where it is and the three of us go in. You, me, and Corry. You inbetween. Got it. Okay?'

No, it was not okay.

'Now once we get through the door, I'll hold up my jacket so you can't see the rack. If you try to look then Corry grabs you, I throw the jacket over your head, and we drag you back outside. Then we try it again.'

It took half an hour's persuasion before the three of us came through that door.

But it worked, by God. Somehow it broke the spell.

Or maybe it was just the fact that I never saw another magazine cover drawn by that particular artist.

And so it was that Jimbo – in a triumph for amateur psychology – took care of the drugstores, took care of the news-stands, took care of the confectioners.

But he didn't take care of the blood.

Good Lord, I don't believe it! I think I'm in love!

I went to the seminar, God knows why – maybe cause Ruryk suggested it and maybe I thought I'd find a key to unlock more of myself. Who knows why! Who cares!

Good God, what a woman! You should see her!

Genevieve, Genevieve, GENEVIEVE – where have you been all my life?

Just my luck she's married – so what if it's one-way love.

Oh God, to have this feeling again.

Genevieve DeClercq – I LOVE YOU.

Oh happy day.

So let's talk about severed heads.

The human brain can live for up to a minute on the blood-oxygen supply within it at any given time. Cut the head from the body and the mind lives on. Consciousness survives.

Why do human beings so fear a severed head?

Is it because we know instinctively that if decapitation should happen to us, our mind lives on?

But tell me something.

If this is everyman's general fear, why must I be plagued with it multiplied a thousand times?

Why must this fear also be my particular neurosis?

Can you answer that, YOU IN HERE WITH ME?

Genevieve, Genevieve, Genevieve! Will you be my salvation?

I listened to every word you said in the seminar tonight. Did I get it right?

Genevieve, will you be my secret therapist?

I hope you will – as long as you don't know.

This will be my secret.

After the seminar tonight I spent some time in the sky. My camera caught a nebula and I saw the canals on Mars. I developed some shots of Jupiter taken the other evening, placing the prints – unenlarged – out on the drying table.

The Polaroids of the severed heads are now *four* in number. They were off to the side.

Genevieve, I've made up my mind to meet this MONSTER! headon.

Tomorrow after work I'm going to rephotograph the Polaroid prints and put the negatives through my enlarger.

I hope it works!

I guess my brother's murder precipitated my decision. But maybe it's deeper than that.

They never found his body so the motive's speculation, but I had seen the needle marks on the inside of his forearm. In this city we all know that the monkey is motive enough.

My mother was devastated: she never came back from it. I watched her spark just fizz away as she aged a hundred years. She used to sit in my father's chair staring out through the shutters. The same chair I used when she died.

I know a guy who was terrified of hypodermic needles. He overcame his fear by becoming a doctor.

I guess it was preordained that I'd become a cop.

God, why did I blow up those heads!

I'm back! You won't believe this! She asked me out to lunch!

'Brunch,' she said on the telephone. '10.45'.

Oh happy happy day.

Another picture arrived tonight, and then the news we got him.

This one was different, not a Polaroid.

It's almost as if the Headhunter knew we were looking to identify people buying that type of film.

Genevieve will be happy now that her nightmare's over.

I never got off the blocks.

'Watch out! Watch out! Watch out! I'm going to take her too.'

Back to you, Cathy Jenkins, high school heart-throb of mine.

I think there are people in this world who Death likes to follow around. People like me.

You know that was a silly argument we had over graduation. I know the lottery meant you went to the dance with some other guy. It was all so adolescent. It's just that you were the only girlfriend I ever had. I wish I'd been able to tell you that before the accident.

Is that why I've got no umbrella in that graveyard driven with rain?

Losing my chance with women, that's the story of my life.

It's time to fade away.

Hey, surprise! I'm back. I guess you can't keep a good man down.

A cop is a cop, I suppose.

Something strange has happened: I don't think Hardy's our boy.

Here's what bothered me. Each of the victims except for the last – and that's because of the interruption – was raped by the Headhunter before her head was carried away. Yet only the body of Joanna Portman showed signs of ejaculation. Now why would the Headhunter come only once: that doesn't fit a pattern?

Okay, start with the assumption that this particular killer is motivated by a sexual aberration.

He gets his rocks off by stabbing woman before, during or after intercourse.

Or perhaps he can get it up but can't get off and holds women responsible. Then he stabs them for mental satisfaction and blows a load in his head.

So what's going on here? The night that John Lincoln Hardy was killed I had missed the seminar. It was my turn on graveyard shift – and besides I had told Genevieve I would help her in every way I could. So I spent several hours that night at my desk reviewing the investigation. That was when I found the note by DeClercq concerning the statement by Mrs Enid Portman.

It read: *Jack – have someone check out the possibility that*

Joanna Portman had a boyfriend. Sperm can be found in the vagina for up to thirty-six hours after intercourse. If she had sex within that period it explains the ejaculation. The point bothers me – DeClercq.

After reading this it bothered me too.

There was a subsequent report which confirmed the Superintendent's query. After a follow-up check by the Squad, a boyfriend had been located. He was a married surgeon who worked at the hospital. He had rented an apartment across the street from St Paul's where he and Joanna Portman would slip away during supper-break when they were both on shift. And yes, during that last day of her work they had met and had been fucking.

Surprisingly, after the death of John Lincoln Hardy there had been no follow-up concerning him. Most cops don't like loose ends even when they have closed a file. But perhaps it was just overlooked in the joy that came with the release of public pressure on the Squad. Who knows the reason? Yet somehow it sat in the back of my mind and continued to bother me.

Now I'm bothered even more.

Because today I got the answer.

It took some time to find her.

First I spent a couple of nights driving up and down the streets of the West End. I checked each face on the boulevard against her mugshot picture. The ones who were young and knew they had it stood directly under the lights, pursing their lips or plucking a nipple as I went by in my car. The ones who were ravaged by age or the needle kept themselves to the shadows. They showed more of their bodies in this competition to grab the attention of passing men. The hookers started at Bute Street, and down about Jervis and Broughton they were as thick as thieves. By Nicola they had relinquished the territory to young boys in their teens waiting for the chickenhawk. I didn't find her there.

Next I checked the Corner and all its greasy spoons, strip joints and shot palaces but she wasn't there either.

Then finally in a pub on Granville Street just before the bridge, I scored. Some score.

The guy at the beer tap must have weighed at least 280 pounds. He had a face that someone had once cut to ribbons with a very sharp knife or a barber's razor. He wore a black patch over one eye. Using his good eye to stare at the mugshot he glanced at me for a moment, then flicked a look at one corner. I found her sitting against the far wall of the pub.

I walked over and sat down opposite her.

Charlotte Clarke was slumped across a cigarette-burned table with a terry-towel cover, one hand clutching a beer glass, her face buried in the crook of her arm. Just to the side of her cheek I could see a fresh needle mark at her elbow with its telltale bubble of blood. I reached out and shook her once – then twice – then I waited a while. After a few minutes she began to come around.

'I got the clap,' she mumbled vaguely, looking at me with these opaque shiny eyes. She nodded once, then put her head back down and I had to shake her again.

'What the fuck do *you* want?' she growled at me from another world.

'Police,' I said softly. 'And I want some information.'

The guy at the next table must have heard what I said cause he got up fast and made for the door. He left a full glass of beer behind on the table.

'Go suck yourself off,' the young lady whispered. 'I ain't holdin' so you can blow it out your sweet ass.' When she went to put her head down this time I stopped her with my hand cupped under her chin.

'You were Hardy's girl,' I said. 'I want to talk about him.'

'Lemme see your shield.'

I flashed her the tin.

As she looked at my ID card this smile came over her

face. Wrinkling her nose like a rabbit she said: 'Eh, what's up doc?' She found it very funny.

I didn't. 'I said I want to talk about . . .'

'You killed him!' she said sharply, then her face changed expression and suddenly she slapped me. I slapped her back. The guy at the table two seats down jumped up and made for the exit. Like the junkie before him he left beer and change on the table.

'I didn't kill anyone. Don't try that again.'

Tears came to her eyes. 'If you're a cop, you killed him,' she said. 'That's how it is for me.'

'Did he do it, Charlotte? Did he kill those women?'

'Aw, shit, man! Will you lemme alone? My old man's dead, can't you understand? He may not have bin worth a turd to you, but he meant a fuck of a lot to me.' The rush was wearing off.

'Try me,' I said.

But she didn't say a thing.

'I'll pay you the price of a cap.'

'Don't con me.'

I counted out seventy dollars and placed it on the table between us. She knocked it onto the floor, but then had second thoughts. I knew I was sure to win the game that junkies always lose.

'Two caps,' she said finally with this smirk on her face.

'Sorry,' I said. 'No can do. This is from my own pocket. It's me as man wants to know, not me as cop.'

'Know what?' she asked – and I knew I had her.

'Did you ever fuck him? John Lincoln Hardy?'

Her eyes opened wide and they were shining like stars. 'Did I what?' she asked of me, incredulous.

'Did you ever fuck him?'

'Come on! He was my old man.'

'Word on the street is he wired you. You peddled your ass for him. Word is he beat you once or twice, beat you up real bad. A girl doesn't need to screw her pimp, you and I know that. Once again, Charlotte: Did you ever fuck him?'

406

'Yeah, I fucked him.'

'Often?'

'Every night. Johnnie was a man.'

'Did he come?'

She frowned at me in wonderment, then tossed away one hand. 'Everyone comes for me,' she said, getting up from the table. She bent down for the money on the floor and stuffed it in the waistband of her jeans. Then she turned to leave, stopped, and this is what she said:

'That's the last of the answers, fuzz, and I don't want you comin' back. But here's somethin' for free. Johnnie was a good man and he was a hell of a lover. He was the one who hooked me on junk, kept me in junk – and he was the only guy in my life who ever made me feel wanted. Do you understand what it means to need to feel wanted? You think I was just some sweet girl working in a Dairy Queen who got fucked over by some black stud who beat her black and blue.' She sat down again, and leaned across the table towards me. 'Maybe I deserved it. I stole from him once you see, when I needed some junk. I stole something precious, I stole this wooden mask. So he beat me, and beat me, and beat me. But I loved the guy: and you killed him. And I'd do it all over again the exact same way tomorrow.'

'Why'd you sell the mask? And not his Polaroid camera?'

'Camera? Don't make me laugh,' Charlotte Clarke said looking puzzled. 'What would Johnnie have done with that? He never owned no camera.' Then she got up and walked away.

I let her go: she'd told me what I wanted.

She got another fix and I got a hundred caps' worth.

But I knew that when that junk hit her vein she'd see it the other way round.

And that was good.

At least someone would be happy.

I found them in the courthouse coffee shop down at 222 Main. They were making cop-talk as I sat down at the table.

'So she told me she stole the lighter because she was so nervous about stealing the other goods that she needed a cigarette, but didn't have a light,' Rick Scarlett said.

We all smiled at that one and William Tipple said: 'Not bad, but I think Mad Dog gets the prize. Anyone dissenting? Okay Rabid there you go. Six quarters.'

'What is this?' I asked. 'Some sort of reunion?'

'Nope,' Bill Tipple said, 'just coincidence. Scarlett, Spann and I are down here to speak to the Department of Justice prosecutor about more charges against Rackstraw. We want him for both importing cocaine and for conspiracy. Macdonald and Lewis are here for an evidence interview on the US application to extradite Matthew Paul Pitt. Mad Dog Rabidowski has a theft under trial.'

'Ain't life a bore,' Rabidowski said, 'since they disbanded the Squad. I wish we hadn't caught him.'

'Maybe we didn't,' I said.

At that moment, with that comment, I learned just how Colonel Tibbets must have felt when he dropped the A-bomb on Hiroshima.

So I told them what bothered me. Why would a man who has a normal sexual release go out and rape and kill women yet never have an orgasm? Why wouldn't he just kill them if it was a psychological thing? Wasn't the killer more likely to be a man in a frenzy unable to ever come? Maybe he picked up syphilis and hated every woman.

My theory wasn't welcome.

First Scarlett looked at me strangely, then he got up and left.

The others for a number of reasons soon followed suit.

I was left alone at the table with a rapidly cooling cup of coffee. I'd hit a dead end and knew it.

As the man says: Nothing in life is ten out of ten.

Is man not lost? Now I ask you: isn't that a hell of a question?

Is that why you started drinking, Dad?

If it is I understand.

It was as I was returning the Headhunter files to the 'morgue' that the negative slipped out of one of them and dropped onto the floor. I bent down to pick it up.

I had decided already that going on was just a waste of time; the investigation was over and Genevieve had surmounted her problem. Besides, I had other work to do. Crime waits for no one.

Strangely, I had completely forgotten about the picture. Perhaps it was repression, something along the line that Dr Ruryk had described. But the moment I held it up to the light I knew I would take it home.

At the present moment it's over there, sitting on my enlarger. I feel a little queasy but I know I'll blow it up. My life has been reduced to mental masochism.

Can you hear me, father? Are you out there listening?

You remember that day you spanked me cause I lipped off our neighbour? How angry I got at you? I told you you were no good cause you couldn't hold a job.

Well father, I'm sorry. Believe me. I wish I'd never said that.

I've atoned a million times since, hoping you were listening.

I killed you, didn't I? It was what I said that day that made you get that job?

If it weren't for me you'd never have been on that plane to Toronto, would you?

I'm so sorry, Dad. Cause now I'm lost too.

I guess we're both a couple of fools. Me with my obsession. You with your booze.

I feel pathetic, father. Can you somehow forgive me? Believe me I'm doing penance.

Watch me blow it up!

There, it's done.

I put the negative into the carrier of my condenser

409

enlarger. I checked the easel illumination and made an exposure. Now the picture of the head is a hundred times normal size.

Look at it with me, father. I don't want to be alone.

I wish you could turn the cover over like you did before.

God, how a negative gives tone separation. It's not like a Polaroid. Look at her face, at the rictus of terror frozen into her muscles. Look at her skin stretched tight and grey and the bulge of her rolled up eyes. Look at her hair, how black it is, all matted in hanks and strands. Look at her mouth open to scream, look at her swollen tongue. Look at the way her nostrils have flared to let out the trickles of blood. And look at how shreds of skin from her neck curl around the pole like snakes.

Hey, wait a minute. That's new. The pole's in a bucket of sand. All of the other pictures ended part way down the stick.

Yes, now I can see what the killer has done.

The Headhunter returns with his trophy and puts it down on the ground. He shovels a pail full of sand and carries it and the head inside. Once there he places the bucket in front of a pinned-up sheet. A pole is stuck into the sand, and the head is rammed down onto the pole. Then he snaps the picture.

Do you think he tried to buy more Polaroid film, saw the trap and therefore changed to an undeveloped negative?

What a joke – his psychosis and my neurosis ending up the same.

Is this all your death is to my conscious mind, Father: a miserable severed human head stuck in a bucket of sand?'

And Dad – there in that bucket – what are those leaves mixed in with the sand?

Fall leaves.

I found a botanist out working in the VanDusen Gardens at 37th and Oak. He was digging over by Olga Jancic's

410

marble, *Metamorphosis*. As I showed him the enlarged, cut-out portion of the bucket of sand and leaves I asked: 'Are those from a maple tree?'

He put on a pair of glasses and looked, and then said: 'Why yes, they are.'

'How many maple trees do you think there are in the Lower Mainland?'

He smiled and shrugged his shoulders. 'A hundred thousand, I guess.' He looked at the photo again, pointing to two of the leaves. 'Those are *acer macrophyllum*. We call it a Big Leaf Maple. The leaf has a classic deep lobe and is native to Western North America.'

I nodded and thanked him for his time. Then as I turned to leave he added: 'Of course you won't find the other type growing anywhere around here. They're from a Sycamore Maple or *acer pseudoplatanus*. That type of tree is native to Europe and Western Asia.'

'Come again?' I said.

'These leaves here in the bucket, mixed in with the other ones.' He took the photo back from me. 'You see how they're smaller than the Big Leaf, about half to three-quarters the size? They're not as deeply lobed, either. They don't grow around here.'

I blinked and I guess my look made him think again.

'Well, not around these parts,' the botanist said, 'unless one of them's been transplanted.'

I knocked on the door and waited.

After a while I heard this sound like a scurrying mouse in the attic. Then the door opened a crack with the burglar chain still fastened. All I could see was one twinkling eye at about belt buckle level. 'Yes?' a brittle voice asked.

'Good morning, ma'am,' I said. 'I'd like to speak to Mrs Elvira Franklen.'

'It's *Miss* Franklen, young man. And just who are you?'

'My name's Al Flood, ma'am,' I said, and flashed her my shield.

The dwarf suddenly opened her twinkling eye very wide (at least she looked dwarf-height to me) and gasped: 'You've come about the library book, haven't you? I told them I'd return it. It's not that long overdue.'

'No ma'am,' I said, 'I'm not here for a library book. I was told at VanDusen Gardens that I'd find Mrs Franklen . . .'

'*Miss* Franklen,' she corrected.

'Sorry . . . Miss Franklen here. I'm a detective with Major Crimes down at the VPD.'

'A detective!' the woman exclaimed, agitated, then she surprised me and swung the door open wide. 'Oh *do* come in Detective Flood. *Do* come in!'

Elvira Franklen reminded me of that little swamp creature in one of those Lucas *Star Wars* films. She was under five feet tall, a pudgy wrinkled little old lady with white hair and bulgy blue eyes that were alight with mischief. I would bet ten dollars that she'd seen seventy-five. She wore this frumpy wool suit and had a brooch fastened at her throat.

'May I see your shield again?' she asked as I was ushered in through the door.

'Of course, ma'am,' I said. I gave her the case with my tin pinned next to the ID card.

'It says here your name is Almore Flood,' she said, looking up sharply. 'A person should use their full name, my mother used to say. That's why you're given it.'

'Yes, ma'am. But people continually equate mine with that rabbit Bugs Bunny.'

Elvira Franklen smiled: 'Just like Meyer Meyer,' she said. 'You'd think people would learn.'

'I don't understand.'

'Meyer Meyer, Detective Flood. The 87th Precinct. Surely they make you read those books when you're in police school?'

'Ma'am?'

'Did anyone ever tell you that you talk like Jack Webb?' She lowered her voice several octaves and growled, 'Just the facts, ma'am.'

She was putting me on. This time *I* smiled.

'Do you remember at the end of *Dragnet* how there used to be that sweaty hand stamp out the letters 'Mark VII' with a heavy hammer. Did you know that was Jack Webb's hand? I like an actor, don't you, who does his own stunts? Would you like some tea?'

'Thank you. Yes, I would.'

'Darjeeling or Poonakandy? Queen Elizabeth drinks Poonakandy. That should be good enough for us.'

'Yes, ma'am,' I said. 'It sounds like that decides it.'

Down a dark hallway she led me, all rich oiled woods and Royal Doulton figurines. She ushered me into a living room to wait while she put the kettle on to boil. That wait was like being in a museum. For there were shelves and these tiny antique tables everywhere around me. On one of the tables she had out on display every Royal Coronation mug since the days of Queen Victoria. China was displayed on another surrounded by photographs of Prince Charles and Princess Diana. Prince William had a wee table of his own. The furniture in the room looked so old and delicate that I was afraid to sit down for fear of breaking it. But the pictures hanging on the walls were the best part of all. I counted fifty-two of them. Detective writers. Each of the photos was autographed and set in a silver frame.

I heard the clink of china and turned to find Elvira Franklen wheeling in a tea trolley. There were two fragile teacups, a silver pot smothered beneath a crocheted cosy, a cream and sugar set, two spoons, two knives, and enough plates of scones and crumpets and muffins and Eccles cakes and pastries to feed the entire British Falkland Islands Expedition.

'I see you're looking at the pictures?'

'Yes,' I said. 'Quite an illustrious company.'

She smiled and the movement made her face crack into a hundred pieces.

'The one of Conan Doyle of course is my favourite. He signed it for me personally just before his death. Will that be one lump or two, Detective Almore Flood?'

'One, thank you,' I said.

She poured me out a cup of tea then offered me the fattening feast spread out on the trolley. I took an Eccles cake. As I munched it Agatha Christie watched me from one of the walls.

'Well now tell me, Detective. What brings you to my door?'

'I was hoping, ma'am, that you might help me catch a killer.'

I'm sure if the ghost of Edgar Allan Poe had walked into the room she would not have been more surprised. Or any more pleased, in fact.

'Me?' she said, sitting bolt upright and putting down her tea.

'Miss Franklen,' I said, lowering my voice so Raymond Chandler could barely overhear, 'we have had a body dug up and dumped in our jurisdiction. This body was covered with dirt and leaves and wrapped in a sheet of plastic. The leaves are of two types of maple. One type is called a Big Leaf . . .'

'That's an *acer macrophyllum*,' she whispered, leaning forward in her chair.

'Yes, which is native to British Columbia. The other, however, is not. It is a sycamore maple, or *acer pseudo-platanus*, which grows in Eurasia. Now if we could . . .'

'. . . if we could find some place where *both* trees grow,' Miss Franklen continued, 'then we might be able to find out where the body was originally buried. And maybe killed as well.'

'Precisely,' I said.

'Well,' Miss Franklen said abruptly, 'I think we'd better get started. No time like the present, my mother used to say.' And with that she sprang to her feet and beckoned me to follow.

We went down a hall that led toward the back of her

Edwardian house, and I found myself looking out at what in spring would be a most magnificent garden. Even though it was late November there was colour here and there, a brown or red or yellow leaf clinging to one of the trees, the pastel shades of Nature's paintbrush splashed within many a greenhouse. At the end of the L-shaped corridor we came to another door. She swung it open.

I was stunned by the number of books. There were probably several thousand more volumes than in the Library of Congress. All of them hardcover.

'I do reviews,' Miss Franklen said, 'for several publications. You don't read mysteries, I gather.'

'Cops don't read detective fiction, ma'am,' I said. 'They read science fiction.'

Elvira Franklen crossed the room to yet another door. She pushed it open and disappeared.

We were now in a somewhat smaller chamber, but just as overwhelming. And I thought *I* was obsessed! For here there were pamphlets and magazines everywhere in stacks around the floor. Tables were spread with sheafs of faded and yellowed newspaper clippings. There were cubbyhole shelves crammed full to overflowing with curled mimeographed sheets and thousands of newsletters. All around there were large-paged books of pressed flowers and leaves preserved between pieces of ironed wax paper. Otherwise vacant patches of wall space were covered with numerous framed certificates.

'I've been President of eighteen different horticultural societies,' Miss Franklen said. 'You take the desk by the window,' she said. 'I'll take the one over here.'

'But this could take *years!*'

'Shame on you,' Miss Franklen said, wagging her finger at me. 'And you a detective.'

And so we set to work.

December

Cold turkey, from that moment on I managed to quit my

smoking. There were rules in this house and that was one of them.

But even more amazing was this woman's capacity for work. She literally left me exhausted. The first day we spent six hours going through her clippings.

By the time I arrived after shift the next day she had covered over seven hundred publications. Having finished with *The Arborist* – June 1931 to September 1952 – she had moved on to *The Horticulturalist's Digest* starting in 1923.

For ten days straight we worked.

By the second week in December I managed to wangle a few days off and we really covered ground (no pun intended). On one of those nights Elvira suggested that I sleep at the house. 'Then we can get a real early start tomorrow,' she said.

'Won't the neighbours talk?' I asked, giving her a wink.

'It wouldn't be the first time,' the old woman replied.

So I stayed.

That night before retiring we had Horlicks and Peek Frean biscuits. When I settled into the guest room I found this book laid out on the table. It was *Ten Plus One* by Ed McBain, and I tell you that guy missed his calling.

Instead of being a writer, he should have been a cop.

You would have liked her, Mom: I felt like I'd been adopted.

We worked for seven days straight, at one point spending six hours in the same room and never speaking a word.

That night I had to work graveyard shift and when I showed my face at her door next day she looked at me sadly and shook her head. She told me to take a day off. That she could hold the fort. But I refused.

That afternoon we were sitting in her sanctuary as I was reading about the Arborist's Convention held in

Stanley Park in 1917, when suddenly Elvira Franklen literally leaped out of her chair. I thought she was having a stroke. 'Oh, my Goodness Gracious!' she squealed.

Do people really get that excited? I wondered, as I watched my Loveable Dwarf wave a mimeographed paper in the air.

'I found it!' she exclaimed – and my God my heart skipped a beat.

In a streak I crossed the room.

Then Elvira smoothed the page out on her desk and pointed to an article in the July 1955 issue of *Pacific Planter*. This is what it said:

READY FOR WAR, BUT HOPING FOR PEACE

Maple trees flourish today above Mr Albert Stone's bomb shelter. Mr Stone acquired his property at a public auction of land confiscated from the Japanese during the Second World War – and this he says accounts for its fertility. 'The place used to be a truck farm before the Japs attacked Pearl Harbour,' Mr Stone informed this columnist. Mr Stone is quite a character.

We stood today in his garden fronting on the mighty sweep of the South Arm of the Fraser River. This writer asked him why he had planted a maple garden above his recently completed atomic bomb fallout shelter. 'Is that not a strange juxtaposition?' your astonished reporter asked.

'Not at all,' Mr Stone countered. 'When the Commies send their nukes and The Big Hot One is on, this is one old man who's going to be ready. But until then me and my wife's memory will sit in our front garden.'

And that, gentle readers, is what brought your columnist out here today. For among the varied saplings of *acer macrophyllum* stands the only Sycamore Maple so far planted in Western Canada. It is a hardy little plant and certainly worth the drive on a Sunday afternoon. It is perhaps the only *acer pseudoplatanus* that you might ever see.

'My wife was from the Ukraine, God rest her soul. She brought that seedling to the West – it was her Freedom Tree. Well when she died . . .'

I stopped reading and skimmed through the rest. When I found the address of Stone's garden I took out my book and made a note.

Then I leaned over to Miss Elvira Franklen and kissed her on the cheek.

The maple trees beyond the fence grew wild in the overgrown garden.

And this was one fence that did not look inviting. Perhaps Mr Albert Stone just got fed up with all those *Pacific Planter* readers scampering about his garden, but whatever the reason, someone had certainly done a number. A very paranoid number, indeed. For the fence was a wire-mesh barrier that ran across the front of the land and back down both sides to the river. The spikes that stuck up skyward would rip your balls to shreds. Not of course that anyone would really want to enter. For the only structure visible on the land was a Quonset hut made of corrugated iron, the roof of which had long since rusted, seeping streaks of orange down its metal sides.

I decided to approach from the water, so I drove by without stopping. Besides, there was no gate.

Steveston is just a small sea-breeze community sitting serenely on the dykes of the Fraser where the marshes of Lulu Island slip quietly into the sea.

A sign in the local hardware store window said: *Small boat for rent. Enquire within.* The store was filled with boiler plugs, blocks and tackle, ship's barometers and lamps, blue yacht braid, anchors, any-sized corks, and Greek fisherman's hats. The man behind the counter was mending a ripped fish net. A notice above the counter read: *People who believe the dead never come back to life should be here at quitting time!*

'Help you, mate?' the man asked.

'I'd like to rent your boat.'

Ten minutes later I set sail heading west toward the sea. Out beyond Steveston Island to my left was the South Arm of the Fraser. I could just make out its choppy waters through a sparse string of trees. There was a shack on the island that looked like an outhouse with smoke curling out of its ceiling. Birds were everywhere. Out on the end of a rotting pier and fishing in the water sat a very old man. He waved at me.

At 2.53 I passed Garry Point and rounded the west end of Steveston Island to double back up the river.

The slough had seen better days.

It branched off the river to the left like a small indent of water snaking off into a field. On either side of its entrance stood a shanty and a houseboat. Up the slough I could make out a row of rundown buildings, some of them made with tarpaper siding, others constructed from split shiplap lumber or old shingle slates, all of them looking as if deserted a long, long time ago.

At 3.09 I sailed into the slough and found the back of the Quonset hut.

The land fell off to the water, ending in a small sandy beach strewn with maple leaves which had once wafted down on the wind. The hut itself sat like a hat on top of a concrete bunker. The bunker was only visible when you came in from the rear. A rickety wooden staircase descended down the backside of the concrete until it ended at a plank and piling pier that jutted out over the slough. That bunker looked as though it could withstand full-scale nuclear attack.

Now it is entirely possible that there was another Sycamore Maple tree within the Lower Mainland.

It is also possible that even if the sand in the bucket was from here it was carted to some other place.

But when you've been a cop as long as I have, you learn to trust your instinct. And my gut told me the Headhunter had been inside this structure. I broke out in a sweat.

For, you see, I had spent my whole life living in fear of this moment. Sure I had become a cop to confront my psychological dread of blood. But the night we caught the squeal on the John The Baptist killing, where an old man in a derelict rooming house had murdered his best friend, cut off his head, put it on a plate and knocked on his landlady's door, I stayed in the squad room and let Leggatt take to the wheels. Sure, I may have confronted those pictures, blowing them up in size. But a photograph is one thing. Butchered human flesh another.

I wanted to cut and run. Instead my right eye started twitching.

'Don't be afraid of fear, son. We all have to conquer it someday – one way or another.'

And I knew my day had come.

I moored the boat to the bunker pier and climbed the rickety stairs. Half-way up I removed my .38 from the holster clipped to my belt.

From the rear the Quonset hut didn't look much different than it did from the front. Same streaked metal. No windows. Only a single door secured with a new combination lock. I knocked on the door and stood off to one side just in case some shots came through. When nothing happened, I waited. Then I knocked again. Once more. Once again. And decided no one was home.

That was when I noticed the smell that was coming from inside the hut. It was like the stench of rotting meat combined with the stench of rotting fish. I knew for certain then that I did not want to enter this place, just as I knew for certain that I would. I'd have to go back to that hardware store to obtain the necessary tools. So I climbed back down the rickety stairs and cast off in the boat.

It was as I inched off to the left of the pier to make for the open slough that I saw the gap between the back of the dock and the concrete wall of the bunker. The wall was shadowed by the ladder down to the pier but in the murk I could still discern some sort of opening. I secured the boat again to a piling and stepped into the water.

Knee-deep in sludge I waded up onto the sandy, leaf-strewn shore.

The space behind the dock was no more than three feet wide. It was a day of cold clear weather and sunlight stabbed deep into the shadows through cracks in the plank-joins above. Where there was protection from the rain I saw a mass of tangled spiders' webs and the oozy trails of summer slugs.

The opening was a square wooden door, more a hatch, set into the concrete wall just over five feet up from the ground. The high tide mark was a foot below it. This door was secured with a padlock that it took me ten minutes to pick. In my job the tools for this sort of work are constantly on your person.

The hinges squealed as I eased open the hatch.

I removed the police flashlight from my back left pocket and shone the torch inside. The beam illuminated a concrete passage about three feet square. The tunnel sloped down at an angle, then straightened out again so I couldn't see its end. Taking a deep breath, I used the pier supports to hoist myself up so that I could wriggle in through the opening. Working my feet and using my hands I inched my way down the narrow passage – until I got stuck.

Have you ever had claustrophobic fear slip inside your skull and begin eating small chunks of your brain? Well there I was, half-way down this incline, the slope of it making blood rush to my head, my body stuck, my arms confined. I thought my mind would snap if I couldn't move my arms. I'd be stuck like this until what? I starved to death?

Details began to flood into my senses. A smell within this tunnel, the smell of burnt human flesh. Two red eyes of a water rat just up ahead and sniffing at my fingers. Green slime on the roof, shaded a glistening black where the torchlight died away. The squish of rat shit in small lumps on the floor beneath my face. And then into the realm of my misery intruded this germ of an idea.

Pulling with my fingers, pushing with my toes, then reversing direction, I began twisting and turning my body, trying desperately to coat both my skin and clothes with the foul-smelling ooze. Rat shit and slime: that might just get me moving.

And it worked.

Soon I was once more advancing, centimetre by centimetre down this mushy incline. I reached the bend in the tunnel where the passage opened wider only to find myself confronting yet another barrier – this one a crosshatch of iron bars with a padlock on the other side.

Twenty-five minutes it took me to do a job on this one. I had to work my fingers with the pick through a couple of the crosshatch holes, moving the flashlight with my chin to get the right illumination. If the pick dropped from my sweaty fingers there would go the ball-game. But I finally did it and pushed the bar-door open. Wiggling through I dropped head first six feet down to the floor.

Thank God the flashlight survived the tumble. I picked it up and shone it around.

Mr Albert Stone's fallout shelter was something to behold. The walls were of concrete, no doubt many feet thick, surrounding a room ten feet by twelve. The floor was of concrete. The roof was of concrete. And there was a concrete slab off to one side of the tunnel I had just come through, positioned so that it could be slid across as a radiation barricade. A second slab of concrete stood to the right of some stairs, and these I immediately climbed.

The stairs ended abruptly at yet another door blocking my progress. This door was of steel sealed by a combination lock set right into the metal. So much for that. I had no doubt that this threshold led to the Quonset hut.

As I began to descend the stairs I heard twigs crunching underfoot. When I shone the light down I saw that I was treading on hundreds of little rat bones. Then as I reentered the fallout shelter I was met by another uneasing thought. With the door at the top of the stairs locked, the only way out of here was back the way that I had come. And I was not yet ready for that.

Stalling, I began to examine the details of the room. Before long I had reached the conclusion that I would rather fry in a nuclear war than spend a couple of years in here.

There were stacks of canned goods and rows of glass bottles scattered around the floor, one wall nothing but shelves of tins, their labels long since disintegrated, piled up to the ceiling. Here was a rusted First-Aid medical kit; there a coal-oil hurricane lamp. There were several boxes of 35¢ paperbacks, all of them science fiction. There was a. . . .

There was a water rat with beady eyes watching me intently from a breach in one of the walls. I hadn't noticed the opening before.

I crossed over to this alcove door and shone my torch inside. Instantly I was horrified, shocked almost numb by what met my eyes.

The chamber was approximately ten feet by ten. Once again it was constructed entirely of concrete. Against the wall to my left there was an old-fashioned full-length mirror. In front of me, raised up from the floor, was this square slab of cement that looked much like an altar. On top of it were two candlesticks and a very large silver box. The surface of the slab was stained and streaked by puddles and rivulets of dried and clotted blood. Fingers of blood ran down its sides and across the floor. In a semi-circle behind this altar were seven sharpened poles. And rammed down on each pole, the sticks bursting through the bone at the top of the cranium, were seven grinning skulls.

It was at that moment that the rat bit me on the ankle (*rabies!*) and I dropped the flashlight.

This time it broke and the room went black.

O God! I cursed myself. Why did I give up smoking?

But on fumbling in my pockets I found I still had a box of matches. I lit one and put it to the wick of one of the candles. Then I approached the silver metal box.

As I touched the lid my palms were sweating, and as I began to lift the cover hackles rose on my neck. I was so sure – so certain – that inside I was going to find a severed head.

When I peered inside what I saw was even worse than that.

There were eight of them, plus the other object.

And then it all came together, at last.

TZANTZA

Thursday, December 23rd, 7.10 p.m.

Genevieve DeClercq closed the notebook and then sat very still. She was curled up in an easy chair and she was wearing a formal dress, the green velvet low-cut and tight-waisted, its shade the colour of a glade in late spring. Her hair was combed up at the sides of her head, there held by two mother-of-pearl clips before tumbling back down to her shoulders. She had kicked off her shoes and had tucked up her feet into the folds of the skirt. Now she was playing with a strand of her hair and asking herself quite seriously: *Do I believe him?*

She was afraid of the answer.

Across the living room of his apartment Al Flood stood at the large front window and stared down four floors to Lost Lagoon in Stanley Park. Beyond Genevieve's reflection in the glass he could see the stream of Causeway traffic streaking through the night. *Everyone rushing*, he thought to himself, *with nowhere important to go*.

He abandoned her image on the window-pane and

turned back into the room. 'Would you like another brandy?' he asked quietly.

Genevieve nodded her head. 'Please,' was all she said.

Flood walked over to the small bar set beside the window. He selected a bottle of Remy Martin which he carried across the room to pour two fingers in her glass. The woman held out the snifter. She drank a third of the refill in a single gulp. Flood watched her wince and thought, *I love you even more*.

'How do you feel,' he asked her, 'about what I wrote in the book?'

'Flattered,' she said. 'Sceptical. Sorry. And somewhat afraid.'

'Not afraid of me, I hope.' And he struggled to give her a smile.

'Afraid *for* you, Al, if what you wrote is from your imagination.'

'*Do* you believe me?' he asked.

Genevieve took another sip and then looked him in the eye. 'Before I reply to that will you answer a couple of questions?'

'Sure.'

'What did you do after you opened the box?'

'Took off my jacket and placed the contents inside. I added the unlit candlestick, then carried both my satchel and the burning candle over to the hole in the wall.' He paused. 'I put the light down on the floor and piled up some boxes as a ladder. Then pushing the sack in front of me I crawled back out the way I had come. It was easier without the thickness of my overcoat.'

'Why the candlestick?' she asked.

'Fingerprints,' he said. 'I took the boat back to the hardware store' – he laughed – 'and you should have seen the look on the owner's face when I came in covered in shit. Then I stopped at a doctor's for a rabies shot and came back here to clean up. That's when I called you.'

'Why?' Genevieve asked.

Flood's eyes wavered from hers as he said: 'You're the

425

wife of Robert DeClercq. Besides, didn't we make a compact, that day that we had brunch? What was it you said?'

Her face took on the hint of a frown. 'I told you that I was desperate and asked for your discretion as a friend. I said that my husband was . . . well having problems and that I had to help him somehow. I had stayed up all night reading those files and I didn't know where to start. Then about five in the morning I came upon your name listed as the Squad liaison officer with the Vancouver Police. I recognized you as the fellow auditing one of my seminars and . . .' Her eyes wavered.

'And what?'

'And I knew that you were in love with me and would do anything to help. So I suppose I used you, didn't I?'

'I don't mind,' Flood said.

'It's just that I had nowhere else to turn. I couldn't go to the RCMP and say that Robert was . . . was cracking up. He was senior officer, with everyone else below him. Besides, there was so much public pressure they'd have pulled him in a minute. So I came to you and asked for secrecy. I made you promise to tell me first anything you found out. I hoped your feeling for me would both make you want to help me and also keep you quiet. God, I sound awful, don't I?'

'No, it was good for both of us. If you hadn't motivated me I'd never have seen it through. But to answer the question *why did I call you first?* – it's both to keep our pact, and also to now use *you*. I need access to DeClercq. You can give me that.'

'Why did you start the diary?' Genevieve asked, changing the subject abruptly.

'My life was getting out of control, what with the Headhunter crimes playing on my neurosis. I had to set things down to get them in perspective. Catharsis, I guess.'

'So John Lincoln Hardy was framed?'

'Yes.'

'And all those things in that mountain shack – they were all planted there?'

'Everything but the masks and the cocaine.'

'Why?' Genevieve asked.

'I can only guess. Maybe the Headhunter felt like I did, that things were out of control and a little too hot to handle. Maybe the killer's psychosis – and I'm sure we're talking psychosis after what I found in that box – was slipping into recession. Who knows? Maybe the hope of promotion that might come from solving the thing. You understand a mad person's mind far better than I do.'

For a moment there was silence, then Flood asked a question: 'Tonight you've got the Red Serge Ball to attend, so why did you come when I called?'

'Because you sounded desperate. Because you were my friend when I needed help so bad. And because I like you.'

Then she surprised him. Leaning forward, she took his face gently in one hand and kissed him lightly on the lips.

'Do you love me enough,' she whispered, 'that you could just be my friend? Believe me, inside I'm old fashioned. I really am a one-man-woman. And Robert is the man.'

Al Flood shook his head. 'I love you that much,' he said.

'Good, then I'll love you too.'

'Even enough to believe the things that I wrote in that book?'

'Even enough for that. What did you find in the box?'

'Tzantzas,' Flood said.

The detective held out his hand and helped Genevieve out of her chair. He led her toward his bedroom and motioned her inside. Then he turned on the light – and the woman audibly gasped.

For each of the heads, except for the nun, had long black flowing hair. The eyes of each had been sewn shut and so had each pair of lips. Each head had skin that was shrivelled and cracked and was now almost pure white. Each head was no larger than the size of a navel orange.

'Mother of God!' Genevieve said as one hand involuntarily rose to touch her open mouth.

427

But it wasn't the sight of the eight shrunken heads that filled her with shock.

It was the dull black gleaming object lying in front of them on the bed.

PART FOUR

Death Rattle

As I was going up the stair
    I met a man who wasn't there!
He wasn't there again to-day!
    I wish, I *wish* he'd stay away!
        Hughes Mearns.

Ambush

6.15 p.m.

'They're gone! My God, they're gone!'
  'Easy, Sparky. Easy.'
  'Somebody knows! Can't you see I'm fucked?'
  'And I said take it easy. Panic never helps.'
  'Ah God, Mommy. This is it. I'm finished!'
  'Cut the bullshit, Sparky. Let's think this through.'
  'Daddy, where are you? Help me, Daddy! Please!'
Back and forth, back and forth, Sparky paced the room. Leaning against one concrete wall was an antique full-length mirror. Candlelit, the mirror reflected Sparky pacing in distortion. The figure that appeared, then disappeared, then reappeared on the glass surface was wearing the tattered Scarlet Tunic of an RCMP Corporal.
  Crunchh! There was the sound of plastic cracking underfoot.
  'What was that?'
  'I've no idea.'
  'Well, go on. Take a look.'
Sparky picked up the candlestick and bent down toward the floor. Broken plastic shards winked back at the flame.
  In ever wider arcs, Sparky swept the candlestick back and forth across the concrete.
  Then something blinked. Another reflection, over against the wall.
  Extending the light in that direction Sparky saw the broken flashlight lying in the corner. Sparky set down the candlestick and picked up the electric torch.

'Well, what is it?'

'A flashlight. I guess I stepped on it and broke it.'

'But we don't use a flashlight. You stroke my hair by candle-light. That's what we've always done.'

'I know.'

'Whoever took my heads away also dropped that thing.'

'I know.'

'Cut the bullshit babble, Sparky. Think, Sparky. Who?'

'I don't have to think, Mother. I already *know!*'

It had been a sudden thought, an off-the-wall connection, but now the tension screwed up another notch. Sparky looked at the words stamped into the plastic handle: VANCOUVER POLICE DEPARTMENT.

'Oh, God,' Sparky whimpered, slumping down to the floor. 'Now I'm really fucked. Everyone will know.'

'So that's our thief? That city bull? The one asking all the questions?'

'Yes,' Sparky nodded. 'It's all gone down the drain.'

'Maybe. Maybe not. Just do what must be done.'

'Mother, don't you see, there's nothing we can do. They're gone!'

'Oh shut up, child. What the hell do you mean, nothing we can do? My heads are out there somewhere in some stranger's filthy hands. My hair, my beautiful long black hair is under some alien touch. I want my heads back. And I want them back tonight!'

'But how, Mother? How?'

'Our cop will have a list of all the bulls on the Headhunter Squad. Names, addresses, telephone numbers: our cop will still have that. The city bull was part of the Squad – VPD liaison. Now take that bloody rag off and put on your own red serge. We've got work to do. I don't know why you insist on wearing your father's uniform. It makes me seething mad. He's dead, Sparky. He's gone.'

'No, you're wrong. He's not dead. He's hiding here inside.'

'He's dead, fool. We killed him. You saw him die out in the Arctic snow.'

'I didn't kill him! You did. God, I was only two years old!'

'*You were there, Sparky. You're a witness and a party. You saw him puke his guts out when the poison got him. You saw me chop a hole in the ice and push his body through. You saw it all and you didn't stop it. That makes you guilty too.*'

'But I was only two!'

'*SHUT UP, you snivelling piece of shit! You sound more like your father every frigging day. Is that what you want? To be just like him?*'

Sparky began to cry, great body-racking sobs and tears that fell like Westcoast rain. 'You can't talk like that! My Daddy's still alive!'

'*Look at you. You're just like him. Quivering mush inside. He was hung up on his old man, just the way that you are. Wanted to be just like him and carry on tradition. Thin red line and "get your man" and all that Mountie crap. Do you think his father, if alive, would have given a fuck? The old man cared so much for him he refused to pass on his name. Is your last name Blake? So don't make me laugh. Your father was a bastard in every sense of the word.*'

'Mommy, why do you hate me? I was only two.'

'*Look at yourself in the mirror, Sparky. Can't you see the reason? How much you look like him? I never wanted you, you were his idea. All you mean to me is a link to get back at him!*

'*Do you know what he made me do? Each night up in the Arctic? He made me dress up like a whore and traipse around before him. I'd stand there in the freezing cold while he looked me over like some piece of meat. "I like to see you cold," he'd say. "It makes your nipples hard. Now turn around. Bend over. And roll your panties down. That's the way Suzannah, get your husband hard. The bigger and harder Alfred gets, the more you're going to like it."*

'*God, I hated him. He was like my father. "Shhh. Suzannah. Come in here,* cherie. *Don't let your mother know. That's my girl. Now take off your pants. Let Pappa see what you've got."*'

'Ah, go away, Mother! Leave me alone!'

'*You'll never get rid of me, Sparky. I'm inside your head. You*

433

think that rag of a uniform gives you some protection. You think you want to be Alfred's child? You want to worship him? Go fuck yourself, Sparky. You know I always win. You were trained forever down in that dungeon in New Orleans. And you'll pay for what your father did anytime I want.'

Suddenly Sparky's lips wrenched back in a grimace of teeth-clenching agony. Pain like splintering shards of shrapnel ripped through Sparky's head. Sparky's mind screamed but not an utterance came out.

Sparky leaped up off the floor and with stunning force heaved the candlestick at the image in the mirror. The glass shattered and a shower of fragments rained down. The room went dark as Sparky fell among the pieces.

Pain settled in, then after a moment's silence, Suzannah's voice came again. *'Stand up, Sparky. You're going to do as I say?'*

'Yes.'

'I killed your father, but you have harboured his murderess for all these years in your mind?'

'Yes.'

'So you are as guilty as I?'

'Yes.'

'And you're going to follow orders?'

'Yes.'

'Like all the other times?'

'Yes.'

'I want our cop to find that prick and get back my heads.'

'Yes.'

'Find that city bull.'

'Yes.'

'Kill, Sparky, kill.'

7.19 p.m.

It had all been rather easy, really.

Sparky had gone upstairs to the Quonset hut, unlocking the door at the top of the steps that led up from the bomb shelter. Removing the tattered uniform with its

434

streaks of dried blood, its tarnished buttons, its torn red fabric now more than fifty years old, the killer had quickly redressed in modern red serge. An odour of rotten fish and cooked meat from the upper room clung to the material, but once outside, the wind blowing in from the mouth of the river would soon dissipate any lingering smell. It was the second time within an hour that Sparky had put on the uniform. The uniform was The Royal Canadian Mounted Police Full Review Order Of Dress. Now to go find Flood.

The cocaine was only an afterthought.

There were two plastic bags, a half pound each, still sitting up on the highest shelf in the boathouse. The bags were buried back behind several cans of CIL Paint where they had been hidden the night that John Lincoln Hardy had died. The coke had gone missing when Sparky had B & Ed that shack on the mountainside in order to make the plant. That was half an hour before the flying patrol had gone in.

Originally Sparky had taken the coke as a source of ready cash. In Vancouver, should things ever get too hot, the wheels of the underground railway out are best greased with drugs. In Vancouver, if you have contacts and coke, you can get to Timbuktu with no questions asked. The drugs had seemed like a good idea – insurance, so to speak. But depending how things turned out tonight, there might be another use.

Sparky had taken down one of the bags and then had left the Quonset hut, locking it up tight.

Outside the wind had been freezing and it felt like it would snow. Winter had come at last.

The patrol car had been parked several blocks away, secreted in an old abandoned run-down garage used for camouflage. It was dangerous to bring the car out here in the first place, dangerous to walk the roads dressed up for the Red Serge Ball, but Mother had wanted her hair stroked so there was nothing else to do. Besides, it would be two hours before the Ball was well under way.

435

Sparky had found the Headhunter Squad list in the glove compartment of the car. On that list were Al Flood's name, address, and phone number. That's how easy it was.

Thirty minutes later, it had started to snow. The wind was roaring through the apartment canyons of the city's West End, freezing the marrow and freezing the heart of anyone out on the street. White spilled from the sky. The faces of the buildings glowed with wary wakeful eyes. Sparky checked the apartment block numbers against the address on the list.

Al Flood's apartment was only a block away.

7.23 p.m.

'How do they do it?' Genevieve asked. 'Shrink down a head like this?'

'You mean "what do I know about death?"' Flood said, putting down his drink.

'Sort of,' the woman replied, and she looked once more at the *tzantza* that she now held in her hand.

'The technique of shrinking heads was developed in Ecuador by the Jivaro Indians. Though it's now against the law, the practice still continues.'

Genevieve DeClercq said: 'There's a shrunken head in the Vancouver City Museum. I remember seeing it once.'

Flood replied: 'As a psychologist, don't you deal with "head-shrinkers" every day at work?' He cast her a watered-down smile.

'You mean: When you've got a problem with your head, it's best to see a shrink! That's just gallows' humour. I'm not always this macabre.'

'Lucky you,' Flood said. 'I am. All the time. Anyway, once a Jivaro cuts off a head he puts it in a wicker basket and allows the blood to drain. The Indian then spreads banana leaves out in a small clearing and builds a fire over which a large clay pot is suspended. The pot is filled with water. Once the head is white from loss of blood it is

436

removed from the basket and, held by the hair, immersed in the bubbling liquid for from fifteen to thirty minutes. When it's finally taken out, the skin is white as paper and it smells like cooked human flesh. The pot is then filled with sand and cooked up once more.

'Next a machete is used to make an incision from the top of the head vertically down to the base of the skull, ending at the neck. The skin and hair are carefully peeled back to expose the skull, which is skilfully removed.

'First the opening in the back of the head and both eyelids are sewn shut. Using an instrument shaped like a trowel, the shrinker begins to fill the hollow skin with hot sand from the pot, feeding it in through the open neck. After three or four minutes the skin is emptied and the process is repeated. Eventually the head is reduced to the size of an orange – except for the hair which doesn't shrink. The process therefore seems to accentuate its length.'

Genevieve DeClercq slowly turned the miniature head round in her hand. 'It's horrible, isn't it,' she said, 'to imagine who this woman was, and who she might have been? She could have been *any* woman in this city setting out on a normal day, going about her business just as she always had before. Then she gets picked at random – to end up like this!'

Al Flood walked over to stand at her side. 'If you want to free her spirit, you unlace the mouth.' He placed his left index finger on the *tzantza's* lips.

'By Jivaro tradition that's the last act they perform. Sewing the mouth shut brings the shrinking process to a close. The Indian takes a needle made from bone and stitches the lips together with a leather thong. He leaves several strips of fine cord dangling from the mouth. The Jivaro say this last act traps the victim's spirit. If the mouth were to remain open, the soul could slip away. It would then be free and would have a choice to make. Either haunt the shrinker. Or dissolve and rest in peace.'

Genevieve looked once more at the head held in her palm. The Headhunter had pierced the lips with several small gold rings, and used a leather thong to connect the rings together. 'I wonder why the killer went to all the extra trouble to do that with the mouth?' she asked. 'That head I saw in the City Museum was finished just like you say, with the lips stitched together.'

'Good question,' Flood said. 'I have no idea.'

7.24 p.m.

Shrouded by the falling snow and keeping close to the building so as not to be seen, Sparky reached the front door of Al Flood's apartment. The patrol car was parked half a block away at the end of Lagoon Drive. It couldn't be seen from Flood's apartment. The front door was locked. An A. Flood was listed in Suite 404 on the face of the intercom.

Furtively, Sparky ran around to the alley behind.

Al Flood's apartment block was divided into eight suites, two on each of four floors, each apartment fronting on Lagoon Drive with a view of Lost Lagoon and Stanley Park beyond. On a clear day, beyond that you could see the North Shore Mountains. Right now, with the snow, you couldn't see the park.

The building was much older than most of the high-rises that now cramp the West End of Vancouver. A zig-zag iron fire-escape snaked up the rear of Flood's apartment block connecting all four floors. Off the alley beneath the building was an underground parking lot. A concrete ramp sloped down to several parking stalls, each one lettered in white. A blue 1971 Volvo sedan with a dent in its right front fender stood in space number 404.

Sparky recorded the licence number, then returned to the patrol car parked down the street.

Some 2,500 police units are linked to the Force computer system. Each police unit has a computer terminal attached to the dashboard of the car. The central computer holds *every* query for up to seventy-two hours.

Tonight it took the cruiser computer less than two minutes to check the vehicle registration for the licence plate number on the blue Volvo car. Sparky used the time to flip open the chamber of the RCMP standard issue Smith and Wesson .38 Special and check the mechanism. All six chambers were loaded. The gun was ready to fire.

In answer to the query the screen above the computer terminal keyboard lit up with green letters: *Query vehicle registered MVB Victoria: Almore Flood, 307 Lagoon Drive, Apt. 404, Vancouver*.

Below this there was a postscript note: *A. Flood is detective. Vancouver Police Department. Major Crimes squad*.

You're kidding! Sparky's fingers typed into the computer.

Then snapping the .38 cylinder shut, Sparky removed the half pound bag of cocaine and a screwdriver from under the passenger's seat and climbed out of the car.

7.31 p.m.

'Where do we go from here?'

'I think you should phone your husband and tell him we're on our way. He can take it from there,' Al Flood said.

'Have you told anyone else about all this?'

'No. You're the only one. It's a tricky situation. A Vancouver Police Detective can't just march into the RCMP Red Serge Ball and arrest one of the dancers. Not for a crime which is closed and already filed away. Besides, your husband was head of the Headhunter Squad and I was working under him. He should know first.'

'God, there's going to be hell to pay somewhere down the line. Not only does the Force have a multiple killer in its midst, but it also shot down the wrong man.'

Al Flood nodded. 'The shooting of Hardy itself won't hurt. He was going for a knife and had lit a cop on fire. He was also involved in cocaine trafficking. But as for the Headhunter case, the shit will hit the fan.'

Genevieve sighed heavily. 'Poor Robert,' she said.

Al Flood reached out and put his arm around her. 'Let's make the best,' he said, 'of a dirty situation. The killer will be there tonight at the Red Serge Ball. Am I correct that this particular celebration is to honour the members of the Headhunter Squad?'

'Yes. In fact both the Commissioner and the Governor General of Canada will be attending. Robert is to receive the Commissioner's Commendation. That's the highest honour that the Force can bestow.'

'Then let's you and I go to the Ball and take the evidence with us. We'll get your husband aside and tell him what I found. I'll keep out of sight just to stay on the safe side, and you bring him to me. All three of us can then decide what to do and how best to protect the Superintendent. If he makes the arrest personally it might help salvage something from the wreckage. The phone's in the kitchen.'

They were still standing in the bedroom at the rear of the apartment. For a moment Genevieve DeClercq glanced out through the window that faced on the alley and noticed for the first time that it had begun to snow. Then she turned from the window, from the heads on the bed, and went out to the kitchen in order to make the call.

Not until the ninth ring was the phone at the Seaforth Armouries answered. Whoever it was who picked it up he was very, very excited.

'Armouries,' the man said. 'Daykin speaking.'

'Hello. My name is Genevieve. Superintendent Robert DeClercq is my husband. May I please speak to him?'

'Sorry, Ma'am. Don't know him. I'm just a caterer. If you'll hold on a second I'll get a Mountie for you.'

'Thanks,' Genevieve said.

As she waited the woman could hear pandemonium in the background. It seemed to her as if a hundred voices were all talking at once. There was no music. Her eyebrows knitted in wonder.

'Mrs DeClercq?' A voice asked through the telephone receiver.

'Yes.'

'Jim Rodale here.'

'Sergeant, I've got to talk to Robert. It's imperative.'

'He's not here yet. We expect the G-G, the Commissioner and the Superintendent any moment. They went for a drink at the Governor General's club.'

'What's going on in the background? It sounds like a drunk.'

'Do you know Bill Tipple?'

'Yes, I've heard of him.'

'We think he just got killed. Not minutes ago a bomb blew one of the cars in his garage apart. We fear he was in it.'

'Good God!' Genevieve exclaimed.

'I just sent Rabidowski out to join the VPD who are already at the scene. Jack MacDougall is also on the way. I'm waiting for Robert, to tell him, then I'm going too.'

'How, Jim? Why? What could be the reason?'

'Bill had just started an investigation into West Coast organized crime. He might be on to something. It might be a hit. We think he was leaving his home for the Ball and had just got into his car. Bomb probably worked off the ignition. We'll know more shortly.'

'My God!' Genevieve said. 'Will the horror ever stop?'

'The party here is over. That's one thing for sure.'

'Jim, if you're waiting for Robert, you *must* give him a message. Tell him that I'm on my way and to please wait for me. Tell him that it's urgent. I'm with one of my students and he has a very serious problem. Tell Robert that he's a policeman, that it's a matter of life and death.'

'I'll make sure he gets it,' Rodale said.

'Good, I'm on my way.'

They both hung up.

By the time Genevieve returned to the bedroom Al Flood was packing up. He had wrapped each one of the shrunken heads in a piece of tissue paper, and after

441

placing his diary in the bottom of an Adidas athletic bag, had packed them in on top. As she came into the room he was placing the dull black object into the towel pouch at the side.

'There's a modern theory,' the woman said, 'that the strong compulsions of many sex offenders have more of a biological origin than previously believed.'

'Why's that?' Flood asked, zipping up the bag and crossing to his dresser where he pulled out a drawer. He removed a holstered gun from inside and clipped the Smith and Wesson .38 snubnose to his belt.

'At Johns Hopkins Medical Institute in Baltimore they've been studying sex hormone levels, brain metabolism and brain structure in deviant offenders. The results indicate that psychological problems may not be the dominant cause of perversion. They've also found that a chromosomal abnormality called Klinefelter's syndrome offers a clue linking deviant behaviour and gender identity. Children born with the disorder have an unusual arrangement of chromosomes in their cells. This syndrome appears a lot among sex offenders.'

'Do you think the same sort of thing is going on here? I think this one's psychological.' Flood picked up the Adidas bag and moved toward the door. 'My Volvo's parked downstairs. We'll take it and talk on the way.'

He reached for the light switch. The last thing that Genevieve saw in the room were all the magnificent photographs of planets, of stars, of asteroids and nebulae tacked up on the walls.

This time she did not look out the window at the snow falling in the alley beyond the zigzag fire-escape attached to the rear of the building.

Nor did she see the pair of eyes peering in at them.

7.42 p.m.

So, Sparky thought, descending the fire-escape steps three at a time, *no one else knows. Unless she yakked on the phone.*

The parking lot was deserted.

It was dark down there with only the occasional naked lightbulb protected by a wire cage throwing off a dim light. Concrete support pillars cast great shafts of shadow. From far off, somewhere hidden, came the throb of a boiler. There were no people. Just cars. Parked between white lines.

Sparky went straight to the Volvo and, using the screwdriver, pried off the left front hubcap. The space inside the disc was small but it would hold the cocaine. Working the plastic bag in around the wheel nuts, Sparky replaced the cap and hammered it back on with the handle of the screwdriver.

Suddenly there was a sharp sound, a scraping off to the left.

Then there was laughter.

Sparky drew the Smith and Wesson from its Sam Browne holster, ducking at the same time in behind the car.

'Bet you can't do this!' a young voice yelled.

As the killer peeked over the hood, two boys, aged seven or eight, came down the concrete ramp into the parking lot. One of the youngsters was balancing with one foot on a skateboard. The other ran beside.

'Come on! Gimme a try!'

Out in the alley behind the boys the world was turning red. Night had come down and the snow was falling thickly, collecting on the ground. Across the lane a burning tin was spewing forth red sparks that lit up the snow.

Damn, Sparky thought, crouching by the car.

There was nothing to do but wait.

Then kill the two boys as well.

7.46 p.m.

'I spend half my life in this elevator. It's the slowest one in town.' Al Flood punched the button a third and fourth time. Finally the doors closed and the elevator jerked.

It took its time going down.

'Donny! Kevin!' a voice called from the alley.

The two boys in the parking lot turned to look up the ramp.

'Where the hell are you two? I said to watch this fire. Burning's against the law.'

'Oh!' one lad said. 'Now we're in for it!'

'Down here, Mom!' yelled the other boy.

The woman who appeared at the top of the ramp was heavy-set and angry. Her hair was up in curlers and she was wrapped in a fake-fur coat.

'I thought I told you two to watch the tin till the fire died. Can't you do anything right? The house could have burned down while you were having fun.'

'Ah, Mom,' one boy said. 'We can see it from here.'

'That's not the point, Kevin. If your father were alive you wouldn't act like this.'

The taller boy bent down to pick up the skateboard. Single file they marched up the ramp and out into the snow.

'Leave the embers,' the woman said. 'Let's go inside.'

The three of them disappeared just as another noise filled the parking lot. It was the sound of muffled voices from beyond the elevator door. Pistol in hand, Sparky left the Volvo and moved into the shadow of a pillar fifteen feet away.

The elevator opened.

'This snow will slow us down,' Genevieve DeClercq said. She stepped out in the open, followed by Al Flood.

7.48 p.m.

The passenger side of the Volvo was no more than eight inches away from one of the concrete pillars supporting the roof. A person would have to be Plastic Man to enter the car from that side. 'A tight squeeze,' Genevieve said as they approached the vehicle.

444

'You'll have to wait till I pull out or get in by the driver's side.'

'I'll get in your side,' she said as they reached the left front door.

Flood was unlocking the door when he noticed the marks and glove smudges on the hubcap of his car.

Vandals? he wondered, stepping forward toward the left front wheel.

'What's wrong?' Genevieve asked. 'Is some – '

Fifteen feet away there was a flash of brilliant yellow from within the shadow cast by one of the pillars. Then a shocking explosion. Echoing wildly the sound of the blast boomed around the cavern. The bullet hit Flood in the side of the chest, spinning him back along the driver's door of the car. Blood spattered the roof of the Volvo as his left lung collapsed.

But wounded though he was, the cop reacted fast.

With his left arm extended, he pushed away from the side of the car with his right hand and gave Genevieve a hard shove to clear her out of the way. Then the muzzle flared yellow again. This time the thunderclap seemed even louder. It boomed in Al Flood's ears like a nuclear explosion. His head was going light.

Veering insanely off the chrome, the slug whacked home against the metal rim of the driver's door and ricocheted. Had Flood not moved a second earlier it would have ripped through his heart. Instead it struck Genevieve in the eye. The velocity of the shot slammed the lead through her brain. It bounced off the inside of her skull and blew out through the top of her head, opening her cranium in a shower of blood and bone.

Genevieve DeClercq was dead before she hit the ground.

Then the muzzle flared again. But by the time the third shot came, Al Flood was on his belly with the .38 in his fist. He was rolling underneath the Volvo when the bullet hit the concrete floor and deflected up under the car. A moment later crankcase oil spewed from the oil pan. Flood felt sick to his stomach for out of the corner of his eye he saw Genevieve in her death throes. He knew that she was gone.

With his heart now beating frantically and pumping his blood away, he scanned the parking lot floor for any sign of the killer. Pinned beneath his car he was like a fish in a barrel; if the assassin bent down and saw him that would be it: a spray of shots along the floor and he would be gone too.

Gritting his teeth against the pain, he rolled out on the other side. He staggered to his feet. And then he began to run.

The fourth shot, triggered off in haste, missed him. He was still on his feet and moving as the bullet hit the concrete at the mouth of the ramp to his right. Flying pieces of soot-stained grey burst out into the snow.

When the fifth shot missed, Flood felt an adrenaline pump of hope that he'd get clean away.

Then the sixth shot hit him high in the back and knocked him to the ground. The slug tore through his shoulder in a line of searing pain. The force of the shot, like a sledgehammer, had knocked him face down in the snow that was blowing along the ramp.

Flood heard movement behind him. Footsteps light and swift across the concrete floor. A whisper in the cavern. The click of an empty pistol. A second click as the hammer once more hit a fired chamber. Then he rolled on his side, screaming out in agony, and pulled off three quick shots in succession.

As the slugs careened around in the lot, Al Flood struggled to his feet and stumbled out into the alley. Here the ground was now white with a thick blanket of snow.

Still on his feet, still moving, Flood staggered off into the storm, leaving a trail of blood behind.

7.51 p.m.

Damn! Sparky thought as the pistol clicked again, then

446

the lot was filled with roaring noise, explosion on explosion, and a slug whizzed by to the right. Ducking behind the Volvo, the killer tripped over the bag. The Adidas bag was on the ground beside the driver's door.

Sparky crouched low until the booming faded and died.

Reload first. Destroy the heads. Then blow that fucker away. No room for an error at this stage of the game.

Flipping open the cylinder and emptying the casings, Sparky fed the .38 six new cartridges. *That's it. All right. Fingers steady. Don't shake. Flick the weapon shut. Now you're ready to go.*

At this very moment half the West End of Vancouver was probably phoning the VPD to say that World War III was on. Magnified by the cavern, the shots would travel far and wide. By now the VPD would be dispatching patrol cars and calling out the SWAT squad. There was not a second to lose: the heads had to go.

As luck would have it all eight heads were in the Adidas bag. So was Al Flood's diary. Sparky glanced quickly at one page. *'Why do human beings so fear a severed head?'* Sparky read. *'If this is everyman's general fear, why must I be plagued with it multiplied a thousand times?'* A flick through a couple more pages brought home to Sparky the diary's chilling implications, and what must be done.

Someone had left an oily rag on the floor after working on a car. Grabbing it quickly, Sparky soaked the cloth in crankcase oil now spreading out across the concrete from beneath the Volvo. Then grasping the Adidas bag, gun still in hand, the murderer ran up the ramp and out into the snow.

Flood was not around, neither right nor left.

Across the lane embers glowed in the burning can.

Half expecting a .38 shot and still clutching the Adidas bag, Sparky skirted the alley and tossed the oil-soaked rag into the tin. It ignited at once. With a whoosh the flames shot up, dyeing the snowflakes orange. Holding the gym bag open with both hands Sparky shook the contents into the burning tin. The shrunken heads caught fire immediately amid the stench of burning hair. The skin ignited like paper. The lip rings turned red and glowed. And then the heads were gone. When the diary burst into flame, its pages curled like fingers as each sheet charred black and then crumbled, sifting down as ash.

Fuck you, Mother, Sparky thought. *Burn, witch, burn.*

Then with an intense feeling of satisfaction and new-found freedom, Sparky lifted the lid of a nearby garbage can and stuffed the Adidas bag inside. As soon as the lid was replaced it began to recollect snow.

Turning out into the alley, Sparky surveyed the ground. A second later, gun in hand, the killer set off to follow the trail of blood that the detective had left in the snow.

Okay, Mr City Bull, now it's you and me.

Shootout

7.56 p.m.

Al Flood had never been shot before so he didn't know what to expect. It was true that he had heard from cops on the Squad who had received gunshot wounds and survived, and had also spoken to a few who had later died. One and all, they had informed him that you could tell if you would live or die from the thoughts that ran through your head. But that did not mean much. For as the man says: *you had to have been there, right?*

Al Flood was there now – and he knew he was going to die.

So go on and die! he thought. *What's so wrong with that?*

We all have to face this fear one day or another. Are you so afraid to die if your time has come?

No, Al Flood thought. *I'm not afraid to die.*

There, he felt better for that. After all there are many more things in life far worse than death. Things like loneliness and not being loved, and he'd had his share of them. Yes, when you got right down to it death could be a blessing. A good, clean release. Perhaps his own salvation. Death was only bad when it hurt so much or took so long that it humiliated you.

Well, it sure the hell hurts, Flood thought, and his head began to spin.

It had been a mistake – Flood knew that now – to have made for the loading bay. At the time he had made the decision, however, all that seemed important was to escape from the line of fire, to get away from the killer as quickly as possible. Turning into the loading bay off the alley had accomplished that. But it was a mistake all the same. For now Flood found himself trapped on his hands and knees in a dead-end alcove. He was cornered in a three-sided box no more than twelve feet wide, and for anyone looking in from the alley he was an open target. He was totally unprotected, with only three shots left. Once those rounds were gone he had no extra shells.

To make matters more precarious, dizziness was coming at him in nauseating waves. Here one moment . . . gone the next . . . then surging back again. At certain times he thought that he could hear the wail of police sirens through the wall of snow, rising and falling, rising and falling, very far away. *It's foolish*, his mind told him, *to place any hope in that. Far, far better than most you know that this is a crime-plagued town. They're not even heading this way.*

Al Flood had collapsed on his stomach and was facing into the alcove with his back to the alley. He had not the energy to turn himself around, to at least face the direction from which an attack would come. Instead he let his head drop and his face fall into the snow.

449

Al Flood allowed his thoughts to lightly drift away.

The visions began with a man, an old man with a wrinkled face wearing wire-rim glasses, a man whose hair was sparse and sweptback and greying at the temples, a man who smoked a cigarette below a thin moustache. The old man was sitting in the back of a sleigh, wrapped in a warm fur blanket. He was reading a newspaper. The paper was yellow and dog-eared, covered by snow. Al Flood recognized the man: he'd once read one of his books.

The man in the sleigh turned toward him and held out the yellow paper. In a voice thick with smoke he said: 'It says here this snow is general throughout the entire province. It's falling further westward into the dark Pacific Ocean. It's falling on every peak and summit in the Rocky Mountains. It is falling also on that lonely mountain graveyard . . . lonely mountain graveyard . . . lonely, lonely graveyard . . .'

And then the man was suddenly gone, obliterated completely by a rage of swirling snowflakes, disappearing beyond a curtain of white that parted several seconds later to reveal a precipitous slope with banks of snow that lay thickly about a shattered fuselage and plane cockpit. This vision, Flood knew, was his father's grave.

Off in the distance beyond the slope he could also discern the angry black waves of an ocean pounding against a shore, throwing out spray to mix with the snow that tumbled down upon crooked crosses and headstones in a deserted, abandoned churchyard.

'What you see – ' it was the old man's voice again ' – is a Christian Indian graveyard, the West Coast of Vancouver Island. One of the graves has been redug and your brother is buried there.'

Then once more Flood could just make out the sleigh within the blinding storm, only this time there was another figure standing behind the old man wrapped in the blanket. This second figure was a much larger individual, full-faced with a bushy beard and one hand on the shoulder of the older one in the sled. *They're friends*, Flood thought, comparing them. *An incongruity*.

'Can you hear the snow,' the old man asked, 'falling, faintly falling through the Universe? The snow is falling, my son, on all the living and dead.'

'She's dead,' the big man stated, 'but you are still alive. If you can do nothing for yourself, then do something for her. Each one does what he can. Take another look.'

Then Al Flood saw the alley all white with its sheet of snow. He could see himself in the alcove, face down as flake by flake enveloped his prostrate form and buried him in a shroud. And he could watch as that same snow blew into the parking lot, its whiteness stained red in the pool of blood that spread out from Genevieve.

'Die for a reason,' Hemingway said. 'Don't throw your life away.'

'Die for a cause,' Joyce added. 'Let's have one last fight for the dead.'

And then they were gone, both of them, leaving nothing behind but the snow. Al Flood heard his breath come in gasps as phlegm caught in his throat. *Death rattle*, the man thought. *I guess my time is near*. 'One more fight,' he said: then slowly he found himself coming around and moving across the ground.

Now he was turning, cutting a ragged circle in the snow, endeavouring to gain a position from which he could make a stand. Inch by inch, like the hands of a clock, he rotated around.

Eight o'clock . . . nine o'clock . . . you're half way there, he thought. *Think of her . . . don't pass out . . . do what must be done . . .*

And then he saw the window.

The window was set in the alcove wall now in front of him. It was long and narrow and two feet high, eight inches up from the ground. Though Flood had passed here countless times he had never seen it before. Whatever its use – perhaps as a light source for a building basement – it had not been opened in years. The windowpane

451

was grimy and caked with layers of soot.

Flood used the butt of his .38 to smash through the glass and clear away the shards.

The pain was fierce, but he crawled in and fell eight feet down to the floor.

8.00 p.m.

Sparky heard the crash of glass and moved toward the alcove.

Easy. Take it very easy. Don't expose yourself.

Gun in hand, crouching low, Sparky peered around the corner just in time to see Al Flood's legs disappear in through the window.

The killer moved into the alcove, closing the gap between them.

8.01 p.m.

It was strange down here.

It was so eerie, so weird, so surreal, that at first Flood thought he had passed out again and that this was another vision. Who were all these people and what were they doing? Living in a madhouse?

For a moment the cop was certain that he had stepped back in time, that now he was a younger man lost on a carnival midway.

Was this some sort of nightmare? Was this what you saw when you died?

Mickey Mouse and Mortimer Snerd and the Count of Monte Cristo? The Connecticut Yankee, Marie Antoinette, the Last of the Mohicans? Alonzo from *The Tempest* leaning against the wall?

For there were costumes on tables and draped on the floor and hanging from the ceiling. Lurking in shadows about the room were men in uniform: a Russian Cossack of the Guard, a Sepoy of the Second Gurkhas, a Hussar, a Roman Centurion.

452

Between two tables and blocking the end of one aisle were a French *Poilu* in his *horizon bleu* greatcoat from the trenches of Verdun and a red-coated Scottish Highlander of the Ross-shire Buffs, ostrich feathers in his bonnet and a goatskin sporran at his groin.

There were clowns with red noses, and Hamlet. There was the Scarlet Pimpernel.

There were Yoda and Punch and Judy and Azuncena from *Il Trovatore*.

Off in one corner by herself was Lady Livia from *Women Beware Women*.

And everywhere that Al Flood looked there were Monster masks.

Each head was stuck on a hat hook that angled out from one of the walls. In his fall from the window Flood had knocked two of these masks to the ground. They now lay beside him: the face of Fu Manchu to his left, and to his right, Fredric March as Stevenson's Mr Hyde. When Flood glanced up, the other heads still on the hooks were beginning to come alive.

That's it, he thought. *You're going.* Then his mind was in a whirl.

'I'm Count Orlock,' Max Schreck said, 'from Murnau's *Nosferatu*.'

'And I'm the Frankenstein Monster,' whispered Boris Karloff. Then the walls were rife with laughter.

Al Flood felt sick. Bile rose to his throat.

Think of her . . . forget them . . . just keep moving . . .

'He's moving,' hissed Vincent Price with his face from *House of Wax*.

'Out of sight, out of mind,' screamed the Phantom of the Opera.

The Mummy did not say a thing.

Flood felt empty, drained, exhausted, as he crawled beneath the table spread with props. He could hear the sirens drawing near, close now, closer, but he was aware that they would never arrive in time. His chest was leaking blood in a trail smeared across the floor. 'He's hiding in here,' the blood mark said, pointing in his direction.

Flood put down his head. *Too late*, he thought as tears came welling to his eyes. *Sorry, Genny. I should have stayed back there in the alley. Should have given it all I had* . . .

Have, you mean.

All right, have. What's the difference now?

Think of her.

I can't.

Fight for her.

I can't.

Die for her.

I can't.

Then die.

Yes, that I can do.

He hit the leg of another table with his shoulder and the table began to rock. Something above him was moving, rolling, now falling over the edge. Each time he took a breath there was a wheeze from his punctured lung. He felt himself slipping away – like snow must slip in the springtime from the slope of his father's grave – and he knew that whatever he had to do was never going to get done.

Something hit the floor to his left and rolled in his direction.

His eyes took a look.

And then he wanted to laugh.

God, how he wished he had the strength to laugh as loud as he could, just to go out laughing at this Joke we know as life.

Is this it! Flood thought. *Is this my final vision!*

Then the pod that looked like it belonged to *Invasion of the Body Snatchers* bumped against his gun and came rolling to a halt.

Flood opened his mouth, thinking, *I'll damn well laugh if I want! Here's one for you, life! Here's how I go* –

But he didn't laugh after all: his muscles froze instead.

For now there was another sound with him in this room. The sound of someone at the window through which he had come.

The sound of someone falling, feet on the floor, a body rolling, feet on the floor again.

Then came the sound of a .38, the unmistakable click as its hammer cocked.

8.03 p.m.

Sparky crouched among the theatre costumes, taking in every sound.

The whistle of the wind blowing in through the shattered window. The rap of a pipe as it rattled deep within one of the walls. The wail of the police sirens less than a block away.

The hiss of Al Flood's wheezing lung near the centre of the storage room.

Then like a cat ready to pounce, Sparky began to move. *Circle the room*, the killer thought, *and keep yourself down low. Use the figures for camouflage and come up from behind. Take him from the rear*.

Furtively Sparky moved past the wrinkled, warted faces of a Witches' Sabbath, past an orange orangutang, past the Mummy of Kharis with its rotting bandages, its cracked and withered and dry facial skin, its one remaining eye.

Keep low. Keep listening. Keep moving. Keep circling behind.

Then suddenly both eyes of the Mummy snapped open, the bad one dripping blood.

Involuntarily, Sparky gasped.

'*Did you really think you could kill me?*' a voice from the Mummy asked.

'Mommy?' Sparky whispered.

'*Yes, child. I've come back.*'

8.04 p.m.

The mummy is hanging suspended from a meat hook in the ceiling. At least it looks like a mummy, this trussed up thing – except that both its arms are stretched out as if in crucifixion.

But for a number of holes the man inside is completely encased in bandages and plaster of Paris. There are four holes in the face-casting for his eyes, his nose, and his mouth. There are two large holes in the body casing: one for the man's genitals and the other for his anus. The mummy is now swinging slightly to and fro in chains. An enamel tray sits on the floor below his dangling feet. This drip tray is filled with colours: yellow, white, red and brown. The mummy is screaming in terror as shrieks bounce wildly off the stone walls.

'Oh God! Woman *please!* No! I'm so afraid of neeeeeedles!'

The scream, however, ends in a choke as the man's voice breaks and degenerates into gibberish. The man is blubbering now through the mouth hole in the plaster. His lips are moving continually, beseeching, yammering, but only whines come out. The man is also grinding his tongue between his teeth.

'There, there,' Suzannah says. 'Just two more.' And she steps forward to shove another silver needle through the head of his penis.

The mummy man shrieks once more as a part of his throat tears. Suzannah steps away and turns toward Sparky. 'If only I'd had your father in a similar position.'

Crystal is standing next to the child, crying in pain for there are welts on both her back and buttocks.

'Just one more,' Suzannah says, moving toward the mummy. She stabs the final needle through his scrotum between his testicles.

'NOOOOOO!' the man screams and his muscles form a rictus of terror about his mouth.

The room is a large grey stone vault with an arched ceiling. There are several flambeaux burning in brackets on the walls. Crystal and Sparky are standing in front of the blood-stained rack. They are both naked now and they are both weeping silently. Their bodies are streaked with the sweat of fear for they are both afraid, very much afraid of this man who hangs from the ceiling. The axe which the man has brought with him tonight is leaning against one wall.

Wildly, screeching insanely, the mummy now begins to thrash and spin suspended from that meat hook in the ceiling. The man's penis is erect as white liquid squirts from the end. Then . . . *craccck* . . . *craccck* . . . *craccck* . . . the plaster of Paris starts to fall away. Chunks of it come raining down upon the flagstone floor. A choking mist of white powder now floats about the room. Then the man releases himself from the hook and tumbles to the floor, his penis still erect though pierced with fifteen shiny needles. As he reaches for the hatchet, Crystal begins to scream.

'You killed my mother,' the man accuses, raising the axe in the air.

Terrified, Sparky is frantically looking around for a place to hide. Finally the child scrambles underneath the rack, crawling back as far as possible against the dungeon wall. Crystal is yelling in horror and now running around the room. From under here you can only see her shadow on the floor. The shadow is shaking violently. Then it stops. Then it's missing an arm.

The blade of the axe comes clanging down, striking one of the stones set into the floor. A chunk of rock goes spinning off trailing sparks behind.

'ARGH!' Crystal chokes out, more a gargle than a shriek. Then the severed arm hits the dungeon floor. It continues to quiver spasmodically for the nerves are not yet dead. The fingers close in a fist. From above a gout of arterial blood splashes down upon the stones.

Suzannah laughs suddenly. From this side of the room.

Crystal's shadow jumps once more and convulses about on the floor.

'You killed my mother, bitch!' the man snarls in a hiss. Again the shadow of the axe strikes the image of

Crystal. Then again. And again. In a steady rain of blows.

Amid the waterfall of blood there is the sound of bones cracking. Scattered chunks of flesh are plopping down on the stones. A wave of red washes in under the rack to inundate Sparky. Then the man falls down on his hands and knees, chopping in a frenzy at what remains of the girl. 'Bitch!' he spits in counterpoint to each blow from the hatchet. 'Bitch! Bitch! Bitch! Bitch! Bitch! Bitch! Bitch!'

By now Sparky is shaking totally out of control. Boots – black boots with red laces and six-inch spiked heels – come slowly across the floor to stand beside the rack. The tongue of a whip hangs down like a snake to curl in the pools of blood.

'Will you come out, Sparky my love? Or does Mama come in and get you?'

Sparky knows already the price of disobeying Mother. So slowly the child crawls out and looks up at Suzannah.

The woman now stands in her black leather corset cut low to show her breasts. Suzannah wears a garterbelt and blood spattered nylons. A collar of leather and iron studs encircles her neck, while straps run down from the collar to where her nipples are rouged and exposed. Suzannah is dressed so that her crotch is bare, the light of the torches now glittering from the golden rings which pierce her labia, a thong of black leather criss-crossing the gold and lacing up her sex. Her head is bald.

'Sparky, are you your father's child? Or do you belong to me?' The voice of the woman is no more than a hoarse, throaty whisper.

Behind Suzannah, the girl once known as Crystal has now ceased to exist. Crystal is nothing more than very small pieces on the floor. The man with the axe begins to move the first piece toward his mouth.

'Show me you're mine,' Suzannah says. 'And no one's going to hurt you. Unlace me gently, Sparky. Then kiss your Mother's lips.'

Abruptly Sparky starts to scream and weep out of control.

458

'DADDY, WHERE ARE YOU, DADDY! HELP ME, DADDY! PLEASE!'

('i'm here, Sparky. i am you.')

8.05 p.m.

Al Flood heard the gasp of shock and the single word 'Mommy?' but he could not place the direction. His head was spinning; his mind was growing darker by the second; the sound was no more than an echo. He dragged himself halfway out from under the table and part way into the aisle, but that was as far as he got. His strength had ebbed completely. He couldn't go on any further. Not one single inch.

End of the line, Al Flood thought. *All aboard for the ever-after.*

Now suddenly a flash of red burst through the broken window. Then there was another and he knew the police had arrived. He heard footsteps running through the snow, but what did all this matter? Help had come too late. Al Flood was going to die.

One last look . . . at life, he thought *. . . it's time to say . . . goodbye . . .*

Then unable to raise his head from the floor, the dying man turned it sideways. All he could see was a costumed figure blocking the end of the aisle – that red-coated Scottish Highlander late of the Ross-shire Buffs.

So long, buddy, Al Flood thought, *au revoir to the French Poilu . . .*

Then in dull shock he realized that the *Poilu* wasn't there. Now what in hell could that mean, unless . . .

. . . unless the red-coated figure is not the Highlander!

Two feet were planted firmly upon the concrete floor. Blue showed below the waist, scarlet at the chest. Several buttons shone. Both arms were outstretched, steadying the pistol. The head was thrown back, the eyes gone dull, the brain running on instinct alone.

Then there was a whisper escaping from the mouth:

'Daddy, where are you, Daddy! Help me, Daddy! Please!'

Somehow, from somewhere deep inside, Al Flood tapped a well of strength he never knew he had. With a push of effort, he raised the Smith and Wesson.

'For her,' Flood said. And then he pulled the trigger.

Four shots rang out.

RICOCHET

Christmas Day, 7.00 p.m.

He stood at the window, staring out, and watched the snow come down. Six floors below the traffic along Burrard Street was almost at a standstill as cars skidded and lurched and struggled to move inches along the road. Across the way a snow-plough was working the thoroughfare, piling up mounds of whiteness as its flashing amber light cut like staccato notes through the monochromatic hush. From far away came the sound of bells calling the faithful to worship, but the man who stood at the window did not feel a thing.

Robert DeClercq loathed hospitals and the memories they held.

Behind him, from the corridor beyond the open door, the newly-appointed Chief Superintendent could hear the hum of rubber wheels rolling across a tile floor, the vibration of metal on stainless steel, and – from somewhere off in some far room – a moan of forlorn resignation. The voices of nurses echoed down the hall just above a whisper.

Inside this room the only sound was the steady *blip . . . blip . . . blip* of an electronic heart monitor.

DeClercq turned from the window and walked over to the bed. There he turned a chair around and sat down with his arms and chin resting on its back. The person lying on the bed was now sound asleep. The smell of antiseptic agents crept up the policeman's nose. Audibly, he sighed.

'Can you hear me?' DeClercq asked, his voice no more than a whisper. 'You're going to make it through,' he said. 'I want you to live. Strange, but somehow I feel that you're my only hope.'

There was no movement from the bed, and for several long minutes the man did not say a word.

Eventually, however, he began to speak again.

'The shot that killed Genevieve was a ricochet. I feel this need to talk to you . . . this need to let you know that I don't hold you to blame. I . . . I know her death wasn't your fault and . . . and I admire what you did. I do hope you can hear me . . . Do you mind if I speak to you?'

From the corridor outside came the sound of gasps, of choking, then the sound of running feet. Crêpe soles squeaking swiftly across tile. Then there followed the closing of a door.

'I . . . I almost killed myself once. That I want you to know. I actually had the gun in my mouth and was going to pull the trigger, but I didn't. Two friends saved me . . . and one was Genevieve. She made me promise after that . . . promise that no matter what happened to me again, I'd never take my life. Yet when they told me she was dead I almost broke that promise. I still wish I could do it . . . but I can't . . . for the sake of her. God knows I love her still.

'It's ironic, don't you think, how the line between life and death is always in shifting motion? We never seem to know where it is at any given time. Any act at any moment might be the little shove that pushes us across. You see she was trying to help him!'

There was the wail of an ambulance outside, the eerie Doppler effect of its siren closing on the Emergency arcade below.

461

From the corridor, the same door opened as had closed a minute before. Now there was no gasping. There was no sound at all.

'This fellow Flood never should have been allowed to be a cop. Do you want to hear about him, this man who you brought down? We're slowly getting the facts.

'Flood has a background connected to drugs. He came from the East End. His father was an alcoholic and his brother was a junkie. His brother was evidently murdered because of his drug connections. The man was recruited into the Police Academy under serious reservations. I wish he'd never got in.

'For the past few months Flood had been seeing Dr George Ruryk, a psychiatrist I know. Ruryk says the man had problems and that he had been depressed. Doubted himself as a man, doubted himself as a cop. I suppose he had the cocaine as his ticket out. Stole it from some busted pusher's stash to traffic it himself and retire on the profit. Is that how you got onto him? An underworld tip?'

Out in the corridor, a hospital morgue bed was being rolled into the room from which had come the gasps.

'Ruryk suggested that Flood attend a seminar at UBC. Genevieve taught the class. I guess he fell in love with her, perhaps it was obsession. Avacomovitch saw them once having lunch together. Genny was always doing that, reaching out to help anyone who had a problem and who was struggling to cope.

'He must have called her on that night and begged her to come over.

'I guess she realized when she got there that matters were out of control. Maybe he told her about the drugs, the money they were worth, and asked her to run away with him. Who knows? Maybe he was just acting out his dead brother's trip.

'Anyway, she called me at the Armouries the night of the Red Serge Ball and told Jim Rodale that the guy had a problem. I must have received the message just about the

462

time she died. Just about the time that you closed in to make the arrest and Flood pulled the gun.

'You know, I wonder if the guy would ever have let Genevieve bring the problem to me? Perhaps he had snapped and was going to take her hostage cause she wouldn't go along. Or maybe she succeeded in convincing him that it was wrong. What does it matter now?

'In a way I'm glad you killed him. The man was a disgrace.'

Out beyond the window a car was stuck in the snow in the hospital quiet zone. Its speakers were blaring rock and roll, the electric scream of Led Zeppelin's *Whole Lotta Love*.

DeClercq, in a whisper, leaned closer to the bed. 'I had a child once, I want you to know, and I loved her very much. She was stolen from me and I never got to watch her grow up. I want you to understand that your father felt the same way about you. If he were alive today, he'd be very proud.

'When I was your age, your father was my mentor: Alfred taught me most of what I know today. He was then even older than I am now, but there was this bond between us. I met your mother only once, just after you were born and shortly before the three of you went North. She was a very beautiful woman and I wish we'd kept in touch. I was very surprised to find that you had grown up to join the Force. When I saw your name on that list of members as I was drawing up the Squad, I was stunned. I'd only seen you once before, that time in Montreal, but I remember clearly to this day the pride your father felt. You could see it in his face as he watched you trying to learn how to crawl across the floor. He was a very good man.

'Before your father went missing in that blizzard on the Arctic Patrol I saw him one more time. He came to see me in Quebec City and asked me for two favours. One was to keep something safe for him, that he would pick up later. The other was to ask me – should anything ever happen

463

to him – if I would see to it that you were taken care of.

'It was shortly after that he disappeared and your mother took you away.'

Outside in the street some carollers were singing *Come All Ye Faithful*. Robert DeClercq reached for his coat and removed something from the pocket.

'Soon you're going to be better, and I hope we will be friends. It may be late, but I'd like to keep that promise to your father. Just as he was to me, I'd like to be your mentor. I'd like to think that in a way you are the replacement for my stolen child.

'Here . . . I have something for you.'

Slowly DeClercq reached out and placed the Enfield revolver on the bedside table.

'This belonged to your grandfather. To Inspector Wilfred Blake. Your father left it with me, the last time we met in Quebec. I want it to be yours.

'But there's something else I have to say, and I hope I say it right.

'That time in Montreal when you were just a baby crawling on the floor, your father turned to me and said: "Robert, do you see it? There's something in those eyes. Have you ever seen a child's eyes sparkle quite that way?" And then he turned to you and said: "Sparky, come to Daddy," and you began to crawl.

'Even then it showed, though you were just a child. That determination in your eyes. That will to be somebody.'

Abruptly there was a jerk, and then a movement on the bed. DeClercq leaned even closer, emotion in his voice.

'I know you're going to do it. That you'll carry on the legend. Just keep on going like you are and you might – just might – outdo even Wilfred Blake.'

Slowly, the eyes opened and looked up at him.

Then from the bed, ever so faintly, Katherine Spann smiled.

EPILOGUE

Delighted and surprised, I embraced her; but as I imprinted the first kiss on her lips, they became livid with the hue of death; her features appeared to change, and I thought that I held the corpse of my dead mother in my arms; a shroud enveloped her form, and I saw the grave-worms crawling in the folds of the flannel. I started from my sleep with horror; a cold dew covered my forehead, my teeth chattered, and every limb became convulsed; when by the dim and yellow light of the moon, as it forced its way through the window shutters, I beheld the wretch – the miserable monster whom I had created.

Mary Shelley, Frankenstein.

THE MASK

Tuesday, December 28th, 10.15 a.m.

It could have been 1944, deep in the Ardennes.

For it would have looked like this at dawn that bleak December morning, when General Omar Bradley's GIs awoke to face Hitler's Sixth SS Panzer Army. Their first warning would have been the explosion of shells on the woodlands and ridges around them. For at H-hour – 5.30 a.m. precisely – two thousand German guns on one second fuses had opened up on the American positions all along the Bulge. There would have been the roaring noise of V-1s overhead, and the rumble of Panther and Tiger tanks sliding down twisting roads. There would have been also the voice of war in the shouts and the cries of the dying. And then – as now – there would have been the snow and the swirling fog.

Not forty feet away, the tank appeared in the mist and vapour.

He could hear the whir of its motor and the mesh of its turret gears, and from where he stood he could just make out a ghost in the murky gloom.

And then the tank began to move and he knew he couldn't wait. He raised his rifle. He sighted the ghost in the fog down its long, cold, blue-grey barrel. Abruptly, the tank stopped. Now another figure appeared in the mist, stepping down from the driver's door to join the man on the ground. And he was just about to pull the trigger to cut the German down, when through the mist there came a shout that smashed the scene to pieces.

'Hey, kid. You can stop your dreamin'. It's time for a coffee break.'

Yes, it could have been 1944 at the Battle of the Bulge. But it wasn't.

With a sigh, the young man picked up a garbage can in each gloved hand and walked over to the rear of the truck. He dumped the refuse into the collecting trough at the back, then pulled the hydraulic lever. With a whir of meshing gears, the mechanism began to lift, rolling the garbage up and into the dustcart. He put the second can down and took off his gloves, then he walked around to the driver's door to join the other two men.

'First day's a little early, kid, to be gettin' bored with the job.'

The man who spoke was a string bean who went by the name of Slim. He was a tall, skinny dude somewhere in his late fifties. Dressed in a floppy farmer's hat and baggy blue coveralls, he had the face of a man who has spent all his life working outdoors. As he spoke, Slim was pouring coffee from a beat-up thermos into a styrofoam cup. When he handed the cup to the young man he flashed him a stained-tooth smile. Slim rolled his own.

The other man was short and squat, with a ruddy drinker's complexion. He too was in his fifties, but a year or two younger than Slim. He was wearing overalls with a seaman's stripes on both arms. This man was called the Perfesser by those in the sanitation department, and if he had another name the young man hadn't heard it. The Perfesser was sitting on the driver's doorstep, spiking his steaming coffee with a shot from a silver flask. As Slim spoke, the Perfesser was watching the young man intently.

'When you bin at this job twenty years,' Slim said, 'then you can start to git bored.'

The young man merely nodded, for to speak would be an impertinence.

'Jest how'd a young fella like you git this job anyway, son? These sure ain't the very best of workin' times.'

'Just luck,' the youth replied.

'Job as a garbage collector ain't really what I call luck.'

468

The young man sipped his coffee and looked at the Perfesser. The Perfesser had yet to speak.

'I just finished first semester out at UBC. The city's got a programme to help us students find jobs. Mine's just over Christmas, so the Union doesn't mind. Besides, I need the money. Every little bit counts.'

'Ah,' said the Perfesser, finding a point to interrupt. 'So we've an academic in our midst. Do tell me, Jeff, just what is your field of expertise?'

'History,' the young man said.

'Ah, history,' the Perfesser said. 'A Sherlock Holmes of the past.'

'Well, actually history is just the beginning. I really want to be an archaeologist.'

'An archaeologist! My, my!' the Perfesser said slyly as he slipped a look to Slim. 'And you thought he was bored with the job. What better job could he have, to practise his future craft?'

Slim shook his head sadly, chagrined at his own stupidity, and fished a package of Export rolling papers out of the pocket of his overalls. The Perfesser took a slug straight from the silver flask. 'Are you bored, kid?' he asked, looking the youth in the eye. 'Do you think this job is beneath you? Is that your attitude?'

Jeff blinked. 'No, no, of course not,' he said.

'I hope not. Cause if you do, son, it's time that you grew up and opened your eyes. I don't like to see anyone look down on another man's job. Most of all I don't like arrogant pricks who think they're better than everyone else. Every job can teach you something about life. And this one more than most.'

Slim began tapping some loose tobacco onto the rolling paper. 'Perfesser says a man ain't worth shit if he thinks he's above cleanin' up the garbage in the world around him. You should listen to the Perfesser, kid. He's a man who's bin around. World's foremost authority, for my money, on women, liquor and life.'

With one hand Slim rolled the paper into a perfect

cigarette. He licked the gum, sealed it, and stuck the fag in his mouth.

What is this? Jeff thought. *The vaudeville of the alley?* But he kept the thought to himself.

'An archaeologist, eh?' the Perfesser said, revolving the word on his tongue. 'That's one of those fellows who digs in the ground, looking for the garbage left behind by past civilizations to figure out how they lived. To try and figure out who they really were. A bit like an academic garbage collector. Have I got that right, son?'

'Sort of,' Jeff said.

Slim lit a match on the zipper of his crotch and blew out a grey cloud of fog. 'Perfesser says that garbage is the true reflection of life.'

'Ah, *garbage!*' the Perfesser said wisely, and he took another shot straight from the flask.

'Ever found yourself with a day off, Jeff, and nothing to do? I have. Lots of days since my wife up and left. At first I didn't know what to do with myself – then I struck on this idea. An experiment, so to speak. I got dressed up in a shirt and tie, and walked my garbage route. Only this time, kid, I walked down the *front* of the street. And I've been doing that once a month ever since, just slowly walking by and taking in the front that people put out, the masks they wear, if you get my drift. Cause sometimes their masks get so solid, they think that's who they really are. I go looking in people's windows. Listening to them chat with their neighbours. And then I started keeping track of the garbage that came out the *back*.'

'We slit two or three bags open every trip,' Slim said. 'Perfesser says a man's trash is the true reflection of his life.' He blew out another billowing cloud of grey smoke.

'So you see, Jeff,' the Perfesser said, standing up and stretching, 'why not use this job to learn a little bit about life? Come on. I'll show you what I mean.'

The Perfesser walked down the alley, and stopped in front of a wooden pen containing two metal garbage cans. Reaching into the pocket of his overalls, he brought out a Swiss Army knife and fingered open one of the blades. As Slim and Jeff joined him he removed the lid from one of the cans and slit open the uppermost black plastic bag inside. With both his hands he ripped the slit wide-open.

'Well, kid,' the Perfesser asked. 'What do you see?'

Jeff peered into the rent in the bag and began to list the contents, starting from the top: 'One box of Shieks, empty. One box of Ramses, lubricated and also empty. Two Swanson TV dinners, eaten. Two Chun King frozen chow mein dinners, also eaten. One copy of *Hustler*. One copy of *Gent*. One copy of the *Hite Report on Female Sexuality*. Several dozen Kleenex, most of them smeared with lipstick and make-up. Two Canadian Pacific Airlines travel folders for tickets. Several pamphlets on Hawaii. Several mimeographed sheets of paper. And I can't see what's below that.'

'Okay,' said the Perfesser. 'Now add this. Those mimeographed sheets are Sunday school papers. These garbage cans belong to the manse of the Baptist Church down the street. In the manse live the minister, his wife – who wears no make-up – and their pious fifteen year old son. Put it all together and what have you got . . .'

'Why that horny little bastard!' Jeff said, and the three of them laughed. Slim flicked the butt of his cigarette into the snow in the alley.

'Okay, you try, Mr Holmes. Pick any can.'

Jeff looked around pensively. Twenty feet up the lane he saw a burning tin across from the underground parking lot of a West End apartment building. Behind the tin were two garbage cans.

'That one,' Jeff said as he left the two older man. He walked over to it, removed the lid and looked inside. As they both watched him with smiles on their faces Slim and the Perfesser saw the young man lift an Adidas athletic bag out of the can. They saw him look inside the main pouch of the gym case, close it and then unzipped

471

the side pocket. After several seconds they saw Jeff shrug and heard him say: 'Beats me, Perfesser. What do you make of this?'

The two older man sauntered over to join him. Together all three examined the object that the youth held in his hand.

The object was made of ebony and it shone dull black in the diffused light that struggled to seep through the fog. It consisted of two small faces, back to back, each one about two inches high, each with a large rounded nose. One of the noses was smooth, but the other was jagged at the end where it had cracked and several small splinters had chipped off. Each miniature face had an open mouth and from each mouth protruded an eight-inch rounded tongue. These tongues curved in a slightly upward arc in opposite directions.

'Well?' Jeff asked, bewildered. 'What do you make of this?'

Slim looked to the Perfesser, a smile upon his lips.

'That, son,' the Perfesser said, 'is what we call a Dyke's Prong. You want another name, call it the Horns of Venus. Call it a Devil's Tongue. That's a pretty fancy one but you can buy a simplified plastic version in any sex shop in this city.'

Jeff stared at the double dildo for several long seconds.

'Down in the Caribbean there's this place called Nick's Nitery. When I was in the merchant marine we shipped into that island port one day and the whole crew went to Nick's. If you got enough of the green stuff that man really puts on a show; in season tourists flock there by the thousands. In one of the shows, two women make the two-back-beast using one of those, matching each other thrust for thrust. The night we were there at least one-third of the audience was female. In the second act, Nick had two men get it on.'

Jeff looked up at the other two and a wordless communication passed among the three of them.

Finally Jeff said: 'Hidden lives, huh? I'm just trying to

imagine a woman using one of those things.'

Slim grinned and said, 'Frankenstein's monster was made up from parts of several *different* human beings.'

The three of them turned from the garbage cans and walked back to the truck. As they passed the burning tin Jeff glanced inside and saw nothing but yesterday's ashes. The Perfesser climbed in behind the wheel and once more the team was moving. The ebony object went into the collecting trough at the back along with the Adidas bag. Then Jeff pulled on the hydraulic lever and the trough took the refuse away.

It was as Jeff was turning from the rear of the truck that Slim stopped him with a wink of his eye.

'Didn't I tell ya?' Slim said. 'World's foremost authority, for my money, on women, liquor and life.'

'You told me,' Jeff said.

'But what I didn't tell ya – an' ya should know – is the garbageman's lesson of life.'

'And what's that?' Jeff asked, grinning from ear to ear.

'Perfesser says that in this city – in *any* city – the *real* garbage ain't what we take outa the cans. It's some of the people that fill 'em.'

Author's Note

This is a work of fiction. The plot, the characters-in-action are a product of the author's imagination. Where real persons, places, or institutions have been used for background to create the illusion of authenticity they are used fictitiously. Facts have been altered if necessary for the purpose of the story.

It would not have been possible to write this novel, however, without the generous help of certain individuals who aided in the research and to whom the author owes a debt of gratitude:

To Dr James S. Tyhurst of the Department of Psychiatry, University of British Columbia, for directing my reading toward *The Psychology of Insanity* by Bernard Hart.

To The Clash of London, England – both for their music and for permission to use the lyrics of 'Jimmy Jazz'.

To Earl Hall of the RCMP Crime Detection Lab, Vancouver BC, who – without knowing the plot or where I was going – helped with the ballistics.

To Gerald Straley of Vandusen Botanical Gardens, Vancouver, BC, for a short course in botany.

To Pacific Press Ltd for the consistent quality of *The Sun* newspaper, Vancouver, BC.

To Annie Hill, for translation.

And to Bill Duthie, who for thirty years has provided the best library in town.

In addition, I must acknowledge the influence of, and the wealth of knowledge contained within, the following non-fiction sources:

Burroughs, William S. *Junky*, Penguin, 1977, London

Butler, William F. *The Great Lone Land*, Hurtig, 1968, Edmonton

Dolinger, Jane. *The Head With The Long Yellow Hair*, Robert Hale, 1958, London

Greene, Gerald and Caroline. *S-M: The Last Taboo*, Grove, 1974, New York

Hart, Bernard. *The Psychology of Insanity*, Cambridge University Press, 1957

Haskins, Jim. *Voodoo and Hoodoo*, Stein and Day, 1978, New York

Hogg, Garry. *Cannibalism and Human Sacrifice*. Pan Books, 1958, London

Horrall, S. W. *The Pictorial History of the Royal Canadian Mounted Police*, McGraw-Hill, 1973, Toronto

Huxley, Francis. *The Invisibles: Voodoo Gods in Haiti*, McGraw-Hill, 1969, New York

Keating, H. R. F. *Whodunit? A Guide To Crime, Suspense and Spy Fiction*, Van Nostrand, 1982, New York

Stone, Alan A. and Sue Smart. (Editors). *The Abnormal Personality Through Literature*, Prentice-Hall, 1966, New Jersey

Tierney, John. 'Common Threads From Atlanta.' *Science 81*

Wilson, Colin. *Order of Assassins*. Panther Books, 1975, London

Wilson, Colin. *Origins of the Sexual Impulse*. Granada, 1966, London

And finally, my sincere thanks to those who – one way or another – saw this into print:

To Bob Tanner, publisher *extraordinaire*, who plucked it from the mail.

To Hilary Muray, who turned the lens and brought it into focus.

To Lee, who gave birth to Michael Slade.

To Kevin Williams, for his counsel.

To the management and staff of the Sylvia Hotel, Vancouver, BC, and to the Mills of East Lothian, Scotland, beneath whose warm hospitality it all came together.

Of course, to Lois McMahon, Slade's right arm, for everything.

And to Evan Hunter, Timothy Findley and Howard Phillips Lovecraft for inspiration.

Mike Slade
December 23rd, 1983